Cara Colter shares
British Columbia, C
more than thirty yea
several horses. She has three grown children and
two grandsons.

Karin Baine lives in Northern Ireland with
her husband, two sons and her out-of-control
notebook collection. Her mother and her
grandmother's vast collection of books inspired
her love of reading and her dream of becoming
a Mills & Boon author. Now she can tell people
she has a *proper* job! You can follow Karin on X,
@karinbaine1, or visit her website for the latest
news—karinbaine.com.

A BILLIONAIRE
FOR CINDERELLA

CARA COLTER

KARIN BAINE

MILLS & BOON

First published in Great Britain 2025
by Mills & Boon, an imprint of HarperCollins*Publishers* Ltd,
1 London Bridge Street, London, SE1 9GF

www.harpercollins.co.uk

HarperCollins*Publishers*, Macken House, 39/40 Mayor Street Upper, Dublin 1, D01 C9W8, Ireland

ISBN: 978-0-263-41759-3

10/25

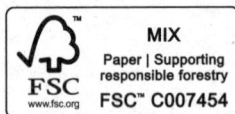

MIX
Paper | Supporting
responsible forestry
FSC
www.fsc.org
FSC™ C007454

This book contains FSC™ certified paper and other controlled sources to ensure responsible forest management.

For more information visit www.harpercollins.co.uk/green.

Printed and Bound in the UK using 100% Renewable Electricity at CPI Group (UK) Ltd, Croydon, CR0 4YY

THE PRINCE FROM HER PAST

CARA COLTER

MILLS & BOON

Dedicated to the memory of first loves.

CHAPTER ONE

GABRIELA OLIVERA SAT down on a stone bench in the walled garden. The bench was warm from the caress of the sun, and she lifted her face to that same kiss. The scent of the olive tree—said to be the oldest tree on the island—tickled her nostrils with its sweet spicy aroma. The tree was in full flower, and butterflies danced amid the thick clusters of creamy white blooms.

She breathed in the sensations that enveloped her, relishing the scents and the silence, so different from what she had experienced over the last two years in New York City.

There could only be one name for these feelings of history, of deep familiarity, of contentment, of safety.

Home.

She was home, at last, to her island that bore the name of those endemic butterflies—slightly larger than monarchs, with a brilliant blue heart-shaped dot on their hind wings—that floated around the olive tree.

Isla Hermosa Mariposa was a nation in the western Mediterranean Sea. Governed by monarchy, the small but extremely prosperous isle was most famous for olives. Gabriela's father and his father before him, stretching as far back in the history of Hermosa Mariposa as could be traced, had been keepers of the Royal House of Falcon groves, hence her family's surname.

Her mother—and also her mother before her—had been in charge of the palace kitchen.

And so Gabriela had grown up in the white-walled cottage that sat on the edge of the castle wall and at the beginning of the acres and acres of ancient olive groves that stretched over the slopes and down to the very private and sheltered turquoise Bay of Butterflies.

That sense inside her—of being home—did not erase the challenges of her world. Her beloved father, always so robust and vital, had been ill for weeks, too weak to get out of his bed this morning. His health was the reason she had taken an indefinite leave from her job.

Or at least it was the biggest part of the reason. The truth was her life was in flux, at a crossroads since the end of her engagement to her longtime fiancé, Timothy Hardy, had been triggered by her decision to come home.

Timothy has been absolutely right, of course, that *something* was missing, which, also of course, meant the walls she had put up throughout their relationship had not gone unnoticed. He had thought he should be invited to come to the island with her when she'd made the decision to come home.

The truth was she could not imagine Timothy here. The truth was she had not wanted to see him against the backdrop of the place where she had loved a different man.

And perhaps loved him still, a voice inside her whispered.

She did not! She had left her childish fantasies and infatuations behind her. She had long ago accepted the love that could not be.

But if that was totally true, why had she felt something akin to panic when Timothy had suggested he come back with her, particularly when she had thought of him possibly meeting the forbidden love of her younger self?

Gabriela firmly put the tumultuous thoughts behind her and focused on the sensation of home and all it brought with it. Her sense of her own strength, her ability to handle what life gave her, had come from within the thick, sturdy walls of that kitchen cottage, and her days growing up playing in this garden.

As if summoned by her memories of a childhood in this garden, the tall wooden gate that connected the cottage to the pathway to the palace creaked open, and a little boy slipped in.

Gabriela's heart went still.

She knew instantly who the boy was because he was identical to the child she had once spent endless sun-filled days in this garden with.

She knew he was five, of course, and his name. The whole world knew his name, though he had been, as much as possible, fiercely guarded against a celebrity-and-royalty-besotted world.

He was sturdy, as his father had been at that age, and sported the same mop of dark, unruly curls. He had huge brown eyes, golden skin and a mouth set with determination that did not match his age.

Gabriela sat very still, and he didn't notice her, squinting with a singleness of purpose underneath the shrubs that lined the walls of the garden. She followed his gaze to see what he was so intent on and bit back a chortle when she saw what he was after.

The ancient black cat, Geraldo, notoriously cranky, was doing his very best to shrink back into the shadows of the wall, but to no avail.

Marcello's eyes lit up, and he gave a little cry. "Aha!"

He dropped to all fours, darted under the shrub and made a grab for the cat, who had missed his opportunity to slink away.

Gabriela watched, ready to spring to the rescue, if needed. This morning when she had cuddled the cat, aside from noticing his fur was beginning to mat with age, she had also realized he was unable to retract his claws, which had been momentarily caught in her blouse. She had made a note to make a vet appointment, knowing her mother was distracted.

These small things that she could do to take some of the burden off her parents made her so glad she had come home.

As she watched, the boy emerged with his prize, the cat hanging with limp resignation in the grasp of the chubby fists that were knotted under its stomach.

Marcello brought the cat to his lips and covered the furry face with kisses, unaware of Geraldo's trying to squirm away in aversion to all this affection.

"You are my best friend in the whole world," Marcello announced to the cat.

It seemed like a sad statement for the little boy to make. Still, Gabriela, satisfied the cat was too old to make a strenuous effort to escape the attentions—or perhaps even secretly was enjoying them—looked at the gate.

Where on earth was the nanny?

Or was this another way the Prince took after his father? Adept at escaping the necessary strictures of being born royal?

Though not when it had mattered...

She stopped herself. She would not go there. She would not go to the secret place within her that had longed for this boy's father, Prince Enrique, to rebel against being ordered to marry...

The little boy's mother, Princess Amelia.

The fact the Princess was now dead made the thoughts seem even more like something that Gabriela must forbid herself.

It had been nearly a year since the Princess—and her baby—had died in childbirth. The palace's official year of mourning would be over soon. Already, rumors swirled in the palace, on the island and beyond about whom Enrique would marry when—not if—he married again.

Some of the most famous women in the world were being bandied about, with the name of Princess Bettina rising most often.

Marcello suddenly realized he was not in the garden alone. His eyes fastened on her, and very slowly—and with one last kiss—he surrendered Geraldo to the ground, then marched toward her.

He stood before Gabriela, regarding her with solemn eyes. She could see the beautiful thick fringe of lash, so like his father's.

"Hello," she said. She greeted him in English. The island's official language was one all its own, a dialect that was an archaic mixture of Spanish and Portuguese, but English had been the go-to for most of the population for decades.

"Hello," he answered in perfect, unaccented English. "I'm Marcello. You may call me Cello." He pronounced it *Chello.*

"I'm Gabriela," she said.

He tilted his head at her and nodded. "I know," he said, and then, "I know you."

That was fitting because even though they had never met, Gabriela also had a sense of knowing him.

"You are Guido's little girl," he said.

For some reason, that simple statement brought stinging tears to her eyes. Because she was, still and always, her father's little girl, and it made the fact that he lay inside that cottage, so desperately ill, feel like a pain she could not bear.

"I've come to see him," the child announced.

"But shouldn't someone be looking after you?" she asked. "Shouldn't you be with your nanny?"

He considered this for a moment, then leaned into her and announced in a rather loud whisper, "I don't like Miss Penny."

"Yes, well, even if you don't like her, Cello, she's probably very worried, and we need to let her know where you are."

Her first impulse was to reach for her cell phone to alert someone to the whereabouts of the wayward Prince, but she remembered her device from New York had proved not compatible with the antiquated island system.

Marcello flicked a wrist, dismissive, and she honestly didn't know if she was amused or irked that he had somehow reached the conclusion that the rules of mere mortals did not apply to him.

That was very different from Enrique, who, raised under Queen Katalina's iron will, had carried the knowledge rules applied *more* to him. Even if he had defied them from time to time, he had always been aware he would pay a steep price for infractions.

Gabriela stood up and held out her hand to the child. "Let's go ask my mother if Guido is up to a visitor today," she suggested.

His hand slipped trustingly into hers, and she was stunned by the level of longing—and sadness—that sturdy, small hand in hers caused.

That hand represented the life she had been told, by a formidable Queen Katalina, that she could not have, that she should not even dare to dream of. And then she'd been exiled to America just after she turned eighteen, supposedly to get her marketing degree in service to her island home.

But really it had been to keep her and Prince Enrique, childhood friends—newly aware of each other in exciting and dangerous ways—apart.

Gabriela had done as she was ordered. There was really no other choice in a society stuck in ancient traditions and ruled by centuries-old laws as Isle Hermosa Mariposa was.

The Queen had sent her away, with a scholarship and an order to learn.

And so she had. She had worked hard at university, graduated with the highest honors, and then been asked to head a marketing department for the exclusive Royal House of Falcon Olive Oils, the most sought-after in the world.

And as she had done those things, she had watched from afar as Prince Enrique, the boy she had played with in the garden, the man she had first kissed, the person who had owned her heart since she was five years old, became betrothed to someone else.

Of his own station.

Of another powerful royal family, rulers of the neighboring Mediterranean island of Xavier.

The wedding, of course, despite the royal family's normal aversion to publicity, had been celebrated worldwide. You were not able to turn on a television, be on the internet or see a newspaper without finding images of the two powerful royal houses being joined together by a marriage.

And so Gabriela had experienced layer upon layer of heartbreak. She had watched, along with the rest of the world, as *her* prince had given himself to another, committed his life to a gorgeous woman worthy of any fairy tale.

As the whole world had invested in happily-ever-after overdrive, had it only been Gabriela who could *see*? Despite all the trappings—gowns and carriages, cakes and ceremonies, well-wishes from the most famous names in the world, wedding gifts of priceless jewels and astounding properties—the bride and groom did not look genuinely happy. Their smiles were fixed and strained, their first kiss was perfunctory, the way they touched each other was stiff and formal.

Not that those things mattered in the worlds that Enrique and Amelia came from.

All that mattered in their realms was duty, and obedience to that duty.

When, a year later, the pregnancy had been announced, and then the baby born, Gabriela told herself she had to let it all go. She had hardened her broken heart, allowed scar tissue to strengthen the cracks around it.

It couldn't hurt her any more.

What was one stupid heart in the way of the world?

She had moved on. She had recognized the foolish naivete of some dreams. She had met Timothy and seen that they were compatible. Eventually—and admittedly reluctantly, something he had called her on when he ended the relationship—she had agreed to marry him.

Nearly a year ago, Princess Amelia—and the second royal baby—had both died during a nightmarish childbirth.

And now Gabriela's father was sick.

It was as if the universe was conspiring to bring her home.

But, she told herself firmly, not to fan long-ago and forbidden sparks of dreams back to life, but to douse them, to lay them to rest, once and for all.

CHAPTER TWO

WITH THAT STURDY little hand in hers, the garden space that had felt like a sanctuary just moments ago, that place that was as much a longing as a reality—home—suddenly felt like the most dangerous place of all.

Gabriela and Marcello moved from the brightness of the garden and through the Dutch door—the top portion open—directly into the kitchen. The cottage was constructed of thick whitewashed stone and so the interior was dark and cool compared with outside.

"Maria!" Marcello let go of Gabriela's hand and flew across the cool tiles of the kitchen floor into her mother's embrace.

"Your Highness," her mother said, contradicting the formality of the title by covering the little upturned face with as many kisses as Marcello had bestowed on the cat, "where on earth is Miss Penny?"

He shrugged.

"I've come to see Guido."

Maria and Gabriela exchanged a look over the child's head. Would Marcello be shocked by the swift changes illness was bringing in Guido? Would it be best to protect him? Was Guido up to a visit?

But Marcello broke free from Maria's embrace, and familiar with the cottage, just as his father had once been, he raced down the hall and threw open the sickroom door.

"Guido! Cello is here!"

"Where is his nanny?" Gabriela asked.

Maria shrugged, distracted, sad. She picked up the old wall phone receiver and said something into it—no doubt alerting the palace to the whereabouts of their missing prince—and then she turned back to the stove. The aroma of soup—her father's favorite—filled the space and increased Gabriela's awareness of how much she had missed home.

She followed Marcello down the hallway and arrived at the bedroom just in time to see Marcello launch himself onto the solid, antique bed, where her father was sitting up against pillows, and into his arms. Guido's face was alight as Marcello twined his arms around his neck and pulled himself deep against the man.

And then he was sobbing, as Guido patted his back.

"Are you going to die? Just like my mommy?" he wailed. "Don't die, Guido! Don't!"

He was saying out loud the words that Gabriela wanted to say, too, and with the same amount of feeling. She could feel the tears she had been holding in since her arrival back on the island spill down her cheeks. She scrubbed them quickly away with the back of her hand, not wanting to upset the little Prince—or her father—any further.

But she had not hidden her sadness from her father, who looked at her and smiled softly. He patted the bed on the other side of him, and she went to it and sank down beside him and the little boy.

"Listen," her father said, "both of you. I will tell you the story of an olive tree."

And so he did. He told them the story of how each tree was born, and eventually each tree would die, but when it died it would become part of the soil that nurtured the trees, born of its seeds. He talked of how each of the trees was born with new life inside it already, and that would mean it never really died; in fact, it multiplied.

"And it is the same," he said quietly, "with all living things.

The cycles of life have sadness in them, but in the end, it is what is most beautiful that remains."

Both she and Marcello were calmed by him, the little boy nestled into his chest, sucking lustily on his thumb, and she in the crook under his shoulder, her eyes closed, feeling her father's heart beating still, and being so grateful for one more moment of that steady thud being in her world.

She had a sudden sensation of being watched that made her open her eyes again.

Prince Enrique was standing in the doorway.

Gabriela drank him in, thirsty, as if she had dragged herself across a desert and caught sight of water.

She had seen photos of him, of course, since she had left the island, but photos did not do justice to reality.

Enrique now, as always, radiated presence. He did so even though he was, at the moment, dressed very casually, in pressed khakis and a navy blue polo shirt, the royal emblem ever so subtly emblazoned over his right breast.

Gabriela knew, from the photos she had seen, that his curls had long since become a thing of the past. His hair was very short-cropped, obviously an effort to keep those wayward loops at bay. Still, it was shiny and sleek, as black as a raven's wing.

The short hairstyle drew attention to the chiseled perfection of his features, the broad forehead, the slash of his dark brows, the fringe of his lashes and, of course, the amazing melted dark chocolate of his eyes. He had high cheekbones and a perfect nose, full lips, a faintly clefted chin. All that, coupled with the natural tones of his skin kissed golden by his Mediterranean heritage, made him unfairly gorgeous, like a film star or a male model.

His looks, when taken together with his status as a *real* prince, had made him a global phenomenon. Media clamored for his pictures, young women lined streets hoping for a glimpse of their heartthrob, the internet lit up with excitement at any news of him.

Even as a young man, he had disliked the celebrity status he could do nothing about.

He was largely protected on this island, but as soon as he set foot off it, he was besieged. Early in his life, the worldwide media had discovered the marketability of a real-life prince who also happened to be utterly gorgeous. The royal family was constantly seeking the balance between how celebrity helped them promote Hermosa Mariposa and its products and allowing the royals to have some semblance of privacy. Still, Prince Enrique was one of the most recognizable and sought-after celebrities in the world.

Added to his natural good looks was an incredible physical presence. He stood just a hair over six feet tall, was broad at his shoulders, deep through his chest and narrow at his waist. Even in trousers, the strength and length of his legs were evident.

His wedding had been the most-watched event of the decade, easily surpassing royal happenings in more well-known countries.

Though the island was in a unique position to protect his privacy, it found the balance it needed to capitalize also on his popularity so its products remained in the public eye. Carefully controlled photos and news items about the Prince, the Princess and then Marcello were released to a world hungry for details.

Gabriela had been as hungry as anyone else for details of him.

But she also saw things that no one else would see in those artistic shots released by the palace.

Something remote in Enrique's eyes, even when he was smiling down at his wife and his baby. Some rigidity in Amelia's body language as she turned ever so slightly away from her husband, instead of toward him.

Still, the palace had managed to maintain the illusion of the fairy tale that the world wanted so badly.

Even so, Gabriela was aware that, no matter the circumstances of his marriage, Enrique's character was such that he would have given it his all, he would have been steadfast in his loyalty to his partner, that his grief for both Amelia and the daughter he had never met would have been overwhelming and real.

He'd be devastated and angry that now, with Amelia gone, a new industry was springing up around the Prince: bereaved husband, single dad. The interest in him was more lascivious—and intrusive—than it had ever been. Enrique, excused by his year of mourning, now rarely left the island. Photos of both he and his son were extraordinarily rare.

Which meant Gabriela had not seen him—not even in a photograph—for a long time.

Would it have helped if she had? She doubted it. She doubted if anything could prepare a woman for the impact of Enrique in the flesh.

And that was probably doubly true of a woman who had loved him.

And not the public image of him.

The *real* him.

Just as he stood before her now, she saw him as she had always seen him. Stripped of his royalty and as a man. A spectacular man, no doubt, but beyond that, beyond the compelling nature of his appearance, she saw a man of deep complexities, now layered with sorrow for a lost wife and child, and a helpless love for his son.

It occurred to Gabriela that what Timothy had implied he always knew—*you aren't completely in this, it's as if part of you is not here*—had truth in it. Her heart had never received the memo that loving Prince Enrique Falcon was like standing outside the wall of a fortress that could not be penetrated, that could not be breached.

To try would be to end up bloodied and beaten, as she already well knew.

And yet her heart rose at the sight of him, wanting desperately to break through the new remoteness in his eyes, the walls around him. Her heart was entirely indifferent to all the lessons that had broken it the first time.

But she was not the same young woman, still in her teens, who had left this island.

She had a new maturity, and new sophistication of thought, and Gabriela knew she had to use every tool she had developed over her years away to fight her instinctive attraction to Enrique, her heart's cry that somehow he formed part of the equation that made this place home. But more, that made her complete.

Enrique stood in the thick doorframe of the small cottage he was so familiar with. In the days of his boyhood, he had torn through this small space as if it was his own. He had felt things with the Oliveras that he had never experienced with his own family.

Family being his mother, the Queen. His father had died in a horseback riding accident when he was a baby.

So maybe it had been the masculine influence of Guido that had drawn him, as a fatherless little boy, to this house, to this man whom he had trailed through the olive groves, over and over again.

But no, he was certain, especially looking at the three people on that bed now, that it had been more.

It had been the warmth in that kitchen. The good smells. The teasing between Maria and Guido, their utter and undisguised delight in Gabriela, and in him.

In this house, he had come to know what the bonds of family were. In these walls Enrique had encountered, for the first time, the warmth, the laughter, the closeness of people who loved one another, deeply and unconditionally.

In this house he had experienced a family, people who saw each other, not through the lens of their usefulness, their role, their duty, their lineage, but through the window of their hearts.

Since the death of his wife, Enrique had seen his son, Marcello, drawn to the same things in this cottage and in the olive groves that Enrique had once experienced himself.

His young son was inserting himself into Guido and Maria's lives like a puppy who had been neglected and finally found affection. Marcello was drawn to this place like a magnet to steel.

The irony that it was this humble space, and not the grand castle they lived in, that nurtured a sense of true enchantment was not lost on Enrique.

Looking at those three people, unselfconsciously cuddled together on the bed, the Prince tasted the bitterness of his failure.

He had vowed his son would know a less rigid upbringing than he had known himself. He had vowed his son would feel loved.

While Amelia had lived, Marcello had flourished under the brilliant light of his mother's love. It was after her death that Enrique had to face the truth that he had somehow been excluded, that his son regarded him as outside the circle of that love, and woefully unqualified to give him what he obviously craved now, more than ever.

Enrique stood in the irony of the fact he was a man who looked to the entire world as if he had everything.

And yet all his power, all his wealth, all his influence—the station in life that had cost him so much personally—had been worthless in the face of preventing the tragedy that had taken his wife and his unborn daughter. It seemed to have no value at all in developing the bond he wanted with his son.

Enrique allowed himself, finally, to look away from his son and toward Gabriela.

He had been steeling himself for the moment, but once again he faced his own powerlessness.

Because he felt his heart drop into an endless abyss, one that felt as if it had no bottom. Maybe it even stopped beating altogether.

CHAPTER THREE

GABRIELA HAD BEEN just on the cusp between being a girl and being a woman when Enrique had last seen her. He had been on the same cusp, between boyhood and manhood. Of course, they both would have denied it. How grown-up they had felt at the heady ages of eighteen and nineteen!

That was eight years ago. That was a very long time not to see a person.

Of course she was changed, and yet he was startled by how the coltishness of her late teens had evaporated as completely as fog before a warm sun.

Gabriela, in a modest skirt that was now rising immodestly up her leg, and a light mauve button-up blouse, was 100 percent woman.

Her eyes were closed, and her expression was peaceful as she listened to her father's calm voice. Even in his grave illness—why on earth was he refusing the best medical care the world had to offer?—Enrique noticed that Guido had no thought for himself. He was weaving this beautiful tale of life and death as a gift to comfort those who loved him.

Marcello.

Himself.

And, of course, Gabriela.

Enrique took advantage of the fact her eyes were closed, and she did not yet know he was here, to note the changes in her. The most obvious thing was that she had cut her hair. On this island, most women had long hair that they wore proudly, and once she had had the most beautiful hair of all, straight and dark, dark brown, hanging in a shining wave nearly to her waist.

Still beautiful, the shimmering wave now ended at her chin. It was a chic, sophisticated cut that mirrored, he supposed, her success in the business world, her immersion in American culture.

When she'd left his island, Enrique had never seen her wear makeup, nor would he have felt her perfect features needed it.

But now he saw how makeup accentuated her beauty—a touch of shadow on her eyelids, a brushing of mascara on her lashes, a sweep of blush across her already high cheekbones and a glossy hint of color on her full, sensuous lips.

The memory of the taste of those lips blasted through his brain with scorching intensity.

And then, she opened her eyes.

Hazel. Huge. Amazing. A kaleidoscope of gold and green and brown.

But more. There was *that* look. As if she had never gone away at all.

That look that said, in all the world, she was the one who had always seen him, not as a prince so much as a fellow human being who longed for all the things that each member of the human family—with the possible exception of his mother—longed for.

Her eyes met his and he steeled himself against the feeling of his heart dropping further into the abyss.

Enrique felt as if he was a man who had wandered, lost, in the wilderness, and suddenly, when he had given up all hope, found the way home.

The feeling, he told himself sternly, was a flash, like a fire that had to be put out immediately, before it gained strength. Little fires, ignored, could burn down the whole world, if they were not checked.

Of course, he had thought he loved Gabriela, once upon a time, just like in stories that ended with happily ever after. Why couldn't he, a prince, after all, have his own fairy tale?

And why, in his youth, wouldn't he think that? That Gabriela would play the central role in his future happiness? He had grown up with her, they had chased each other through their childhoods, shared secrets, become the best of friends.

Once upon a time, ridiculously, naively, he had thought it could be more.

But, of course, it could not be. His destiny had been mapped out for him before he drew his first breath.

His destiny did not include the daughter of the olive grove keeper and the head of the kitchen.

Though, still, even knowing that, even having had that bitter truth shoved at him, over and over, he had been stunned to come home after completing his studies at a private school in Switzerland to find Gabriela, recently graduated from the island's only high school, gone.

Without a word of goodbye.

With no answer to his increasingly pleading phone calls and letters.

He could still, in his mind, hear her recorded voice, at the end of too many rings: *Hi, it's Gabriela. Leave a message. I'll get back to you!* But she never, ever had, leaving him behind as completely as if he had never been.

Of course, now, nearly a decade later, he could see the good sense in her decision. Perhaps, if they had never kissed, never tasted the sweetness of each other's lips, never shared that magical *first* together, they could have been friends.

But after that kiss?

Then what? She had known, with maturity beyond her years, that such an attraction was doomed.

He had known he was expected—no, compelled—to marry Princess Amelia from the island nation closest to theirs.

He had resigned himself to what the fates had deemed for him before he was even born.

And yet, now, looking deeply into those oh-so-familiar hazel eyes, he could feel his commitment to the order of his life absurdly shaken.

"Your Highness," she said formally, scooting off the bed, and finding her feet. She smoothed her skirt around her legs, and inclined her head to him.

"Gabriela," he said, his voice cool, not giving away the downward swoop of his heart at all, "You look well."

"Thank you. As do you," she said stiffly.

He deliberately turned his attention from her. "Guido, how are you?"

The man smiled tiredly and lifted a shoulder. Accepting his fate, surrounded by love, at peace in a way Enrique almost envied.

"Marcello," he said more sharply than he intended, "please don't suck your thumb."

His son glared at him and took two more defiant slurps before removing his thumb from his mouth.

The thumb-sucking was a regression that had occurred after Amelia's death. Enrique—as with most things to do with raising a child as a single parent—wasn't quite sure how to handle it. One part of him was sympathetic, while another part felt, acutely, the responsibility of raising a young man who would, someday, be constantly in the public eye.

Everybody had advice. People skilled about all things childhood were on nanny staff. Outside experts had been consulted. And yet, in the end, he felt very alone with this journey.

"Your nanny is nearly out of her mind with worry," he told his son sternly. Why hadn't he said *he* was nearly out of his mind with worry?

"I don't like her," Marcello said, with that mutinous look on his face that had become more and more familiar since the death of his mother. He scowled at Enrique, his expression saying, *And I don't much like you, either.*

His son's inexplicable antipathy toward him cut like a knife. He could not understand what had caused it, and worse, he could not seem to overcome it.

Again, he was aware of the irony of being seen as one of the most powerful men in the world, and yet he could not even coax the most reluctant of obedience—never mind affection— from his five-year-old son.

"Come," he said, holding out his hand. "We will find Miss Penny."

But embarrassingly, Marcello rebelled, folding his arms firmly over his chest, and nestling farther under Guido's arm.

Everybody in the room had now been placed in a terrible position, by a five-year-old!

Guido either had to force Marcello away from him, which Enrique did not want him to do, or Enrique had to repeat his order and if it was not followed, this time, physically remove his son from the bed. He really did not want a tantrum or tears in the Olivera cottage. The family was dealing with enough without his unruly son bringing more drama to their household.

But in a blink, before either man had to decide what to do, Gabriela cocked her head toward the open window.

"Cello," she said, wide-eyed, "do you hear that?"

Enrique tilted his head. Gabriela had *already* been invited to use the nickname? Miss Penny had not.

"Hear what?" the child asked. "Birds?"

"I'm sure I hear Geraldo in the garden," Gabriela said. "Sometimes he climbs the olive tree—probably after one of those birds! But he's become so feeble he can't get back down. His claws are not working right anymore. Shall we go rescue him before you go with your papa?"

Papa.

Enrique longed for that more casual endearment from his son, but no, Marcello addressed him always, formally as Father.

Enrique debated this new parenting skill Gabriela had just presented him with: Was it okay to tell a little story—even if it wasn't true—to get your child to do what you wanted?

There was no arguing with the result. His son left the bed and placed his hand in Gabriela's with a trust that sparked some emotion behind Enrique's eyes, though he deliberately hardened his features as Gabriela and Marcello moved by him and into the hallway.

"Is there anything I can do for you, Guido?" he asked quietly, when the two had left the room.

"You know what I want from you," Guido said.

I do?

"Look after what is most precious to me."

And he could have been talking about the olive groves.

But Enrique knew he wasn't.

"I will," he vowed, and he knew that was already true. He would look after the Oliveras as if it was a sacred duty.

Even if it added an extra layer of complexity to the rush of feelings seeing Gabriela again had caused in him.

He moved beside the man's bed, and took his hand. Just like that, years evaporated and he remembered being a little boy, and finding Guido for the first time. Their relationship had strengthened as time went by, Guido acting as a mentor, passing on his formidable volume of knowledge about the trees of this island to the heir apparent, who felt it was his duty to know.

Again, Enrique felt emotion stinging behind his eyes.

"I'm sorry," he said.

"Ach," Guido responded. "For what?"

Suddenly, Enrique wasn't sure. For the unruly behavior of his son? No, deeper, for a loss that this entire island would feel for a long, long time. That he would feel in his own heart for the rest of his life.

"There is nothing to be sorry for," Guido said. "My beautiful angel, Gabriela, has come home. I was blessed with a visit from Cello. The birds are singing. Geraldo, the horrible, is stuck in a tree and soon I'll have the pleasure of hearing the Crown Prince scrambling up a tree after him."

Impossibly, Enrique found himself going from sadness to a shared chuckle with Guido.

"I thought the cat in the tree was just a story to persuade obedience from Marcello."

Guido's eyebrows shot up at the insinuation that Gabriela had lied. "Can you not hear the cat? He's making quite a racket."

Enrique tilted his head, and sure enough the cat was now howling piteous outrage at his predicament.

"Your Majesty," Guido said, closing his eyes, "I fear I have failed you. You must learn to hear with your heart."

Enrique stared at the beloved old face, and felt it was, somehow, not Guido who had failed him, but he who had failed Guido.

For it had been a very long time since he had listened with his heart.

He left Guido and gave Maria a quick pat on her shoulder as he went through her aroma-filled kitchen. She responded by laying her hand on top of his and leaving it there for a moment. In that simple gesture, he felt what he had always felt here in the Olivera house: welcome, a member of the family.

He went into the garden to find Gabriela and Marcello standing beneath the thick branches and foliage of the tree, looking helplessly up at the cat, who was loudly ordering his own rescue.

"We're not tall enough, Father," Marcello said sadly.

It felt good to have a problem to solve for his son.

"I can put you on my shoulders," he said. "And then you'll be tall enough."

His son's whole face lit up, and Enrique crouched down and Marcello scrambled onto his shoulders. "Don't get scratched," he warned his son.

"He won't scratch me!" Marcello declared. "We're friends."

That cat was at least seventeen years old. He had been skulking around this garden since Enrique and Gabriela were children. Enrique was pretty sure Geraldo considered all humans his servants, not his friends.

He stood up, feeling the warmth of his son's legs on his neck, the hands folded across his forehead, the small muscles bunching as Marcello stretched upward. Enrique savored the moment, more connected to his son than he had been since Amelia's death.

"I nearly have him," he shouted, squirming. "Geraldo, come."

Enrique tilted his head and peered upward.

"He won't listen to a dog command," Gabriela said. She made a little clicking sound with her tongue, to try to encourage the cat over the one inch that separated him from Marcello's eager grasp, but the cat sat frozen on the branch.

Marcello settled back on his father's shoulders. "Darn! I still can't reach. And he won't come. Put me down!"

Enrique set his son down, and Marcello stepped away from him.

"I suppose he'll figure out how to get down when he gets hungry enough," he told his son.

Marcello gave him a disdainful look that said he didn't understand anything, which felt uncomfortably close to the truth these days.

"I know what to do!" his son declared. He gazed intently between his father and Gabriela, clearly calculating.

"Yes, it will work," he decided. "Put Guido's little girl on your shoulders. It will work. I know it will!"

CHAPTER FOUR

GABRIELA FROZE. Of course, Marcello's suggestion was absurd. More than absurd! Prince Enrique was not going to invite her onto his shoulders.

But the man in question was looking at her quizzically. She smoothed her skirt uneasily. He lifted an eyebrow at her.

Just like that, she was young again, and knew what he was saying without him speaking a word.

Was she game to try?

And just like that, the Prince was young again, too, some mischief lighting the dark depths of his eyes, that formidable remoteness gone from him.

He squatted down and tapped his shoulder. Marcello shrieked his approval.

It was a moment that, if a person thought about it for too long, would become way too evident it meant too much. And then the moment would be gone, but the wash of awkwardness would remain.

Gabriela made her choice, if it could be called that. The two princes were quite irresistible.

She strode toward Enrique, kicked off her shoes, tucked her skirt firmly against her thighs, took a deep breath and stepped onto his shoulders.

It was really everything she could do not to gasp as she placed her legs on either side of his neck. Even with the slight barrier of the thin fabric of the skirt, heat radiated from him onto the delicate skin of her inner thigh.

"Okay?" he asked.

She was not okay! She was being swamped with primal feelings that were stunning in their intensity. Of course, she would die before she let him know that.

"Yes," she lied, through clenched teeth. "Fine."

He rose effortlessly, lifting her with grace and strength, the soft curve of her legs and bottom molding to his hard, muscular strength way too easily. She wobbled. The truth was, Gabriela felt off-balance in every way it was possible for a woman to feel off-balance.

She folded her hands over his forehead in an effort to stabilize herself. Again, nothing could have prepared her for the deepening of her searing awareness of him as a man. The skin-on-skin contact, and the springy sensuality of the silk of his hair beneath her fingertips, made her feel as heady as if she had consumed too much champagne. She wobbled again.

His hands closed around her shins, and he pulled her legs tight into his chest. This new area of contact, the warmth and strength in his touch, made it very difficult—nearly impossible—to focus on the mission.

The electrical jolts of pure awareness threatened her precarious balance even more, and they both tightened their holds.

She forced herself to focus, glad Enrique could not see her, as she could feel a blush rising hot in her cheeks.

Geraldo—the mission—peered at her from the branches of the tree. He meowed piteously. She reached. Enrique adjusted, just a hair, to compensate for her movement.

She felt the broadness of his shoulder shifting under the curve of her bottom, the back of her thigh.

Good grief! She was not an innocent, freshly released from a convent. And yet, there was no denying the ripple of pure *want* that this unexpectedly intimate encounter was creating in her.

"Geraldo!" she said, out loud, sternly, hoping her tone

would disguise all the helpless sensations coursing through her. "Come here."

She leaned closer to the tree, and held out her arms, hoping the cat would walk into them, but no, he yowled pathetically, and sure enough, when she looked closer she could see it was the non-retracting claws that were causing his difficulty.

Leaning in, her every micro-movement causing a micro-adjustment from Enrique, Gabriela had to get a finger under the cat's paw, and loosen each of his claws, one at time. The first paw freed, and while she cajoled him not to reengage it in the tree, she got the other one free. Finally, after what seemed to be a very long period of extremely intimate contact with Enrique's neck, she got her hand under the cat's belly, lifted, and then Geraldo's substantial weight settled against her breast.

"I have him!" she called, finally, triumphantly.

Enrique lowered himself slowly into a crouch, bracing one hand on the ground. She considered her options. It had been easy to step from behind him to get on his shoulders, but it seemed as if it would be much harder to dismount that way.

Sensing her dilemma, he ducked his head. With as much dignity as she could muster, she slid off his shoulders, over his lowered head. For one stunning moment, her skirt caught, and she felt the heat of his breath on her thigh.

The Prince was under her skirt. It was a millisecond, if that, before she stepped away. She knew there was no way the redness she could feel burning in her cheeks could be possibly attributed to the rescue. Had there ever been a more embarrassing predicament?

Thankfully, there was the distraction of a very excited Marcello.

"Geraldo," he crooned, holding up his arms for the cat.

She went to pass the feline to its most ardent admirer, only to find Geraldo's claws were as firmly caught in her blouse as they had been in the tree branch.

She tugged, and nothing happened. When she tugged a little

more firmly, the cat, who had thankfully not panicked at his predicament while in the tree, panicked now. He tried, with increasing franticness, to jerk his paws free from the fabric of her blouse.

"He's stuck," she told Enrique, trying for a calm tone, but hearing the faint edge of desperation. "It's that problem he's having with his claws. If you could get a finger under his—"

But they both froze at the very thought, because the Prince's finger under the cat's paw would put it directly on her breast.

"Here," Enrique said, "I'll put my hands around the cat's middle, and you can disengage him."

But when he reached for the cat, Geraldo hissed and tried to scramble away, climbing her blouse with his back paws, while his front ones remained firmly caught in the fabric above her breast.

As the cat became more panicked—writhing mightily in his determination to free himself—his trapped claw met her skin. She gave a little cry of pain and could feel her own panic rising.

Quickly, operating on what seemed to be pure instinct, Enrique reached past the cat, flicked open the buttons of her blouse and slid it open and off her. He guided it to the ground with the cat still stuck in it, howling his indignation at his predicament.

Marcello darted toward the cat, but without taking his eyes off her, Enrique ordered his son to stop. Even though the little boy looked like he had a tendency not to listen, some note of pure authority in his father's voice stopped him in his tracks.

Gabriela was standing in front of the Prince in her bra! The gods had apparently decided to show her there was, indeed, more embarrassing predicaments than having the Prince under her skirt!

It was as if everything went very, very still. Even the yowling of the cat seemed to be far off in the distance.

She watched Enrique's stunned expression as he took her in. She watched his eyes darken with something so smolder-

ing it jumped the small space between them and lit an answering fire in her.

Ridiculously, she glanced down at herself, and found a moment's satisfaction in her choice of underwear this morning:
her bra was a blush of pink, spider webs and lace, sophisticated and sexy. It was standard fare in New York City bou-
tiques. Here on the island? Not so much.

She folded her arms over the confection of silk and lace.

"You're bleeding," he told her, but there was a hoarse catch
to his voice that she suspected had nothing to do with blood.

Gabriela glanced down at herself. A tiny, thin line of red
was appearing, above her folded arms, but between her breasts.

"It's nothing," she said, meeting Enrique's gaze again. Was
there a certain hoarseness to her own voice? "Superficial. A
scratch."

For a suspended moment, it looked as if he might move
closer, to get a better look. Perhaps to touch the blood-lined
scratch.

The tiniest shiver—anticipation of being touched by him
again?—went through her. She took a small step back from
him, and from the magnetic field that had sprung up, powerfully, between them.

In a blink, Enrique unbuttoned his own shirt, stripped it
off and closed the small distance she had managed to put between them.

His naked chest inches from her own, she took him in. He
looked like one of those warriors that graced the covers of
romance novels. She made herself look away from his chest
before she licked her lips in pure hunger.

But looking into his face was almost a worse torment. She
could see the fine shadow of whiskers on his cheeks and chin.
She could see the small dent, like a thumbprint, in the plump-
ness of his lower lip. She could see the sooty tangle of his
lashes, the multiple shades of darkness in his eyes.

His scent, beautifully clean, seductively masculine, tickled her nostrils and then embraced her completely as he swung his shirt gently around her own naked shoulders and tucked it protectively around her.

Now, it was her turn to be stunned.

Oh, how the boy of her memory had matured! He was deep-chested, breathtakingly sculpted, as perfectly made as the marble statue that graced the front courtyard of his palace home.

They stared at each other for a moment, some forbidden and primitive awareness absolutely raw between them.

The intensity of the moment was shattered when the garden gate was flung open and a harried-looking young woman tumbled through it.

Enrique moved a quick step back from Gabriela. She turned from him and took in what could only be Miss Penny.

The poor girl looked young and terrified. Her eyes found Marcello first, and she started to call out his name.

But then she froze, and took in the scene before her: bare-chested prince, strange woman with a man's shirt draped around her.

The girl glanced over her shoulder, debating escape, but instead dropped into an awkward curtsey.

"Your Highness," she said.

"Miss Penny," Enrique replied. Without an ounce of self-consciousness, he reached down to the discarded blouse on the ground and flicked at the cat's paws.

With a final yowl and furious tug, Geraldo was free. He held up his front paws, one then the other, inspected each for damage, shook them and leveled each of them—Enrique, Gabriela, Marcello and Miss Penny—a regal glare, before marching off to his sanctuary under the shrubs.

"Your Highness," Miss Penny said to Enrique, her voice quavering, "I have failed you. And your son."

"You are not the first person Marcello has managed to escape," Enrique told her, and Gabriela noticed how deliberately tempered his tone was.

It was clear the young nanny worshipped him and that a harsh word at this moment could have destroyed her.

She was unable, however, to accept forgiveness.

"Your Highness, I can't do it," she said, dropping her eyes from Enrique's, sending a bewildered gaze at Marcello. "He dislikes me. He won't listen to anything I say. He ran away, and could have been in terrible danger. It would have been my fault if something happened."

"Miss Penny, the thing is, nothing did happen, and we could take it as a learning experience—"

Miss Penny stunned all of them by interrupting the Prince. "You'll have to find someone more suitable. For his sake, and yours, I resign. As of this very moment. Your Highness."

Enrique's mouth fell open. "Miss Penny, I really think—"

But Miss Penny was flustered beyond measure. Her cheeks red, her lip trembling, her eyes sparkling with tears, she whirled away and ran out the gate. For a moment, it hung open behind her, but then she tiptoed back and shut it with a gentle click.

"I fear she's gone to fall on her sword," Gabriela said wryly.

"Really?" Marcello asked, far too eagerly.

"It's a figure of speech," Enrique told him.

"I didn't know Miss Penny had a sword," Marcello said, and looked at the gate wistfully, as if he might have given her a second chance had he been armed with that knowledge.

"She doesn't have a sword!" Enrique said.

"Guido's little girl said she does," Marcello said, stubbornly.

"I didn't mean she had a sword," Gabriela said. "I'm sorry I confused you. It's a very grown-up expression. It means people are really sorry. Miss Penny was really sorry she lost you."

"She didn't lose me," Marcello said, not the least repentant now that he'd discovered there was no sword involved. "I lost her."

And then he looked at his bare-chested father, Gabriela in his father's shirt, and gave a chortle of pure delight at all the unexpected turns his morning had taken.

But it wasn't the gleeful Marcello that captured Gabriela's attention. It was Enrique, and the light that came on in his face at the music of his son's laughter.

Still, he said firmly, "You've been very naughty, Marcello."

"I will fall on my sword," Marcello decided.

Enrique had to bend over and scoop up Gabriela's blouse to hide his laughter from his son. She had to bite the inside of her cheek.

He straightened and extended it to her. She could see the suppressed laughter dancing in his dark eyes, like sunlight glancing off water.

She wasn't quite sure what to do, but it was not put her blouse back on in front of him! And so she shot a hand out from under his shirt, and grabbed her blouse with that hand, and tightened the one that clutched his shirt closed at her throat.

"You need to look after that scratch," the Prince said gravely. "It will need antiseptic."

It was dismissal. In her own yard! And then she noticed that the remoteness had crept back into his eyes.

For a moment, she debated the same exit as Miss Penny, including a curtsey!

But no, with as much dignity as she could manage, she said, "Cello, it was so nice to meet you."

Marcello did not answer, so Gabriela glanced over at him.

He pretended to lift an imaginary sword from a belt at his waist. He placed it solemnly in front of him.

And then he fell dramatically on top of it. He lay there, still, and then opened one eye to gauge the reaction of his audience. Pleased with himself, he burst out laughing, hugging himself and rolling on the lawn, delighted at the unexpected hilarity in his world.

Gabriela returned her gaze to the Prince, who was taking in his son with a look that clearly said nothing about being a prince had prepared him for the rigors of parenthood, particularly the unexpected crisis of being an only parent.

Ridiculous to feel pity for him, but here he was, arguably one of the most powerful men in the world, overwhelmed by a five-year-old.

"He's very precocious," she said, "and very, very bright."

"I'm in over my head," he admitted, "Way over."

She could feel some longing in her breathe to life, some desire to step in, to help him, to fix it all. But she could not encourage those kinds of feelings!

Just this brief encounter had shown her how vulnerable she was to every single thing about Enrique. She could not make his problems her problems.

Not that he had asked her to, she reminded herself. She had to bring this encounter, fraught with so many subtle dangers, to a close.

She debated, briefly, how to address him. Formality would be good for rebuilding some barriers between them. On the other hand, given their location, her current state of undress and his shirtlessness, it seemed as if the circumstances were somewhat less than formal.

And she certainly did not want Enrique to know how unbalanced this whole encounter had made her feel.

Some little devil inside her was prompting her to remove that remote expression from his face.

"It's a good thing," she said solemnly, leaning toward him, and whispering for his ears only, "that I put on panties this morning."

She watched, with satisfaction, when his jaw dropped. Mission accomplished: nothing the least remote about that look.

And then, shoulders proudly back, she turned on her heel, to her house, and left him to deal with his son.

The victory of her exit, of having the last word, was marred, somewhat, by her father's laughing face at the bedroom window, and her mother's astonished one at the kitchen.

And the fact she just knew she was going to keep that shirt forever.

CHAPTER FIVE

As Enrique walked the well-worn Mediterranean cobble pathway that began outside the Oliveras' gate and led to the back garden of the palace, he contemplated Gabriela, and her last statement.

His whole body had felt as if it was humming with awareness of her, even before she had said that.

It all was a stark reminder she was not the girl she had once been. Her statement, the loveliness of her bra, told him her years away from this island had made her more sophisticated. Bolder.

It made her—a person he had known his entire life—feel a bit like a stranger, as if there was an exotic, secret side to her that she had never revealed to him.

But once that had occurred, could you ever *not* see it again? He felt the danger of his intrigue with her.

As soon as that gate had closed behind them, he gave Marcello a stern lecture about escaping from his nanny, but even as he had given it, his heart wasn't in it.

He was grateful that, in all the world, there was not a safer place than this island. The palace, and the grounds on which the Olivera cottage sat, were further protected by an ancient stone wall that a five-year-old had no hope of scaling.

He was reminded that he, himself, at the same age Marcello was now, had begun to escape to the warmth of the Olivera cottage. Because of the safety on the grounds, he recalled his own escapes had been treated with sternness, but there had been no mistaking a certain tolerance ran beneath the obligatory reprimands.

Marcello skipped ahead of him, swinging an imaginary sword, but abandoning it to stop, get down on his haunches and inspect an interesting bug or stone or blade of grass. Enrique was aware of wishing his son would share some of his observations with him, but no, every time he drew close, Marcello would take up his imaginary sword, again, and run ahead.

Still, there was some happiness around his son, and he could feel the relief of that. Marcello had become so somber since his mother's death.

Enrique contemplated what had just taken place in the Olivera garden, and it was not the resignation of the nanny that was foremost in his thoughts!

No, his mind went to that impulsive moment he had crouched down, and Gabriela had stepped toward him, and straddled his shoulders, the moment his hands had closed around the silky skin on her shins, the way her heat had radiated onto his neck...

It had been crazy, of course, to lift Gabriela up. It had been pure madness. Why had he given any credence, at all, to a five-year-old's suggestion?

It was simple, really.

He had wanted to make his son happy.

How had something so simple become so complicated? Not just the sudden physical contact between him and Gabriela, but that startling moment afterward, when he had found himself under her skirt, and then, worse yet, when he had freed her from her blouse—and the cat—to leave her to stand there exposed.

Utterly gorgeous, the blush in her cheeks matching the blush of that exquisitely feminine piece of fabric that had covered her.

Enrique could not *unsee* that. He could not *unfeel* the sensation of her strong legs bracketing his neck.

He could not unhear, *It's a good thing I put on panties this morning.* He forbade himself to go down that road, though his wayward thoughts blithely ignored his command. Did that mean there were mornings—

Stop, he ordered himself. *I mean it.*

But still his thoughts, uncharacteristically undisciplined, like a puppy eager to please, but easily distracted, continued to drift back to the encounter in the garden.

There was no denying it was a *new* Gabriela, light-years removed from the young girl he had grown up with, and shared so many memories of. In warm weather—which was nearly always here on the island—they had lived in bathing suits. Was that much different from what he had just seen?

Yes.

Nothing could have prepared the Prince for how much Gabriela had changed since those long-ago summers, and he had seen, from the sudden heat in her eyes, that so had he.

They'd been children.

And now they were grown-ups. He reminded himself, sternly, that aside from growing up with Gabriela in her bathing suit, as an adult, he had been on some of the most beautiful private beaches in the world and onboard yachts where scantily clad women were the norm. Why had he been, well, so shocked? So aware?

It was the unexpectedness, he assured himself, it was the fact that the situation was so out of context, that had caused such a deep visceral reaction on his part.

A warning, he told himself firmly, that their worlds had been separated for a long time. He did not like his thoughts acting like an unruly puppy, running amok. His position in life required great composure and great control. To react in such a primal way to Gabriela was, as his mother would point out, unbecoming to his station.

He was going to have to avoid his childhood friend. It was

that simple. Until he remembered his vow to Guido, which made it more complicated.

The encounter this morning had shown him his vow would have to be kept at arm's length. Hopefully, he would not have to keep that vow for a long, long time. He felt his heart clench at the thought of losing Guido.

At the thought of Gabriela losing her father.

And of Marcello facing yet another loss.

There was a shortcut through a hedge that would bring the princes, father and son, to a courtyard off the set of doors that led into Enrique's ground-floor bedroom, but he didn't think it was a good idea to show his already wayward son yet another route to the Olivera cottage. When he cast a look at that secret passageway, he saw it was now almost completely grown over, anyway.

Instead, they crossed the formal back garden of the palace. It was shaded by huge palm trees and resplendent in colors and scents of shrubs and flower beds. The gardens spread out like spokes from a wheel around a central fountain that gurgled pleasantly. It was incredibly opulent, so very different from the cottage garden they had just left.

The palace, Casa del Falcon, was not like the intimidating stone fortresses of European royalty. Constructed over five hundred years ago out of a very rare local marble—brilliant white shot through with subtle veins of rose—its exterior lines were sweeping, and hinted of the soaring ceilings, held up with huge dark beams, within.

The windows, with the exception of his own main-floor quarters, had no glass, to better invite ocean fresh breezes into the interior, already cool because of the thickness of the walls. There were heavy wooden shutters that could be closed in event of storms. Centuries-old flowering vines climbed the walls and framed the windows, their scent perfuming the interior.

Many of the corridors were open-air, as was the one they entered now, through a pillared, vine-covered archway.

If they went right, it would lead to the kitchen and utility areas. But they went left, toward the public areas of the castle. The princes ended up in the massive, breeze-swept foyer, with doors off it open to the grand salon, the formal banquet room, the ballroom.

On the far wall, a matched pair of curving marble staircases bracketed the foyer. The right staircase led to more rooms that were for official use: the Queen's study and his own, a library and staff offices. The hallway off the left of the upper staircase went to guest suites.

Tastefully hidden behind a heavy antique carved wooden panel was the entrance to the elevator that went to the third floor, where the smaller of two personal suites was located. Queen Katalina had taken that one when he and Amelia had married, giving him the larger ground-floor unit with its nursery wing.

He had been in some of the most beautiful spaces in the entire world, but none had ever compared to his magnificent home. And yet, still, for all that it was inordinately beautiful, it could never achieve the coziness—the *feeling*—of the small cottage they had just left.

In the hallway on their way to their quarters, Marcello paused and squinted up at a framed sword, sheathed, that hung on the wall, beside a tapestry and framed portraits of their ancestors. The sword's jeweled hilt glinted in the sun that poured into the space.

"Can I have a sword?"

"No."

It should have been a simple question, and a simple answer, but nothing, Enrique had discovered about the world of parenting, was ever simple.

"I meant a toy one," Marcello said.

Was a toy sword acceptable? Little boys played with little-boy things. But toy guns were long since seen as politically incorrect. Where did a sword fall on that continuum of correctness?

Better to play it safe. He had done enough risky things today in service of his son's happiness.

"No," Enrique said, hesitating a moment too long, as they continued down the wide hallway to their personal wing.

His son, the only one in his world who would dare to question him, gave him a look Enrique could only interpret as challenging.

"You have a sword," Marcello pointed out, pouncing on his father's hesitation.

His son, sadly, had seen his father in full formal dress uniform only once. At his mother's funeral.

"Yes, it's ceremonial. It's not a toy."

"But there could be a toy one," Marcello insisted, as they proceeded down the wide marble-floored hallway to the double doors to their quarters.

Enrique opened the door.

The space was, of course, less formal than the spaces seen by the public. Amelia had, for a while, been able to assuage her great unhappiness at their arranged marriage by pouring herself into the renovation of their suite. The result was an extraordinarily modern space within the ancient walls of the castle. With its sleek lines and a sophisticated palette of neutrals—with the odd splash of color in an abstract canvas—it could have been an apartment in a penthouse in Los Angeles. It was tasteful, and beautiful.

And not the least welcoming, warm or cozy. It reminded Enrique of some of the very posh hotel presidential suites he had stayed in.

Why had he really not ever noticed that before?

Gabriela.

Without even trying, he could feel his perceptions of everything shifting. And he didn't like it.

"We'll ask Miss—uh—" He remembered Miss Penny had just resigned. Still, there was an entire staff of nannies, one of whom was coming toward them now.

"Caravanno," he remembered her name.

"Your Highnesses," she greeted them quietly, giving Marcello a warm smile, which he did not return.

Enrique was not unaware of his own desire to abscond on the responsibility of making the decision, and it bothered him. Still, he did not want to play the bad guy—to deepen already existing fissures—between him and his son.

Marcello's brows dropped.

"Yes, Miss Caravanno will know," Enrique said firmly.

She raised an eyebrow at them.

"We wanted to know about the appropriateness of a sword as a toy."

"Oh," she said, uneasily, "I don't think that's a good idea."

His son gave him, not her, a withering look, and Enrique could not help but think how Gabriela had used distraction so masterfully.

"Isn't it time for tea?" he asked.

"It is indeed. I have it all ready in the nursery," Miss Caravanno said, holding out her hand to Marcello, who ignored it and marched by her with his chin in the air.

Much later, Enrique went into the nursery to tuck Marcello into bed and say good-night. Thankfully, after the distractions of this morning, his day had gotten back on track, filled with business meetings, phone calls and one charity event that had just ended. He was still in his formal tuxedo.

"How was the rest of your day with Miss Caravanno?" he asked, perching on the edge of the bed.

"I don't like her. I don't like any of them," Marcello declared, pulling his sheets up around his chin. "Guido would know about the sword."

His son was *still* on about the sword. And it was very likely true that Guido would have a good answer, but Enrique didn't think he should undermine the authority of the nanny by revisiting the question.

He tried the distraction technique. "What was your favorite thing that you and Miss Caravanno did today?"

"Nothing," he said darkly. And then the darkness suddenly left Marcello's face, and a beautiful light went on. "I will have Guido's little girl for my nanny!"

This suggestion was posed with utter confidence, in the same way his son had posed Gabriela climbing on Enrique's shoulders as a solution for getting the cat. The result should serve as a warning about taking suggestions from his son.

Besides, after seeing Gabriela in a state of undress, Enrique was not sure he could ever think of her as a little girl again.

And secondly, he had just decided, because of that encounter, that he needed to avoid Gabriela, not invite her to join his personal household staff!

"That won't work," he said, firmly.

The happiness went from Marcello as if a needle had pierced the outer shell of a balloon. His face crumpled and he burst into tears. "I want *her*," he sobbed.

"We can't have everything we want."

His son gave him a look that said, without words, he already knew that, thank you very much. Then he rolled over, putting his back on his father, and defiantly put his thumb in his mouth.

Enrique didn't have the heart for a correction. "Good night, Marcello."

No response. Enrique turned and left the room, closing the door quietly behind him. He had sent the staff away, and he took off his jacket, loosened his tie, made himself a drink and wandered over to the window.

Over the garden wall, he could see lights on in the Olivera house.

It made him think of the predicament Marcello had put them in on the bed with Guido, refusing his father's instructions, and of Gabriela coming to the rescue. She would know the answer to the sword question even better than Miss Caravanno or Guido. He knew she would.

He didn't want to think about Marcello's impossible suggestion! And yet, gazing at the lit-up cottage, his mind turned over the possibilities.

Having Gabriela as a nanny would be difficult and fraught with complexities. But now that the idea had been planted, Enrique was not sure he could think of a better person to coax some happiness back out of his son.

And in the end, wasn't this what a good father did?

Put the well-being of his child ahead of his own?

Gabriela would be good for Marcello. Did anything, beyond that, matter?

Startled, he realized he had made the decision. Equally as startling, it was an impulsive decision, an unexpected turn of events, in a world where he relied heavily on complete order.

He debated how he should approach Gabriela, and decided it would be imperative that he kept things on a strictly business footing. Nothing but trouble could come from revisiting the bonds of old friendships.

Particularly now, after the unexpectedly sensual events of the morning with Gabriela were emblazoned on his brain, and he would probably wonder, for the rest of his life, whether she considered panties optional.

"Ouch!" Dr. Leon Ferreira said. Like many of the people of this close-knit island nation, Gabriela recognized the veterinarian from her childhood, a boy who had gone to school a few years ahead of her.

The cat writhed mightily, and the vet let go. Geraldo bolted away. Leon was wearing huge leather gloves, but Geraldo had managed to bite right through one.

He slipped it off and looked at the damage. "I think the large animals are less dangerous," he decided.

She looked after Geraldo, who had planted himself in the middle of a clump of oregano, and was glaring at her with betrayed indignation.

And indignant he should be! He had escaped with his clump-ridden fur only partially shaved, so he was down to his dusty scalp in some areas, while black spikes of hair stood straight up in others.

"He looks like a mini-monster," she said ruefully.

Leon laughed. He was an attractive man. No wedding band, though perhaps his work would make him remove rings. Still, she found herself not interested. At all. And not because of her recent breakup, either.

Had she been waiting, this morning, hopeful for a gate to squeak open, for a small escapee to find her? For his father to come looking?

"Should we catch him and finish?" she said, annoyed with the direction of her thoughts.

"I don't want to seem like a sissy, but given the go-for-the-jugular look, I'm going to say no. On a professional note, let's leave it. We're both bleeding already, and I think we've stressed him enough for the day. At least we managed to get all his claws done."

"I'll get you some antiseptic," Gabriela said, slipping off the pair of gloves Leon had provided her with.

"He got you pretty bad, too."

"Yes, he did. Poor old guy. He had no idea that was for his own good."

"Don't worry about the antiseptic," Leon said. "I'll look after it when I get back to the stables."

She stood up and brushed mud and grass off her shorts. "Thank you for coming."

Leon stood up, too. "Gabriela—"

The gentle tone in his voice made her attention snap back to him.

Please don't ask me out.

"He's very old," he said softly.

"Seventeen," she said. "At least."

The doctor nodded. "The clumping is a sign he can't groom himself anymore. And the claws. Well, you saw the claws."

Geraldo's claws had splintered into dust, like rotten wood, when they had cut them.

"What are you saying?" she asked, though her falling heart told her she already knew. She would have preferred being asked out to *this*.

The vet looked at her gravely. "That the time is coming when you will have to make a decision."

For some reason his statement, and the sympathy in it, felt as if it knocked the wind out of her.

Of course, she had known her cat was getting old. But somehow, *that* had never occurred to her.

Thankfully, the back gate opened and a young man slipped in. She was aware of how much she wanted it to be Marcello. It wasn't, but it still allowed her to avert her attention from the vet and the terrible message he had just delivered.

"Are you Miss Olivera?" the young man asked.

"I am."

"I'm Phillipe, from Prince Enrique's office. I have a message for you."

Once, she had known everyone who worked in the palace offices, and they had known her.

Gabriela stared down at the creamy white piece of paper Phillipe placed in her hand, the familiar House of Falcon crest subtly embossed letterhead.

The young man waited, expectantly, and she opened it. A thick sheet of paper unfolded in her hand and she scanned it, bemused.

She'd been summoned to the office of the Prince! The time was impossible. In an hour? She looked down at herself. She was an absolute mess.

And suddenly it all felt like too much for her. All the

changes. Palace staff not knowing her, and her not knowing them. Her father's illness, the vet giving her a warning about the cat's longevity.

She thought of the last royal summons she had received, the one from the Queen, and all the years she had missed with both her father and her cat, because of *this* family, with their crests and impossibly thick stationery and regal summonses.

Enrique couldn't just call the cottage phone if he needed to speak to her? He had to summon her, to remind her of yet another change in her life, another place she could never go back to, that was lost forever?

Gone were those sunny endless days from her past that they had spent together, unburdened by their different statuses in life.

She felt an insult in the piece of paper she held. Enrique was obviously and deliberately putting up the barriers of their stations between them by asking her to meet him so formally.

The way it used to be, if he had something he wanted to say to her, he would have come to her, crossed the path between the two homes without a thought.

Or flashed a light onto her bedroom window—one garden—and a whole world away.

Or maybe he would have picked up an old rotary-dial phone and called her, perhaps suggested a meeting at one of their old haunts.

But no, a summons. He was making it clear that none of the old existed between them anymore. Was he letting her know how totally inappropriate her final remark had been? Rather than being humbled by that possibility, it made her sense of herself rise up.

"Tell the Prince," she said haughtily, raising her chin, "I will not be available in an hour."

There. Hermosa Mariposa was her world, too, and he was not going to make all the rules in it. He was not going to do a full retreat into the kind of remoteness that people like him and his mother wore like shields.

Leaving both the men in shocked silence, she turned her back and walked, with what she could only hope was regal grace, into the humble cottage of her childhood.

CHAPTER SIX

ALMOST THE SECOND Gabriela shut the cottage door, there was a tentative rap on it, reminding her that you could not shut something so flimsy as a door against a world pushing its complications at you.

Her father.

Her cat.

Her heart belonging to…

"Miss?"

She threw the door back open. "What?"

The young messenger took a startled step back from her.

"Might I tell Prince Enrique when you *would* be available?"

"I'll be at his office at five p.m. He can call me if that's unsuitable. I believe he has the number."

The young messenger seemed to be considering how his commander would react to that news. "I will pass on your message," he said uncomfortably.

She snapped the door shut again without saying thank you.

She turned to see her father and mother at the kitchen table, staring at her, open-mouthed and wide-eyed. They were both holding cards, a pegboard between them.

"What?" she asked them, in the very same tone she had used on the messenger.

They both quickly focused on their cards. She might have tried to soften the *what* by saying how nice it was to see her father up at the table, except that he seemed to be trying to hide a smirk from her.

"What?" she asked, again.

He glanced at her and smiled, all innocence. He showed her his hand.

"Twenty-four," he said, but she was pretty sure that wasn't what he'd been smirking about. But then Guido called her his little angel, in three different languages, which made her feel guilty for snapping at him, though not guilty enough to apologize.

Now that she had set the appointment, Gabriela took her time. She took the traditional midday nap, then got up and showered. She blew her hair dry, put on makeup and added a few bandages to her fresh Geraldo wounds. She dug through the things she had brought home for an outfit that might be suitable for an audience with a prince.

What she needed was a power suit. Naturally, it had not even occurred to her to pack such an item for a trip to Isla Hermosa Mariposa.

She had to settle for wrinkle-free black slacks. She coupled them with a highly structured white linen shirt. The shirt was not wrinkle-free, she had to press it, and, of course, now her mother was smirking as if she was getting ready for a ball rather than answering a rather rude summons.

She put on the string of Hermosa Mariposa pearls her father had gotten her for her sixteenth birthday. At the time, his gift had seemed impossibly extravagant, but the rare and expensive pearls had elevated many an outfit to the next level of chic.

Thankfully, she had packed a single pair of high heels. The gleaming black stilettos took Gabriela from all business to ever so subtly—but powerfully—sexy. As she looked at herself in the mirror, she was pleased with what she saw. A confident woman, not the least put out to be summoned by a prince, not the least hesitant to turn the tables on him and answer his summons on her own terms. Not the least like the little peasant girl that had been ordered to the palace—and away from her beloved home—so many years ago.

Taking one final deep breath, and smoothing her blouse unnecessarily, she stepped out the cottage door and through the gate toward the palace. Of course, she had crossed this pathway a zillion times as a child, going to visit her mother in the kitchen, playing hide-and-seek in the back passageways with the Prince.

Since the summons had been official, she did not go through the back door, but walked an open-air corridor around the palace to the side entrance that was generally used for royal business.

The palace commissionaire was at a desk at this door, and it was still Angelo Madero. Most of the palace staff, like her parents, held positions that had been in their families for generations. Their social circles consisted of each other, and the Maderos had been her mother and father's best friends. Angelo was her godfather.

He leaped from behind his desk and greeted her by holding her shoulders, and scanning her face, then kissing both her cheeks.

"Beautiful!" he decided. "Oh, it makes an old man's heart happy to see an island daughter come home. I wish the circumstances were better. How is Guido today?"

"He seems a little better," she answered truthfully. "He had a good laugh yesterday when our cat got stuck up in a tree and I had to rescue it." She did not offer the detail that she had not been alone in her rescue.

"Ah, laughter," Angelo said. "Such good medicine. We have not had enough of it here."

It reminded Gabriela that the whole palace was still under the shroud of the death of the two princesses, Amelia and her unborn child.

"The Prince has asked to see me," she said.

"Yes, yes, I have it written here. I'll take you."

Which was good, because after her long absence, she had

no idea where Enrique's office would be. Of course, he had not had an office when they had been teenagers.

If Angelo thought the summons was odd, after practicing generations of decorum and navigating royal protocols, he never let on. And so, they went through the palace, with Angelo filling her in amicably about his children and his grandsons.

She was glad for his chatter, for even though she had grown up in the shadow of the palace, she had rarely found herself in its formal spaces.

The grandness—the priceless paintings, the hand-knotted carpets, the crystal-dripping chandeliers, the centuries-old furniture—was all stunningly gorgeous, of course, but more than a little intimidating. The confidence her outfit had given her could only go so far!

But she realized she could not imagine laughter in these spaces, and it made her feel faintly sorry for Enrique, but more so for Marcello. No wonder both princes had found their way to the cottage!

Angelo led her up the grand staircase and down a hallway, then knocked on a door, and opened it for her. She stepped into Enrique's office.

In the course of her work, she was well accustomed to the opulence of very rich men's office spaces.

In fact, Enrique's office space was toned down compared with some of those that Gabriela had been in. Still, the space was subtly elegant, and very masculine. There was a meticulous and precise order to his desk; nothing was out of place, a man in control of his world.

In the garden yesterday, she had still caught a glimpse of the boy he had once been. But here, his space spoke of a man of confidence, power and authority.

She allowed herself to look at him. Ah, yes, that professional remoteness was firmly in place. Still, everything about him was a perfect fit for his office. He was impeccably and beautifully groomed, not a hair out of place, freshly shaven. His silk tie was gorgeous, as were the gold cuff links. He had on a crisp white linen shirt, not unlike her own, though it had probably cost thousands of dollars. And it had not been pressed by him, of course! He probably didn't even shave himself!

He rose to his feet. "Thank you for coming. Would you like to sit?"

Gabriela had planned to be completely professional, as versed in and as accepting of strict royal protocols as anyone who had grown up in close proximity to a royal family should be.

Instead, she found herself ignoring his invitation to sit. She cocked her head at him, letting the silence draw out between them, until she saw him shift a little uncomfortably.

"A summons, Your Highness? I could hardly not come, could I?"

"Though not at the appointed time," he said, and something twitched around his lips. Annoyance?

Or amusement?

And then he disarmed her, when she most needed to be armed.

"How is Guido today?"

"Beating my mother at cribbage."

She had a sudden unwanted memory of her family teaching Enrique to play that very game on a rainy day around their kitchen table.

"She's letting him win," he said, his smile full of fond remembrance. "No one beats Maria at crib."

But then, a shadow crossed his face as it occurred to him why Maria would be letting Guido win.

"Gabriela, what's wrong with him?"

His concern was so genuine. How could she not be disarmed by him? Still, she needed to keep her defenses strongly in place.

But she did sink into the chair in front of his desk. But he did not sit down.

"I don't know for sure," she admitted. "I hoped maybe you knew. I've been assuming cancer, but neither he nor my mother has said that word."

As if by not saying it, they could hold back the truth of his new thinness, the grayish tinge to his skin, the weariness that settled around him like a cloak.

"I've tried to persuade him to go off island," Enrique confided in her. "I can access some of the best care in the world, but he won't hear of it."

"Would it involve flying?" she asked, dryly.

"It would."

Together they said, "It's unnatural," and shared a wry laugh. A little more of the chinking in the defensive barrier she had erected between them fell away.

"I told him I'd bring experts here, if he didn't want to fly. Same answer."

"Nature had been my father's church for his entire life," she said. "It would be an affront to him to suggest it has made a mistake."

"I know," he said softly. "It is hard not to admire a man who will stand by his beliefs even when his own life is at stake."

"I agree. Thank you for trying."

"Of course." He surveyed her for a moment, and then, his gaze fell to her sleeve and he frowned.

"Are you bleeding?" he asked.

She glanced down. Sure enough, one of her scratches was bleeding through the plaster she'd applied. It was her best shirt! She wanted to flee the room and put club soda on it.

Or maybe the reason she wanted to flee the room had nothing to do with her shirt. It was the weakness that his genuine care for Guido had caused.

Her sensation of weakness—when she so desperately needed to be strong—only intensified as Enrique came around his desk and stood before her, then leaned over her arm. He gently pushed up the cuff of her shirt, his touch cool and blistering at the very same time. He laid a finger on the bandage with the blood seeping out the edges.

"That's nasty," he said. "That didn't happen yesterday, did it?"

"No."

She did not miss his look of relief that he might have missed an injury on his watch. Another chunk of chinking fell out of her defensive wall at his protectiveness.

"How did you do that?"

"Leon—Dr. Ferreira—came over to help me with Geraldo. Geraldo objected."

He lowered her sleeve and his frown deepened. "Why were you holding the cat? Why didn't you call for an assistant?"

There! That was exactly what was needed as she was nearly melting under the warmth of his touch, his proximity and his concern for her and her family.

"Your Royal Highness," she said with deliberate stiffness, "we don't all have assistants at our disposal."

"Dr. Ferreira should have brought one with him."

"Don't be ridiculous. He was coming to help with a small cat, not to deal with a tiger." She caught the stunned look on his face. She suspected it had been a long time since someone had told him not to be ridiculous. "Do you have any club soda?"

"Can that be used as a disinfectant? I'll send for some."

She didn't bother to tell him she was more anxious to save her blouse than to stave off possible infection. He didn't have a bar in his office. For some inexplicable reason, she liked that. She really didn't want to like anything else about him!

"Of course you can send for club soda," she said coolly. "Perhaps a glass of 1959 Dom Perignon at the same time?"

He took a step back from her, but did not go back around his desk, nor make any effort to order a club soda. Instead he leaned his backside on the desk, crossed his arms over his chest and narrowed his eyes at her.

He was really impossibly good-looking when he did that!

"You seem a little angry," he noted after a moment.

"An official summons when you wanted to see me?" she said. "Really, Enrique? You couldn't just pop by the cottage? Or pick up a phone like everyone else?"

CHAPTER SEVEN

THE PRINCE LOOKED at Gabriela, and though he was plainly exasperated, he proceeded carefully. "Given the, er, incident, yesterday, I thought you might not appreciate me being overly familiar."

"Oh," she said. "When you sent the summons you were being considerate. I see. How nice."

"Well, yes, so I hoped. Plus, I wanted to discuss a proposition with you and I thought we should keep any arrangement we came to on a professional level."

"A proposition?" she echoed, caught off guard.

"Yes, a business proposition. As you witnessed yesterday, Miss Penny has suddenly resigned. I watched you with Marcello yesterday. He likes you. You like him. Of course, the remuneration will be very generous, and you will immediately be assigned as his primary caregiver."

Will. Immediately be assigned.

As if all of this was already decided. As if she had no choice.

"My life," she said icily, "beyond servicing the royal family's needs is of no consequence at all, is it?"

"I don't understand."

She didn't even mention that she had a degree in marketing and had been steadily climbing the ranks of the corporate ladder. She loved her job! She'd been given a leave of absence from her position in New York, but she had no doubt she would return there eventually when Guido's situation resolved, and she had ascertained her mother would be okay. What would the point be of staying here when the thing she wanted the most from this island—her very own prince—was an unrealistic fairy tale.

And here was that very prince presuming she'd give up her very satisfying life on his whim, to be a nanny, a field she had absolutely no qualifications in?

Even as some weak part of her actually *longed* to be with Marcello. But what if that longing was really about being with him? Prince Enrique? The hopeless love from her past?

No, this door had to be shut, quickly, firmly, irrevocably.

"This is eerily like the last time I was summoned," she said. "Now, as then, it's not an offer, it's an order."

"I'm sorry. I don't know what you're talking about." There was a certain edginess in his own voice now, too.

And she *liked* it. She liked that she was getting under his skin.

"Don't you? Don't you know your mother, Queen Katalina, summoned me here the day I finished high school?"

The expression on his face said he really had not known this.

"Yes, I was *offered* a scholarship, at a fine university in America. And then, when I graduated, I was *offered* a position with the Royal House of Falcon's head office in New York City. But they weren't really offers. They were orders. I was ordered by your mother to leave this island and I was never invited back."

Prince Enrique looked genuinely stunned by this information.

"And because of that," she finished, softly, "I have missed the last years of my father's life."

"Gabriela—"

"And now Leon has warned me I should prepare for the worst with Geraldo, too. I've had that cat since I was nine years old. My father found him in the olive grove when he was so tiny. He gave him to me."

"Gabriela—"

"So, I've missed the last years of my cat's life, too."

"Gabriela—"

She held up her hand to stop him, but to stop herself, too, from leaning toward the comfort she heard in his voice, to stay strong. There was strength in anger.

"So," she said, springing from her chair and whirling toward the door, "you can take your offer and shove it right up your Royal Highness."

She honestly did not know whether she was appalled or pleased at her uncharacteristic punchiness!

Prince Enrique stared at the empty place where Gabriela had sat, totally flummoxed. He'd been wrong that Marcello was the only one who dared to say no to him!

In the space of a few minutes, Gabriela had told him he was ridiculous, and now this. Had she really told him to shove his offer?

In no uncertain terms, actually.

She was also on a first-name basis with the vet, which should be of no importance at all, and yet it needled him, in a way he couldn't quite define.

Enrique took a deep, steadying breath. He contemplated his mother's interference in his life. It certainly explained Gabriela's radio silence when he'd tried to contact her. He felt a rare, burning rush of resentment, not just at his mother, but at a life that was mapped out, and exploring beyond the designated boundaries of that map was thwarted both secretively and openly.

He was reminded, with an ache, what Gabriela had been to him: his breath of fresh air, his intoxicating brush with freedom. She had been the one person in his world who had never seemed intimidated by his status, who had always spoken her truth to him, who had always allowed him to be himself in a world that required him to play roles.

He went back around his desk and sank into the chair. It was so good that she had said no. His heart was racing like crazy, as if he had just survived a hurricane. Or a wildfire. Or a storm at sea. Or all three.

He realized, absurdly, when she had sprung to her feet and stood inches away from him, the air around her crackling with her indignation, he had sensed the passion between them. Had he actually considered stepping toward her and claiming her lips with his own?

Of course he hadn't!

Well, all right, maybe for one heated second, he had felt the raw pull of an essential force between them.

That pull had been there, he remembered, the last time he had seen her, too. Almost a decade ago, and yet his memories were as fresh as if his first—and only—taste of her lips had happened yesterday.

He'd been home from his private school in Switzerland on a spring break. He'd met her in the garden on the eve of his return to school. There had been something in the air between them since the day he'd arrived home. Not new, exactly; it had been bubbling beneath the surface since they had both hit puberty. An awareness, an almost electrical tingle, an aching hunger to know more, to explore brand-new territories.

They had never talked about it.

Neither of them had ever mentioned it.

But there it was, in the accidental touching of hands, in lingering gazes, in the ways they moved around each other.

There it was when they swam together in the turquoise waters of the Bay of Butterflies, sensing each other's youth and strength and beauty in brand-new ways.

Resisting. Resisting. Resisting.

Like an elastic band pulled tighter and tighter and tighter.

Until—*SNAP*.

They had parted ways, that final day before he had to go back to Switzerland, but he'd been restless that night. Apparently so had she. He'd used the childish signal between them, a flashlight turned on and off directed at her window. The answering signal had come from the Olivera garden.

He'd gone to her, and they had sat on the wall in a darkened corner of the garden, the scent of herbs and olive flowers heavy in the warm night air around them.

He had taken her hand, oh, so tentatively. He had turned it over, and kissed her palm.

She had turned to look at him, her face uplifted, painted in moonlight, her eyes—those incredible green and gold and brown eyes—luminous with need.

She had leaned toward him, and he toward her.

The elastic band stretching.

Snap.

Their lips had connected.

Did a man ever forget the tender awkwardness of a first kiss? The joyousness of it? The door to new and enticing worlds squeaking open? A door that could never be shut once it had been opened?

To this day—right now—he could remember, with aching melancholy, the sweet taste of her lips, her openness to him, the trust between them. Kissing her had felt like the most natural step in the world, an evolution of everything they had been to each other forever.

Kissing her had felt as if the very stars danced in the sky, celebrating all that was meant to be, coming to fruition, a universal force that would not be denied.

Maybe that was why he'd felt a little prick of—What? Jealousy?—when she had casually mentioned the palace veterinarian by his first name.

Now, of course, he could see how hopelessly naive he had been, how blinded he had been to the realities of his life.

And tonight, she had revealed to him the realities of hers.

Had his mother caught wind of that innocent garden tryst? Or had what had been growing between them been obvious to absolutely everyone who had stood on the perimeter of what was unfolding?

He digested the fact his mother had sent Gabriela away, and he digested the fact that she had not seen her leaving as her own choice.

No wonder, he thought, not without sadness, she had never answered his pleas to have contact with him.

And no wonder she did not want to work for him now.

Enrique was seething from the Queen's intervention. The rawness of his emotion would not be a good place to confront her from, and yet he knew he could not allow this to pass un-addressed. But he would have to choose the time and place of that battle very carefully.

Gabriela was absolutely fuming as she crossed back over to the cottage. A nanny! Just give up her life...

She was stopped by the scent of smoke as she entered the Olivera garden. She saw her father sitting quietly on the stone bench, puffing contentedly on his pipe, stroking Geraldo, who was on his lap.

She crossed the garden and sat beside him. The cat shot her a baleful look, got up and leaped off Guido's lap and onto the ground. With one last look, loaded with the accusation of betrayal, the poor partially shaven cat stomped off into the shrub bed.

"You're not supposed to be doing that," she told her father, mildly.

He took a long and unrepentant pull on the pipe. "An old man takes his pleasure where he can find it. Don't tell your mother."

"All right."

The silence was comfortable between them. She felt wrapped in the cocoon of the familiar scent of his pipe.

"Papa, what's wrong with you?"

"How very insulting," he said, teasing. "There is nothing wrong with me."

"I meant your health."

"And still my answer is the same. The laws of nature are immutable. A man is born, he lives, he dies."

She sighed. "Prince Enrique said he has offered you some of the best medical help in the world."

He made a scoffing sound. "What could be better medicine than to be in my own home, surrounded by all that I love?"

How could you argue with that? It didn't seem to be working, that was how!

"Is that what he wanted?" Guido asked, his voice now tinged with amusement. "To let you know he can be in charge of my destiny?"

"Actually, it seems to be my destiny he wants to be in charge of."

"Oh? How so?"

"He wanted me to look after Marcello."

"Ah," he said, drawing in a deep breath, content. "I'm glad. They need you."

"Oh, Papa, I said no."

"Why?"

She slid her father a look. "You don't want the Prince to be in charge of your destiny, but you want me to turn mine over to him?"

"It's not the same," he said stubbornly. "Why did you say no?"

"All those years in university, and building my career, to drop everything because the Prince thinks I would make a good nanny?"

He was silent for a long time, and when he spoke, there was faint reproach in his voice. "You think it's a menial job?"

"I guess," she admitted uncomfortably.

"Our family has never done that," he chided her softly. "We

have never considered one job more or less important than the other. We have always done what is given to us with honor and integrity. That is what elevates us in life. Not the job we do, but the spirit we do it with. Besides, there could never be anything menial about playing an important role in the life of a child."

"I can't, Papa," she whispered.

Guido sighed heavily. "I know how you feel about him," he said softly. "I've always known."

There was no point in protesting the truth of what her father was saying.

"It's all the more reason to say no."

"I don't see it that way," Guido said. "You are worried about your own heartache, but Enrique needs help. What would he know about being a father? He's never had one. And that poor little boy, my Cello. He doesn't have any friends. His mother was lonely here. She didn't teach him about friendship. She smothered him with neediness masked as love."

How did her father, a humble keeper of olive groves, know these things about human nature and its frailties?

Because it was exactly as he said. He had used every opportunity given to him to become a better human being, wiser, kinder, more compassionate.

Gabriela wondered how she was going to survive without him as the constant in her life, the compass, the steady source of radiant light.

"Think of the child," Guido said. "When love asks something of you, the proper answer is never *what is in it for me?* The proper answer is never *will I be hurt?*"

"What is the proper answer?" she asked him, through tears.

He took her hand and squeezed it. "The proper answer is, love, how may I serve you?"

And then he patted her leg, snuffed out the pipe and hid it under the bench, and got up and went to the house. Geraldo detached himself from some shadow, and followed her father, followed the trail of love he left in his wake as if it were scented with catnip. Guido paused in the doorway, leaned over and scratched Geraldo behind his ears, and then went in the door, leaving the cat outside.

The house lights went off, and Geraldo sent her a look of naked dislike before stalking off into the shrubbery.

"Who knew cats could hold grudges?" she called after him.

Then, Gabriela sat in the dark, lost in thought. She did not want to be persuaded by her father. She wanted, despite everything he had said, to protect herself. After a while, she got up, went into the house, washed the makeup off her face, put on her pajamas and climbed into the narrow bed of her childhood.

But she tossed and turned, unable to sleep. Her bedroom seemed hot and stuffy and she found herself back in the garden, going over the same mental ground again and again.

Was it possible she could do both? Help those two princes and protect herself?

If she set the perimeters, it was possible, wasn't it?

But how did she tell Enrique she had changed her mind after that terrible parting line? Was she even sure this was the right decision?

Impulsively, she went to the garden shed. There was the flashlight, sitting on the sill of the dusty window as if it had not been touched in eight years.

She would flash the light at Enrique's window, the same signal they used since they were children to meet in this garden. *If* the flashlight worked, *if* he answered *her* summons, she would follow Guido's advice.

If the flashlight did not work, or if Enrique did not respond, she would leave the Prince in her past.

Where her head told her, firmly, he belonged.

CHAPTER EIGHT

BUT GABRIELA'S HEART told her something completely different from her head, because when she pushed the button on the flashlight, there was no denying she felt a quick jolt of elation when the beam did, indeed, come on.

Of course, the businesswoman in her pointed out, it was not any kind of a miracle. Of course her father would have changed the batteries.

The shaft of light illuminated the garden shed, throwing eerie shadows, and she acknowledged that she felt excited, as if she was embarking on a great adventure.

She took the flashlight outside, then climbed on the bench so she could look over the wall and at the moon-washed marble of the palace.

Everything, she knew, had changed. Enrique probably did not even have the same window. And yet, this was how she was going to make this decision? It was like flipping a coin, heads for no, tails for yes.

It was whimsical, and irrational, and dreamy, the antithesis of everything she had learned at university, of every lesson being in the business world had taught her.

But there she had it.

If Prince Enrique got her summons, and answered it, she would make an arrangement with him. On her terms. Not his.

And if he didn't answer, it was over before it began.

Noticing her hand was trembling, ever so slightly, she aimed the beam of the flashlight on the darkened window that had once been the Prince's bedroom.

On. Off. On. Off. On. Off.

Pause.

And then she repeated the pattern, twice more. She set the flashlight down, firmly. She was not going to flash that window all night, as if she was leaning toward one answer and not the other.

She realized she was in her pajamas: a silky combination of a pair of smoky-gray shorts and a matching camisole. Entirely inappropriate to meet Enrique in the darkness of the garden.

Where once their lips had met...

She leaped up from the bench, reentered the house quietly. Should she get dressed? Redo her makeup? Do something with her hair?

Of course not! For one thing, she did not want to risk waking the soundly sleeping household. And for another, she did not want to look as if she was trying too hard.

She sighed heavily. This was *exactly* why becoming Marcello's nanny, even temporarily, was going to be fraught with complications. Even the simplest decision suddenly seemed to be weighty with repercussions.

Gabriela threw a housecoat—lightweight and silky, chosen for its ease of packing and suitability for warm weather—over her pajamas and went back into the garden, then again sat on the bench.

When she saw Geraldo still lurking under the shrubs, she patted the bench beside her and softly called his name.

He ignored her.

The minutes ticked by, each one an eternity.

So, Enrique was not coming. There. If the universe really aligned for human purposes, as her papa believed, she had her answer. The great coincidence of the Prince being in the right place at the right time—standing at the window she had flashed that beam at—had not occurred.

Things were as they were meant to be, though she was very aware she had been leaning in one direction more than the other.

Despite all the complications it would give rise to in her life, she had hoped he would come.

She pulled her wrapper tighter around her, and got up from the bench. She tried, one last time, to reconcile with Geraldo. She crouched beside the shrub bed trying to coax him out, but the cat withdrew deeper into the shadow.

Just as she straightened, the gate squeaked open. Enrique paused there, bathed in moonlight, and then stepped inside. Gabriela's heart went very still.

And she could not hide from herself that what she understood rationally, and what she had hoped for, were two entirely different things.

He scanned the garden, saw her, and she thought she saw something in his face, a lowering of barriers, an absence of remoteness. Had she secretly nurtured the hope that she would see that look on his face again someday?

Was it part of what her fiancé had seen in her?

Some unspoken holding back on her part? As if her heart already belonged to another.

On the other hand, it could have been a trick of moonlight.

"You called?" His tone was light. He crossed the garden in a single stride, coming to her. "I saw the light on Marcello's window. I had heard a noise in there. He has my old room. I have the master suite, now. The Queen has her own suite on the second floor."

She saw he, too, must have been in bed, or close to retiring. He was not in pajamas but the crisp shirt of earlier had been replaced with a slightly rumpled tee and a pair of running pants that looked as if they had been pulled on hastily, as if he slept naked.

Now there was a place she could not let her mind go!

His substantial *presence* was not in any way lessened by

the casual clothing. She suspected it would not be lessened by nakedness, either. He carried it within him, like a flame.

He stood in front of her, gazed down at her face, and there was nothing lighthearted in his eyes to match the tone he had used coming through the gate.

But it was not that remoteness, either.

In fact, there was a stunning intensity sparking in those dark depths. He lifted his hand. She held her breath. For a moment, it seemed as if he was going to brush her cheek with his palm.

But then he thrust his hand into his pocket.

She sank onto the bench, and he took the seat beside her. She could smell the warm masculine scent of him mingling with the garden herbs, the blooming olive trees, all of it woven against the backdrop of the scent of the sea.

Geraldo, who had been so pointed in his rejection of her, emerged from the shadows, gathered himself and jumped on Enrique's lap.

"Are his claws going to get stuck in my shorts?" he asked.

"Probably. Don't worry. You can take them off."

Suddenly, the thing she was least expecting happened. They were both laughing, softly, trying desperately not to wake the sleeping household just steps away from them.

"I don't think I could get them off without serious damage from Geraldo. You'd have to help," he told her. He was teasing, and yet there was an undertone of seriousness that whispered along her skin like a touch.

She gulped. He was joking. So wrong to envision her fingertips skimming the waistband of those shorts, tugging...

"And what if I don't have on underwear?" he said, softly, the taunt she had thrown at him being tossed back at her.

Something electric, like a broken wire snaking across the ground, snapped and crackled between them.

She reminded herself there were going to be consequences if she touched that wire. She was going to be burned. And probably badly.

Still, she didn't want him to think she was a gauche girl who couldn't handle a slightly risqué interchange, particularly since she had been the one who started it, even if it had been a day ago.

"Sadly, I'll never know about your commando status," she said.

"Commando?"

"Slang for no underwear."

"Ah," he said, "You've gone away and become a woman of the world."

It was the very impression she had hoped to give, so why was she reacting to the faint regret she heard in his voice?

Could she really be having this conversation with a prince? With both of them in their pajamas? She had to get this back on track. Obviously, inviting him to the garden had been a misstep on her part. It would have been much easier to keep the atmosphere strictly professional between them if she had just swallowed her pride and requested another audience with him to discuss his proposal.

"Your Highness, I am happy to inform you Geraldo is not going to be getting stuck on your pants."

She said it lightly, but she knew Enrique registered the wall of propriety she was trying to erect between them.

He was silent.

"That's why Leon was here. To trim his claws, and try and clip the clumps out of his coat. You can see only one job got completed."

"The important one," he said. "The one that allows me to keep my pants."

And then, despite her best effort to keep things somewhat official between them, they were laughing again.

Their eyes met. The electrical charge between them was stronger in silence than it had been with the slightly ribald teasing.

Enrique looked away first, and turned his attention to Geraldo.

"Hello, my old friend," he said, running his hands over the butchered haircut, and eliciting a deep purr. "Such a trouble-maker, this last while. Did you scratch your mistress?"

He lowered his head pretending to listen to the cat's response.

"Well, I agree the haircut is humiliating in its awfulness, but you can't scratch the people who love you." Enrique lifted his head, and met Gabriela's gaze.

"He says he's sorry."

And somehow, the apology was not just for the cat or from the cat.

"His apology is accepted."

"What did Dr. Ferr—Leon—say about him?"

"Just that he's very old, and that I should prepare myself." She felt an unexpected catch in her throat, and a smart in her eyes.

"I remember when you got him," Enrique said. "I was here. Guido came up from the olive grove and there was a little bulge under his shirt, and he opened the buttons, and we heard this pitiful little sound. You raced over and took that little black ball of fluff from him."

"Don't," she warned. "You're going to make me cry."

"Then you passed him to me," Enrique recalled, softly. "I'd never had a pet before. When he snuggled against my chest and started purring, it felt like one of the best moments of my whole life."

She was crying then.

His hand came around her shoulder, and he tugged her gently into his side. She hesitated, and then gave in. She rested her head on the broadness of his shoulder.

In this moment, finally, he was not a prince, at all, but her lifelong friend and companion. She could feel the warmth and strength of him, though the hum of that electrical current was in the background, now, being replaced by something just as strong.

The bonds of experiences shared. A life shared, really.

"Remember the time he brought the mouse into the kitchen?" Enrique said softly. "It was raining. We were playing a game at the kitchen table. I remember how you used to show me games, and it was like being invited into a brand-new world. I think the game we were playing might have been Sorry."

"He dropped the mouse," Gabriela remembered, "and it was alive."

"And you upended the board game—I'm sure I was winning—and then you were standing on top of the table screaming."

"A pretext," she said, "just to keep you from knowing it was because you were winning. Because we both know I am not the hysterical type."

We both know and that was so true. They both knew so much about each other.

As if to confirm what they both knew, he said, "And of course, I am the save-the-maiden-in-distress type."

She pushed the thought that he had not saved her, not when it mattered most, to the back of her mind, not wanting to sacrifice the connection they were experiencing right now. She acknowledged it was probably dangerous, and that they were getting far off track from the original reason she had flashed that beam at his window.

Or, had some part of her known, as soon as she took up that flashlight, that this very thing was a possibility? That in this garden, she would find remnants of whom she had always known? In this garden, she could chase the remoteness from him?

"And then," she continued, even though she could sense the danger of going too far down this road of shared memories, "you were chasing the mouse around the table, and I was begging you not to kill it."

"And I caught it inside my hands, and raced to put it out the door. And it bit me, ungrateful cad!"

From tears, to laughter, as they remembered that moment.

"And Geraldo," he said to the cat, "you just watched, amused, a troublemaker even back then."

The cat delicately lifted a paw and licked it.

His arm was still around her shoulder, but he seemed to realize it, and he took it off, and shifted slightly, so that there was space between them on the bench.

Given what she was feeling—warmth, longing, hunger for his touch—she should really not say what she was about to say.

She was being shown how dangerous it could be to intertwine her life with his. She had to remember the Prince was a broken heart in waiting.

It was not lost on her that he had broken the contact between them, that he had shifted away. So, she moved down the bench, even farther away from him.

"I've decided to accept your proposal." She was shocked at herself. She had fully intended—rehearsed even—to use the same word as him. *Proposition.*

Because, somehow, the word *proposal* was horribly loaded with unrealistic and romantic notions.

CHAPTER NINE

ENRIQUE BECAME VERY STILL. He turned and looked at Gabriela.

She wouldn't meet his eyes.

"But on my terms," she said sternly, as if anything as flimsy as terms could keep all this dangerous awareness between them at bay, could take the charge out of her inadvertent use of the word *proposal*.

He snorted quietly, and she did glance at him then. He lifted a shoulder as if to say he had expected nothing less.

"These are my terms. First, it can only be temporary."

"No," he said. "That is not acceptable."

Did he not know what he was asking her? How cruel it would be to hang out on the periphery of his life, forever?

That was the problem with dealing with a prince! All his life he'd gotten his way, he'd dictated the terms. No wonder he felt her boundaries would be up for negotiation.

"So," she snapped, "you think I should just put my life on hold until Marcello is, what, eighteen or so?"

It might have made the barriers that had come down between them come back up if he had answered her in kind, but instead his voice was pensive.

"Gabriela, he's lost his mother. Guido's sick. You tell me our friend Geraldo is on borrowed time. My son does not trust life, as it is, and I see so much more loss—that I can't stop or protect him from—coming at him. What if he becomes attached to you—and how could he not—only to lose you, too?"

And how could he not. Without even trying, Enrique was making her feel precious and valuable. And very, very vulnerable.

Plus, his voice was raw with pain for his son. It made her want to throw her whole life at his feet if it would ease his torment.

But she forced herself to be firm.

"Enrique, it's you—not me, or Guido or the cat—who must be the constant in his life. You must be the one he turns to and can rely on. You must be the one who will teach him, that yes, bad things will happen, but that you will have his back. You must be the one who helps him uncover his own strength. That's *your* job."

His gaze met hers. "It is this, exactly," he said softly, "that makes me so sure you are perfect for the position of his nanny."

"Temporarily," she reiterated stubbornly.

He, just as stubbornly, said nothing, but his silence spoke volumes.

"Surely you can see paid companions will always have the potential to be temporary? You, on the other hand, are not. You are his forever."

She wished she had not spoken that word, taken aback at the stab of longing in her for things she could never have. Not with him.

And because of him, possibly not with anyone.

Forever.

Enrique sighed heavily. "I want it to be as you say, but Marcello and my relationship is strained. I want to be the one he sees as completely reliable in his life, the constant—"

"The one who loves him best of all," she inserted in a whisper.

"—but that does not seem to be what he wants from me."

"You can't let a five-year-old decide what he wants! Good

grief, he'll be having cookies for breakfast and ice cream for lunch. He is not the boss, Enrique."

"See?" he said with satisfaction. "You are perfect for the position."

"But not," she said, exasperated, "as a substitute for his father."

"What I'm trying to tell you is that Marcello doesn't seem to like me. I wasn't as close to him as I should have been when his mother was alive. She made him her whole world, and to be honest, I was content to let her."

Guido had already hinted at a less-than-ideal relationship.

"Before she died, he seemed indifferent to me. And after, downright hostile."

To be entrusted with these confidences rattled her, and made her weak with wanting to take his pain away. But to preserve herself, she had to fight the impulse to reach across the space between him, touch the troubled lines of his face, assure him that love would make everything right in the world again.

Love.

The secret she kept, even largely from herself. She'd never fooled Guido, though. This was a complicated space she was stepping into, a difficult dynamic to navigate. How was she going to not get hurt?

Her father would tell her that was the wrong question.

She drew in a deep breath. When she spoke, she was trying desperately to channel the television super-nanny who was so popular in New York.

"Well, it seems our work is cut out for us," she said, her tone completely no-nonsense. "But meanwhile, he needs to know his hostility means nothing to you. That you will always be his father, you will always be there for him, you will always be consistent, you will always protect and guide him. You must be the constant in his life."

"I needed to hear that, Gabriela, thank you. You will be good for us."

But would they be good for her?

Or, between the two princes, Enrique and Marcello, was her heart going to end up shattered into a trillion tiny fragments?

Guido, she reminded herself, again, would say that that was not the right question.

"If you come to the palace, first thing in the morning, I'll have Phillipe work out the details of a contract with you."

He was trying to find familiar footing, to put some barrier back up between them. As much as that would be to both their benefits, this relationship, even as a working one, simply was not going to be on his terms.

She got up off the bench. Her wrapper had fallen open, and she pulled the lapels closed and tightened the belt at her waist.

"I think it would work better if you brought Marcello here, tomorrow morning at ten," she said, still channeling the super-nanny, Jo-Jo. "*You* bring him. Do not assign it to someone else. And do not, under any circumstances, tell him or anyone else I am his nanny. Am I clear?"

Even Geraldo seemed to get that she was not a woman to be trifled with. He got up silently from the Prince's lap, and slid off the bench into the darkness.

Gabriela watched with some satisfaction as Enrique's mouth fell open, and he nodded.

"You may tell him you've been invited for a visit." Then she turned on her heel and left him sitting on the moonlit bench by himself.

Enrique watched her go, her head high, in defiance of that dressing gown that had slipped open and shown him the mist-and-smoke lingerie underneath.

He thought over the unexpected twists and turns of the garden meeting they had just shared.

He would have to cancel a number of engagements and an important overseas business call to answer her summons in the morning.

"Hey," he called softly after her, still trying not to wake up the rest of her household, "how long should I plan on being here in the morning?"

"As long as it takes," she called back, and then slipped in the door and shut it with a firm click behind herself.

It occurred to him that nothing with Gabriela was ever going to go quite as he expected. And in a life where everything was arranged, always, to meet his expectations, to fit in with carefully choreographed plans, and highly structured days, he had to admit, even if reluctantly, that not knowing exactly what tomorrow held was like an invigorating breath of fresh air.

It had always been like that with her. She had been the one who had given liveliness and life to the days of his youth. Even before that kiss they had shared, his heart had belonged to her, even though he had never said it. How could he say it? Even as a young man, he had known Gabriela would not be considered a suitable match.

It was after she was gone that he had known, acutely, how much light she had brought to his life. For months after, it had felt as if he walked in the shadow of a dark cloud of loss. But then his responsibilities had increased exponentially, and one step at a time, life went on. Once he was married, he had not allowed himself to think of Gabriela, their warmth and their connection. Thoughts of her would have made the life he had to live too hard to face. Maybe, for that reason, secretly, he'd been happy she was gone, that he did not have to face, every single day, the haunting loss of her laughter and her light from his life.

Even now, he was aware these kinds of thoughts had to be curbed, that no good could come from them, that he had to keep his desire for the happiness and well-being of Marcello at the forefront of all his dealings with Gabriela.

The next morning, Enrique was in his office early to try and rearrange his schedule and get a few things crossed off his to-do list for the day.

Phillipe, as always, had beaten him there.

"I've moved your morning appointments, and assembled the paperwork Miss Olivera, er, requested," he said.

So, Gabriela had also been up early this morning.

Phillipe looked slightly caught off-balance, which was unusual. The uncomfortable way he said the information had been *requested* made it seem as if it might have been more of an order than a request.

"What did she *request*?"

A look passed between them, an age-old look between men that said a bomb was about to go off in their world. And that it was a woman.

"I've put together the structure of the childcare service for her, and the names and background information of each of the nannies. She said she wants to review it."

Enrique was suddenly reminded that she had a world that did not include him. He'd heard reports that she was very good at what she did, and he could see, now, that she was a force to be reckoned with.

"She also *asked* for the names and contact information of every four-to-six-year-old boy within these criteria."

Again, the emphasis on *asked* suggested she might have ordered what she wanted. Phillipe passed him a neatly typed piece of paper. Enrique glanced at it.

Had Gabriela been up all night? It felt like a whirlwind was moving on the periphery of his world.

"Is that all right, sir?" Phillipe said uneasily. "I mean, can she just *ask* for all this?"

Order it.

The unspoken question: *Who was she? What was she to the household?*

Questions he realized he had not given nearly enough thought to. Again, he'd approached her about taking over as nanny on an impulse. Impulses were not a norm in his world.

No. Worse than an impulse.

On the advice of a five-year-old.

"Wouldn't she need some sort of security clearance, Your Highness? To be looking at the personal information of royal staff? To be inquiring about their children and grandchildren?"

Enrique shot him a look. It was clear that while Phillipe obviously knew *who* she was, he had no idea *what* she was to this household.

A member of the most trusted family on the island, a family whose fates had been intertwined with that of his own since the dawn of time.

And whose fault was that, that she was an unknown in her own home?

She had made that quite clear yesterday. The blame fell solidly on his family.

"I'll vouch for her," he said, taking the thick sheaf of papers from Phillipe. "She's agreed to assist with Marcello's care, for the time being. Give her whatever she asks for."

"Yes, Your Highness."

Leaving a rather astounded Phillipe, Enrique went to fetch Marcello and found a flustered nanny—Miss Helena?—rattling the handle of the nursery bathroom door. The sound of water running, while Marcello sang lustily behind it, penetrated the door.

"Your Excellency," she said, stepping back from the door, "I'm sorry. I wanted to have him ready, but he won't come out. He's jammed something against the door so I can't get in, either."

"Marcello?" he called.

The singing stopped, while Marcello registered his father had arrived on scene, but then resumed more loudly than before.

It was a sea ditty.

What do you do with a drunken sailor? What do you do with a drunken sailor? What do you do with a drunken sailor ER-LYE in the morning?

Where had he learned that?

Admittedly, Enrique's first impulse was to force the door open, to show his five-year-old son what every other single person on this island—with the exception of Gabriela—accepted without question.

He was the *boss*.

Instead, he switched direction. "Miss Helena," he said loudly, "Marcello and I have been invited to the Olivera cottage this morning. Could you tell him I had to go without him? Geraldo will miss him, of course, as will Guido and Gabriela. However, I don't want to be late."

The door swung open a bit.

His son was still in his pajamas, soaked to his skin. He seemed to be standing in a puddle.

"Good morning," Enrique said, resisting the impulse to scold.

"Good morning, Father," Marcello said, all wide-eyed innocence, as if he wasn't behaving like the naughtiest boy on the planet.

Instead of pointing that out, Enrique said, evenly, "Where did you learn that song?"

"My mommy and I sang it together. And 'Row, Row, Row Your Boat.'"

Ah, the world he had been excluded from. "Perhaps," he said tentatively, "you could teach it to me, sometime."

Marcello considered this, then lifted a shoulder, hurtfully unwilling to commit.

Enrique did not let his hurt show. "Can I ask what you're doing?"

"I'm making a magic potion," his son responded solemnly.

"A potion? For what?"

"That's a secret."

Terrifying, Enrique thought, and also another part of his son's world that Marcello was unwilling to share with him.

CHAPTER TEN

"WOULD YOU LIKE to join me at the Olivera cottage this morning?" Enrique asked his soaked son.

"Yes, I would," Marcello said and ran past him and down the hallway—leaving wet footprints the entire way—toward his bedroom. Miss Helena raced after him. Even though Enrique was annoyed beyond measure at his son, what mattered most to him was the light that had come on in those big, somber eyes at the very mention of the Oliveras.

Enrique realized they were *his* magic potion.

Because Marcello had needed to get ready, they were late, and as they went through the gate to the cottage, Enrique felt the strangest little shiver of trepidation, like a schoolboy tardy for class.

Was his world going to be constantly off-balance now that Gabriela was back? Would being around her renew his deep feelings of longing for a life he could not have? Would some awareness of her always form a background hum to every interaction between them?

He caught sight of her. The answer was *yes*.

She was sitting in a child's chair at a small red table. It was the set Guido had built for her—for them—when they'd been children. Memories of long-ago tea parties—sunshine and fresh-made scones from Maria—came to him, vivid and compelling.

Though not quite as compelling as this moment. Gabriela

was wearing a simple cotton dress, white, with small blue flowers in the pattern. It was a summer dress, with wide straps that left the soft swell of her shoulders bare. The dress was riding up the curve of her thighs. Her feet were also bare, and the sun was making her dark hair shine as if it was spun through with threads of gold.

A little boy sat in the chair adjacent from her. There was a container of soapy water in front of her, and she held a wand in her hand.

As Enrique watched, she dipped the wand in the bucket, and blew gently on it.

He felt a jolt of pure awareness that was shocking given the absolute innocence of her activity. But who had known blowing bubbles was so similar to puckering for a kiss? He remembered the knife-like sensations of passion rising that he had felt around her as a young man.

Stop it, he warned himself, but as he watched the bubble break free of the wand and dance, iridescent, in the air, he knew that would be easier said than done.

Marcello darted up to the table and skidded to a halt. He stared at Gabriela as if she was spinning pure enchantment out of plain soap and water.

Which, of course, she was.

"Can I do it?"

"Marcello," she said, ignoring his question, "this is Henri. He is Mr. Madero's grandson. Henri, this is Marcello."

"Your Highness," Henri squeaked, obviously coached for this meeting.

"In this garden, and when you play together, you may call him Cello," Gabriela said, straightening.

"That's not what my grandfather said," Henri said, uneasily.

"It's like when I'm with my father and my grandmother," Marcello explained, patiently. "When you're in pubic, you use their titties, but when you're by yourselves, you don't."

Enrique bit back his own snort of laughter and watched, delighted, as Gabriela tried to contain hers.

"What he means, Henri, is in *public* places we use *titles*, but when we're just among friends in the garden, it isn't necessary. Cello, say hello to Henri."

"Lo, Henri," Marcello said as he reached for the wand in her hand.

"Lo, Cello," Henri said cautiously, obviously worried about disobeying his grandfather's instructions.

Ever so gently, Gabriela held the wand out of Marcello's reach, and then handed it to Henri.

"I only have one," she said, and Enrique clearly saw she had done this by design. "You will have to share it. Perhaps you could take turns seeing who can blow the biggest bubble?"

She watched for a moment, and then satisfied the boys would take turns, she got up from the table and turned to Enrique. He was surprised to see she was wearing glasses. Considering he was bracing for a reprimand, the glasses did make her look like a schoolteacher. The exact kind who did not brook any type of nonsense, like tardiness.

But right underneath that, he detected a sort of radiance about her that seemed to stop his world. Everything seemed to blur together: the radiance, the laughter of the two little boys as they shared the bubble wand, the sun in the garden, strong aroma of the blooming olive tree.

Every man, he realized would, at some time in his lifetime, be given a cruel glimpse of the life he was not able to have.

This was the life he was not able to have: laughing children, a carefree moment in the garden, a woman who would have loved him best of all.

Checking one more time to make sure the two little boys were practicing sharing—a concept that was obviously more difficult for Marcello than Henri—Gabriela turned her full attention to him and came across the garden.

She looked searchingly at him, and then laid her hand, soft, on his forearm. He had not put on a jacket yet, his dress shirt rolled up at the cuff. Her touch, meant to be soothing, instead felt like a brand, as if she was marking him for life.

"Enrique, what's the matter?"

He looked down at her arm, and then into her face. He drew in a deep breath. "Nothing. My apologies for being late."

Those beautiful eyes, so deep, so perceptive, searched his own in a way that made him feel as if no matter what he said, she would see the truth.

"You look as if you've seen a ghost," she said.

How tempting it would be to tell her seeing her in the garden, laughing with the children, had brought him to stand on the edge of an abyss of a life that was shockingly lonely, that was bereft of the kind of dreams most men were allowed.

Still, even without saying a word, it felt as if she *knew* somehow. He should have realized that there was no hiding anything from her. Her perceptive abilities were at least as terrifying as Marcello conjuring potions in the bathroom sink.

He realized she was still touching him, and that the touch, while comforting now, would increase his sense of being bereft later. He withdrew his arm, sharply, from under her touch, and thrust his hand in his pocket.

"I'm fine, really," he said.

She scanned his face once more, not believing him, but then she took a deep breath, and followed his cue.

"Let's get down to business, then," she said, looking at the folder of papers he carried. "You've brought what I asked for?"

She relieved him of them, and took them over to the bench and sat, opening the first folder.

"So," she said, "I see there are four nannies, three now that Miss Penny has resigned."

"Except, you would be the fourth."

"Temporarily," she reminded him. She scanned the documents quickly. He sank, his reluctance palpable to him, onto the bench beside her. He should have remained standing, but he was aware that brief touch had done the most dangerous of things.

Made him aware of a *need*.

A simple need. For connection. She did not ever have to know what sitting on the bench so close to her did for him. And to him.

"Which one of the nannies is Cello's favorite?" she asked, not looking up.

He had no idea, but he tried to cover up what suddenly seemed like a shameful lack of knowledge by saying, "I think he dislikes them all equally."

She looked up at him, then drew her glasses down to the end of her nose and peered over the rims. Again, he had the frightening suspicion that he could not hide anything from her.

"Okay, then, which one is *your* favorite?"

Enrique managed to quell the urge to squirm like a school-boy not doing very well on a pop quiz. "I don't think I should discuss the palace staff behind their backs," he said uneasily.

She was not fooled—of course *she* wasn't fooled—by his effort to turn his lack of knowledge into looking as if he was taking the high road.

"We're not discussing the staff," she said softly. "We're discussing Marcello's life."

Henri started shouting it was his turn, not Marcello's, and Marcello shouted back that it wasn't. Enrique, thankful for the excuse, started to rise. She laid her hand on his thigh. It was worse—much worse—than her hand on his arm had been, even with a layer of fabric between her touch and his skin.

She seemed to realize it was a horrible mistake and snatched her hand back. Something that had nothing at all to do with small boys sizzled in the air between them.

It was as if a fire-breathing dragon had stepped from its lair. How did you put that back, once it had been let out?

For a moment, both of them lost track of where they were.

But, then with obvious effort, she drew back her shoulders,

and looked back down at the file in her hand. "Who hired the nannies?"

He had to think about that for a minute. The truth was he didn't really involve himself in staff issues, but he knew she'd look poorly on him if she thought he'd taken a cavalier attitude toward his son's care.

Which led to the question: *Had* he taken a cavalier attitude toward his son's care?

"Miss Caravanno has been here since Cello was born," Enrique said. "Amelia vetted her, I believe. She was the only one, until the pregnancy, and then Miss Helena joined the staff. After, more were hired, but none have lasted very long."

"Probably the most plum job on the island, and no one stays," she mused.

"As you've seen, he can be quite a handful."

"Who hires them?" she asked, as if he'd deliberately skirted the original issue.

"I'm not precisely sure which department that falls into."

"Well, let me make it clear for you, then," she said, and he could see little red spots of annoyance rising on each cheek. "It falls into the daddy department."

Daddy. The word, like the scene of the children blowing bubbles with her, conjured images of the life he did not have. A life of tossing baseballs, and wrestling, and laughing over silly things. He realized, envious, that Gabriela had an authority about her when it came to raising Marcello because she had come from a family that knew exactly what a family was supposed to provide.

He, on the other hand, had accepted his wife's lead in the matters of their child because he'd had no framework of family and because duty came first. Amelia, assuaging her own loneliness, had shut him out, and he had felt helpless, and unsure how to breach her boundaries. Now, when his son needed him, and he needed his son, Marcello seemed intent on regarding him suspiciously, the outsider.

Gabriela was watching him, again, way too closely.

"I will find several suitable replacements for Miss Penny," she said, after letting him squirm for a moment, "but you will do the interviewing and have the final say."

"It almost sounds as if you are giving me orders," he told her, stiffly.

"And do you want to know the reason for that? I can't—I won't—care about this more than you do. He's your son, Enrique. What's with this hands-off approach to parenting?"

She refrained from speaking the words *what is wrong with you*, but he felt as if he heard them anyway.

It had been many, many years since he had been called on anything. No one dared to criticize him, or question him.

He realized it was part of the abyss of loneliness that he had gazed into just a few minutes ago. He carried the mantle of his responsibilities alone. Mostly, it was a burden life had prepared him for.

But it was true that he had been completely unprepared to be plunged into the world of parenting, and the biggest responsibility of them all, raising a child who was capable of giving as much as receiving, who knew how to serve as well as how to be served, who understood he was *part* of the great surge of universal energy, not above it.

Enrique sighed. And confessed the truth to her.

"The hands-off approach to parenting is all I know," he said quietly.

"Humph," she said unimpressed, a teacher hearing a lame excuse like the dog had eaten the homework. "All right, go say goodbye to Marcello. Give him a hug, and tell him you love him."

He got up from the bench and looked at his son, and then looked at her.

"What?" she asked.

"I'm not… I mean we don't. We're not demonstrative."

"Are you telling me," she asked, something both incredulous

and furious in her tone, "that you don't hug your son, and tell him you love him when you say goodbye to him?"

He was silent. "Well," he offered finally, "before bed. Sometimes. I mean, a kiss on the top of his head."

"But why?" she asked, genuinely appalled.

"It's as I said. It's all I know. It was never done for me." His throat felt raw, as if he was confessing some terrible secret about his life to her.

Her mouth dropped open.

"Never," he continued quietly. "I have never once heard those words."

She snapped her mouth shut. She looked rapidly back at the file in her hands.

"Never?" she whispered, and glanced up at him.

He braced himself for her pity. But that was not what he saw in the amazing kaleidoscope of colors that were her eyes. What he saw was a compassion so deep it was like a bottomless well. It made him feel as weak as anything ever had, as if he could drop to his knees in front of her and let it wash over him, healing something in him that he had not known was broken.

"Go break the cycle," she told him, her voice soft, but firm.

There was no mistaking it. Gabriela had just given him a command!

CHAPTER ELEVEN

ENRIQUE WALKED OVER to the little red table, to Marcello and Henri. Both boys were soaked, and bubbles danced in the air around them.

He drew in a deep breath, uneasy with the task he'd been given, like a warrior asked to serve tea.

He started with the easy one. "Henri, I'm pleased to have met you."

"You as well, sir," Henri said, leaping up from his chair.

He waved him back down. "Marcello, I'm leaving now."

"Bye," Marcello said, without taking his eyes off the rather gigantic bubble he was busy blowing.

You didn't interrupt a bubble like that!

Unless you could feel a gaze was burning a hole in your back.

He bent awkwardly and gave Marcello a stiff hug. He added a kiss to the top of his head, and said, gruffly, "I love you."

Marcello pulled out of his grasp, gave him a look that was clearly confused, and then a shield went up in his eyes. "Oh," he said, and then, "Henri! It's your turn."

Enrique turned and looked at Gabriela, expecting her to appear exasperated at his attempt at affection. If she was grading it, he had earned a D-minus at best. But instead, she was beaming at him, and it was, unfortunately, a look that a man could carry within himself, like a talisman, against all that was wrong in his world.

He veered away from her and the boys, and knocked softly on the cottage door.

"Come," Maria called.

He entered. Maria, at the stove, of course, was stirring a pot that wafted fragrant aromas. She turned and gave him a tired smile.

"He hoped you would come in. He can hear the boys laughing. A good sound."

He tilted his head and listened. It was such a good sound. His visit with Guido was brief, but his old friend seemed to be in good spirits. He had more color in his cheeks than Enrique had seen in a long time. It made him feel warily hopeful.

But sometimes it felt, especially to a man who had just stood at the lip of an abyss, as if hope was the most dangerous thing of all.

Still, even if he was afraid of it himself, he wanted to hold it out like a gift to Gabriela.

"Your father seems better this morning," Enrique told her when he went back to the garden.

She was deeply engrossed in the papers he had brought, but she looked up at him.

He saw that she, too, was suspicious of hope, because she just lifted a shoulder and gave him a smile that was very much like her mother's had been.

Enrique suddenly felt unbelievably selfish. This family was going through enough challenges. What had he been thinking asking her to take on responsibility for his son at this point in her life?

Himself, was the obvious answer.

"Look," he said uncomfortably, "If you don't want to do this right now—"

She cocked her head at him.

"I don't want you to feel like I ordered you. Or pressured you."

"It's a little late for that," she said dryly. "I made the decision freely, Enrique."

"Okay." He was aware of a wash of pure relief.

"Come back at three," she said. "Don't be late. For his sake, not mine. And don't even think of sending someone else to get him."

He had been nice to her! And she was being snippy in return. He gave her a look that clearly told her he was not used to being addressed like that!

Not the least intimidated, she added, "Your Royal Highness," not even trying to take the cheeky note out of it!

Enrique's entire day was off-kilter. Whether it was because of a schedule hastily rearranged or because of the unexpected emotional intensity of his time in the garden this morning, he couldn't say. It was probably a combination of both, a carefully controlled life roiling dangerously, like a ship encountering an unexpected storm at sea.

Still, he made it back just before three. Henri was gone. Gabriela was back at the little table, and Marcello lay on the grass, on his tummy, legs up and crossed behind him, piling up sticks. Both gave him the merest of glances.

His son was filthy and sunburned. His hair had grass in it, and his jumper was torn.

But he was not sure he had ever seen a little boy look so tired. And so happy.

"What are you building?" he asked.

"A house for Geraldo."

All day, he had debated the wisdom of his decision to ask Gabriela to be the nanny. Because after this morning, it had been clear she would require more of Enrique.

And she would set his well-ordered life on edge, rewrite every single rule he had followed his entire life.

On the other hand, where had adherence to all those rules gotten him? Had they brought him happiness? Had they been able to save the life of his wife and his child?

Gabriela gestured to one of the other chairs at the table.

Enrique actually looked over his shoulder. Surely, she did not expect him to try and fold himself into that child's chair?

Apparently she did.

With a sigh, he went and sat—uncomfortably—at the small table. She smiled at him as if his discomfort was of no consequence to her at all.

She passed him a piece of paper. "I've narrowed down the nanny candidates to these three young women."

It occurred to him his discomfort was of no consequence to her because she was laser-focused on the well-being of his son.

"How did you get these names so quickly?" he asked. "Were you given access to the applications on file?"

"I didn't even know there were applications on file. No, I just asked around."

He looked down at the three names. Beside each, in brackets, was a brief explanation. *Angelo's daughter's sister-in-law, first cousin on Maria's side, Leon's next-door neighbor.*

Did that mean she had spoken to Leon, again? He contemplated the fact that that surely wasn't the most important thing about this list.

"As I put together possibilities," Gabriela said, "I was reminded of the lovely small-town feel of this island, the sense of community here."

Her tone took him aback. Wistful. Homesick.

He felt a bit wistful himself: that always and forever he was set apart from the warmth offered by that close-knit sense of neighbors who had each other's backs.

"My plan," she said, "is to have each one of these young women come spend a few days with Cello. I think here is best. It's informal. We won't spoil any of their chances by mentioning the word *nanny*."

"It would be good if you could set aside an hour here and there, as well, just kind of casually. To see what you think of the interactions."

Casual wasn't really part of his life.

"If you could make a point of being the one to drop off Cello, and pick him up, I think it would really help him to see that he is your number-one priority."

He thought of trying to rearrange his schedule over the next few weeks to accommodate these suggestions and could feel his head starting to ache.

But he could also feel Gabriela looking at him, gauging his reaction, and he knew she was right. His son needed to be his number-one priority and Marcello needed to know that. Isn't this exactly why Enrique had been compelled to ask for her help? Because she *knew* things?

Because he had known Gabriela would find her way, instinctively, to what his son needed?

"Thank you, for all this," he said, and got to his feet. "Marcello, it's time to go home."

"I want Geraldo to try his house first."

There it was, always, that little edge of defiance.

Gabriela also got to her feet. "Marcello," she said firmly, but gently, "your father has said it is time to go home. You can show Geraldo his house tomorrow."

"I'm coming back tomorrow?" Marcello breathed. Here he was, a little prince, with an entire kingdom at his disposal, and ironically, it was *this* that made him happy.

Marcello went and threw his arms around her knees, and when Gabriela bent to him, he captured her neck, and covered her face with kisses until they were both breathless with laughter.

Enrique, surrounded by some of the most priceless pieces of art in the world, was sure he had never seen anything quite so beautiful.

Ah. Not so much *this*—the cottage, the garden, the bubbles, the cat—as *her*.

Gabriela watched as the two princes moved toward the gate. Marcello tugged on his father's pant leg, and Enrique looked down. Marcello stretched out his arms. Enrique looked momentarily stunned. And then, with easy strength, he scooped up his exhausted son. Marcello wrapped his arms around his father's neck and his legs around his waist.

Enrique turned slightly, and gave her a look.

Luminous.

It was the kind of image—the strength of the father, the vulnerability of the child—that could burn itself right into someone's mind.

Still, from that glance back, these moments were rare. Given what Enrique had said this morning, was that so surprising? His words, that he had never heard *I love you*, had haunted Gabriela most of the day.

Her mother came out to snip herbs from the bed beside the door, and she looked at the departing princes, and smiled indulgently.

"Enrique said this morning no one has ever told him they loved him," she confided in her mother. "Can that possibly be true? It seems as if pretty much the whole world loves him."

"The whole world bandies that word about much too lightly," her mother said. "They think they love him, based on his status and his looks—he's handsome, eh? Even an old heart like mine beats a bit faster when I see him."

"Mom!"

Maria laughed. "But he knows they don't know the first thing about who he really is. He walks a lonely road."

"You don't think his mother ever told him she loved him? *Ever?*"

Her mother snorted. "Queen Katalina? Can you even imagine that?"

The truth was, she could not.

"He was here a lot, growing up," Gabriela said pensively. "Didn't you ever say to him you loved him?"

"Gabriela!" Her mother slid her a look. "Your time away has made you forget some of the differences between Hermosa

Mariposa and the rest of the world. Maybe in America, everyone is the same, everyone is equal, but not here. He's a prince. I'm a cook. Of course I did not overstep the boundaries."

Of course, that was understandable, but still—

"I think," Maria said, "we told him how we felt about him without words. Sometimes, it's even better that way. I believe he knew he was loved here."

She used past tense, a reminder whatever had been was gone now. Little princes grew up. Someday they became kings. And every decision that shaped their lives was made with that in mind.

"Enough of this," her mother said.

"Can I help you with dinner?"

"You have no gift in the kitchen, Gabriela."

"I can set the table!"

"Go spend time with your father. He's driving me crazy with his demands. Does he think I have nothing better to do than play cribbage with him all day?"

In her voice, despite the fact she was trying to hide it, Gabriela heard a note of what her mother was most afraid of.

Hope.

And when she saw Guido, she felt that same hope and the same fear that accompanied it. He looked so *well*. Was it possible he could get better?

He looked at her brightly, almost like his old self. "Do you want to walk in the olive grove with me?"

"Are you sure you feel up to it?"

"Don't treat me like an invalid," he warned her.

"All right," she said, and looped her arm through his. Since walking through the groves with Guido was something she had resigned herself to never experiencing again, it felt as if every slow step they took through the blossoming olives was lit from within, a gift from heaven.

"It was a good day, eh?" her father asked her.

Gabriela thought of the boys playing and the laughter. But

what she thought most about was Enrique and the light-filled moments with him and how, even when she was trying desperately not to show it, those moments had turned her life from drab to dazzling in the blink of an eye.

CHAPTER TWELVE

"YES," GABRIELA ADMITTED to Guido, "it was a good day."

But even as she admitted that, it felt as if there was a storm on the horizon. Where was it all going? How could it end in anything but hurt and heartache? Enrique had been worried about Marcello forming an attachment only to experience yet another loss, but now she could see the same thing looming on her horizon.

Her father stopped, and looked at her, having heard the hesitation in her voice. "My angel," he said, "you know I don't like to give advice."

They both laughed at that obvious fib.

"Don't worry so much," he said softly. "Take it from me. There comes a point when you realize the secret to happiness is to just enjoy each moment."

"You're right," she said, softly. "Especially this one with you, Papa."

It seemed as if Guido's message to just enjoy each moment was foremost in Gabriela's mind when Enrique brought Marcello again the next day.

For the longest time in her life, she thought she would never have moments with Enrique in this garden ever again, that that part of her life was over. And yet, here they were, sitting on the bench together.

To Gabriela's secret delight, the Prince had accepted the invitation for coffee this morning. The rich aroma of the brew, blended with the gorgeous scent of him, especially against the backdrop of the laughter of children, was a heady way to start the day. Their shoulders were nearly touching as they shared the bench, and she could feel the subtle warmth radiating from him.

Still, even doing her best to immerse herself in the moment, Gabriela could not help but notice the differences between them, and they were acute.

She had chosen a bright yellow sundress this morning, belted at the waist, with short sleeves and a full skirt. When she'd put it on and twirled in front of the mirror, she had been quite pleased at the balance the outfit struck between being attractive and playful but remaining practical and professional.

But now, sitting beside him, she felt like a peasant.

Because, he was exquisitely put together this morning, 100 percent pure prince. He could easily have been chosen for the cover of any gentlemen's magazine.

Enrique was beautifully dressed in a custom dark gray suit that showed off, rather than hid, his amazing physique, the broadness of his shoulders, the narrowness of his waist and hips, the length of his powerful legs.

He had on a crisp white linen shirt, beautiful shoes and cuff links, and a dark, narrow silk tie that had a hundred shimmering shades of gray in it.

The scent of soap and aftershave was subtle and masculine in the air around him. He was, of course, completely ready for whatever the official business of the day was.

"Marcello is very taken with Henri," he told her, apparently unaware of the differences between them.

"Yes, they are on their way to a good friendship."

"All last night," he continued, his deep, beautiful voice tinged with humor, "I heard about Henri. Henri has a dog. Henri has a baby sister—*awful* apparently—Henri shares his room with his brother. Henri this and Henri that until I could have covered my ears and begged for mercy. If I wasn't so happy that he was talking to me."

Gabriela felt the sweet satisfaction of being a part of beginning to repair the puzzling rift between the father and son.

"Did you know Henri has swords?" Enrique asked with a sigh.

"Henri has swords?"

"Light sabers. I'm afraid the possession of such items has raised Henri in a status that far eclipses anything I could ever hope to achieve."

"Oh, the irony," she said.

"I'm aware," he said, "a pair of light sabers trumps royalty."

"Every time," she agreed solemnly, and then they laughed and they clicked coffee cups in their shared amusement.

"They're from a movie, apparently. The light sabers."

"Yes, *Ryder of the Lost World*."

"I haven't heard of it."

"Ah, well, a hit with the under-ten set."

"How is it you've heard of it, then?"

"In New York, you'd have to be living under a rock to have not heard of it. The merchandising is phenomenal."

Then, just like that, just like old friends, they were catching up. They were talking about her job, and New York City, and favorite movies. It was easy between them, just as it once had been, just as if eight years had not flown by and taken their lives in totally different directions.

She *loved* this moment. When the future tried to intrude on her pleasure at just sharing time with Enrique, his deep voice washing over her, she reminded herself of Guido's advice.

"He fell asleep in my arms on the way back to the palace yesterday," Enrique confided in her.

Not *home*, she noted.

The way he said it, it was clear it was one of the best things he had ever felt.

Little boy asleep in arms trumps pomp and circumstance, she thought, but didn't say.

Every time.

"You've decided Marcello needs mates," Enrique said, taking another sip of his coffee and smiling out at the boys tumbling around the garden. Today, Henri had been joined by his cousin Emilio.

"Job one," Gabriela said, marveling at how the ease of their conversation had dissipated most of her self-consciousness at sharing the bench with the suave man beside her.

"I thought that was finding a nanny."

"This is just as important, I think. The first day I met Marcello, I heard him telling Geraldo he was his best friend. He needs friends who aren't cats. Friends his own age."

"I never had friends my own age," Enrique said.

She let it go for a beat, and then she corrected him. "Yes, you did. You had me."

Spontaneously, he took her hand, and squeezed. "Yes, I did," he said, and they looked at each other for a moment, everything that they had ever been to each other laid raw between them.

The self-consciousness disappeared completely as their shared history welled up.

Even when he let go of her hand, she thought, but didn't say, *and you still have me.* She realized her father had been right, as he so often was. And not just about doing her best to stay in the moment.

Gabriela had been given this job to do, to help this man find his way through the perilous new territory, of being a single parent, that he found himself in.

To be, to him, what they had always been.

Friends.

And more than friends. The words that must not be spoken sizzled between them, more powerful than if they said them, just as her mother had pointed out yesterday.

She loved him. She always had and she always would and

it made things between them unbearably complex, though in this moment they simply felt blissful.

The gate squeaked open and a young woman came in and took in the garden at a glance. She strode to the bench and Enrique rose.

She dropped a curtsey and introduced herself as Matilda. Ah, Angelo's daughter's sister-in-law. She seemed respectful of the Prince, but not ingratiating or intimidated by him. Gabriela liked her immediately.

"I'll introduce you to Marcello," she said, but Matilda turned and looked at the rambunctious boys, her nephews both of them, careening around the garden, and smiled.

"I know, of course, who Marcello is. From what you told me, he's allergic to the idea of a nanny, so I'll just go insert myself without a formal introduction," she said.

Within moments, she had gained the acceptance of the troop. Then, she inspected the Geraldo house from yesterday, now just collapsed sticks, and soon had all three boys eagerly organized to build a new one.

"Wow," Enrique said, pleased as the boys marched out of the shed armed with hammers and scraps of wood. "I think she's a winner."

"Agreed."

He was still on his feet, and he looked, ever so reluctantly at his watch. "I'm sorry."

"No, no, don't be. Go."

Go to your life outside this garden. Go to that place of power and wealth and prestige. Go to that place I can never be a part of.

But a little voice inside her insisted on adding, *But come back to me.*

They fell into an easy pattern for the rest of the week. Enrique would come with Marcello in the morning. He and Gabriela would have coffee together in the garden while Marcello got to know potential nannies and new friends. They shared memories. And laughter. And looks that said everything their voices did not say. The morning visits were a tingling combination of tension and complete ease with another person.

Sometimes, Guido and Maria would join them, which acted as a buffer to the growing tension.

But now it was Friday.

The bench had come to feel like *their* place. Today, Geraldo had found his place on her lap, and her fingers combed his mangled fur. She was pretty sure it was not total forgiveness, but a relatively safe place from the little troop of sweaty boys rampaging through the garden in a rough-and-tumble game of tag.

Absently, Enrique's hand also moved to the cat.

And then, to background shouts of *You're it*, their fingers collided.

One of them, or both of them, could have moved their hand. But neither of them did. Instead, they stroked the cat together, their hands touching, moving in perfect sync, as if they had choreographed this moment.

How could such a simple thing, petting a cat together, be one of the most deliciously erotic things Gabriela had ever experienced?

She pulled away first. She folded her hands primly onto her lap. She cast a glance at him, and saw his hands, too, had been placed in detention. He was looking straight ahead, but then he, too, cast a glance at her.

An ember smoldering enough to start a forest fire leaped in the air between them, before they both, still in sync, ordered their eyes front again.

He cleared his throat. "I've never played that before," he said, nodding toward the boys.

Handsy over a cat?

"You've never played tag?" she caught his meaning.

"No," he said. "Never."

"Well, maybe you could include it this weekend," she said,

trying, but not completely succeeding, to strip the croak from her voice. "What are your and Marcello's plans?"

"The weekend?"

She glanced at him again. He was frowning.

"In my world," he said, and she could hear a faint weariness, "there are no weekends."

"I don't understand."

"Those are the busiest two days of the week, generally. That's when most official duties take place. Building openings. Fundraisers. Speeches. Attendance at sporting or charity events."

"But surely you set aside family time, don't you?"

His silence was her answer.

"Do you work every day?" she asked, appalled.

"I have been," he admitted.

"Well, that's not fair to you."

"I gave up my expectation of life being fair quite some time ago," he said.

This was the part people did not see when they looked at royal families. They saw the wealth, the prestige, the fairytale balls, the extraordinary castles.

They did not see the sense of duty, the weight of responsibility, the ingrained sense of a life that did not belong to you, at all, but was to be used in service to your people.

"It's really not fair to Cello," Gabriela said, after a moment. "Enrique, you really have to have time set aside to spend with him. Designated time that he counts on every single week to be with you."

"But what would we do?" he asked.

She looked at him fully to see if he was serious. "What do you mean, what would you do? Anything. Play tag. Throw a ball back and forth, finger-paint, go to the beach, take a trip to the zoo, walk in the forest, lie in bed all day and read books, color, watch *Ryder of the Lost World*. Or just do whatever you normally do to have fun."

Enrique felt Gabriela's words landing on him with a sting, as if he was being hit by little pebbles.

When was the last time he'd had *fun?*

He could recall a ski trip to the Canadian Rockies a few years ago. And, there were, of course, endless balls and red-carpet events that people probably thought were fun, but were not.

There were invitations to sporting events, time spent on private yachts and private islands, visits to some of the most incredible places and the most exquisite residences in the world.

But underlying each of these things—even when it seemed as if it might be for fun or for leisure—there was always an official note.

It was forwarding a business relationship, it was cementing friendships with allies, there was *always* an agenda that was separate—but just as important, or more important—from the stated reason for being there and the event itself.

At all times, Prince Enrique was aware he was representing his family, and the island. There was no off time; you were always *on.* There was no letting your guard down.

There was no sitting with a beautiful woman, stroking a cat, in a garden.

"Take tomorrow off," Gabriela said softly. "Build on what you've started developing with Marcello this week. You could take him to the Mariposa Garden. It's a beautiful place to have a picnic. It's actually closed to the public, right now for a cleanup, but, of course, they'd make an exemption for you. You could have it to yourselves."

Enrique thought of clearing his schedule for tomorrow.

There would be people who would be disappointed. His mother would be irritated when she found out.

On the other hand, that would be the same mother who had sent Gabriela away. He suddenly didn't give two hoots if she was irritated. In fact, he hoped she would be. A discussion needed to be had with her, obviously, and that might be just the thing to bring it about.

But it wasn't really about the Queen. He realized he wanted, more than he had ever wanted anything, to have a day like the one Gabriela was conjuring in front of him.

A day of freedom. How rare was that in his life? A day with no appointments, no phone calls, no royal duties or engagements.

A day of no obligations.

Except the obligation to the person who meant the most in the world to him.

Or was that two people who meant the most in the world to him?

"I'll take tomorrow off," he said, after a moment, shocked at what an act of rebellion that giving in to that simple impulse felt like. "On one condition."

"Which is?"

"That you come with us."

CHAPTER THIRTEEN

ENRIQUE BRACED HIMSELF for Gabriela's rejection. She was going to say no. What kind of person put a condition on something that had been suggested for his own good, for the good of his family? What kind of person placed a condition on the suggestion that it would be wise to spend some time with his son?

The truth was, he'd had very little one-on-one time with Marcello. The truth was the prospect of trying to entertain a faintly hostile five-year-old for the day filled him with a sense of being in over his head. Way over.

And buzzing just beneath the surface of those truths was an even deeper one.

He *wanted* to spend time with her. So much so that he felt himself holding his breath, waiting for her answer.

"I'm a little unsure what Marcello and I would do together," he said, which was true, but he was also hoping to persuade her.

"Oh, it's easy," she said. "A picnic. A ball. There's a wonderful walking trail through Mariposa Garden. The butterflies float around you. It's completely magical."

He could not imagine experiencing that without her.

"Come with us," he said softly, and he was surprised by the faint pleading in his tone.

Apparently, she was, too, and totally disarmed by it.

"Sure," she said. "Why not? Should I bring a picnic?"

"I'll look after it."

When Enrique left the garden, he was aware of something flitting delicately about him, like one of those dancing butterflies Gabriela had promised.

He contemplated it for a moment before he recognized what it was.

It was happiness.

But he should have learned a long time ago a man's happiness was an elusive thing, beckoning him to follow it, and then darting away when it looked as if he might catch it.

Because instead of it being a day out of a dream, by the time the royal limo pulled up at the front of the Olivera cottage the next morning, a nightmare was unfolding.

Gabriela was waiting on the curving front walkway. Despite the ruckus unfolding inside the vehicle, Enrique realized how few times he had seen the front of the Olivera home, since he almost always came along the path that joined the cottage to the palace. The tiny, vine-covered building reminded him of a cottage that might sit on the edge of a fairy tale. Cute.

And she was also very cute. She was dressed casually, a baseball cap, NYC embossed on it, covering her glossy hair. She had on pressed beige shorts and a pink V-necked T-shirt, sturdy walking shoes. It was nearly the exact outfit he had on, except that his T-shirt was navy blue and had the House of Falcon coat of arms embossed subtly over his right breast.

Her look was completed by an enormous bag draped over her shoulder. It was a bit of a middle-aged bird-watcher look, one any sane man would not find sexy.

And yet, when it came to her, where was his sanity? It flitted about him like those butterflies that they might not see today, after all. To Enrique, Gabriela looked incredibly sexy.

His driver would have normally come around and opened the door, but Enrique didn't wait. He got out of the car, and slammed the door behind him.

It reduced the sound of the caterwauling, but didn't eliminate it.

She came toward him, her eyes huge with concern.

Just her concern calmed some agitation within him.

"What is going on?" Her voice was so soothing. "I heard him as soon as you opened the door."

"He's having a meltdown."

"Yes, I can clearly hear that. He doesn't want to go to the Mariposa Garden?"

"Henri invited him to his birthday party. Today. Unfortunately, he didn't tell me. There was an invitation."

He produced the crumpled, filthy piece of paper from his pocket. She took it and smoothed it with her hand.

"Oh, dear," she said. "Poor kid."

"Henri?"

"Cello! He's probably never been invited to a party before."

She meant *his* kid, that thrashing, screaming, snot-flying-from-his-nose little monster currently taking out his fury on the window glass of the limo.

Bulletproof, thank goodness.

"Usually," Enrique said, "invitations come through normal channels. They have to be vetted."

"In other words, normally he wouldn't have even known he'd been invited."

"It's not as if he can just go to a party on a whim," Enrique said, tersely. "There are security issues."

"I wasn't aware the threats on Hermosa Mariposa were so severe."

"There are protocols."

"Look." She gave a pointed glance at the dark gray sedan that had pulled up behind the official palace limo. "There's plenty of security right there. We can drop Marcello off at the party, and they can sit unobtrusively in front of the house, ever alert to danger."

She was saying that as if it was actually a possibility.

Was it actually a possibility? The truth was he would consider just about *anything* to stop that whirlwind of unfettered anger and emotion being contained—barely—inside the bomb-proof vehicle.

"He'll need a gift, of course," she said, as if it had been de-cided. She looked at the invitation again. "Oh, it's at noon. It's got a Ryder theme. It'll be tight, but it's doable."

She cast him a look. There was something faintly pleading in it. The fact that she was so genuinely on his son's side made him feel weak when he needed to be strong.

She was asking him to make a spontaneous decision, some-thing his life had not prepared him for, at all. She just didn't know the reality. It took days and weeks of preparation for ei-ther of the princes to make public appearances.

So, he was shocked when he heard himself say, without an ounce of tentativeness, "Okay, then, change in plan."

She beamed at him. He figured he'd enjoy that look while it lasted, which should be precisely until the moment she opened that car door.

"Marcello," she said, opening the door and not even raising her voice above the ruckus, "that's quite enough."

Her voice was firm, and cut through the racket with ease. The screaming came to an abrupt and startled end.

"That is an absolutely appalling way to behave."

"I want to go to the party!" Marcello shouted, obviously ready to ramp it up again.

"Can you go to a party with your face all swollen and your nose running from crying? Here, let's go into the cottage and clean you up."

She held out her hand, and after a moment, Marcello slid out of the car and took it.

"Am I going to the party?" he whispered, wiping his nose on his arm, and sniffling.

"Is he going to the party?" she asked Enrique.

He saw, gratefully, what she was doing. Allowing him to be the good guy, in his son's eyes. He nodded, and Marcello gave him a look as if he had personally ordered the stars to line up.

Gabriela was right. Why not? The island was safe, there was security and the very spontaneity of the decision meant absolutely no one would know Marcello was in attendance until he was actually there.

"Can you ask your driver to leave Marcello's car seat?"

"What?"

"Well, obviously he can't arrive in an official vehicle with a crest on the door and flags flying. I can't even imagine the fuss that could cause. It would probably spoil the party."

Enrique felt chastised, somehow. He watched as Gabriela and Marcello walked, hand in hand, up to the front door of the cottage.

"Please don't tell Guido I've been naughty," Marcello said before they went in.

Enrique contemplated that. It was perfectly fine to be naughty—an understatement if he'd ever heard one—to his own father. But not Guido.

The driver, trying not to let his utter astonishment show, moved Marcello's car seat onto the walk.

"Will you be needing the basket, sir?"

The basket? Ah, the picnic lunch from the now-aborted plan. Why not? He wasn't sure what the day held, but he felt as if he was going to need nourishment at some point.

The huge wicker basket the kitchen had prepared was set beside the car seat. And then with one more *are you sure about this* look, his driver got back in the official royal vehicle and pulled away. Enrique went and apprised the security team of the change in plan. Both men's mouths flattened into disapproving lines. They, like him, enjoyed solid plans, immutable schedules, predictability.

But no member of his staff would ever argue with him.

In a few minutes, the pair reemerged from the house. Marcello's hair was freshly combed, his shirt had been straightened and he was holding a cold cloth on his tear-swollen face.

"Now what?" Enrique said. Were they squeezing in with the security team?

But no, Gabriela pointed a set of keys at Guido's ancient jalopy. Enrique was pretty sure the vehicle predated his mother's coronation and had not been moved since Guido got sick.

Then she took the baseball cap off her own head, and pulled it low over Marcello's brow. She handed Enrique one of Guido's familiar newspaper-boy hats.

And a pair of sunglasses.

He put them on, and a little smile tickled her lips as she surveyed him and Marcello. "You look just like a pair of American tourists," she said. "You could be anybody!"

He felt that first delicious breath of fresh air that was anonymity.

"Except," she said, "for the shirt. Could you take it off, and turn it inside out?"

He pulled the shirt off from the hem, pulled it over his head. He paused for a moment, aware of her eyes on him, and absolutely relishing the look in them.

Pure, unadulterated *want*.

He played with it a bit, taking his sweet time turning the shirt inside out. He pulled it back over his head very, very slowly.

And when his head came back out the neckline, he could see her little pink tongue caught between her teeth.

"Chasing witches," she said, as if she was trying very hard to distract from the look in her eyes.

"Sorry?"

"A line about inside-out shirts from a children's book. While you figure out the car seat, I'll go ask them," she said, not able to disguise the hoarseness in her voice and jerking her chin at security, "to follow us."

"To?"

"To Lido's Toy Store, of course. Where else are we going to find a birthday present at this late time?"

"Where else, indeed," he said. The truth was he had never been inside the only toy store on the entire island.

He watched for a moment, as Gabriela approached the men, stuck out her hand and introduced herself.

He noticed that William, the younger of the two, said something that made her laugh. He looked at the man more closely. William would probably be considered very good-looking. Single, if he recalled the personnel file. His behavior was utterly professional, of course, but still, Enrique picked up the subtle signals.

Was he ever so faintly jealous, the same way he had been after she'd called the vet by his first name, Leon?

"Do you know how to drive a stick?" she asked, when she came back. He'd successfully wrestled the car seat into place and put the picnic basket in the trunk.

Her tone suggested it was some sort of test of manhood and that if he did not she would not think as highly of him. He was somehow unwilling to surrender even a little bit of the appreciation of his masculinity that had stormed through her eyes moments ago when he had taken off his shirt.

"Of course I know how to drive a stick!"

And then, he was in the driver's seat, trying to figure out the operating system of the ancient car. It lurched to life, and soon they were careening down the narrow road toward Hermosa Mariposa's main village, Benito.

The car had no springs. The clutch was cranky, and he was out of practice. The brakes seemed, if not iffy, at least very tired. There was no air-conditioning, so dust flew in the windows, and clouds of it came out of the seats every time he hit a bump. Which was often.

The heat inside the vehicle was suffocating.

So even though the old car was impossibly uncooperative when he was trying to show off for a pretty woman, and even though he was choking on dust, and the interior heat of the car was probably only slightly cooler than a lava lake, he felt a tickle of pure delight at the unexpected twists and turns of the day.

He started to laugh.

And then so did Gabriela.

And then Marcello joined in.

They were three people experiencing the utter and pure bliss of finding themselves on an unexpected holiday from regular life and on a rough road that seemed to lead to pure adventure.

CHAPTER FOURTEEN

GABRIELA LET THE laughter wash over her. It felt like a healing balm, being poured over the wounds of her losses, so many of them recently. The loss of her fiancé felt as if it hardly rated compared with the loss of eight years from her home, the uncertainty around her father and the recent news that Geraldo was probably coming to the end of his nine lives.

And then there was her impossible love for the man beside her.

Still, for all that, she had been given this incredible, totally unexpected moment, a pure gift from the universe, and she planned to enjoy it.

They entered Benito. It was Hermosa Mariposa's largest village, and Gabriela felt a sigh of homecoming.

The village dated back to medieval times, and clusters of white homes, their vine-covered stone exterior walls touching, marched up and down the cobblestoned streets of the steep hills that surrounded the village center.

The square—the heart of all of Benito with its shops and theaters and cafés—consisted of narrow, cobblestone pathways that beckoned intriguingly away from the central park with its fountain and gardens. The pathways were shaded by bougainvillea dripping off archways above them. The doorways of the stores welcomed with hanging baskets and clay pots spilling over with fragrant, colorful flowers.

The roads in this old part of the village were so narrow cars could not pass, and so the core was, charmingly, vehicle free. They found parking and got out of the car, releasing Marcello from the bonds of his seat.

"I'm sweaty," Enrique said, appalled.

She laughed at the look on his face. "All the better for your disguise! You look like a normal person on a hot day."

As they moved away from the car and toward the heart of the village, she glanced back at the security team, who had had to park some distance from them and were hurrying to catch up. Both men looked as if the stress of this unscheduled excursion to such a difficult-to-protect area was going to cause them heart failure. And that was even though they both—but particularly William—looked as if they were in optimal condition.

She saw that, even with the rather handsome William trailing them, and even with the Prince disguised, it was Enrique that women sent looks to.

Her hand slipped into his on one side and Marcello's on the other as they moved into the narrow crowded street that would lead to Lido's.

"To look like a family," she whispered to Enrique. "No one's expecting you to be part of a family."

But was that really it? Or was it to send a message to all those women who slid him interested looks?

He's mine. Of course, he was not, but on this splendid day, what would it hurt to pretend, just for a little while?

"I think being sweaty is a pretty good disguise," he whispered back. "Not to mention an inside-out shirt."

"Both are barely noticeable," she assured him. Now that she had taken his hand, she saw the looks they attracted were indulgent, people enjoying seeing the little family out for a Saturday excursion.

Indulgent except for the grim-faced men who followed them, radiating tension. Gabriela led the small troop to their destination, Lido's Toy Store.

"Sir," William said, "would you let me go in first?"

There was something faintly beseeching in the man's voice. *Please let me do my job.*

Enrique nodded. This, Gabriela realized, not without sympathy, was his life. Simple freedoms that most people, including her, took completely for granted were not his to enjoy.

William went in the shop, while they took in the display in the front window. Marcello could not contain his excitement as he looked over the treasure trove of toys behind the glass.

"Clear," William said tersely, when he came back out, and then he and his partner took up stations on the street, watching it warily.

Enrique held open the door for Gabriela and Marcello, but she turned, wanting to see both their faces when they walked into the store.

Both he and Marcello looked as if they had entered a magic kingdom. She realized that neither prince had ever actually been in this store before.

And perhaps not any store in Benito or anywhere else on the island where they would be so hugely recognizable.

It felt as if it was an unexpected gift she was giving them. She would have liked to spend hours exploring this space with them. The shelves were crammed with wooden trucks and toy trains, teddy bears and board games, puzzles and craft kits.

Poor Marcello, mouth open, hardly knew where to look first.

The clerk, a young woman, with a huge name tag that said Darla, acknowledged them with a nod but her attention was outside the window. She hovered, frowning out at the security team.

"Did you see that man come in here?" she asked them, not looking away from the window. "Comes in and looks around and leaves again. What do you suppose he was looking for?"

Enrique and Gabriela exchanged amused looks.

"Men like that don't come in places like this," Darla decided. "He doesn't look like a child snatcher, but who can tell these days? He's with another man, now, both just standing out there eying up the store. I don't like it one bit."

But Gabriela saw the clerk's focus being outside of the store as an unexpected bonus since it kept her attention completely away from their little "family."

She asked Darla where to find the Ryder-themed toys, and the clerk flapped her hand toward the back of the store. When they found the huge section, Marcello let out a screech of pure delight. She had to remind him the mission was to find a birthday present for Henri. Surprisingly, he focused immediately on finding the perfect gift for his new friend.

Gabriela helped him narrow it down to three, and finally, he settled on an action figure set for Henri.

"And I will have these light sabers for myself," he announced. "And this and this and this."

She glanced at Enrique. Clearly he had been totally intimidated by this morning's tantrum and was prepared to buy the whole store if it would prevent another outburst.

Firmly, she put each of the items Marcello had chosen for himself back on the shelves.

"Let's add all those things to your birthday list, when we get home," she suggested.

"Will I be having a party?"

"Of course you will!" Gabriela assured him. She raised her eyebrows at Enrique. He lifted a shoulder, indicating he knew nothing about the party status of his son.

They made their way to the front register, selecting a gift bag on the way. The cash register looked like possibly the first such device that had ever found its way to the island, but Darla was not behind it.

Though not difficult to locate. She was leaning out the open front door, yelling at the two security men, who looked on, resolute and immovable.

She came back in, slamming the door behind her, her cheeks flaming with color.

"I told them to clear off," she said. "I told them they can't stand in front of a children's store as if they're looking for a child to grab. Look at them! Haven't moved an inch. You'd think I hadn't even spoken to them. I'm calling the police."

Enrique moved forward, cleared his throat.

But he didn't have to say anything, because the clerk was frowning out at the men. "But come to that, they kind of look like police, don't they?"

As if the pieces of a puzzle suddenly fell into place, she swiveled all her attention to Marcello. The baseball cap did not hide his dark curls. He blinked those unmistakably Falcon eyes at her charmingly. She completely froze and then recognition blazed across her face. She looked swiftly to Enrique. Her mouth fell open.

"Your Royal Highness?" she whispered. "Your Royal Highnesses."

She dropped into a curtsey and nearly took out the cash register with her forehead.

"You have a lovely store, Darla," Enrique said, taking adulation and awe completely in stride. "Have you worked here long?"

Gabriela could see the inbred graciousness in him, the effortless way he turned the focus away from himself, and made the clerk feel as if only she existed for him in that moment.

"It's my mum and dad's," she stammered. "It belonged to my grandparents, on my dad's side, before us. I help out whenever I can."

"Do you enjoy it?"

"I adore it," she said, shyly. "It's what first gave me my love of children. I've just graduated with a degree in early childhood education."

"I appreciate you being so protective of its clients," he told her with utter sincerity. "Miss Lido, I think you are going to be a great teacher."

Gabriela noticed how carefully he listened, how he respectfully didn't use her first name, even though it was emblazoned on the huge name tag, but the last name she had revealed by saying it was her father's parents who had owned the store.

"Oh! Why, thank you, Your Royal Highness."

He cast a look at Gabriela and then leaned into her. "I don't have any money," he confessed in an undertone.

Of course he didn't have any money. Of course he would not even have a credit card. He did not shop for himself!

"Go," she said, matching his hushed tone. "I'll catch up with you. Go before this poor girl has a heart attack." The hospital was soon going to be filled with all the people they were causing heart problems for today.

When Enrique left, holding open the door for Marcello, Gabriela slipped her own credit card out of her purse. And then she saw a bookcase behind Darla.

"Oh!" she said, "and a copy of *Snuggle-Uffle-Gus*. And *I Am Loved Best of All*? And we'd better have *The Illustrated Hermosa Mariposa Alphabet* book, as well. Oh, and there's Roald Dahl, *The Witches*. We were just talking about that book."

"Those are my favorites," Darla said, though still in a daze. She plucked the books from the shelf and put them in a separate bag, and rang in the purchases, which Gabriela paid for.

"Was that really them?" the young woman asked, breathless, staring out the window, and looking dangerously close to swooning. "I'm not being pranked, am I?"

Gabriela smiled. "It was really them."

"I can't believe it. I'm going to call my sister right this second."

"I know this is going to be difficult, but if you could not say anything, we might be able to come back another time. Prince

Enrique did notice how protective you were of the store's clients."

What Gabriela was weighing was, if Darla did say something, did call someone, how fast would word spread? Even with the island's archaic cell phone system, it would be like a wildfire. How long would they have before the two princes were mobbed?

It felt as if, if there was an incident, it would be her fault for pooh-poohing royal security measures and protocols.

The girl stared at her, obviously thinking about the choice between basking in the glory of her brush with the island's royal family and having them come back.

"Their visit will remain my secret," she decided, raking her hair back off her forehead. Her hand was trembling.

How did Enrique live like this? How did it feel to be worshipped by complete strangers? By people who didn't really know the first thing about you, but were completely bowled over by your status, by the station you'd been born to?

He'd handled it so well—out of long habit, no doubt—but didn't he ever find it tiresome?

As Gabriela gathered up the packages, the girl said, "Could you tell those men I'm sorry? I practically accused them of being perverts. And the younger one was so handsome! Just standing there, letting me go on and on, not saying a word in his own defense."

"I'll tell them," Gabriela said gently, and she was almost out the door when she stopped.

She looked back at Darla. A love of children. A degree in early childhood education. Protective. Loyal. Able to make good decisions under pressure. Able to offer an apology when she was wrong.

The star-struck factor could probably be overcome.

"The royal family has just had a nanny leave their employ," she said. She went quickly back to the counter and asked for a piece of paper and a pen. She wrote down her name and the cottage phone number. "Give me a call if you think it would interest you."

She had the fleeting thought that William and Darla would make the cutest couple. But then she was amused with herself. Who was she to be matchmaking? What about her own life would qualify her for that?

Gabriela went out the door to catch up with the two princes, who were sauntering down the street, enjoying the gift of their anonymity for a little while longer.

She passed on the apology to the security detail, as they returned to the car. A few minutes later, they pulled up at the house where Henri lived.

"I'll go to the door with him," Gabriela said. Newly aware of the security predicament she might have put them in, she said, "Stay in the car. Don't take off the hat, or the sunglasses."

"I'm a little scared," Cello said, as they went up the steps to the house. He was clutching his gift to him as if it was a shield.

She realized this was a brand-new experience for him. She crouched down in front of him, and straightened his shirt, ran her hand through his curls.

He'd been in her care less than a week.

She loved him madly, already. She was not going to spoil the day by asking herself what that would mean when she had to leave him. Guido would tell her that was the wrong question.

"It's just the boys you've been playing with in the garden. You are going to have so much fun!" she assured him.

And then the door opened, and she was relieved that it was Henri's grandfather, Angelo, who was standing there. He would know to keep the visit in absolute confidence. Plus, Marcello knew him, of course, from the palace.

Angelo took in the situation in a glance, and mouthed to her, *I'll take care of him.* Out loud, he said, "Welcome, Prince Cello." And to her, "Come back around four."

She turned back to the car, to find Enrique standing outside it, fanny leaning against the door.

"I told you to stay in the car," she said to him.

He lifted an eyebrow at her, a reminder people did not tell him what to do. Even in his disguise, he was unreasonably attractive, like a film star. There was no way they could hang out here without someone noticing him. He was that kind of man. He had the kind of sheer presence that would attract attention no matter where he went.

Gabriela realized how lucky they had been to escape the village square with only Darla figuring out who he was.

"It was too hot to stay in the car. I'm dying, Gabriela."

"Unaccustomed to the discomforts of us commoners," she said with an unsympathetic sniff.

"You could save me," he said, with an easy smile, not rising to her attempt to bait him.

Oh, that smile! It drew her eyes right to the full, sensuous curve of Enrique's lips.

For some ridiculous reason, mouth-to-mouth resuscitation came to mind. Her heart was starting to pound way too hard.

"How?" she squeaked.

CHAPTER FIFTEEN

IT OCCURRED TO Gabriela that the time they had spent together in the last week in that sun-drenched garden, they'd had Marcello to act as a buffer between them. Not to mention her parents a few steps away!

Now, they were a grown man and a grown woman alone together, the chemistry between them unmistakable.

Well, alone, except for his security.

"Let's go to the beach," Enrique suggested, his voice soft. "Just you and me. Butterfly Cove. It's always secluded."

"What about them?" she said, nodding toward the security team.

"I told them to stay with Marcello."

The full impact of what he was suggesting hit her. Not even security. They were going to be alone. Entirely alone.

It was a terrifying—and absolutely thrilling—new twist in the wild and unmapped road she found herself traveling down today.

"What did your security have to say about you ditching them?" Gabriela asked the Prince.

Enrique raised an eyebrow at her. "The only one who ever dares to question my decisions is you."

"Well, maybe your decisions need to be questioned."

This was madness. She didn't feel quite so cavalier about his security as she had when they had started out on this excursion. She clutched for an excuse.

"I didn't bring a bathing suit," she hedged. They were walking toward danger. Possibly from several different directions. Someone had to be the sensible one!

He grinned wickedly at her. "Neither did I."

The sense of danger went off the charts. "Oh," she managed to croak out.

And then he leaned in close to her. "I guess I'll find out if you put on your bloomers this morning."

She smacked him smartly right on his shoulder.

He cupped his hand over his shoulder, pretending hurt. "And you're the only one who has ever done that, too. You're also the one who introduced the whole concept of *commando* to my sheltered world."

She snorted at that, a sound designed to hide exactly how hard her heart was beating. He held open the door of her father's car for her, just as if she'd said yes to this crazy idea to ditch his security and spend time together. In a state of undress!

It occurred to Gabriela, as she slid by Enrique—just as if she *had* said yes—that she didn't want to be the sensible one anymore.

She wanted to leave that behind. Maybe not forever, but for the delicious space of the *now*. She wanted to flirt with danger. She wanted to feel what being with him made her feel.

Alive.

She could live one heartbeat at a time, couldn't she?

She plopped into the passenger seat.

Enrique had been absolutely right.

The heat inside the car was enough to melt her.

Maybe he was not motivated by wanting them to be alone together. Maybe he was just hot and it was as simple as going for a swim.

But whatever it was for him, the fact that her actions were signaling a strong yes instead of no was turning her world into an inferno.

That feeling of being *alive* intensified, the heat playing across the newly sensitive surface of her skin, along with a hyperawareness of color and sound.

And scent.

The tangy aroma of him tickled her nostrils, despite the open windows. He found the switch for the radio. She noticed the squareness of his wrist, the masculine appeal of his hands tapping on the steering wheel as crackly music filled the car. It was a well-known love ballad by a local musician.

Enrique began to hum along, and then sing.

His voice was raspy. Terrible, really.

"Don't give up your day job," she advised him.

He only grinned and sang louder. Even this—the fact he was comfortable revealing such a flawed singing voice to her—made her feel a deepening sense of intimacy with him.

By the time they reached Butterfly Cove, she was ready to ignite.

She got out of the car. As he had guessed, the beach was completely theirs. It really was one of the best-kept secrets on the island, a tiny half-moon of fine white sand tucked between towering black volcanic boulders. Protected turquoise waters lapped gently at the shore.

Without waiting for him—feeling as if her sensation overload might explode if she looked at him—Gabriela ran across the sand and down toward the water, shedding her clothes as she went, not being the sensible one.

At all.

She plunged into the sea in her underwear.

But if she had thought that was going to put out the fire, she was wrong. Because when she turned, finally daring to look, Enrique was standing there at the shore.

He had brought the picnic basket, and set it at his feet. Was he waiting for the exact moment when she turned and looked at him?

His gaze locked on hers, he flicked open the top button of

his shirt. With exquisite slowness, sure that he had her full attention, he moved to the next one. When he had dispensed with all the buttons, the shirt gaped open, revealing the hard washboard lines of his perfect abs, the jut of his hips, the muscular arrows on either side of those abs that dipped into the waistband of his trousers.

Still with tormenting slowness, he slipped the shirt off one broad shoulder and then the other, peeling it from his arms, letting it drop in a heap in the sand.

And then his hands moved to the button on his trousers, and then the zipper. He bent, and peeled down the trousers, stepped out of them one leg at a time.

Black boxer briefs clung to him, and he stood there for a moment. He had shed his identity as a prince as completely as his clothing. Enrique stood before her, 100 percent pure man.

Radiating certainty.

Radiating confidence in himself and his innate masculinity.

He stood there, still, letting her drink him in, letting her know that sometimes not even water could put out a fire.

And letting her know this was not a man whose only agenda was a cool dip on a blistering-hot day.

He knew exactly what he was doing.

Enrique let the water close over him, a refreshing burst of coolness on this sweltering day.

And yet the chill of the water hardly cooled the heat inside him, as he swam out to where Gabriela stood, the water lapping just below her shoulders.

Her hair was soaked, otter-slicked against her head. Her thick lashes were tangled with crystal drops of water.

What had been building between them for a week, since the moments that followed Geraldo's rescue from the tree, burst open like a storm cloud on a summer day.

He put his hand behind her neck and drew her lips to his own.

As soon as he tasted her, he knew the truth.

What had been building between them had been building for a lifetime, not a week. Her lips under his tasted of homecoming.

Of the place where he most wanted to be in the entire world.

Her lips tasted of the promise of being accepted, not for what he was, but for who he was.

Just a man.

With her, with the ocean all around them, cradling them, and her arms twining sweetly around his neck, her lips answering the invitation of his, he was nothing else.

For a suspended moment in time, he gave himself to every sensation, gave himself to her. It felt as if they were young again, experiencing the startling bliss of discovery. The time they had been apart evaporated as though it had never been.

Though he had been kissed many times since—and so, he was sure, had she—it was now, as it had been then, as if this was the very first time for both of them.

Her lips tasted of salt and need. There was no resistance in her; the opposite of that, an opening, like a flower opening to sun.

All that mattered, to Enrique, was this moment of pure connection between them. There was no future. And really no past, either. All that existed was this, an experience so profound he could feel himself beginning to tremble in its majesty.

It was an enchantment that drew them both into the circle of its power, that held them fast in bonds stronger than steel and softer than the petals of a rose.

At the back of his mind, he registered the irritation of a dog barking frantically.

"There's someone on the beach," she whispered.

It felt as if he was, indeed, trying to break bands made of iron, as he turned and looked over his shoulder. A middle-aged woman, wearing a rather daring bikini—probably because she had thought she would have the beach to herself, just as they had—was throwing a ball out into the water for a shrilly excited terrier.

"At least we know she doesn't have a place to hide a phone or a camera," Gabriela said. "So, no nearly naked prince cavorting in the water as tomorrow's leading story in the *Tribute*."

Interesting that she would think of protecting him, when he wanted to protect her. He placed his body so that he completely blocked the woman's view of Gabriela in her underwear.

Gorgeous underwear.

It seemed to have been spun from silk threads, moonlight and enchantment.

Reluctantly, Enrique realized what a good thing it was that woman had arrived and interrupted them because didn't protecting Gabriela go a lot further than making sure a stranger didn't see her in her underwear?

Despite the fact it felt as if he had waited a lifetime to have this—to taste her lips, to know her, finally, as a woman—he reminded himself that not only did she technically work for him, but this was Guido's daughter!

Could Enrique ever look at himself in the mirror again if he treated her with anything less than complete honor?

How could he respect himself if he gave in to an impulse, rather than making a conscious decision?

The woman seemed to realize, suddenly, she was not alone at the beach. She squinted out at them, her mouth fell open and she glanced down at herself. She called the dog and scurried away.

Gabriela leaned into him again, her eyes closed, her lips ready.

He put a finger on her lips, and she opened her eyes and saw the *no* in the gesture and in his eyes.

She looked stunned by his withdrawal. And hurt. It was almost enough for him to say, honor be damned.

But before he was pulled back into the pure temptation

of her lips, she masked the look on her face, and cocked her head at him.

Then she reached out, her arm flat against the water, and delivered a mighty splash to his face. While he choked on water, she punched him—a little too hard—on the shoulder.

"You're it," she said, the game he had watched the boys play in her garden. And then pulled completely away from him, turned, tried to run, gave up and swam away.

She'd always been a strong swimmer, and for a moment he just watched her, admiring her beauty and strength and grace, feeling the ache of the lost moment he had refused.

After a second, he followed her through the water, accepting her invitation to play, though admittedly he was not trying nearly as hard as he could have to tag her. A man could only test his resolve—and win—so often.

That moment that had sizzled between them had finally fizzled out as they chased each other through the water until they were utterly exhausted.

Now, back on the sand, Gabriela watched as Enrique scooped up his heap of abandoned clothes, and acted as if the excursion was over.

"She's gone," she said. "Let's dry off before we get dressed. I'm starving. Let's see what's in the basket."

His eyes drifted to her underwear, which she knew was very nearly transparent. She knew he'd come to his senses, and that she should be nothing but glad that he had, but she at least wanted him to regret that he had done so.

He hesitated, then dropped his clothes. He opened the picnic basket and took out a blanket, then flicked it open.

She sat on it, and after a moment, glancing around to satisfy himself there were no other dog walkers about, he sat down, too.

The contents of the picnic basket were, of course, exquisite. Baked-that-morning flaky croissants, excellent cheeses, a selection of Hermosa Mariposa's finest olives, ice-cold artesian well water in glass bottles, strawberries and grapes.

Gabriela deliberately made him regret the interrupted kiss even more with the way she ate the strawberry, closing her eyes, biting into its plump flesh delicately, darting out her tongue to catch the delicious juices. She opened her eyes. She had his complete attention. She smiled, all innocence.

CHAPTER SIXTEEN

AN ALMOST INAUDIBLE groan escaped Enrique, but he yanked his gaze away from Gabriela. After he had finished eating, he flopped down on his belly, his head resting in the crook of his elbow, his powerful legs splayed. His golden skin was covered in water droplets, clinging and sliding. The sight made the strawberry taste like dust.

Gabriela realized that he could do to her, effortlessly, what she had needed a strawberry to do to him!

She lay down on her tummy on the blanket beside him, her head turned toward him. They weren't quite touching, but so close she could see the water beaded in the thickness of his lashes, and feel the puff of his breath on her wet skin. She looked at his lips, and thought of the taste of them, *yearned* for it. His lips had been better than that strawberry by a long shot!

But, he had chosen to be the sensible one, and really she should be nothing but grateful for his discipline and wisdom.

Still, she had to close her eyes hastily against the visual temptation of him.

"Can I ask you something?" she said.

"Of course." But there was trepidation in his voice, as if he feared she might ask why he had not resumed kissing.

"It's a funny question."

"The best kind," he said, but he still sounded faintly wary.

"Who buys your underwear?"

She opened her eyes. He looked into her gaze, genuinely shocked.

"What?"

She closed her eyes again. "Well, obviously you can't run down to Bella's Department Store and rummage through the bins yourself."

"Gabriela, I have absolutely no idea who buys what."

"Seriously?"

"Yes."

"So, you just open your bureau drawer and it's magically stocked with everything you need?"

"That about sums it up, yes."

"You don't even know if it's a woman or a man picking out your personal items?"

"For God's sake, Gabby!"

He hadn't called her Gabby since they were kids. She felt like a cat stretching upward toward a comforting scratch from familiar hands.

She *liked* it that he was off-balance; the legendary composure that had allowed him to break off that kiss seemed to be on very shaky ground.

"The reason I ask," she said huskily, "is that they're very sexy."

She opened her eyes again. He was looking at her with extraordinary intensity.

"Who buys yours?" he asked huskily.

"Me, of course!"

"Because they're very sexy, too."

And here they were, a man and a woman, back at the point he had just backed away from, a man and a woman alone on a beach and feeling as if they were alone in the entire universe.

"I've missed you so much," he said, his voice raw with surrender. "I don't know how we could have lost everything we once were to each other. But I don't blame you for not answering my calls, after you told me about my mother interfering in your life."

Something went very still inside her.

"What?" she said. "Not answering what calls?"

He frowned at her. "When I got home from school, the year you left. I must have left a hundred messages for you."

"I never got a single one."

"But it was your voice on the message."

"How could it have been?"

But suddenly, she had a vague memory of one of the Queen's staffers calling her to his office and giving her an answering machine as she was packing, getting ready to leave. He said because of the time differences, the Queen never wanted her to miss a call from her family.

Gabriela had actually been touched that the Queen understood how lonely she was going to be so far from home.

The staffer had showed her how to use it, and insisted that she "practice" making a recording. But had he given it to her? No, she remembered, he had said it would be shipped later, as an electronic device might flag her through customs.

She'd gotten to the US and received not the machine but a gift card saying that the original machine would not be used with American electrical outlets, which was true!

How naive she had been. And what extraordinary measures Queen Katalina had gone to sever the relationship between Gabriela and Enrique.

"You never got my letters, either," she said, flatly.

"Your letters?"

"I wrote you for the longest time. Until I realized you weren't going to answer."

He took that in, drew in a deep breath and tried, not entirely successfully, to mask his anger.

"Once again, I find myself having to apologize for my family."

He reached out and touched the wetness of her hair. Though there had been lots of physical contact as they played tag, this was different, a reopening of a door that she was pretty sure he thought he had shut. And certainly that his mother had thought was shut all those years ago.

She touched his chest, laid her palm flat against the warm, water-encrusted silk of his skin. Below the skin, she could feel the sinewy strength of him.

He leaned closer to her.

But this time, it was Gabriela who found the strength to pull away. She just wasn't sure she had the fortitude to go down this path, only to be rejected again, only to find there were powers that be intent on keeping them apart.

Her head felt as if it was swimming with so many conflicting emotions: anger, betrayal, hope, elation.

And, even with all that, a desire to *know* him, in this deeper, more adult way, a desire to understand how his deep sorrows had changed him and become a part of him. Really, it seemed as if that should have come before the kiss they had just shared, and the one he was now inviting.

"Enrique, how are you still standing after the loss of Amelia, and your baby?"

He was startled by the question, but then he ran a hand through his still-wet hair and drew in a deep breath. When he looked at her, she saw unmistakable relief in his dark eyes. She realized he'd had no one to talk to, no one to take his heartaches to. While it had seemed as if the world grieved with him, the fact was Enrique had carried the burden of his terrible loss alone.

And so he told her. He spoke of Amelia only with the deepest respect, even as he acknowledged he and his wife had been virtual strangers trying to navigate the intimacies of the situation they found themselves in, to the best of their ability. Amelia had given up her home and the secret love of her life to fulfill her royal obligations to her family and her island.

"I know she tried to overcome it, but she had understandable resentment, and that came across as a certain coldness toward me, and an immersion in Marcello.

"But in our last year together, I felt we had turned a corner. We had genuine respect for each other, and enjoyed each other's company. She began to love the island, and became involved in some very important local charities.

"It was Amelia who wanted the second child, and by wanting that, it felt as if, for the first time, she was embracing, not just life here, but me. There was a kind of hopefulness in both of us as we looked forward to her arrival, and some kind of new beginning between us.

"I remember Amelia showing me this tiny little dress she'd found, and me touching it, and something in my heart opening like a flower that had needed water and sun.

"It was the dress we buried her in." His voice cracked, and Gabriela's hand found his and held it. Tight.

She was not sure she had ever felt so honored by a confidence, as if some hidden part of Enrique—his vulnerability—had been laid before her.

The silence between them was long, but comfortable.

And then he said, his voice still hoarse with emotion, "That's enough about me. I want to hear about you."

And so she told him. About life in New York and her surprising affinity toward marketing, and finally, about Timothy and her broken engagement. "I think it's time to go get Cello," she said, a bit later, startled by how fast time had gone by.

As they pulled their clothes on over their underwear that had partially dried in the sun, but were still wet enough for the damp to seep through, she was aware of something different between them.

Something more mature, and deeper than it had ever been before. It was a feeling of finding a part of your heart that you did not know had been missing.

When Marcello tumbled out of Henri's house, holding a balloon and a bag of party favors in his hand, it felt as if even her affection for him had been deepened by Enrique's revelations.

"My present was Henri's favorite," he said. "Guess what we had?"

"What?" Enrique asked, his eyes settling on his son in the rearview mirror.

"Hot dogs! They are the best thing I ever tasted."

"Are they?" Enrique said.

Gabriela shot him a look. "You haven't had a hot dog?"

"Sorry. I keep trying to tell you I've led a sheltered life."

"Have you, Gabriela?" Marcello asked.

"Oh, they sustain life in New York City. You can buy them at stands on practically every street corner."

Marcello contemplated that as if he had just heard that heaven really did exist.

She felt as if she had made the same discovery when Enrique's lips had beckoned to hers, when she had tasted him.

But once you had tasted heaven, how did you ever stop yearning for it?

By the time they pulled back up at the Olivera cottage, Marcello was fast asleep. Enrique got him from the back seat, and stood, for a moment, looking at her.

So much in his eyes, the same overload of confused feelings that she herself was experiencing. Regret. Hope.

And most dangerous of all. Hunger.

She passed him the Lido's bag with the books in it.

"What's this?"

"A little gift for you and Marcello."

"As if you haven't given us enough, already. Thank you for today," he said huskily.

It was there between them, like magnets being pulled together. He wanted to kiss her. She wanted to kiss him.

Instead, he turned and went to the vehicle behind them. One of the security men held open the door for him, obviously relieved that things were back under control.

But were they?

CHAPTER SEVENTEEN

"WOULD YOU LIKE me to read you a story before bed tonight?"

It hurt Enrique how carefully Marcello seemed to be considering this decision.

"Gabriela gave me some new books," he added persuasively.

That clinched it! And so Gabriela, without even being there, gave him yet another gift. Soon, he sat beside Marcello on his son's bed, both of their backs against the headboard, their legs stretched out in front of them.

He noticed Marcello had on blue pajamas with little ducks on them. Who bought his son's pajamas? And didn't they know he liked Ryder themes?

It was the same with the bedding. And the entire nursery. Enrique noticed the room in ways he had not before. The walls were wainscoted halfway up the wall. Above that, they were dark blue, tasteful, with fluffy sheep cavorting across them. Everything in it, from the mobile to the framed pictures, was lovely but distinctly babyish. It occurred to him the room was photo-shoot ready as the perfect nursery, and yet did not reflect his son, at all.

Amelia had planned this room and furnished it She had chosen each stuffed animal and mobile and wall print. Enrique had been pleased she had found something to be excited about and accepted her rebuff of his interest. Did Marcello feel his mother's love in these choices? Or would he be ready to move on to a room that better reflected Marcello's growing-boy passions?

Since he hadn't known, until recently, what his son's interests were, it felt as if he had no one to blame for these lapses but himself. He hadn't even known if Marcello had a birthday party.

Of course, there was always a small family event, but had children his own age ever been invited?

Enrique doubted that.

His son was only five. For most of his life, his mother had been enough for him. Friendships outside the palace walls were a recent development.

This was another way Gabriela was inserting herself in his life, without even having to be here. He was thinking of things in a different way from how he had before.

He opened the stiff cover of the brand-new book, *Snuggle-Uffle-Gus.*

In moments, both he and Marcello were completely entranced by the beautifully illustrated story of a renegade monster, Gus, who was supposed to like scaring people, but instead liked hugs best of all.

Without even realizing what he was doing, Marcello cuddled in closer to his father, traced the pictures with his fingers, made delighted oohs and aahs at all the unexpected turns the story took.

But it had been a long, exciting day, and Marcello's comments grew fewer and his finger slipped from the page. His warm weight settled more heavily against his father and his breathing deepened.

Enrique stopped reading.

His son, in what seemed to be an act of complete trust, had fallen asleep against his chest.

Enrique's fingertips found his son's curls and combed through them. He was reluctant to get up, not just because he didn't want to wake Marcello.

But because he never wanted this moment to end.

He dropped a kiss on the top of Marcello's head, and the words he'd had trouble saying just a few days ago felt like the most natural thing in the world.

"I love you," he whispered.

And still he stayed with his sleeping son.

How did a man let go of the best day of his life?

The last thing he wanted to do was go and see his mother—that would be a sure way to take some of the shine off the day.

But after what he had discovered, how could he not confront her? And one thing he had learned about dealing with unpleasant matters was the longer he put it off, the more difficult it became to address.

He went and knocked softly on the door of his mother's suite. It was answered by the Queen's longtime assistant, Mabel, who looked surprised to see him. Of course she was surprised; nothing in the Queen's world unfolded with spontaneity.

"I'll see if she's receiving," she said uncertainly, standing back to let him in the door.

This, he thought, was his world, a place where there was no spontaneity, where you didn't even pop by unannounced to see your own mother. It had made the unexpected freedom and pure spontaneity of the day all the more intoxicating.

While he waited, he took in the grandness of the suite. It was extraordinarily formal, furniture, paintings, carpets, all of them hundreds of years old and all of it priceless. The effect of it was cold and museum-like.

Mabel ushered him through to his mother's inner sanctum, a den and TV room. It looked faintly shabby and entirely lived in.

His mother sat in a recliner, a blanket over her legs, and tray on her lap, the large wall-mounted TV across from her muted. He noted, amused, she was watching a show about housewives in America, not the news. They had not had pets, ever, while he was growing up but now she had a dog, Beau. He was at her feet, apparently too weary to raise his head. His tail flopped twice in greeting.

That dog, he realized, a little sadly, was really her only friend.

Despite the blanket over her legs, he could see his mother was still dressed, a businesswoman just home from a busy day. Her makeup was still on. Her hair, gray now, but as unruly as his and Marcello's, was still pulled back in a stern bun, not a hair out of place.

"Enrique," she said. "What an unexpected pleasure."

Her emphasis was on *unexpected* rather than *pleasure.*

She looked beautiful and regal. He realized he had never seen her dressed casually, never once seen her drop the role.

"Come have a seat," she said. Her expression was neither welcoming nor unwelcoming, but completely neutral. She cocked her head at him. They were not, after all, a family that did spontaneity.

He saw no point in beating around the bush. "I found out that you sent Gabriela away. Today, I found out that communication between us was thwarted after she left."

"And what are you looking for from me, Enrique?"

What was he looking for? An apology, he supposed.

She took the tea from the tray on her lap and took a sip. "I did what I could to prevent an absolute disaster," she said, not the least apologetic.

"It was despicable," he said.

She lifted a shoulder. "Despicable, but necessary."

"It was necessary to send an eighteen-year-old girl away from her home, to a place where she knew nothing and no one? It was necessary to keep her there, away from her family, and every single thing she knew and loved?"

"Well, that was the problem, wasn't it? She loved you."

He wanted to say he had loved her, too, but it was not the

kind of information you gave to someone who would be prepared to use it as a weapon.

His mother sighed. "Enrique! You were both teenagers. You have to think about where it was heading, and where it would have gone. What good could have come from it, if you would have followed all that youthful lust to its natural conclusion?"

He winced at her reducing what had happened between him and Gabriela to *that*. Lust.

"No good could have come from it," she answered, softly, when he did not respond. "Would either of you, in the throes of young passion, considered protection? Would you have even known what that was? You weren't in a normal position, Enrique. You couldn't go down to the chemist and get some condoms."

He was a little shocked that his mother knew what a condom was!

"What if she'd gotten pregnant?" his mother pressed softly. "It didn't just involve you and her. It was Guido and Maria, and everyone on staff."

What did he hear as Guido's name came off her lips? He wasn't sure.

"It was centuries of working relationships," she continued, "that could have been lost in bitterness and divided teams. Sacrifices had to be made."

"You sent her away, and made sure she never came back," he said.

"Again, Enrique, what good could have come from her coming back? After she'd finished university, you were a married man."

"To your choice," he pointed out with bitterness.

"Yes! To a partner who had been carefully selected for you, without the complication of emotion. Of love. An arrangement beneficial to Princess Amelia's island and ours and both our people. That's what comes first, Enrique, the people. A relationship like the one you enjoyed with Amelia is *safe*. There are no fireworks and no potential for the dreadful kind of accidents that happen when fireworks are involved."

"Is that the kind of relationship you had with my father?"

"Exactly," she said, and yet something flickered behind her eyes, and he wondered, just for a second, if he was the only one who had had sacrifices imposed on him.

He also realized that though his mother said everything was for the people, she didn't mean for individual people. She meant for people as a whole. She concerned herself with her subjects' standard of living, and access to medical care, to good jobs and prosperity.

Everything else—the needs of one person, or two—were not of consequence to her. She was single-mindedly devoted to the big picture, and she had been willing to forfeit everything for that, including her own happiness.

"Have you ever loved anyone, Mother?"

A look crossed her face that was heartbreaking and intense, but then it was gone as if it had never been.

"Of course I love you and Marcello," she snapped. She waved her hand at the television set. "But I don't subscribe to romantic notions of love. Here on Hermosa Mariposa, we're not like Americans, constantly bleating about love, constantly letting our lives be disrupted by a force that can be so destructive if it's not kept in check."

His mother saw love as the archenemy of order and control. And in that she was not wrong. Look at how his unexpected day with Gabriela had spiraled completely out of his control.

"You would have found your way back to each other if she'd come back here," his mother said. "Is that what you would have wanted for her? The tawdry life of the other woman?"

She suddenly looked small to him, sitting with her dog, her only true friend in the entire world. She looked small and lonely.

The woman who had forgone everything for duty.

He thought of the absolute delight of his day, and knew he was not prepared to make those same sacrifices.

Nor would he ask them of his son. His son was not going to be sitting, alone, in a recliner, sixty years from now, with a cat, still, as his best friend.

"Do not," Enrique warned his mother, "interfere in my personal life, again. Ever."

His mother looked shocked, as unaccustomed as he himself was to being challenged. But then her expression was quickly masked. And he was confused to see something flash through her eyes before she dismissed him by turning the sound back on to the television show, her only window into the havoc love wreaked on lives.

But for a moment he was fairly certain what he had seen in her face was that she had been pleased.

By him standing up to her.

But was that because she was pleased for him, or because she was pleased at the prospect of a clash of wills, a good fight, brightening up the dull landscape of her life?

He went to leave.

"Wait," she said. She put aside the blanket and got up from the recliner. She moved to her desk, not looking the least small or lonely anymore, but looking regal, powerful and untouchable.

She went to her desk over by the window, and opened the bottom drawer. There was no rummaging. She knew exactly where everything was.

She handed him a packet of letters, tied with a ribbon. It wasn't quite an apology, but there was something ever so faintly contrite in it.

Later, he opened those letters one by one. Read each of them, and then read them again more slowly.

He ran his fingers over Gabriela's girlish cursive.

And then he held the letters to his lips and kissed them, thanking them for making plain to him what he had really known all along.

What his mother had known all along. Gabriela had loved him then.

And he loved Gabriela.

It felt as if he loved her still and that he was always going to love her.

But he was not the boy he had once been, impulsive and callow, unable to see the consequences of loving her.

He needed to make sure that he was not mistaking friendship for love. He needed to make sure he was not mistaking gratitude over the changes she had brought about in his relationship with Marcello for love. He needed to make sure that what he was feeling was real and rooted in today, and was not the residue of an eight-year-old kiss. He needed to make sure that it was more than passion between them.

He needed to do all those things before he got either of their hopes up that there could be a future, before he took on the formidable task of challenging age-old rules and protocols.

But if it was true—if their time had come—he was aware he would fight to the ends of the earth to give them the future they both deserved.

He was aware that his hope was mixed with fear.

Because he had never allowed himself to think he might one day have his own happily-ever-after.

CHAPTER EIGHTEEN

GABRIELA WATCHED, a touch ruefully, as Darla and Prince Marcello bent over a paper at the small table. The little Prince's tongue was caught between his teeth as he earnestly practiced the alphabet Darla was showing him. Darla had come every day this week. Her absolute affection for Marcello—and his for her—practically shimmered in the air around them.

The gate squeaked open and Enrique slipped in, came and sat beside Gabriela on the bench. Cello's concentration was such that he had not even noticed his father.

"She's a treasure, isn't she?" Enrique asked.

Gabriela was so glad he saw it, too. "Yes. She wants to start taking Marcello, Henri and a few of the other boys on excursions. Mariposa Gardens. The museum. She has come up with lesson plans, intent on teaching them in such delightful ways they won't even realize they're being taught. She wondered what would be involved in setting up something like that."

"Well, security, of course. As soon as she has a schedule, I'll see to it."

Gabriela passed him a piece of paper. Their hands touched. And lingered. She pulled her hand away. Where was all this going? How naive to think it was going anywhere at all!

"She's already done a schedule. It might be nice if you put William in charge of the security."

"William?" For a moment, a look crossed his face that could almost be interpreted as jealousy. "Why William?"

"He kind of has a swoon-worthy way about him, doesn't he?" she couldn't resist teasing.

"How would I know?" he sputtered, and then, "But I suppose *you* find him good-looking?"

"Good-looking," she agreed, "but it's more. Supremely masculine. In charge."

Enrique was scowling at her.

"Perfect for Darla," she said, after a beat.

He glared at her when she giggled, seeing how completely he had walked into her trap.

"Ah, Darla," he said, apparently quite happy to change topics. "What a wonderful string of coincidences brought *us* to her."

"Yes," she said.

He heard some hesitation in her voice.

"What?" he asked. "You don't think she's working out?"

"Oh, no, she's working out. Too well, maybe."

"How is that possible?"

"She's going to start transitioning to the palace nursery next week."

It dawned on him, just as it had on her, what this would mean.

"I think my time as your nanny is drawing to a close," she said softly.

The morning-coffee time they'd come to share would be over. The easy conversations, the lighthearted kidding, the crossword puzzles, the cat between them.

Over, too, would be those lingering afternoons when he came to pick up his son, that time when he'd told her about his day and she'd told him about hers.

Those times had been different since the kiss, since their exquisite brush with freedom. Both of them were deliberately keeping a lid on the chemistry that was so strong between them. But something else, even deeper, was unfolding, and it felt as if she would be bereft without the routine, without the possibility of seeing Enrique every single day. What would there be to look forward to?

No more long, easy talks about everything and anything. No more games with Marcello. No more laughter.

Oh, the laughter! For some reason, Gabriela had allowed herself to believe these times between them could last forever, to avoid the question, *Where was it all going?*

She, of all people, in the face of her losses—her childhood love of Enrique, in particular—but also the more recent loss of Timothy, and now her impending losses, her father and her cat, should know better than to invest in a childish belief of forever.

Of a happily-ever-after.

To nurture dreams of these two beautiful princes being part of her daily life for as long as she had a daily life.

She slid a look at Enrique, and was shocked to see he appeared as happy about her impending end as his nanny as she was dismayed by it.

Silence spread between them. Eventually, he broke it.

"I wondered," he said. He suddenly stopped. He looked at his hands, then over at Marcello and Darla. He gazed everywhere but at her.

"You wondered?" she prodded him.

"I wondered if you'd have dinner with me tomorrow night."

Not with Marcello and him.

It was the first time *this* was out in the open between them. He, one of the most sophisticated, sought-after, sexy men in the world was asking her out! And he seemed as nervous as a schoolboy, worried he had rivals in someone like William.

"Since you don't work for me, anymore," he added hastily.

She felt something tingle along her spine at how *everything* seemed to be working together, how the sheer coincidence of finding Darla was having a domino effect in the best possible way.

Was that why he had called an abrupt halt to that kiss at the beach? Bound as her employer to act with complete honor?

"I would love to have dinner with you," she said.

What had seemed like a terrible thing only moments ago, Marcello moving back to the nursery, had turned completely on its head. A window had closed and a door had been flung open.

A door to possibilities, the likes of which she had never, ever allowed herself to contemplate.

"I'll send a car for you."

"Can I just meet you?"

He cocked his head at her.

"Guido. Maria," she said. Why didn't she want them to know? Because they would make too much of it, that's why.

Maybe she was making too much of it. They were going *out* for dinner but maybe it wasn't a date, despite his nervousness in asking.

It was likely just his way of thanking her for helping him and Marcello.

"Meet me outside the back gate, then," he said. "At seven."

How did you get dressed for a special dinner without letting the other members of your household know it was a special occasion?

As it turned out, the universe lined up for her again, because Guido was having a good day and he and Maria went to have supper and play cards with friends, something they had not done for a long time.

And so she was alone.

To curl her hair, and apply her makeup, to spray the air with perfume and walk through the mist, so the scent just hinted.

She was alone to slip on the dress she had gone to find in the village that morning. Sometimes, Benito shocked, in the best possible way, with what you could find there.

And she had found, in the same little cubbyhole of a shop where she had found her dress for graduation, a dress out of a dream.

It was bold by Hermosa Mariposa standards, which probably explained why it was gathering dust on a sales rack in the back of the store. It didn't look like much on the hanger, a limp clump of smoky-colored pleats, and yet as soon as she saw it, as soon as she felt the filmy fabric under her fingers, something in her had sighed.

She had gone into the change room, taken off her clothes and put on the dress, with her back to the mirror.

The dress had settled around her, like mist cascading down a mountainside, and when she turned to look in the mirror, she saw it was an enchantment.

She had been transformed, a Cinderella. She had gone from being Guido the olive keeper's daughter to a goddess bathed in moonlight. The structure of the dress was deceptively simple, falling in an A-line from her neck to her mid-thigh. But the light played in the constant movement of the pleats. One moment, it looked like that silvery mountain mist, the next white as snow and, after that, the tumultuous gray of lightning-lit skies.

It was, she realized, a dress a woman intent on seducing a man wore.

Was she bold enough to pull it off?

The intensity of her answer rippled through her.

Yes.

Enrique was waiting for her outside the gate. She saw from the look on his face that the dress had accomplished everything she might have wanted. He looked utterly bewitched.

He leaned toward her.

She readied for his kiss, but instead, he kissed both her cheeks, quite formally. When he took her hand, it was lightly, as any gentleman might take the hand of a woman in high heels on uneven ground.

He was dressed as beautifully as she was: a dark dinner jacket, a white dress shirt, a dark tie, knife-creased pants, shoes so shined they reflected the moonlight.

They had known each other since they were children.

And yet, suddenly, it felt as if they were strangers to each other.

He guided her along the path, and then around the palace and past the garden. She could hear a sound, but she didn't connect it to them, until they came to the helicopter pad, and the shiny machine, embossed with gold royal crests, waited for them, its engines throbbing.

"I thought we could enjoy ourselves more if we were off island," he said.

The pilot held open the door for them, and Enrique helped her to get in. She settled and he took the seat beside her, picking up the earphones and setting them over her hair, adjusting them for her, before he put on his own.

The pilot got in, joining a copilot who was already seated.

"Your Highness, miss, we have a clear night for flying, and we're expecting no turbulence. It will be a half hour airtime to Isle Santiago. Enjoy your flight."

Gabriela, of course, had flown a great deal since she had left this island, but on commercial flights, not private helicopters! She was not sure she had ever experienced anything quite so dreamlike as the flight to Santiago.

First, they lifted, and she watched the palace and her own home become toy-like, lit up in the darkness beneath them. Then they could see the lights of Benito and finally they left that behind them, and it was only them and the stars, inky ocean water beneath them, broken only by the odd light of a ship.

The lights of Santiago started to come into view a bit later.

Was it so magical because it was a first, or because Enrique's hand remained in hers, his voice melodic through the headsets, as he pointed out various landmarks along the way, and then constellations?

A long, dark limousine picked them up from the helipad and whisked them through Santiago City, which had much the same style as Benito, except it was much larger. The streets were full of summer crowds. People stopped to stare at the limo, but the darkened windows protected the privacy of the passengers.

At the edge of town, they took a twisting road upward, until they reached a castle at the top of a mountain.

The door was opened for them, and with her hand in Enrique's, they followed a black-jacketed man to a huge patio at the back of the castle, which sat on the very edge of a precipice that overlooked the sea and the city below them.

It was obviously a restaurant, but only one table was set, and only one candle burned.

"Is this Café Allegro?" she asked, awed. It was, arguably, the most sought-after reservation in the world.

"It is."

"But where are all the other customers?"

"It's closed. For tonight."

She let the impact of that hit her. He had presumably commandeered one of the poshest restaurants in the world for his own personal use. She did not even want to think what that cost.

This was not the boy she had grown up with in her parents' garden; not Marcello's father, either.

This was one of the most powerful men in the world holding out her chair for her.

CHAPTER NINETEEN

GABRIELA ACTUALLY FELT tongue-tied, as if she did not know him at all, but Enrique was an expert at overcoming people's awkwardness, and soon he had her laughing and feeling at ease. Though that might have had a bit to do with a very expensive wine!

With her mother being in charge of a royal kitchen, Gabriela had grown up on really good food.

And yet nothing compared to this meal, under a star-studded sky, with Enrique's attention focused solely on her.

As dessert was brought out, he lost his lighthearted tone.

"I spoke to my mother," he said. "She admitted it was true, that she not only sent you away, but that she kept us from getting in touch with each other. She was, of course, not the least apologetic. She claims to have saved us from ourselves, that she felt we were barreling toward catastrophe."

Gabriela contemplated that, and reluctantly could see there was some wisdom in it.

"She was concerned the fallout from young love would change the dynamic between our families."

Again, reluctantly, Gabriela could see the point. They had been eighteen and nineteen. An adult observing would see the naivete, the intoxicating power of first passion that might lead to poor decisions with far-reaching repercussions.

"I question her motives were purely altruistic," Enrique went on, "because by allowing me to think you wanted nothing to do with me—"

"And me to think the same thing."

"She was able to engineer the relationship she wanted for me, the one with maximum benefit to Hermosa Mariposa and Amelia's family, also."

"And if I could put back time," he said pensively, "would I? I cannot imagine a world without Marcello."

His love for his son was so beautiful, and yet she could hear something in his voice that she felt compelled to pursue.

"I've seen many changes in him in a very short time," she said.

"Yes, I have, too. And I'm very grateful for that."

"But?"

"But it seems every time I almost get to the place of trust and connection that I hope for between us, he slams up a barrier, as if I am his enemy, not his father."

"It'll come, Enrique. It's just going to take time."

"It's come farther since you've been back than it ever had before." He lifted his wineglass in salute. "Thank you for that."

So, this *was* what this dinner was about, then. An expression of gratitude. She needed to be very careful not to read more into it.

"It'll continue with Darla. She's extraordinary with him."

"You are, too. You seem to have a natural gift. You want children, don't you?"

That question seemed far more complicated than it might have before her return to Hermosa Mariposa. Of course she wanted children one day! And yet, there was only one man she wanted children with.

"Timothy was a really good guy," she said, to hide her new truth from Enrique. "Solid. Reliable. The kind of guy you look at, and go, *Wow, he's going to make a great daddy someday.*"

She saw Enrique flinch, ever so slightly, insecure about being a great daddy himself.

"So, what happened?"

She gazed out over the view, the sparkling lights of Santiago reflecting in the dark waters of the bay.

"When Guido got sick, Timothy wanted to come back here with me."

"That seems very supportive."

"I couldn't picture him on Hermosa Mariposa," she admitted to Enrique softly. "I realized I couldn't picture him against the backdrop of my world. Or maybe didn't want to."

She didn't mention that she had certainly not wanted him to meet the Prince. Because the comparison would be inevitable, like a racehorse standing beside a plow horse.

"And then he called me on it. He said I held a piece of myself back from him, and that he wanted more for himself and me."

"I'm not sure love should be comfortable," Enrique said, and then grinned, self-effacingly, "not that I am any expert on the subject."

She didn't tell Enrique that Timothy had called her out on the lack of passion. It had always been comfortable between them, but there were none of the sparks of pure chemistry between them.

Of course, having had her world burned down once because of those sparks, she had been wary of them. In that way, Timothy had seemed like a good pick.

But now, sitting across from Enrique, the sparks practically falling down around them when they weren't even touching, she saw she had very nearly missed something that suddenly felt essential to life.

When he walked her to the garden gate, hours later, she felt blissful. There would only be one way to feel more blissful, and that was to recapture what had started to unfold between them at the beach.

But when she leaned into him, and touched her lips with his own, he answered tenderly, but chastely. He put her away from him.

And then took the sting out of his rejection completely, by saying: "Can we do this again?"

And so they did it again. The most amazing week unfolded. He invited her to a movie night at the palace theater, which they had all to themselves. And then to a picnic for two at the Butterfly Garden.

And finally, he had invited her for a private evening in the small, walled courtyard, outside his quarters, the open patio doors giving a glimpse of his bedroom.

There had been a table set up, and candles, wine and chocolates. Music filled the space.

And after they'd had a drink, he'd invited her to dance. For all that they had known each other forever, they had never danced, that most intimate of courtship rituals between a man and a woman.

Gabriela had hoped the close proximity to his bedroom might have meant he had something more planned, but no, he said good-night to her with the same chaste kiss, and then walked her to her own gate.

When it closed behind her, she hugged herself and twirled. She contemplated the feeling inside her: so alive, so excited by life.

So in love.

But there was that doubt. How could Enrique be courting her? She thought of the evening they had just shared, so perfect in every way, the sensation of being in his arms, gazing up into the liquid brown of his eyes. She sighed.

Wouldn't he need now, as he had then, to make a strategic match? Wouldn't he need to marry a woman from his own background? Surely his mother would not be happy for him to enter a relationship with an ordinary woman, much less the daughter of staff members?

Gabriela realized that as blissful as it was to just immerse herself in these moments that she spent with Enrique, neither of them was addressing the elephant in the room.

Which was *why*? Why were they doing this? To what end?

She moved through the garden and into the house. It seemed strangely empty, and then she saw a note on the kitchen table. Maria and Guido had gone to the other side of the island to visit his sister, Gabriela's Aunt Sophia. They would stay the night.

She smiled as she contemplated that note. Guido was up to an overnight trip. He just seemed to be feeling so much better, stronger, more himself.

Geraldo strutted into the kitchen, and demanded attention, so she picked him up. The radio was playing softly, and she danced around the small space with him cuddled against her.

"You're nearly as good as a prince," she lied to him. He purred deeply. He, too, seemed healthy and vibrant.

The storms that had gathered around her life felt as if they were dissipating. She allowed herself to dismiss the cloud of *why* that hung over her, and luxuriate in the feeling of all being right in her world.

She allowed herself to luxuriate in her sense of happiness.

She should have known, by now, that was like throwing out a challenge to the gods.

The phone rang. She glanced at the clock, alarmed. It was very late. She put down the cat and snatched up the phone receiver, terrified it was bad news about her mother and father.

But no, the familiar voice of her boss, Peter, in New York reached her. He'd obviously forgotten the time difference.

She let relief sweep her.

"Gabriela! I've been trying to reach you for days. I seriously cannot believe you don't check your phone or your emails."

"My phone doesn't seem compatible with the system here. The internet is, um, cranky."

Though this was true, the biggest part of the truth was that she had let go of her other world, so as to more completely immerse herself in this one.

"It's absurd," Peter said. "I don't think I could live a day without checking my email and watching a few reels on my phone."

Just a short time ago, she would have felt the same way. Now she felt reconnected to life in a way she cherished.

Though, how much of that had to do with the enchantment of Hermosa Mariposa and how much had to do with dancing with her very own prince tonight, she could not determine.

"Listen, I've got some exciting news for you. Are you sitting down?"

She wasn't. What kind of news would she have to sit down for? Her feeling of relief ebbed away.

"You're being offered the Madrid office."

"I'm not following."

"They want you to head it. Our biggest office, the hub of all our international trade. I've got the offer in front of me, and it's unbelievable." He named the salary. "Shares! A house comes with it."

She could feel the blood draining from her face, the joy sliding out of her. "I have to think about it," she said.

"What's to think about?"

Enrique. Marcello.

"You know my father isn't well."

"Well, yeah, but what are you going to do? Put your life on hold forever? Like are you sitting around there *waiting*?"

She knew this bluntness was the American way, that family was not the same priority for them, and yet still it stung that he was making her sound like a vulture in a tree.

"The Madrid office is the perfect solution," Peter said. "What's Madrid from your airport there? An hour?"

She knew, of course, what Peter did not. It was more subtle than last time. Far more subtle. But the reasons were the same. While she thought her and Enrique's deepening relationship was unfolding in private, there was really no such thing in this royal world. She knew exactly who was behind this spectacular offer, and why.

"Let me think about it," she said again. She was only twenty-six years old. Even though she knew she was good at her job—maybe even spectacularly good—the position was way above anything she had earned.

"Really? What's to—"

She hung up on him. She picked up Geraldo again, but the music had stopped—it felt like literally and figuratively—and the news was on.

Hermosa Mariposa news. A traffic light not working in Benito. A baby being welcomed by the Gonzales family. An international grant for Mariposa Gardens. A burst water main in the Colombo district.

And then, "And Queen Katarina has just announced that Princess Bettina of Isle Xavier will be arriving on Hermosa Mariposa on Monday for an extended visit. Though no official reason has been given for the visit, it is largely thought that she and Prince Enrique will announce their engagement—"

Gabriela felt blindsided, and then despised herself for being so naive. What had she thought? All this time, enjoying him, lapping up his attention and affection, allowing herself to believe... What exactly had she believed? That he was going to marry her? That love was going to win this time?

Yes.

That was exactly what she had thought. She had thought he was courting her! But now what had seemed like his desire for privacy felt instead as if it might have been secrecy. Hiding her, hiding how he felt about her.

Why had she not asked him the obvious question? *Will you have a need to remarry?*

But she knew the truth. She had not asked it because she was a coward. Because she could not bear the answer.

In her naive love for him, she had missed all the signs.

This was not meant to be. It could never be. Guido had told her love didn't ask what's in it for me, it asked how to serve.

She could not put Enrique in the position where he had to choose to give up everything for her. The Queen would never consent to a union between them.

So, would he? She thought of the time they had spent together, and figured it was possible he would.

She knew what it was to give up a world. She knew the agony of it. How much worse for him, who had been born to his life and his role and his obligations, who knew nothing else?

She thought of another poor lost prince who had famously given up everything to follow his love of a woman, and how he seemed now to be rudderless, without a place for his heart to call home.

Gabriela called on every bit of her inner strength. Her fortitude. Her love.

She would serve love one last time. She would give to Enrique—freely, knowing there was nothing in it for her, no possibility of a future—what he had never had. Not once in his whole privileged life.

And, if the radio was correct, that he was heading back into.

A loveless arrangement between two powerful families.

He had a duty. He had been born with obligations. He had learned that in his world it would always be service above self. He could not break out of it. He had a life that was bigger than himself, and he was a prisoner to that life.

They had, both of them, succeeded in "living in the moment" the last while. But maybe they had been too successful, not giving enough weight to the future and decisions that would have to be made.

She knew he loved her. She knew that suddenly and deeply and wonderfully. But that knowledge made her aware he might think he could choose her. Maybe that's what all this, in his mind, had been leading toward.

But if she really loved Enrique, could she put him in that

position? Could she ask him to make a choice that would reverberate through not just his life, but Marcello's, as well?

She had been naive to think he could ever be free to choose his own partner And while he did not seem like a naive man, he seemed to be under that illusion, as well.

She would save them both from the illusion.

Yes, she would give him something, but she would take something back.

A final memory to sustain her through the lonely road she saw unfolding ahead of her. In permanent exile from her family, because she would never be able to bear to come back here to see Marcello with a new mother, to witness Enrique's life unfolding, once again, with another.

CHAPTER TWENTY

THIS IS WHAT the Queen had always known, Gabriela thought. Katalina had been right the first time, to break it up. It could only cause distress to everyone it touched, and it wasn't just Gabriela and Enrique involved. It was Maria and Guido, and even Marcello. She had to leave the little boy or he might never bond properly with his new mother.

She fought back the tears the very thought of that gave her, when in truth she wanted to drown in self-pity at the enormity of the sacrifice that was being required of her.

But no, self-pity was for tomorrow.

Tonight, there would be one more moment. And she intended to make it a glorious one.

She had never been so certain of anything in her life as when she crossed the path to the secret place in between the hedges that she and Enrique had discovered when they were children. She slipped through the thick foliage, for the second time tonight, and found herself back in the private courtyard that led off Enrique's bedroom.

The table they had shared was still set up, the white linen lifting gently in the breeze, though the candle had sputtered.

She found the French doors, still open to the evening air, and slipped through them. She had not put on shoes, and she could feel the cool marble on her feet. Her eyes adjusted to the dark and she went across the room.

He was asleep, naked, a tangle of white sheets around his

lower body. He was, painted in moonlight, as beautiful as she had ever seen him.

She drank in all that beauty with all the hunger and desperation of one who was saying goodbye.

She saw a bundle of letters tied with a ribbon beside his bed, and recognized, with a poignant ache, the younger self who had yearned for the same things she yearned for today.

Tonight, finally, she would have it. Not forever, that unrealistic dream of the naive, but for that one glorious moment.

After a long time, Gabriela reached down and touched Enrique's shoulder. She didn't shake him, she just laid her hand against the warm, silky texture of his skin, and closed her eyes at the sensation that washed over her.

He didn't start awake. His eyes blinked open, slowly, and for a moment he looked dazed. And then a smile of pure welcome slid across his lips. In his eyes she saw the truth of what they were to each other.

"Gabriela?" he said, his voice husky with sleep. "What—"

She touched her finger to his lips. At the beach, he had stoked a fire in her by undressing slowly, and now she did that to him.

With only moonlight illuminating her, her fingers moved slowly to each button of the dress. She undid them, one at a time, then peeled the garment down off her shoulders, over her arms, tugged it down around her waist and then her knees. Then she stepped out of it, leaving it in a puddle on the floor.

She was only in her underwear now, beautiful underwear that celebrated and honored a woman's curves, her innate sensuality.

She reached behind herself and flicked the clasp on the bra. It fell away. She stood there, owning the power of herself as a woman. And then she caught the waistband of her panties and pulled them down, stepped out of them.

She never once took her eyes off his. It felt as if the most real part of her was being revealed to both of them.

A woman.

A warrior.

Who knew exactly what she needed.

And was not afraid to take it.

It was a sneak attack against every single defense he had put up between them, and finding him at his most vulnerable worked. Any walls he had crumbled. Any shield he had held was laid aside.

Yet, still, he seemed to be fighting some fight.

"I need you," she whispered hoarsely.

And his fight was over. He untangled the sheet from around his legs, and held it open, inviting her in. She slid into the bed beside him.

A sound came from his lips—of wonder, almost of worship—the sound of a man holding out his sword for her to take, a man who could fight no more, a man in complete surrender.

"Gabriela." He whispered her name, and it was like a benediction.

She leaned up on her elbow, ran her finger down the hollow of his throat, circled the pucker of his nipple, opened her whole palm to lay it over the hard washboard of his stomach, feeling the rise and fall of the life force in his belly.

She had a sense of having lived, her whole life, for only this moment. Every single thing had led to here.

She touched him, in this new way. Not as the child-woman she had once been, not as a woman subject to the whims of his family, not as a nanny to his son, but as his complete equal. Her exploration of the hard, beautiful male surfaces of him—skin, bone, muscle—were possessive, intimate, confident.

Every touch made him hers, branding him, as she herself would be branded, for all time.

Finally, when they were both trembling beneath her touch, she sought his lips. These were not the sweet good-night kisses they had shared. This was not the chaste relationship he seemed committed to.

No, this was a veil torn away to what was real between them. Recognition in each of the other's power, beauty, courage, passion.

She tasted his lips lightly, at first, testing, tasting, teasing. She ran her tongue over the edge of his lip, and then over the edge of his teeth, and then over the edge of his tongue.

A groan so primal it might have been born at the beginning of time escaped him. His hands found the back of her head, and he drew her lips more completely to his own.

A fierce note of pure need overshadowed any tenderness between them. The barrier that had held them back from each other broke with all the ferocity of a swollen river breaching a dam.

Just as with that, they were swept up in the current, raging and ravenous, devouring everything in its path.

Then, as currents do, it would calm, slow, meander, only to build intensity again as it found its way back to the rapids where it churned, and foamed and then raged. The surging energy was hurtling toward an edge, and beyond that unknown edge it felt as if complete dissolution, complete destruction, the certain obliteration of both of them, yawned, waiting.

But no, when that wall of pure flowing energy burst its banks, it did not destroy. Instead, it flowed outward, it oozed into every crack and crevice of a parched land that had waited and waited and waited. For this. Rebirth.

The culmination of their loving each other brought not destruction, after all, but life.

She lay on top of him, after, feeling an exhaustion and exhilaration, both in their purest form. His arms locked around the small of her back, their skin hot and slippery, their bodies made to be joined like this.

She freed a hand, touched his face, and said it.

Her voice husky with emotion, she whispered, "Enrique."

He swallowed hard.

And she said it fiercely, huskily, from the place inside her that was joined to everything, the future and the past, life and death.

She said, "I love you."

She watched the tears pool in the darkness of his eyes, spill over and run silently down the rugged, extraordinary planes of his beautiful face.

She caught one with her thumb, lifted it to her mouth and tasted the salty, sweet bitterness of a man who did not want to say goodbye.

And knew he had to.

Enrique, whether he realized it or not, was a warrior being called to a battle that he must go to, even if he had no wish to fight.

She kissed his cheek, lingeringly, slipped off him, and he gathered her to his side, put his arm possessively over her midriff, buried his nose in her hair, kissed her neck. She waited until he fell asleep and then she slid out from under the weight of his arm. She could not resist the temptation of looking at him, once more for a long, long time, trying to memorize every line, every curve, the rise and fall of his chest with each breath.

And then, finally, she pulled on the clothes she had left in a heap on the floor. She looked around his bedroom, taking in the details of it for the first time. It was expansive. The four-poster bed was exquisitely carved, probably at least six hundred years old. The bureau—presumably where he kept the shorts he did not buy for himself—was also old and exquisite.

She compared it with the small room that her parents had spent their entire married life in.

Gabriela realized how far apart their worlds were. She saw, sadly, that Queen Katalina had been right all along.

She could never fit in this world.

CHAPTER TWENTY-ONE

ENRIQUE OPENED HIS eyes to brilliant morning light pouring through the doors to his bedroom. Contentment was mingled with a sense of elation.

He patted the bed beside him, and then lifted his head.

Gabriela was gone. His initial reaction to her absence was alarm, but then he realized she had probably slipped away in case Marcello's habit was to come in here in the morning. It wasn't, but he thought someday—especially if Gabriela was part of their lives—it would be. He pictured that for a moment, the three of them, maybe on a Sunday morning, with newspapers and books.

A family, the way she and Marcello and Guido had been that first morning that he had seen her again.

He closed his eyes, and relived that one moment from last night that rose above all the others.

I love you.

He did not know until he heard those words that he had waited his entire life for them, and that a part of him had always known it would be her that would speak them.

Those words had felt like an anointment. They had oozed over him, and moved inside him, as beautiful as warmed oil and honey.

He had not expected last night, which, of course, had made it all the more exquisite, but it had not been what he planned as he had courted her this week, deliberately holding back, intending to treat her only with the complete honor of the woman he hoped to marry.

Of course, there were obstacles. He had known this all along. The biggest one would be his mother, his intention to do the unthinkable, which was to thwart convention, to stand in the face of strict traditions and expectations, and say, *No, I will claim this part of my life for myself.*

I will have love. I will not sacrifice it again.

In doing so, he was aware he would teach his son the most important lesson of all. While a man had duties and responsibilities, in the end his biggest obligation was to be true to himself and to acknowledge the power of his own heart.

Enrique smiled, the battle he needed to win well worth the future he envisioned. Married to Gabriela. Waking up to her. Sharing life with her. Someday, there would be more babies, brothers or sisters for Marcello.

But first, he needed to make his intentions known to the Queen. As it turned out, not surprisingly, his mother was unavailable. He knew from long experience there was no penetrating the fortresses Mabel set up around his mother. But, what did a small delay matter? He was not asking his mother's permission, he was telling her how it was going to be. He would move ahead with his plans, and announce them to her later.

Enrique had been debating all week how to go about the proposal, what to do about the ring. He had all of the crown jewels at his disposal, of course, but it didn't feel right, somehow. Those rings had been worn by others. They were steeped in the history and tradition of the monarchy on this island.

Enrique felt as if he and Gabriela were starting something brand-new, and that the ring should reflect that. In fact, maybe she should help to pick it.

But he dismissed that idea almost as quickly as he had thought of it because there was one more tradition he was eagerly anticipating.

And that was getting down on one knee, and holding a ring

box out to her, asking her to be his wife, to walk through life with him.

He wanted to run across the garden and be with her, to lift her in his arms, and experience what it was like to see her through the new eyes of her lover.

But no, he wanted so much more than that.

If he went to her now, he would blow everything. He might just blurt out how he wanted to spend the rest of his life with her. No, he wanted this occasion to be special, to be a moment she looked back on for the rest of her life with sweet joy in the memory.

He picked up the phone beside his bed. "Phillipe, cancel my engagements for today. Notify the jet crew that I need to go to Madrid."

He thought of the jewelry stores there, of the famous Venetian style that both reflected their heritage and was exquisitely beautiful. He held up his hand, and saw the faint tremor in it. That's how big getting everything just right felt.

He went and checked on Marcello, who was in the nursery, still in his pajamas, already deeply involved in a card game with Darla.

"I have to go away for the day," he said. "It's unexpected."

Marcello barely spared him a glance, and Enrique reflected that for all the changes in his life and for all the extra time he had created trying to be a better father, the improvements between him and his son seemed barely discernible.

Gabriela, he thought, would work her magic. Some things—perhaps the things people longed for the most—took the greatest amount of time.

His trip to Madrid was swift. Phillipe had arranged for private appointments with several extraordinarily exclusive jewelry designers.

His heart stopped when he saw *the* one. Diamonds and sapphires formed a blue butterfly. For a complex design, the ring was breathtakingly simple. He took it immediately.

He tried to gain an appointment with his mother again on

his return, but again he was stonewalled by Mabel. However, it felt as if there was someone's approval that he needed far more than that of his mother.

As he walked the familiar path between the palace and the cottage, it seemed as if every memory he had ever had of him and Gabriela walked with him, like the ghosts of their younger selves skipped along, delighted.

He was shocked at how nervous he felt.

Of course, he had to take Guido aside first. He had to ask his permission to marry his daughter.

Did Guido think he was man enough for this? Would he approve?

His heart hammering in his throat, a few minutes later he knocked on the cottage door. After a moment, a hoarse voice asked him to enter.

As soon as he walked in, he knew something was wrong. Guido looked white and strained, and Maria had obviously been crying.

"What's happened?" he asked. At first, he thought maybe it was the cat, but then Geraldo appeared and stalked over to him, winding his way around Enrique's pant legs.

Maria got up from the table, and picked up the cat. "My apologies, Your Highness," she said.

Her apologies? What was going on? Why was he catching an overtone of anger? Not like she didn't want the cat shedding hair on him, but as if she didn't want her cat touching him.

"Guido," he asked, desperate, "have you received bad news? About your health?"

"I have received bad news," he said quietly, "but not about my health."

Slowly, he pushed a piece of paper to the edge of the table. Enrique picked it up.

He could feel his heart shattering into a million pieces. Gabriela was gone. He read the note like a man caught in a nightmare.

A new career opportunity.

Her work with Marcello done.

Guido gave Enrique a look that was so sad and so defeated, and right underneath that look was the accusation.

This is your fault.

Guido pointedly turned over the newspaper in front of him. On the front page was a photo of Princess Bettina coming out the door of her private plane on the Hermosa Mariposa runway.

The headline blared "Romance in the Air?"

Their planes must have practically touched wings.

He looked from Guido to Maria, and saw the assumption in their faces. That he had spent the day, as that headline insinuated, with the visiting Princess.

He wanted to tell them the truth. That he hadn't even known Bettina was coming. He didn't even know if she was still here.

He wanted to show the Oliveras the ring that felt as if it was burning a hole in the suit pocket next to his heart.

But the sense that had been building in him with Gabriela—of being loved, of having family, of coming home—felt as shattered as his heart.

They knew him. This family knew him.

Gabriela knew him.

Or maybe they didn't, at all.

Because if they did, how could they believe the absolute worst of him? How could they believe he would woo Gabriela and be open to a romantic visit from another woman at the same time?

Stunned by the level of betrayal he felt, he turned stiffly, left the small kitchen, shut the door with a firm snap behind him.

As soon as he departed, he went to the palace and took the stairs, two at a time, to his mother's office.

Mabel, of course, was on guard in the outer office.

"The Queen is not receiving."

He ignored her, went and rapped firmly on his mother's office door and strode into the room.

His mother was at her desk, Beau at her feet.

"Oh," she said, "Just who I wanted to see."

As if she had not been refusing his requests to see her!

"Princess Bettina is here—"

"So I hear," he said tersely.

"And I was planning an informal dinner tonight for you and—"

"No," he said quietly.

She arched an eyebrow at him.

"No," he repeated. "I told you I would no longer brook interference in my personal life, and I meant that. I am in love with Gabriela Olivera and I intended to ask her to marry me."

She caught the past tense. "Intended?"

"She left the island unexpectedly, I suspect because of Bettina's arrival."

"So, she understands what you do not. I admire a woman who is able to make sacrifices."

His anger at Gabriela crumbled away when he saw her departure in that light. She was trying to do the right thing. For him. The love he felt for her in that moment made him feel stronger than he ever had.

"I'm going after her," he said.

"Enrique," his mother said, with elaborate patience, "this is not how things are done. Our world is not one of decisions rooted in passion, rather than reason. Our systems work, and they work for a reason."

"Do you hear yourself?" he asked softly. "All the world reduced to a system that works? A world devoid of passion? And spontaneity? And love? What kind of world is that?"

"It's presumptuous to think two people can change the way things have always been."

"Perhaps it is presumptuous," he agreed, his voice soft, "but it's not two people. It's bigger than that."

His mother was silent, so he continued.

"It's the biggest thing of all. It's the only force that really changes anything, ever. Love."

CHAPTER TWENTY-TWO

GABRIELA LOOKED AROUND her space. It had no air conditioner, of course, and she was hot and sweaty, dusty from rearranging furniture and unpacking the boxes that had arrived from New York.

The apartment, in the center of Madrid, reminded her of her New York apartment, tiny and humble. Still, it was close to her new job at an up-and-coming Spanish clothing company.

The first thing she had done after she had left Hermosa Mariposa was resign from the House of Falcon. The only thing she was going to take from her phone call with her old boss was his very good suggestion that Madrid would be a great location for her. Other than that, she was divorcing herself, finally and completely, from the interests of the royal family, and from the influence of Queen Katalina.

"She's a hostage taker," Gabriela muttered to herself. For a moment, she felt a wash of pity for Enrique—and for Marcello—so great that it felt as if it might overwhelm her.

But, she had discovered—for the second time in her life—grief did not overwhelm, much as she might have wished it did. Much as she would have liked to have taken to her bed and done nothing but weep, and sleep, she could not indulge in such weakness.

And it was unworthy of a woman who had been strong enough and courageous enough to do the right thing for the man she loved, even at great cost to herself.

Though Guido and Maria were devastated by her choice, wasn't Guido the one who had told her to ask the right questions of love?

So even though grief resided in the background of every single thing, and every single breath, life insisted on going on.

There was a new position to adjust to, there was a new city to learn to navigate, there was a new apartment to settle into, there were the necessities of life that had to be dealt with, whether a person felt like it or not.

A knock came on the door. Her new neighbor had offered her houseplants, and she'd said yes.

To some it might have seemed having plants to care for was a pathetically small undertaking after the life she'd left behind, her weeks back in her home, but to her it was huge to say yes to something to care about, something to look after.

She glanced down at herself. She was in Enrique's shirt, the one that she had kept from the cat-rescue day. She had on nothing else, but the shirt trailed to nearly her knees, providing more coverage than some of the dresses she owned. Still, for a moment, she debated opening the door in such an outfit, but it was only her neighbor, after all.

But it was not her neighbor.

When she opened the door, Enrique was standing there. Marcello was with him. Marcello, with a great cry, let go of his father's hand and wrapped his sturdy arms around her, wetting her bare legs with his tears.

She crouched before him, and gathered him in her arms. How could they do this to her? How could they weaken her when she needed to be strong? That little boy against her, sobbing, made her feel as if she could never be without him—them—again.

But then, it seemed as if there was only one reason they would be here, and it would explain Marcello's sobs.

"Guido?" she asked.

It was probably a terrible mark against her character that

even as she contemplated a great tragedy unfolding, her heart sighed that it was Enrique who was here.

The man she wanted, impossibly, to lean on as life's storms gathered and hit and receded and then gathered again, the man she wanted to share her burdens with, just as she wanted him to share his.

She had been trying to reach her parents for two days, and there had been no answer. She had hoped, foolishly, that it meant Guido was feeling better, that they were both getting back to their normal lives, traveling, visiting friends and relatives.

"No, no, Guido is fine."

"My mom?"

"Your parents are fine."

She looked up at him more deeply then, the circles under his eyes, the gauntness in his face, the shadow of a beard around his mouth and on his cheeks and chin.

She had never seen him anything but impeccably groomed.

"Enrique, what's happened? Is it your mother?"

Again, her heart reached toward him. Would she be the one he came to if he needed comfort?

She knew the answer was yes.

"No, the Queen is..." He stopped, chose his words carefully. "...just as she always is."

"We're here for me," Cello whispered against her, her shirt—the Prince's shirt, had Enrique noticed that?—already damp with his tears.

"Are you all right?" she asked, terrified. What did this mean? A health problem?

"I am now," Marcello said. She lifted him to her hip and he leaned his head, hard, on her shoulder. Marcello was getting bigger, and yet she felt as if she could carry his solid weight forever. She heard him slurping on his thumb.

"I wanted to come see you privately, but as soon as he got

wind that I was planning to visit you, he attached himself to my leg and would not let go."

Enrique looked at his son in her arms and smiled a smile of such tenderness it threatened to melt her whole world.

She had to steel herself against these feelings, these longings. Why had he come here, both he and his son knocking down barriers that she needed to keep in place?

Enrique, sensing how heavy Marcello was in her arms, held out his arms, and she put the boy in them. He gazed down at his son's face, the most gorgeous smile on his lips.

The kind of smile every woman dreamed of seeing on the face of the man she loved as he looked at their children.

"He's totally exhausted," he said.

"You can go through and put him on my bed," she said. She watched as Enrique navigated her space. It seemed ten times as tiny as it had a few seconds ago.

She looked down at her shirt. *His* shirt. She touched her hair. The truth was, she was an utter mess. And now, with Marcello taking over the only bedroom, she couldn't very well go and put herself together.

She suddenly discovered she didn't want to. Her legs were not cooperating, anyway. She sank down on the sofa, and a moment later Enrique emerged from her bedroom. He came and sank down beside her.

"He seems restless. I don't know if he'll stay in there. He's beyond tired."

"Why have you come here, Enrique?" she asked.

"I can't do it alone."

He was here to try and get her back into the House of Falcon's fold. He was here because he needed help with Marcello.

"You want me to come back?"

"Yes," he whispered.

"Darla isn't enough?"

"Darla?"

"The nanny?" she said with a touch of impatience.

"You think I'm asking you to come back as Marcello's nanny?"

"Aren't you?"

"No, I'm asking you to come back as his mommy."

Her breath stopped in her chest. She took in his face, her mind grappling with what she had just heard.

She could see the truth in his face, and his absolute love for her. For the first time since she had left the island, something in her that she did not know had been tense relaxed. He looked unbelievably and uncharacteristically flustered.

"This is going all wrong. I want you to come back to me as my wife."

"Did you just propose to me?"

"No! Not officially."

"Enrique, I thought Bettina—"

"Stop!" he said. "I'm not having another woman's name come up at my proposal."

"But she was arriving—"

"Stop!" he said again. Then, with a shake of his head, "This is not going to plan."

"You are not marrying Bettina?"

"Of course not! What did you think all that courting was about? The dinner on Santiago, the picnic, the dancing? Could you possibly have missed the fact I was wooing you?"

"But you didn't want anyone to know. It all seemed very secretive, all those very private solo outings."

"I wasn't ashamed of you, if that's what you're implying. I was *protecting* you," he said. "Had it gotten out that I was seeing you, the press would have been on you like hounds after a fox. I wanted to give you special moments before that happened."

"Maybe," she suggested, "you were protecting me from your mother. But she found out, anyway."

"And despite my warning her not to meddle in my life, she

invited Bettina to Hermosa, without my knowledge, certainly without my consent."

"And offered me a new and better position at the House of Falcon."

He looked very angry at that. "The Queen has been made to understand my position."

"You've spoken to your mother?"

"I have. We have her blessing."

She felt a shiver go up and down her spine. She would not have wanted to be the Queen from the look on his face. She actually felt a little sorry for the monarch.

"But aren't there many considerations?" she asked, making one last effort to be brave, to put the needs of the kingdom ahead of her own. And his. "Don't you need to marry into your own level of society? For the good of Hermosa Mariposa?"

"Why would I have been courting you if I had not already considered all of that?"

"I—I—I don't know."

"You better not think," he told her softly, "I was grooming you for a lifelong relationship in the shadows."

Something in her was unfolding like a flower before the sun as she accepted this was true. There was nothing left to fight. He had already anticipated the battles and addressed them.

"I think there would have been more kissing involved if that had been your agenda!"

"How could I give in to the temptation to kiss you and still be honorable and decent, the man Guido would expect his son-in-law to be?"

"It seems to me," she said, a bit wryly, "you gave in to temptation rather easily."

"A goddess shows up in my bedroom! How can a mere mortal fight such a thing? Besides, by then I already knew the direction I was going in."

"And that was?"

"Asking your father's permission to marry you, of course.

Really, I should not have been surprised that with you, very little goes according to my well-laid-out plans. Not even this," he said, a bit dourly.

"I'm sorry."

"You're not. You're getting ready to burst out laughing."

"I'm just happy, Enrique."

"Well, let's proceed, then. I have your father's permission."

"My parents know?"

"Of course!"

"That's why they haven't answered their phone in days. My mom might trust herself to keep a secret, but not Guido."

"Gabriela! Please! Let me do this."

"Oh, Enrique," she said, as one last doubt bubbled to the surface, "what if *they* don't like me?"

"Who?" he asked, genuinely astonished.

"The people. Enrique, I am not what anyone would expect of a princess."

"I think you are wrong, there. I think the people of Hermosa Mariposa will embrace you all the more because you are truly one of them. I think, in very short order, they will come to see everything about you that I have seen. Your inner and outer beauty, your humor, your compassion, your delight in life. I could not ask for a more perfect princess to be by my side, and neither could they. Now, will you let me get on with this?"

"All right," she said, waving her hand at him, trying to be regal about it at the same time as trying not to giggle at his earnestness. "You may proceed."

Still grumbling about things not going according to his plan, Enrique took a deep breath, gathered himself and then got off the couch. He went down on one knee before her, and slipped a jewelry box from his inside suit pocket.

He opened the hinged lid of the box.

She gasped at the beauty of the ring, delicate, butterfly shaped, sparkling with diamonds and sapphires.

"Papa?"

Neither of them had noticed Marcello come back out of the bedroom.

Both Enrique and Gabriela let the pure magic of that word wash over them.

"Yes, I'm here," Enrique said gently. "We're both here. We'll both always be here for you."

Marcello's eyes fastened on the ring box.

"Is that candy?" he asked, darting forward.

"No." Too late, Enrique tried to hold the box up out of his son's reach.

But Marcello had the ring. When his father made a frantic grab at it, he popped it in his mouth.

"No!" Enrique cried. "Marcello, you're much too old to be putting shiny things in your mouth!"

"But it's candy," Marcello said defensively.

"Cello, spit that out! Right now," Gabriela said, trying to keep her voice calm.

But Cello, panicked about the imminent loss of his treasure, did not spit the ring out, did not appear to notice it was not a sweet treat, at all. He swallowed.

CHAPTER TWENTY-THREE

ENRIQUE SIGHED HEAVILY.

"This is exactly what I mean," he said, to Gabriela, "about things not going according to plan."

He scooped up Marcello and headed for the door. Gabriela followed. William was waiting at a long black car, with no markings on it.

It was only when she saw the look on his face that she realized she was still dressed in Enrique's shirt.

"Sir?"

"To the nearest hospital," the Prince said.

Because they had gotten to the hospital so quickly, the doctor chose an endoscopic removal of the ring. Whether it was because Enrique had been recognized or because Gabriela looked a little come-hither in her man's shirt, they had been ushered into an office, rather than being put in a public waiting room.

Now, while Marcello recovered from the procedure, the doctor came and gave a rather rumpled tissue to Enrique.

"He's fine," he assured them both.

After the doctor left, Enrique unwrapped the tissue. He looked down at the ring hidden in those folds for a long moment, then gazed around the cluttered office and sighed.

"Why do I have a feeling, Gabriela, nothing with you will ever go as planned?"

And then he got down on one knee, and held the ring, in its bed of tissue, up to her.

Whatever script he had planned, he didn't say it. He choked, but the words came straight from his heart.

"Gabriela, I love you."

From the way he said it, it felt as if she was the first woman who had ever heard those words from him.

"I love you madly and endlessly," he continued. "I have loved you since I was a little boy and, if you'll have me, I will love you until I'm an old man, until I breathe my very last breath."

And then he took the ring from the tissue.

He looked at it, suspiciously inspecting it for stomach fluids. He carefully wiped it on his shirt.

Gabriela thought it was probably the most beautiful marriage proposal in the history of royal families everywhere.

He slipped it onto her finger. Despite nothing else going according to plan, that ring fit her perfectly.

But she didn't even look at it.

She looked right past it into the face of her beloved.

"Yes," she said.

Gabriela and Enrique had decided, together, to have their wedding in the garden, with only a few close friends and family around them. An official ceremony, a royal wedding, would have taken months to prepare. Maybe longer.

After waiting a lifetime, neither of them was in any mood to wait.

They would spend a week on a honeymoon together, on a private island owned by a friend of the Falcon family. When they returned, an announcement would be made and, as Enrique had warned her, her life would change for all time.

Gabriela stood at the kitchen door, with Guido. The top half of the Dutch door was open a crack, and they peered out.

The garden had been transformed.

"The Queen is arriving," she whispered.

"In a few minutes, she will be your mother-in-law," Guido said. "You think she is difficult, but I want you to remember she is the strongest and most courageous woman I have ever had the privilege of serving. The tragedies she has endured and the sacrifices she has made for this island would have shattered a lesser person than her."

The Queen had none of her usual entourage with her. She was shown to the front row, where she sat down, always regal, even in a plastic garden chair.

"She's probably never been in this garden before," Gabriela said.

"That's where you're wrong," Guido said.

Something in his voice—a soft tenderness—made Gabriela turn swiftly and look at him.

"She's just a little younger than me. We grew up in much the same way that you and Enrique did."

"Papa!" She looked at him closely. "You loved her," she guessed.

He did not admit to that, and she realized perhaps Guido was better at keeping secrets than she had given him credit for.

"Love finds a way, Gabriela," her father said softly. "Always. Sometimes, maybe it takes a long, long time. Maybe even lifetimes. But it finds a way.

"Though, sometimes," he continued with a lift of his shoulder, "even love needs a little nudge in the right direction."

There was a mischievous twinkle in his eye, and Gabriela gasped.

"Papa, you didn't pretend to be ill did you, to get me home?"

Guido widened those sparkling eyes at her, as if appalled by the suggestion that he would be capable of such duplicity.

Then he put his hands in his pockets, and rocked back on his heels.

"You know how the nanny, Darla, *just happened* to be in the toy store the day you went there? And how everything *just happened* to line up? Perhaps it was the same with me getting sick. The universe using everything in its considerable power so that what is meant to be finds a way.

"People," he said softly, "should trust *that* power more, and what they perceive as their own power less."

The music started. Enrique appeared through the garden gate, William flanking him.

Proof that Guido was right, as usual. Love would find a way.

Guido swung the cottage door open wide, first the top half of it and then the bottom. He looped his arm through Gabriela's. If there had ever been anything wrong with him, it did not show now, his stride long and proud and confident.

Enrique saw her. His jaw dropped. He swiped at his eyes with the cuff of his shirt.

She moved toward him, and her future. She was wearing the simplest white dress. Her feet were bare. She had flowers threaded through her hair.

As she walked up the makeshift aisle, between the chairs, butterflies danced in the air around her. She caught a glimpse of Geraldo, peering at her from under the shrubs, a put-out expression on his crabby face.

Marcello, she saw, had found a seat on the Queen's lap.

He rested against her, comfortably, and tilted back his head to look at her.

"Granny," he said loudly, "I love you."

His announcement was met with laughter from the wedding guests, but Gabriela slid a look at the Queen's face and at the formidable cast of her features The Queen looked at her grandson, and the sternness in her features melted momentarily with indulgence. And then her eyes met Gabriela's and glanced off Guido, before she looked quickly back to the front.

But in that moment, Gabriela saw Katalina's strength. And her sacrifice.

Gabriela saw the absolute truth in the words her father had just said to her.

Love finds a way.

* * * * *

THE TYCOON'S FESTIVE HOUSEGUEST

KARIN BAINE

MILLS & BOON

For everyone at my lovely pottery class.
You make Tuesdays so much fun xx

CHAPTER ONE

'I REALLY NEED to leave, Mr Thompson.' Aurelia tried again to excuse herself from her position, but the stern store manager fixed her under his steely bespectacled gaze.

'The young Mr Delaney will be here at any second to meet the staff. It's not going to make a great impression if I tell him the head of our toy department has gone home early. We have to do our best to convince him not to sell Delaney's Department Store, not let him think we come and go as we please. That we don't care about the place. We need to give him reason to keep his father's store running, now that Mr Delaney Senior has passed. Our fate is in this man's hands and we could all be out of jobs if we're not careful. I don't know what's got into you today, Ms Hughes. I've already had to warn you about using your mobile phone. Do you want the store to be bulldozed and leave us all unemployed?'

'Of course not. I'm sorry, Mr Thompson.' Thoroughly chastised, but nonetheless anxious, Aurelia had no choice but to wait in line with the rest of her colleagues for what felt like an inspection. Being viewed under a microscope to see if she was worthy of her position. And goodness, less than two weeks before Christmas, she couldn't afford to lose her job on top of everything else.

With the younger Mr Delaney taking over, it seemed a very likely prospect. Delaney's was an aging department store in the centre of Belfast. A throwback to the past which couldn't compete with modern shopping habits, and was only standing because of a loyal customer base and the novelty factor to tourists. People came from all over Northern Ireland, and beyond, for a taste of nostalgia. And it was also the only job she'd ever known.

She'd started as a teenager working weekends to earn herself a few pounds, and her independence. Taking on extra shifts and overtime so she could afford to live on her own. Her mother had given her little choice, throwing her out when her latest boyfriend had made her choose between him or her teenage daughter. Given her upbringing until that moment, Aurelia had never even considered she would be first choice. However, getting that first rented room had been her first taste of security knowing she wasn't living on her mother's whim. At the mercy of wherever her next doomed relationship took them.

After eleven years of working at the store, the staff at Delaney's had become her family. Mr Thompson was like the stern father she always did her best to keep onside to ensure a quiet life. Suzy, a part-time sales assistant in the department, was the gossipy, complaining older aunt. And then there were the young weekend staff who filled in when needed and often felt like kid brothers and sisters. The older Mr Delaney had been something of a Victorian grandfather ruling the roost with a firm hand, but whom everyone respected. His son, on the other hand, was something of an unknown quantity. Rarely seen in the store, and whose disinterest was now causing alarm for the employees.

Gabriel Delaney was a property developer who'd made millions from knocking down old buildings like this and throwing up modern, soulless apartments in their place. Aurelia doubted there was any room in his heart for sentimentality, or loyalty, when there was money to be made redeveloping the land.

Yet that wasn't her biggest problem at present. No, that was her impending eviction, and she needed to phone the council housing office in the hope they could find her some temporary accommodation for over the Christmas period at least.

She was sure if she explained her circumstances she'd be allowed to leave, but as well as making a bad impression on the new boss, it meant admitting how big a failure she was. How big a disaster her life was. Right now her dignity was all that she had. Thanks to Gary.

He'd disappeared after five years of living together, paying the bills together, and letting her think she had the stable life her Bohemian mother had never provided for her.

Aurelia had done her best to keep up with everything, but in the end her wages wouldn't cover everything and the debts had finally caught up with her. The eviction notice hadn't been unexpected but she wasn't able to do anything until she'd actually been ousted from the apartment. Something which was happening today, but she hadn't been allowed time off because of the prodigal son's arrival. And her own pride.

She checked her watch. There was still time. Her belongings were already packed back at the flat. As long as she was able to make a call before the end of the working day, she could still make it.

There was some commotion at the far side of the ground floor where they'd all been summoned to, as the old Victorian elevator descended. One of the suited businessmen contained inside pulled the ornate iron safety gate across, allowing the rest of the group to step out. Even if she hadn't seen Gabriel before in passing, she would have recognized him as the man of the hour.

He was blond, head and shoulders above the others, a serious expression worrying his otherwise smooth forehead, and he just radiated power. It was in the way he stood, upright and confident, and the way he shook hands with everyone he came into contact with. Assertive. Dominant. Aurelia could almost feel the line of staff melt in his presence, toppling like dominoes until he reached her, and she too wobbled, ready to fall at his feet.

He was a handsome man. Startlingly blue eyes, which seemed to home in on her, hypnotizing her to the point she hadn't heard him talking to her until one of her colleagues gave her a nudge. She realized he was holding out a hand and waiting for her to react.

'Nice to meet you,' she said, shaking his hand.

He smiled and ducked his head, whilst the others looked at her in horror, making her stomach plummet. What had she done?

'Mr Delaney was asking how sales are coming up to Christmas,' Mr Thompson interjected.

'Oh sorry.'

'Perhaps you could show me some of our bestsellers.' Mr Delaney stood back and waited for her to lead him through to the toys.

She knew he was trying to show an interest but she was so aware of the extra time this was taking up that she hesitated. Mr Thompson glared at her, his point clear.

Go and show the boss what he wants to see. Keep him onside.

'These are very popular. We can hardly keep them on the shelves.' She led him towards the display of must-have squashy cuddly toys, feeling like some sort of not-so-glamorous game show assistant.

The figure towering over her frowned, making him seem more imposing. 'Do we have a problem with stock control?'

'No. Not at all. It's just like this in December and we have to stay on top of deliveries to ensure the shelves are stocked at all times.' There was no way she wanted to give the impression that they were lacking in the commitment to their jobs in any capacity. Even though it was a struggle at times to keep the shop tidy and stocked, and serve customers at the same time. As far as management was concerned she didn't want to show any weakness lest she was culled in any 'restructuring' of the store.

He nodded, and the scowl evened out again, helping her to relax a little.

Aurelia showed him the Christmas displays they'd arranged to promote some of their other ranges and hoped she'd done enough to keep everyone happy. Her reward came in the form of his thanks as he walked away to talk to some of the other department heads.

She took her place back in line, sending Mr Thompson what she hoped was a beseeching look. His eye-roll and abrupt head nod was her cue to make a discreet exit.

Aurelia grabbed her coat and bag from the staff room

before hurrying down the back staircase to avoid running into the designer suits.

Thankfully she didn't live too far from the store, part of the reason she was a keyholder as well as department head, and so she began running home. She had her phone to her ear as she dodged commuters exiting the train station, her speech prepared in her head for the moment the call went through.

'The office is now closed...'

Aurelia swore and hung up. It was the weekend, then they were into the Christmas holidays. She'd missed her chance, and though she knew there was likely an emergency hotline, she wouldn't be a priority. There were married couples and single parent families who deserved help more than someone stupid enough to think she could rely on the man she'd been living with for years to help pay the bills.

At least she had a job, which was more than most. No doubt she'd be told she simply had to move somewhere she could afford, and that probably wasn't in the centre of Belfast.

However, that didn't help her current predicament.

'What the—' As she arrived at her flat, Aurelia discovered her belongings had been deposited unceremoniously in the front garden she'd so lovingly tended over the years.

'You've had plenty of notice.' Adam, her landlord, was locking the front door behind him, presumably after changing the locks so she couldn't get in again.

'I know, but I couldn't do anything until you actually evicted me. I will pay you the back rent I owe somehow, but I don't have anywhere to stay tonight. The housing office is closed and it's supposed to snow.' Even though she knew it was futile trying to appeal to the young man who'd never done anything for them even when they had been model tenants, Aurelia did her best to locate an empathetic bone in his body.

'No rent, no apartment,' he said abruptly, getting into his flash sports car and driving away, leaving her on the brink of tears in the darkness.

She supposed she was lucky she'd been able to stay as long as she had, and she couldn't say she blamed him. Regardless that she'd been doing her best, and the apartment was as sparkling clean as when she'd moved in. Ready for someone else to call it home.

Aurelia grabbed her wheelie case, and the couple of black bags containing her worldly possessions. Perhaps that was something she'd inherited from her mother— never accumulating too much 'stuff' in case she had to move at a moment's notice. Not a trait she'd ever hoped to emulate, but in this case it was useful.

The snow began in earnest, the cold biting at her nose. Sleeping out wasn't an option, she would freeze to death. Goodness knew where her mother was, she wasn't one for keeping in touch, and Aurelia had never even met her father.

She had no one to turn to. The only friends she had were her work colleagues. Although they were the only people she had in her life, they all had families and lives of their own. There was no way she could impose on them at this time of the year, she'd be mortified having to face them on their doorstep, carrying her belongings in binbags.

Aurelia trudged on, briefly considering spending the

night in the train station, before several drunks lurched out of the exit. She dismissed the idea at once. Besides, it probably closed overnight anyway. Onwards, glancing briefly at dark shop doorways, considering and dismissing them as potential stops. By morning she'd be a frozen front page headline.

Her feet carried her towards Delaney's, now in darkness, and she felt the keys in her pocket. No one would have to know...

She walked around to the back door, and with a quick glance around to make sure no one noticed her, Aurelia let herself in. Despite the icy temperatures, she was sweating as she punched in the security code to turn off the alarm.

Although she wasn't going to steal anything, and she had keys, this was probably still illegal. If nothing else it would see her fired. Surely millionaire Gabriel Delaney wouldn't begrudge her a night in from the freezing temperatures? Still, she couldn't take the chance, so she didn't turn on any lights and used the torch on her phone to light the way.

She was thankful the famously old-fashioned and notoriously tight-fisted older Mr Delaney hadn't felt the need for CCTV. Relying on the elderly security guard they employed during opening hours only.

It was eerily quiet. Not even the sound of the outside traffic seemed to penetrate the dark depths of the store. A sharp contrast to the usual hustle and bustle of the department that she was used to, as though she'd been transported into another world. Alone.

Aurelia made her way to the home furnishing department. There was a tabletop Christmas tree festooned with fairy lights which she deigned to put on. It would give her a little light, and wouldn't be seen outside. After eating the sandwich meal deal she'd bought at lunchtime at one of the dining room tables on display, she washed and changed into her nightshirt in the ladies' toilets.

If she was going to trespass for the night, she might as well be comfortable, so she picked out a king-size bed and made it up with her own bedding before collapsing on top of it. The last thing she did was set the alarm on her phone to make sure she was up and out before anyone else came in. She'd have to be up early to find somewhere to stash her stuff too.

Suddenly, the reality of her dire situation hit home, silent tears falling down her face. She'd worked so hard not to become her mother, not knowing from one day to the next where she'd be resting her head that night. Unlike her mother, she cared. She'd simply made the mistake of relying on someone else to provide that security. Never again.

As exhaustion claimed her, and thankful oblivion called to her, her last thought was wondering where on earth she was going to sleep tomorrow night.

Gabe couldn't sleep. It wasn't unusual for him to stay up late working, making overseas phone calls, and generally being the workaholic he was. This was different. Ever since his father had died and he'd moved onto the family estate, he'd found it difficult to settle.

It wasn't a home filled with cosy family memories, only a constant sense of his father's disappointment in him. He didn't remember his mother, who'd died when he was young, leaving his father to raise him alone. It was no wonder he'd grown up just as obsessed with money, and making it. The only language his father knew. Gabe had soon learned it was the only way to gain his father's respect or a morsel of affection.

So Gabe had followed in his footsteps, desperate to make his own fortune and prove to his father he was worthy of the Delaney name. Of love.

Except his first business venture had ended in disaster when the property bubble burst and he was left bankrupt. A situation which not only alienated him from his father, but saw his fiancée, Emma, pursue his more successful best friend. Proving that Gabe was nothing to anyone unless he had money, success and power. He'd spent his life since working his way back, making millions and amassing a property portfolio anyone would be proud of.

Still, it never seemed to be enough. Now he was here, owner of this dusty old mansion, and the equally dusty Delaney's store. His knee-jerk reaction had been to sell the place, telling the board that he would give them one last Christmas. But he wasn't sure if he was able to completely sever all ties to the place after all, ending the family legacy.

So he found himself at a crossroads, wondering which way to go. His heart told him to leave things as they were, carry on as his father would have done. On the other hand, his head knew that the land the store sat on was worth more than they could ever hope to make selling overpriced fancy goods. And making money was his birthright, not a crumbling old relic.

The store represented the best, and worst, of his father. It was the one thing that he'd truly seemed to love, a position which should have been held by his son. Gabe was torn emotionally, as well as financially, when it came to making the decision about Delaney's future. It was the last tie to his father, and whilst part of him wanted to be rid of him forever, to finally move on without wondering if he'd ever live up to his father's expectations, he didn't know if he could be that callous.

Gabe paced dark halls lined with the expensive antique vases and paintings his father liked to display his status. Which meant nothing to a child who'd only wanted to be loved. This didn't feel like a home to him, more like a mausoleum. A tomb dedicated to the misery of his childhood.

The grandfather clock at the end of the hallway chimed twice, echoing through the house. An ominous sound which wouldn't have been out of place in a horror movie. He half expected to see his father rushing from one of the rooms, checking his pocket-watch to make sure both timepieces were in synch. Not that the prospect of seeing his deceased father in the halls of his new residence was what was currently unsettling him, but this sense of loneliness which seemed to have consumed him.

He hadn't seen much of his father these last few years but now he knew he was truly alone in the world. It wasn't that he was often without company, in his personal or professional life, but there was no one who he was particularly close to. His own doing of course. Since Emma he'd been afraid to open himself up, to share his life with anyone to that same extent.

He'd gone against the instinct that family life wasn't for him because he'd loved her so much, and she'd told him that's what she wanted. Marriage, and babies. He'd done everything he could to try and make her happy, and she'd left him for someone else anyway.

For the past eight years he'd concentrated on making money, rather than relationships. He didn't need a life partner when he had his career to keep him happy. At least that was one area which he could give all of his attention and love to without fear of abandonment. He was in for the long haul, and he was good at what he did. So he didn't have the time, or the inclination, for committed relationships. There was always that chance he'd disappoint another partner too eventually, and they'd leave him the way his mother, Emma and now his father had. With his father's business affairs to look after too, he had enough on his plate without opening himself up to more heartache.

Gabe grabbed his car keys. Unwilling to spend another second here alone tonight. His father often visited the store at night. Probably to indulge himself in self-praise over what he'd achieved. Gabe was simply seeking solace. Though he probably wasn't going to find it somewhere he was contemplating knocking down.

As he entered the store, he switched on the ground floor lights, looking for some inspiration. Something to tell him what he should do.

The glass display cabinets were a throwback to another world. A time where status was everything. A legacy he was still trying to come to terms with.

He made his way up to the next floor, taking the elegant staircase, sliding his hand along the smooth wooden handrail. Every intricate detail, from the swish burgundy carpet underfoot to the huge ornate gilded mirrors lining the walls, he knew would have been chosen with care by his grandfather at the time. It would be a huge decision to simply bulldoze over the history, regardless of the prime real estate which would go up in its place.

He strolled around the shelves displaying kitchen hardware, and through the bedding department. It was the glow of fairy lights in the dark corner of the department which drew him over towards the row of display beds.

And the sight of a beautiful woman curled up in one which made him stop. He peered down at the brunette who was fast asleep as though she had every right to be there and wasn't trespassing on a huge scale. She didn't look like a burglar. In fact, she seemed to be wearing her nightclothes.

Gabe looked closer. There was something familiar about her...

'What the hell are you doing here?'

CHAPTER TWO

Aurelia was fighting her way back from sleep. Some-one was shouting at her. She wanted to tell them to go away and let her be. But something was telling her she had to wake up.

'Hellooooo...'

Was someone actually clicking their fingers at her?

Reluctantly, she opened her eyes and tried to focus. A pair of beautiful blue eyes were peering down at her.

'What time is it?' she mumbled, sitting up and wip-ing the drool at the side of her mouth on the back of her hand. It didn't seem that long since she'd fallen asleep.

'It's 3:00 a.m. Sorry to disturb you, but I'll ask again, what the hell are you doing here?' The voice sounded fa-miliar. Cross, but familiar.

She blinked until she could clearly see who was both-ering her. It took a moment to remember where she was, what she was doing, and...oh no...

'Oh my goodness! I'm so sorry, Mr Delaney. I can ex-plain everything.' Aurelia threw off the covers and got out of the bed before remembering she was only wearing her short nightie. She desperately tried to pull it down over her knees, only for it to spring up again.

'I'm looking forward to hearing it.' He folded his arms

and waited, but she thought she saw a flicker of a smile play on his lips. A sight which had a strange effect on her, and she stopped trying to hide herself from his gaze and fronted it out instead. Letting go of the hem of her nightie and standing taller, as though being caught sleeping in the store wasn't out of the ordinary.

'I needed somewhere to stay for the night.'

'And this was the only place you could go?' He waved a hand around the department.

'Actually, yes.' It was obvious how sad that sounded. A grown woman who had no friends or family to turn to when she was at her lowest ebb. So desperate for somewhere to go that she'd essentially broken into her place of work and jeopardised her job in the process.

'Have you been drinking?'

'What? No.' What did he think? That she'd been out on a pub crawl and had decided to have a sleepover here rather than attempt to get a late night taxi or bus? It was absurd. Not least because she lived five minutes away. At least, she used to. Not that she supposed he knew anything about her other than she was one of his minions.

'Then why on earth would you think that sleeping here was a good idea?' He unfolded his arms with a sigh.

She supposed someone like him would have no idea what it would be like to have nothing. He was a millionaire who'd come from money. So far removed from the real world that he thought this had been a choice.

'I didn't. As I told you, I had nowhere else to go. I got evicted.'

'Couldn't you have gone to the council for rehoming?' See? No clue.

'It's not as easy as that. There are forms to fill in, a

lengthy waiting list and little social housing available. Apart from anything else, they were closed by the time I tried to get hold of someone.' It wasn't as though she hadn't tried, but circumstances seemed to have conspired to make her homeless for the holidays.

'That sounds like a distinct lack of planning to me.'

Aurelia fought to control her temper. It was one thing having people talk down to her here during working hours, but she was off the clock now. Regardless that she was still in the building.

'You can't get on the housing list until you've actually been evicted. Something which happened while I was working. I had intended to go straight to the office from work, but *someone* kept me back.' She narrowed her eyes at him, hoping he would feel a little responsible for her current situation, and give her a break by at least not calling the police on her. It felt as though she had nothing to lose by being rude to the boss, when she was going to be sacked for certain anyway.

He had the decency to look a tad sheepish. 'Sorry about that, but you can't stay here. Can't you go to a hotel, or something?'

'Apart from the fact it's Christmas, and everywhere is fully booked, I'm broke. That's why I couldn't pay my rent.' The concept was apparently completely alien to him that not everyone could do what they wanted, when they wanted. Not that she would have been in this situation in the first place if she'd had the choice.

His frown only served to irritate her further. 'But you're an employee of the store. A department head.'

It was Aurelia's turn to sigh. 'I know you're out of touch up there in your family mansion, but a Delaney's wage is not enough on its own to pay rent and bills in Belfast. If you must know, my boyfriend decided he no longer wanted to be a responsible adult, and left me struggling to pay the bills on my own.'

Okay, so she was being a tad tetchy, but it was the middle of the night, she was homeless, broke and probably unemployed come tomorrow morning. Getting to insult the boss face-to-face was a small victory when he was part of the reason she'd ended up here tonight anyway.

'I'm sorry to hear that.' He seemed to be genuine in what he was saying. At least he didn't appear to have that glazed look of someone simply paying lip service. Like a man asking which were the top sellers in the toy department because he thought he should, not because he was really interested.

'Yes, well, that's the sad tale of how Aurelia Hughes ended up sleeping in a display bed in Delaney's Department Store. Now, if you don't mind, I should get dressed, or I will freeze to death out there.' One of those doorways she'd dismissed earlier was likely to become her new shelter, so she needed something more substantial to wear than a thigh-skimming, cotton nightshirt.

She grabbed her wheelie case and, with as much dignity as she could manage in the circumstances, tipped her head in the air and walked back towards the ladies' bathroom.

A quick change, a few added layers and with a strong attempt not to cry, she walked back out onto the floor. Ready to hand back the store keys and be told never to darken Delaney's doors again.

'Where are you going to go?' Mr Delaney was waiting outside the toilet doors, casually leaning against one of the pillars, looking as fresh as he had fourteen hours ago.

Aurelia, however, had seen her reflection in the mirror and knew she looked as though she'd just been dragged out of bed.

'I don't know. It's not your problem, though, is it?' She tried to smile, but her mouth was wobbling, betraying her shame and fear.

Mr Delaney levered himself off the wall and grabbed the black bags she'd left sitting on the floor.

'What are you doing? That's my stuff. Oh yeah, that's right, just chuck everything out in the snow like it's nothing. Like I'm nothing.' Aurelia followed as he carried her stuff down the stairs, humiliated that she was about to be dumped on the pavement for a second time.

She was surprised when he led her out the back of the store and a snazzy car beeped as he pointed his key at it.

'I'm not chucking anything out,' he said, opening the boot and depositing her stuff inside.

'So…what are you doing?' She didn't like that he was suddenly taking control of her life, that she was at his mercy. For all she knew he could be taking her straight to the police station, or there was the slim chance he might spring for a night in a fancy hotel to salve his conscience. A temporary reprieve for her but would likely help him sleep better.

'We're going to my place. You're staying with me.'

'What? No, Mr Delaney. I can't.' She objected but Gabe didn't see that they had a choice.

It was Christmas, and she was one of his new employees after all. He was embarrassed that they paid their staff so little that a department head had been made homeless. However, the alternative, giving a wage increase across the board, wasn't going to improve finances at a time when he was already looking at potentially closing the store.

'You can call me Gabe, Ms Hughes, if we're going to be housemates for the foreseeable future.' Now he'd said it out loud, it made it real. He'd invited one of his employees to stay in his house for an undetermined length of time. It was crazy. Yet, he didn't know what else he should do in this situation. He couldn't let her keep sleeping in the store, nor could he put her out on the streets. Besides, the house was big enough to share that they weren't going to be on top of each other.

He opened the passenger door and held it open for her, but she hesitated. 'You don't even know my name, do you?'

'It's, uh... I'm sorry.' She had him there. He'd been introduced to so many people today he couldn't remember all of their names. Apart from anything else, his father had always insisted that senior members of staff were addressed 'properly.' He was sure if he'd been told, he would've remembered the pretty brunette's name. After all, he'd remembered her face well enough.

'It's Aurelia. For future reference.'

Aurelia. It suited her. Unusual. Quirky.

'Well, Aurelia, we've both got to get up for work in a few hours' time.' He gestured towards the passenger seat again.

Thankfully, she got in, so he didn't feel as though he was having to coerce her too much. He wasn't sure about this arrangement any more than she was. They knew very little of each other, and neither had time to think through the logistics or consequences of what they were doing.

All he did know was that he was suddenly very weary. They could work everything out once they'd had some sleep and could think clearly, because his actions now would suggest he didn't know what the hell he was doing. His father would probably turn in his grave if he knew he'd just invited a member of staff to stay at the family residence. He would likely have fired her the moment he caught her in the store, or at least demoted her.

But Gabe wasn't his father, and he was still trying to figure out if he wanted to be. In this case it looked as though his conscience was making the decision for him.

'This place is amazing.' Aurelia was wide-eyed and open-mouthed as they drove up to the Delaney family estate. Even in the early morning darkness, she could see the sheer size of the property. The turrets and pillars making it look like something out of a fantasy—or a horror film, depending on what happened next. A place which represented this man's wealth and status, just as the binbags represented hers.

Gabe stopped in the driveway and looked up at the grey stone building as though he'd never thought about it. 'I suppose it is, in its own way.'

Without elaborating, he strode over to the huge wooden front door and unlocked it, before coming back to help carry her things into the house.

It was like a bizarre dream. Nightmare even. In the space of one day she'd gone from being homeless to a trespasser, to a houseguest courtesy of her new boss. If she had any other option she would have baulked at the idea of coming here, but since the alternative was freezing to death, or a police cell, she was thankful for his generosity.

Though she knew it wasn't a completely altruistic move. It would not look good for the new owner if one of his employees was caught breaking into the store because she couldn't afford her bills. Regardless that was exactly what had happened to her.

There was so much she wanted to ask him, and wanted to clarify. Why he was doing this, and how long for, were just some of the questions on her lips. But for now she just wanted to have somewhere to lay her head for the night without breaking any more laws.

'Thanks for this,' she said as he closed the door behind them. It occurred to her that she hadn't said it yet. Probably because she was half expecting the rug to be pulled from under her again, that this was too good to be true.

Although she doubted shacking up with her boss because she was homeless and he felt sorry for her was anyone's dream scenario.

'No problem,' her host answered gruffly.

Away from the gloom of an out-of-hours store, and now fully awake, Aurelia could see he'd changed out of the stuffy suit he'd been wearing earlier. Although he was nonetheless intimidating, he had donned a casual pair of grey jogging bottoms, a black hoodie and expensive trainers. Looking for all the world as though he'd just finished a workout at the gym. Perhaps he had. There could well be a personal gym secreted away in this mansion.

She did her best not to think about him pumping iron, bare-chested, sweat dripping down his muscular torso— because that would be inappropriate. He was her boss, and the only thing saving her from sleeping on the pavement, or in a cell, right now.

'So where am I staying?' she asked, though she'd be happy to kip on the sofa right now. It was bound to be as sumptuous as the rest of the place anyway.

The hallway was every bit as imposing as the exterior of the building. The dark wood panels on the wall, and the huge staircase gave it a Gothic feel. A brooding atmosphere which suited the owner.

'There's a room Mrs Kent keeps made up for…um… visitors. You can stay there.' He started up the stairs and Aurelia assumed she was to follow.

'Mrs Kent?'

'The housekeeper.'

'Of course.' They came from completely different worlds and it had never been more obvious as she carried her meagre possessions up this staircase worthy of its own scene in a movie.

Gabe ignored her jibe and led her down a corridor with several doors on each side. One of which he opened and stepped aside to let her enter.

'You can stay here. My room is at the other end of the hall if you need anything. Mrs Kent will have breakfast ready in the dining room for 7:30, and I can give you a lift to work when you're ready.'

'Work? I still have a job?' She was sure he had multiple grounds for dismissing her, and no one would blame him if he never wanted to see her again.

'Aurelia, it's December. You're the head of our toy department. We need you.' It wasn't a case of helping her out it seemed, but an act borne of necessity. More than she deserved, or could expect, in the circumstances, but it still left a bitter taste in her mouth. Gabe Delaney was just someone else who didn't really want her.

'Thank you.' She supposed she should think herself lucky he was doing anything for her.

He turned to walk away, then stopped. 'I'd prefer if

you didn't mention any of this to anyone. You're my employee.'

Those blue eyes were steely as they locked on to her, making sure she understood exactly what he was saying.

'No problem. My lips are sealed.' She motioned to zip her lips, then realised the implications for her too if word of this got out. 'That goes both ways, right?'

Gabe pretended to lock his lips shut and throw away the key. He was kind of cute when he lightened up.

'Thanks, Gabe.' It felt odd saying his name, but she liked it. As though a barrier had been broached and they both seemed okay with that. It was how it would look to other people which clearly had them both concerned.

He didn't want to appear as a soft touch, or as though he was having an inappropriate relationship with one of his employees. Aurelia didn't want anyone to know about her dire financial status, or her disastrous personal life. She'd kept it to herself this long. It would make things weird at work if people thought she was getting favours from the new boss, regardless that there was nothing salacious about it.

Apart from anything else, she might be out on the streets again by tomorrow night anyway. She made a note to phone around tomorrow and see if there was any alternative accommodation.

'Well, I'll let you get ready for bed, then.' He afforded her a last smile before leaving to let her settle in.

'Good night,' she called after him, waiting until his footsteps faded before throwing herself on the huge bed.

Aurelia could never have predicted she'd end up here tonight feeling like Cinderella after she'd arrived at the ball. Overwhelmed. Grateful. And wondering what was going to happen when it struck midnight.

CHAPTER THREE

'WHAT ARE THE figures like for today, Miss Hughes? It looked as though you had a steady flow of customers.' As ever, the store manager came to check in with her at the end of the day.

'Good. I think we're well over target for this time of year.' It had been a busy shift, but that meant the time had flown by and she hadn't been able to dwell too much on her current situation. She didn't know if Gabe had been on-site at all as she hadn't seen him since breakfast. An awkward enough affair as they'd sat at opposite ends of a huge dining table, served a feast by his lovely house-keeper which had kept Aurelia going all day. It didn't feel right to be asking him what his plans were as though she was an interested partner, rather than an unwanted house guest.

On the drive to the store she had broached the subject of finding somewhere else to stay the night, but he'd simply brushed her concerns aside. Told her not to worry about it for tonight. Which was easier said than done, but she assumed it meant she could stay with him for another night at least. Not knowing for sure meant that weight of dread sat heavily in the pit of her stomach.

At least until her phone pinged with a text. With Mr

Thompson satisfied with her account of her department today, he was already making his way to cosmetics, so Aurelia chanced a peek at the message.

I'm parked out back. Come down when you're ready. Gabe

Aurelia didn't know why the text message from her boss made her heart beat a little faster other than it was confirmation she had somewhere to go tonight.

It seemed an age before the store finally closed and she was dismissed for the night. Aurelia rushed to the back of the building where Gabe was sitting in the car down a side street.

'I'm so sorry for keeping you waiting,' she said, opening the passenger side door and getting in beside him.

'It's fine. I was on a call anyway.' He started the car, and focused on the road ahead.

Gabe Delaney was a difficult man to read. Aurelia was staring at his profile, his chiselled jaw clenched tight, his lips drawn into a thin line. Something had clearly bothered him.

'You didn't have to do this. I could have got the bus back.' The more put-out he felt about her intrusion into his life, the more likely he would be to throw her out on the street again. Her best bet to extend her stay was to be as unobtrusive as possible so he might forget she was actually living in his huge house.

'I wasn't going to let you walk back on your own, in the dark.' His eyes never strayed towards her, and the tension didn't ease from his body. The atmosphere in the car was as awkward and stilted as it had been on their first meet. As if he resented the fact that he had made himself in some way responsible for her welfare.

Aurelia didn't want that. She preferred honesty over passive-aggressive actions.

'Well, you seem pretty ticked off about it. I know I've put you in a difficult position so I'll pack up my stuff and leave tonight.' Not that she had any more idea now than she had last night about where she was going to sleep, but she didn't want to be on tenterhooks waiting for the moment when he'd had enough inconvenience. Regardless of her current circumstances, she didn't intend to be at his mercy. Too many men had dictated the direction her life should take already.

This time he did turn his head to stare at her, a puzzled frown marring his forehead, before evening out again. 'My mood has nothing to do with you, Aurelia. I've been asked to make some difficult decisions which are weighing heavily on my mind.'

She'd been so wrapped up in her own personal problems that she hadn't given a thought as to what he'd been going through lately. 'I'm sorry. I'm sure this has been a difficult time for you, losing your father.'

Gabe gave her a half-smile. 'Thanks. There's just a lot of stuff to sort out. I didn't mean to make you feel uncomfortable.'

'So I can stay tonight?'

'If it puts your mind at rest, you can stay over the whole Christmas period, until you can contact someone at the housing office. I have nothing planned anyway.'

Her relief was slightly dampened with Gabe's own admission. 'Nothing?'

He shrugged. 'I'm on my own. There doesn't seem much point in putting on a big show.'

'Correction, you *were* going to be on your own. Now you have company.' Aurelia could suddenly see how she could pay him back for his generosity. It hadn't escaped her attention that the house had been missing any festive cheer. She could understand his reluctance to do anything, he was still grieving the loss of his father, and in the middle of taking control of his affairs. He likely didn't feel like celebrating anything.

'I'm sorry if my non-plans differ from yours,' he said dryly.

'I just think we're both going through a tough time, and a little tinsel and sparkle couldn't do any harm.' It might help her forget that she was essentially homeless, for a few days at least, if she were to get lost in the wonder of Christmas for a good cause.

'I really don't want to be bothered with interior decorators or stylists. It's a waste of money.' His version of how to do Christmas managed to raise Aurelia's eyebrows.

'That's not going to be a problem... Is that how you really do Christmas?' She couldn't get over the idea of strangers being paid to come into the family home and push their vision of Christmas onto the occupants. It felt so...sterile.

'Well, father wasn't a great believer in wasting money so we didn't really bother. He only did it in the store because it was guaranteed to bring in the Christmas shoppers. Mrs Kent used to put a small tree in my room when I was little, and she cooked Christmas dinner for us. Other than that...'

Aurelia couldn't help but feel sorry for the little boy who probably would've wanted to get excited about the season the way everyone else did. He was lucky he'd had such a kind woman looking out for him. It also explained something about his resistance now.

'Doesn't she have family of her own?'

'Yes.' Gabe didn't seem to understand the question.

'I'm sure she would much rather have spent the day at home with her family, no offence.'

Gabe waited for the electric gates to open onto the estate, mulling over her comment. 'I suppose so. Well, she can have time off this year. I won't be needing Christmas dinner.'

'Christmas isn't Christmas until you've eaten your own body weight in turkey and chocolate. Why don't I cook for us? It can be my way of saying thanks for taking me in.' Besides, she couldn't think of anything more depressing than being homeless, broke and not celebrating Christmas in some fashion.

'If you really want to.'

'I want to. It'll be nice to pretend I have a normal life for a while,' she sighed. Perhaps it was foolish to continue in the fantasy, but she needed something to cling to right now. For someone who'd so desperately wanted to be able to stand on her own two feet, she'd failed spectacularly. The only difference between her and her mum right now, was that she had no friends to turn to for a bed for the holidays, and had to rely on the charity of her employer. The very thought made her cringe, and it was important to her that she was able to feel as though this arrangement was in some way beneficial to him too. So she didn't feel indebted to him as much as she was.

However, as she walked into the grand, stark hallway, it was evident there was a long way to go for this odd situation to feel like Christmas for either of them.

'Are you hungry? Would you like to go out for dinner somewhere? It's just... I don't tend to keep a lot of food in. Mrs Kent will leave me something to heat up, or I order in.' Gabe looked sheepish with the admission he was making, probably so she didn't think he was trying to wangle a date. Not that he was likely to ever have an interest in someone like her.

Aurelia imagined he only dated lithe, blonde supermodels whose daddies had their own empires for them to inherit, not homeless, penniless, curvy brunettes who dressed as though they'd been dragged through a jumble-sale.

'Don't worry about it. I'm not really up to going out again. I'll make myself a sandwich or something later.' The idea of eating out in the sort of swanky establishment Gabe was likely used to, was already making her stomach churn. No doubt the price of a meal out with Gabe would probably have paid her rent for the month.

'I'm sure we can do better than that...'

'No, honestly. I don't want anything. Actually, there is one thing I want...' Aurelia shrugged off her coat, with a burst of renewed energy. There was one thing which could improve her spirits immeasurably in the face of her current situation.

'I'm sure we can get anything your heart desires.' There was something about the twinkle in his blue eyes which went some way to softening his usual stern expression. Regardless that he was teasing, the moment helped her feel as though she wasn't just an unwanted house guest. That the dynamic between them was slowly shifting between them to make her feel more comfortable in her surroundings. Something she intended to capitalise upon.

'Oh good. I was hoping you'd say that.' She didn't try to hide the smile on her face as she lured Gabe into her plan.

He narrowed his eyes, that frown back to mar his forehead. 'Why do I get the feeling I've just agreed to something that's going to cost me a lot of money and peace of mind?'

Aurelia chuckled at his scepticism. It surprised her even more that someone who seemed naturally suspicious of others should even have agreed to let her invade his home in the first place.

'Not at all. I just thought it might be nice for both of us if I put some Christmas decorations up. You know, make the place feel like home for a little while.' She didn't mean to be rude, or diss his family pile, but it wasn't exactly a place that gave warm, cosy vibes.

Gabe pursed his lips into a tight line as he glanced around the vast reception area. For a moment, she worried that she'd gone too far by insulting his inheritance, and she was about to find herself sleeping in a doorway after all.

Until he finally opened his mouth and sighed. 'You're right. This place hasn't felt like home to me for a very long time. If ever. I suppose a few Christmas decorations aren't going to hurt. Knock yourself out.'

He was about to walk away, but unfortunately, words weren't going to be enough to change things up around here.

'Gabe, wait.' It always felt weird using his Christian name. Almost like when her mother tried to get her to call her 'Gloria' instead of 'Mum' because she thought it made her sound too old.

He was Mr Delaney. *Young* Mr Delaney to many at the store. 'Gabe' sounded too...familiar. Though she supposed they were living together, so it might be weirder to be referring to him with a title.

'Is there a problem? I told you, you can do what you want.' He looked annoyed that the conversation wasn't yet over, so he was going to be even more ticked off when he realised what else she had in mind.

'Well, to decorate, I'm going to need decorations as well as a tree. I've only got a couple. Not nearly enough to fill even a corner of this place.' As much as she loved Christmas, she didn't have a lot of stuff. Only a few sentimental pieces she'd kept over the years she'd made with her mum which were past their best now. The cotton wool ball snowman had lost any structure it once had and now resembled more of a cloud with eyes and a cardboard top hat.

'I'm sure we have plenty for you to choose from at the store. We do have a Christmas shop.' Gabe folded his arms, clearly of the impression she was trying to make problems.

They did have a Christmas section but she knew the price of those fancy, fragile ornaments they sold there. As pretty as they were, they weren't really her style. She guessed that was one area where she was a little old-fashioned. She preferred traditional, pretty decorations depicting robins and snow scenes to 'themes' which had been chosen by some young buyer. Though the displays looked good in the store there wasn't anything personal about the tasteful sets of ivory baubles with white feathers, or the blue and gold filigree egg-shaped ornaments which cost a week's wages each. Aurelia liked her decorations to have a little more character and history.

'I know, but it would be nice to perhaps have something that meant something to the family. To you. You said Mrs Kent used to put a tree in your room. Perhaps it's still here somewhere?' Anything would make this place a little homelier than it was, though she was grateful she'd been given refuge in it.

'It might be in the attic. I'm not sure it's going to be quite what you're looking for. It was just a token gesture for a little boy who was missing out on Christmas.' There was a faraway look in his eyes, and a quiver in his voice which made Aurelia see he wasn't as unemotional as he liked to portray.

'Well, that is definitely something personal which I think would be lovely to have out on display. Maybe we can find a few lights and ornaments to decorate it with too,' she said hopefully.

Her heart went out to him and she was grateful he'd had someone in his life to show him some affection. From what she'd seen of his father, he wasn't a man who would've encouraged any frivolity of any kind in the home. Even at Christmas. She imagined it would have been hard for a child to grow up in that environment, regardless of the privileges that came with it.

It made her think back to her own childhood and the experiences she'd had with her parent. Very different to Gabe's, but with no less emotional complications. In her case, she'd had to try and rein in her mother's fanciful ways. Aurelia had been the parent on many occasions. Trying to be practical and logical, when her mother simply wanted to enjoy herself. It had been exhausting for both of them. It was no wonder they'd been better apart. She'd needed stability and security, and her mother needed to be free. Landing wherever the day, or fancy, took her. No longer having to deal with the responsibility of towing a child along with her. Not that her daughter had ever been her priority.

Another heavy sigh and an eye-roll from Gabe. 'I suppose that means a trip to the attic for me, then?'

'I'll help.' It wasn't an altruistic gesture, she wanted to see what a house like this might have in storage. There were bound to be generations of Delaneys who'd stored unwanted possessions up there, and she was keen to have a respectful rummage through the past.

He mumbled something unintelligible before stripping off his jacket and hanging it on the nearby coat stand. She followed suit, though she became distracted when he unbuttoned his shirt cuffs and rolled his sleeves up. Aurelia was so used to seeing him buttoned up in a suit, she'd forgotten he was flesh and bone beneath it. And muscle. Tanned, taut muscle dusted with golden hair.

'Right.' The sudden clap of Gabe's hands together startled her from her ogling, but she blushed all the same for even looking at him that way. He'd been nothing but generous and kind to her since learning of her circumstances and she was ashamed of herself for perving after him. Though it apparently didn't stop her sneaking a peek at his taut backside as he took the stairs two at a time in front of her.

'Are we there yet?' she moaned as they seemed to walk for miles, up stairs, and along corridors in the multi-storey mansion. Until eventually they came to a dark, narrow set of steps up to a locked door. Like something out of a horror movie.

She waited anxiously behind him as he turned the

handle on the door, half expecting a rush of something unworldly to come rushing past them, finally unleashed after years of imprisonment. Instead, there was simply silence and a fug of dust to greet them.

'I haven't been up here for years,' Gabe said as he located the light pull and illuminated the space with a soft yellow glow.

'It doesn't look as though anyone has.' Probably not since the young master moved out and there was no need for any nod towards Christmas any more. It was sad in a way. She could almost feel the neglect, and she related to it. Abandoned, forgotten, no longer of any use, waiting for someone to brush away the dust and take an interest.

Boxes upon boxes were stacked in the rafters, and the floor was cluttered with old furniture covered in dust sheets. No doubt there were antiques galore worth more than everything she had packed in the few bags she'd brought with her, but had been tossed aside like yesterday's newspaper. There were so many pretty glass lamps the Delaneys could have easily opened a shop just for them.

'This stuff is beautiful.' She traced her hand over a brightly coloured glass-panelled lamp which looked as though it had come straight from a study in a period drama.

'I didn't realise I came from a family of hoarders.' Gabe seemed almost as astonished as she was to see the treasures which had been hidden away here, likely for decades.

'This is on a different level. I wouldn't throw any of this out either. If I was stuck for space, and I don't imagine why I would be in a place this size, I'd sell all this and buy myself a private island somewhere.' Maybe she could simply live here. No one would be any the wiser.

She brushed a layer of dust off some of the boxes to find they'd all been labelled in black marker pen. At least someone had been organised. She'd thrown her belongings in a bag in such a hurry she'd ended up with toothpaste all over her work uniform. Thank goodness Gabe had a washer and dryer that she'd been free to use.

She moved the box marked 'China' very carefully to the side, along with one labelled 'Cutlery.' Most likely it was full of the family silver no one wanted or needed. Aurelia checked each of the boxes until she came across one with 'Christmas Decorations' written across the top. Her heart did a joyful skip.

'I think I've found what we're looking for,' she called to Gabe, who was sorting through another stack in the corner.

'Me too.' He lifted a box and carried it over to her, flexing those muscles she'd become acutely aware of recently.

'Can I look inside?' She was fit to burst with anticipation as to what she might find, given the array of delights all around.

'That's why we're here.' Gabe smiled and let her do the honours.

As much as Aurelia wanted to rip the tape off with glee, like a child opening presents on Christmas morning, she did it as carefully and slowly as she could. Inside there were more neatly stacked boxes. Opening one, she pulled back the white tissue paper nestled inside and uncovered the quaintest vintage ornaments.

'They're so pretty.' She held one up and let it spin from

her fingertips. A gold bauble with a painted snow scene of a couple on a horse-drawn sleigh. Gabe reached inside and took out a silver version which depicted two children having a snowball fight.

'I vaguely remember these. My mother must have put them on the tree when I was little. I'd forgotten all about them until now.'

'What age were you when she died?' Although it was nice for him to unlock some other Christmas memories involving his mother, she supposed they brought a sadness with them. As shown in his eyes now taking on a wistful glaze.

'Eight. I don't remember a whole lot, but I think she liked to make a fuss at Christmas.'

'I'm so sorry. We can pack these away if you like?' She didn't want to upset him any more, especially when the grief for his father was probably still raw too.

'No. It would be nice to see them on display again. It might jog my memory of those days a bit more. Though I didn't realise we had so many decorations.' Gabe continued to pull out decorations, tinsel and some vintage candle-shaped lights.

'There are probably layers of family history and Christmases here.' Aurelia inspected a fragile green bell with gold glitter trim and could just imagine the house in the '20s or '30s decorated for Christmas. It seemed a shame that the traditions had likely stopped when Gabe's mother died.

She thought about her own family. The people she'd never met. All she had were the stories her mother had told her. Which, if she was honest, tended to differ every time she told them. What Aurelia did know was that her mother's parents had kicked her out when she was young because she was 'a free spirit.' From her experience she knew that meant Gloria ran wild. Drink, drugs and bad boys were her particular favourite pastimes, and probably did not go down well with her elderly religious parents. Though her upbringing might have explained why she did have a soft spot for Christmas at least. Aurelia was sorry she never got to know her grandparents who'd died before she was born. At the very least she might have had someone to turn to. She might have had family.

Gabe turned over a homemade card in his hands. 'Merry Christmas, Mummy. I hope you feel better soon.'

He passed it to Aurelia. It was a sweet child's drawing of a Christmas tree with lots of presents piled up beside it and a family smiling as they held hands.

'This must have been from our last Christmas together. She wasn't able to get out of bed at that stage. I don't think I really understood what was happening. Thought that she'd wake up some day feeling better and everything would go back to the way it was. She died on Boxing Day.' Once Aurelia handed the card back, Gabe returned it to the box. This was clearly one thing he didn't want to be reminded of.

'I'm so sorry. I didn't realise you lost her at Christmastime.' Not that any other time of the year would have made the loss easier to bear, but it went some way to helping her understand why Christmas didn't represent a joyous time to Gabe, or his father. It was apparent in his every word how much he'd loved his mother. How close they'd been. If Aurelia had lost someone so special, she couldn't guarantee she wouldn't turn against the festivities either. Grieving a loss at a time when everyone else was celebrating.

It made her question if she was doing the right thing now. She'd wanted to make him happy, to thank him for helping her. It hadn't been her intention to bring up painful memories he'd obviously been trying to quell over the years.

'Gabe, we don't have to do this, you know. I didn't realise—'

'I told you, it's fine. I'll start carrying the boxes downstairs.' He got up and brushed the dust from his trousers, grabbed a box and walked away.

Aurelia was grateful that he was letting her do this, regardless of the painful history they would be unpacking along with the decorations. She was more determined than ever to make this a happy Christmas for him. To thank him for the favour he'd done her in taking her in. Not because she felt anything other than gratitude for her boss...

Gabe kept himself busy carrying down the decorations so he wouldn't be tempted to spill any more family secrets to someone he hardly knew. He didn't know what had come over him. It wasn't usual for him to open up to anyone about his background. Then again, he didn't usually invite employees to come and live with him.

He put it down to grief. It was said to make people act in different ways and he had just lost his father. Perhaps he'd simply been feeling lonely living in this big house on his own, having left his apartment to move into the family home. There was just something about Aurelia that made him feel comfortable enough in her company to share. It could simply be down to the fact that she seemed to be on her own too. And it was Christmas. A time when people were sentimental than usual.

'I think I've found a Christmas tree,' Aurelia called from the corner of the attic when he made what he thought was his final trip up there. She was bent over, backside in the air, as she pulled a large, rectangular box from the eaves.

'It's bigger than the one I used to have in my room.' He wouldn't have expected that one to be more than a couple of feet tall, but the sides on this one were so large, they were supported by some sort of metal frame.

'It might be the one your mum used to put up,' Aurelia suggested.

'I suppose so. I might need a hand to get it downstairs though.'

'I can help. Unless you'd rather I kept looking for the other one?'

'No. This one will do.' The sooner he could leave her to it, the better. This whole exercise was bringing up more memories than he cared to relive. Even now he was having flashbacks about helping his mum to hang the decorations on the tree. On the bottom branches only because that was all he could reach. Regardless that his father complained that it looked a mess, she would never attempt to rearrange them, so Gabe felt as though he had helped in some way. He'd forgotten about that until he'd seen the tree and remembered how much his father had hated having to bring this box down out of the attic every year. Gabe made the decision not to do the same. He knew Aurelia needed this and he didn't want to ruin it for her.

Between them they managed to get the box down the

stairs. Stopping every now and then for a breather. Once they manoeuvred it into the living room, he set about dismantling the frame so they could get it out of the box. Aurelia began slotting the sections of tree together and unfurling the full branches.

'You have such beautiful Christmas things, it's a shame they've been forgotten about.' She was stroking the baubles as though they were the most precious things on earth. Gabe felt a tinge of guilt that he'd been complicit in letting these things be lost to time.

'I think we got a real tree that last Christmas, and my dad got someone in to decorate. After Mum died, he said there was no point. I think it hurt too much to be reminded of her.'

'That's a shame. You were just a child. He should have let you enjoy Christmas the way your mother would have wanted.'

Gabe shrugged. He didn't want to go down that route having already given away too much about his personal life. 'What about your parents? Why can't you stay with them over Christmas?'

From what he could tell so far, it was obvious that they weren't a big part of her life, but he wanted to deflect the attention away from his family. Emotions weren't something the Delaney men had ever been too comfortable expressing. As proven by a father who wouldn't even talk to his eight-year-old son about how much he was grieving after losing his mother. Gabe had learned the only way to keep his father happy was to do as he was told, and praise was only earned when he was old enough to make his own money.

Aurelia carried on hanging the decorations on the tree.

'I never knew who my dad was. I can't be sure my mum even knows, to be honest. She's what she likes to call "a free spirit." By which she means, doing what she pleases, when she pleases. So we tended to move around a lot. She did make an effort at Christmas though.'

'Ah, that explains it. It represents happy times for you.' As much as he was trying to suppress memories, Aurelia was trying to recreate them. He could understand that when it didn't sound as though she'd had a particularly happy childhood either. Not that she'd given away too much.

It seemed they were both lonely, wounded souls who'd simply found themselves thrown together because they had no one else.

'Yeah. Actually I have a couple of things of my own to add, if that's okay?'

'Sure.'

Gabe did his best to untangle the fairy lights and test them so they didn't cause a fire and burn the whole place down. Aurelia disappeared upstairs, only to return carrying what looked like a pile of used cotton balls.

'Now, I know these aren't exactly in keeping with the vintage elegance you might be used to, but I'm sentimentally attached to these.' She held out a couple of obviously handcrafted, well-loved items, but he couldn't for the life of him tell what they were supposed to be.

'Not to be rude, but what are they?'

Aurelia rolled her eyes. 'This is Frosty, and this is my toilet roll Santa Claus.'

Now he looked closer, the cotton balls did appear to have eyes, and a little hat. 'Santa Claus' seemed to be a cardboard tube wrapped in red paper with a face drawn on in crayon and some cotton stuck on for a beard.

'If you say so.'

'Rude. I think these are the only things Mum ever took time to make with me, other than her failed attempts to make gingerbread.'

'Sorry.' He was sorry for being rude about her handicraft, and that her parent had been as neglectful as his by the sound of it.

'Do you mind if I put these up somewhere? I know they don't exactly fit the aesthetic here.' She glanced around at the antiques littered around the room. Expensive family heirlooms which had never meant anything to him other than he'd had to be careful when playing as a child in case he broke something. All style, no substance, he supposed.

Much like the family dynamic with his father. From the outside it might have seemed he had the perfect life, but he was realising just how much it had been lacking. Love. When his mother died, it seemed that had died with her.

'I told you, you're free to do whatever you want.' If playing make-believe for a few days gave her peace of mind, he wasn't going to stand in the way of it. He just didn't want to get too caught up in the fantasy that he would ever have a happy Christmas again.

'Thanks.' Aurelia took her precious keepsakes and set them on the mantelpiece beside the gold gilt Victorian mantel clock.

Gabe liked the juxtaposition. Some whimsy pushing out the staid past he'd never seemed to be able to escape. More so these days. Not only was he dealing with the complex grief of losing his father, but his death also seemed to have unlocked feelings surrounding the loss of Gabe's mother too. He'd been too young to really understand what was going on at the time other than he'd never see his beloved mother again. Left alone to deal with his grief, he'd learned to hide the tears from his father, and tried to smother those feelings of loss. Now he was having to find a way to get through double the grief, mourning the relationships he never got to have with either of his parents.

Not only had the untimely death of his mother robbed him of a normal upbringing with a loving mother, but it had also caused his father to withdraw from him emotionally. He'd never had anyone to turn to for support through his adolescence, navigating high school and puberty. It had been down to him to figure things out for himself, leaving him with an intense feeling of loneliness.

He couldn't help but wonder how his life would have turned out if he'd had at least one loving parent to guide him. Perhaps he would've been happily married with a family of his own, unafraid to open his heart. Unfortunately, he'd never know. Life hadn't turned out that way, and he'd been left alone, with no family around him at all now.

Since Aurelia had moved in it seemed as though some light was breaking through the gloom of his grief. Perhaps letting her stay would do them both good.

She took out a leafy green garland festooned with red velvet bows, and draped it around the fireplace. It appeared she was keen to make her mark everywhere and he wasn't going to interfere. As much as this was now his home, he hadn't been able to change anything to suit himself. By letting Aurelia do her thing, it could give him the nudge he needed to eventually make the place a home for himself too.

He heard a stomach rumble and couldn't be sure if it was his, or Aurelia's. Dinner had been forgotten about in the rush to bring Christmas to the house. Gabe left Aurelia humming holiday tunes as she decorated the living room, clearly in her happy place, whilst he headed towards the kitchen. There wasn't much fresh food in the fridge, but he had some frozen quick dinners in the freezer for those nights he didn't feel like going out or ordering in. Which were becoming more frequent. He'd only offered to take Aurelia out tonight as a treat, as well as a chance to get them both out of the house.

The contents of the freezer would've appalled his father, who had been a stickler for a 'proper' dinner, usually consisting of potatoes, meat and veg. Gabe grabbed a pepperoni pizza and put it in the oven, hoping it would at least stave their hunger, even if it wasn't going to impress anyone. He just wanted to do something to repay Aurelia for everything she'd done tonight. It would never have occurred to him to put the decorations up, but they were growing on him. The reminder of past Christmases began to bring back some happier memories than the ones he'd spent with his father.

He considered setting the table in the dining room, but it seemed absurd to go to all the trouble when they were simply sharing a pizza. So, when their late night snack was ready he grabbed a bottle of white wine from the cellar along with two glasses, and set everything on a tray.

'I thought you could do with a break, and a bite to eat,' he said as he carried dinner back to Aurelia. She'd been busy in his absence, the place transformed from a stuffy, formal living room, into a cosy Christmassy room he actually wanted to spend time in.

With the main light turned off so it no longer felt as though he was being interrogated, the fairy lights gave off a warm glow that seemed almost magical. All of his mother's precious decorations hung proudly on the front of the tree so he could see them every time he came into the room, and of course, Aurelia's own handmade memories had pride of place above the fire.

Gabe allowed himself to think about what it would be like to have a family of his own here, enjoying Christmas together. It unnerved him that his mind had ventured there already after opening up the house to one person. He'd never considered another serious relationship since his ex, never mind the commitment of a family. Too worried that he'd let them down the way he had everyone else in his life. That he would open up his life to someone else, only for them to abandon him when he didn't prove worthy of their love in some way.

So he'd let work become his focus, his baby, and he'd done a good job of parenting that. Working, earning money, was where he felt safe, because that's what he'd grown up with. That's where he'd learned to express himself, and where he drew his father's attention and approval.

In hindsight, perhaps that had been a contributing factor to the breakdown of his relationship. He'd thought that his success was the only thing guaranteed to keep Emma by his side. However, his work, his drive to make his mark in business, had taken time away from their relationship. Perhaps it was inevitable she would find solace elsewhere. At the time all he could see was the betrayal by his fiancée and his so-called friend when he'd caught them together half undressed in his home. Kyle, someone he'd known since university, had apparently been stopping by to keep her company on the nights Gabe had been working late to try and save his company. And one thing had led to another.

Beyond that, Gabe hadn't wanted to hear anything else and had thrown them both out of his home. A relationship and a friendship destroyed in one night. He had no idea if Emma would have strayed even if he hadn't been working so hard, and at the time he'd put it down to the failure of his business. A validation that he meant nothing to anyone without money and success. Whatever the reason for the break-up, he only knew how deeply he'd been hurt and had vowed to never be in that position again.

That was where danger lay. When it wasn't simply his bank account at risk, but his heart. And that had been broken once too often by those who were supposed to love him. It had been safer since Emma to simply shut himself off emotionally than being on the receiving end of someone else's disappointment.

That's why a family of his own had seemed like wanting the impossible. It wasn't that he wouldn't have liked a wife or being a father, but he was afraid that he simply wouldn't prove up to the job. He never wanted to be the sort of father he'd grown up with. Cold, demanding and making his son feel like the loneliest child on the planet. For a time, he'd been willing to try if it meant keeping Emma in his life, but once she'd gone, so had any desire for domestic bliss. It seemed like a fantasy completely out of reach.

For almost a decade he'd been used to being on his

own, save for the odd casual relationship. However, being in the family home had really made him feel like that sad little boy all alone in the world again. This was the first time in years he felt comfortable here and it had taken a stranger to do that. Though, now that he'd shared so much of his personal life with Aurelia, she was becoming more than that to him.

'Thanks, but shouldn't we eat that somewhere else? I wouldn't want to get tomato sauce on any of the furnishings.' Aurelia looked longingly at the pizza, but held back from taking a slice.

'It's fine. This is my house now and I'm trying to feel more comfortable in it. The place is well overdue a revamp. I might move some of my own furniture in from storage, and sell some of the contents here. I don't know... I haven't decided yet.'

He'd been reluctant to let go of his own things, hence the storage, but he couldn't bring himself to get rid of the items that had been here for as long as he could remember. Regardless of the fact he would never feel comfortable here until his father's influence wasn't so apparent.

'Well, if you insist...' She grabbed a slice from the plate and took a bite.

Gabe pulled over a table and set the tray down, before joining Aurelia on the sofa. 'Dad would never let us eat or drink in here.'

'Oh, you rebel,' Aurelia teased.

'That's kind of how I feel,' he chuckled. 'As though I'm finally standing up to him.'

Gabe realised he'd said too much again and shoved some pizza in his mouth before he told her anything else. She didn't need to know that he'd lived his whole life simply trying to earn his father's praise. Although, she'd probably figured that out for herself by now.

They made their way steadily through the pizza and wine and as he reached for the last piece, his hand brushed against Aurelia's as she reached for it at the same time.

'Sorry. You have it,' she insisted.

'Not at all. You're the guest here.'

'An uninvited one,' she mumbled, as she withdrew her hand.

'I distinctly remember inviting you to stay. So, you're a guest.' He released his control of the last slice, doing his best to be chivalrous.

'Under duress.' It seemed she was determined not to relax for the duration of her stay, punishing herself needlessly when she was already under so much strain.

Gabe fixed her with the stare he used in board meetings so she knew he was being serious. 'Hey, I invited you here, and you're welcome. I want you to enjoy Christmas, and this delicious pizza I made you specially.'

Aurelia's brown eyes watched him warily as he lifted the last slice and held it out to her. All of a sudden she lunged forward and chomped down on it, taking him by surprise, and making him laugh. Something there hadn't been too much of in this house for the last twenty-five years.

Their eyes locked, and for a split second, the atmosphere seemed to crackle with electricity. He could've been fooled into thinking this was a romantic moment, that the pizza was about to be abandoned so they could devour one another instead. Except Aurelia was an employee, she was living with him, albeit temporarily, but it meant she was not someone he should even be thinking about romantically.

He sat back, and set the pizza down in the box. 'You finish it. I think I'm going to head to bed. Thanks for making the place look festive. I appreciate it.'

Aurelia swallowed down the pizza and wiped her mouth. 'Don't mention it. It's the least I can do.'

The moment, whatever it was, had passed, and they were back to being courteous, temporary housemates. Content that he hadn't done anything he'd come to regret, Gabe took his leave.

Hopefully, now that she'd been given space to indulge her inner child and let Christmas explode over his house, they could avoid each other outside of working hours.

Perhaps it was about time he got back on the dating scene. Fulfill any urges on strangers he wouldn't see more than once or twice, instead of someone he was currently living with.

CHAPTER FOUR

AURELIA STIFLED A yawn as the irate customer in front of her raged about how useless the store was because they no longer had the must-have toy of the year in stock. This was the part of the job she enjoyed least. Staff at Delaney's were supposed to smile and placate, even when getting abuse for something that was beyond their control.

'I'm sorry, sir. I'm afraid the manufacturers themselves underestimated the popularity of the toy and they haven't been able to keep up with demand. Everywhere sold out weeks ago, it's not just Delaney's.' She managed not to laugh in his face at the fact he thought he could stroll in and lift one from the shelves this close to Christmas. It wasn't her fault there was likely to be a disappointed little girl on Christmas morning. Some parents had been ticking off their children's Christmas lists for months.

'Well, it's not good enough,' he blustered, red in the face, and spit collecting in the corners of his mouth. 'I'm going to put in a complaint.'

'You're very welcome to do so, sir.' She kept smiling until he eventually took the hint that ranting at her wasn't going to get him anywhere and he walked away, swearing under his breath.

'And a merry Christmas to you too,' she called after

him. The season tended to bring out the best, and the worst, in people, and she saw it all working in a toy department. At least she had the pleasure of watching children enjoying themselves to counteract the occasional difficult customer.

This time she didn't manage to catch the yawn in time, only to find Mr Thompson glaring at her.

'Is there a problem Ms Hughes?' he asked, staring down his nose.

'Not at all.' Instead of explaining that she'd lain awake half the night thinking about their boss, she made her way over to the till where she'd be constantly busy, and unable to take time to chat to the store manager.

Last night with Gabe had been all kinds of weird. It had been fun uncovering all of the vintage decorations and getting to put them up so it felt like Christmas. She'd even appreciated the fact he'd been able to open up to her a little bit about his personal life. From what she could gather, despite his privileged upbringing, he hadn't had the happiest childhood either.

It had been nice to have someone make her something to eat, and just to chat with. For a while she'd been able to forget her dire personal circumstances, and the fact he was her boss and had only let her stay with him out of pity.

That lapse in concentration had let her start romanticising what was happening between them. He was a handsome man being kind to her, and for a brief moment she'd wanted him to kiss her. Thought he *was* going to kiss her. But the look of horror as he pulled back from her soon put the record straight. She was still cringing now.

Aurelia supposed it was only natural to be attracted to

someone who'd effectively rescued her. Her white knight was handsome, rich and could offer the sort of stability she'd never had in her life. But that was all it could be, a fantasy. He was her boss and if she wasn't careful she wouldn't even have a place to stay over Christmas. She certainly didn't want to wear out her welcome before she could find somewhere else to live.

Besides, romantic relationships never worked out well for the Hughes women. Her mother was a prime example. Always on the move from one toxic partner to another, living at the mercy of a man's fancy. Aurelia had sworn never to be like her and she'd valued her independence. Until she'd begun to feel lonely and think there was more out there for her than working at Delaney's.

She'd been young and naive, with no one to guide her when she'd first ventured onto the dating scene, but she'd also been careful not to get too carried away by the notion of a happy-ever-after. There hadn't been a problem finding men who weren't interested in long-term commitment, and she'd got to keep her independence.

Then she'd met Gary, who'd swept her off her feet. He'd promised her the world, and for the first time she'd begun to believe in the fairy tale. That she could have a husband, a family and live happily ever after. So she'd gone against her promise to herself to never end up like her mother, only for it all to come crashing down around her anyway. She supposed falling for the wrong men was simply a genetic disorder she couldn't escape. Although she hadn't seen it until it was too late, Gary was the same as every other man her mother had brought into her life. Unreliable and too immature to deal with a serious relationship.

Since Aurelia couldn't be trusted to make the right decisions when it came to men and relationships, it was better for her to avoid them altogether from now on. The most important thing in her life right now was making sure she held on to her job long enough to get back onto her feet.

'Excuse me, can you help me please?' A young woman approached at the side of the till, clearly not making a purchase. At least not yet.

'Of course. Tommy, can you take over here, please?' She waited until their part-time sales assistant came before leaving her place.

'How can I help you?' Aurelia escorted the woman to the side of the shop where it was less busy and they could talk in private.

'I'm actually here to ask if Delaney's toy department would consider donating some gifts to the local children's home? Our young residents are often overlooked at this time of year and I would really like the opportunity to do something for them. It doesn't have to be anything expensive. I just thought it would be nice if we could give them a few presents to open on Christmas morning.' The hope was there in the woman's face, and it was obvious she wanted to give the children in her care a happy Christmas.

Still, it wasn't within Aurelia's power to give the go-ahead.

'You'd actually have to speak to the owner, Mr Delaney. I could take you up to his office and see if he's available to speak to you.' She would never have had the audacity to go to Gabe's father's office without an appointment, but she hoped the young Mr Delaney would be more receptive. They were living together after all.

'That would be great, thank you.' The relief was obvious on the woman's face when she'd clearly been nervous about asking in the first place.

Aurelia knew a little of how it felt when you were that desperate. Except in her case she hadn't been able to ask for help. She was lucky that Gabe had caught her that night, and offered her everything she needed when he could easily have had her prosecuted. Hopefully his generosity would stretch to others who could use a helping hand at this difficult time of year.

'Do you get any donations for the children?' Aurelia asked as they got into the old-fashioned elevator and pressed the button for the top floor.

'A few. We tend to get more for the younger children, and the teens get stuck with toiletry sets and socks. Not that I'm complaining of course, but I would just like to be able to give them something a little more exciting.'

'What about Christmas dinner?' After her conversation with Gabe last night she'd begun to realise the impact that missing out on the small things as a child had on the adult. She was still carting around some pieces of cardboard and cotton wool simply because her mother had once spent some time with her. These children were already being deprived of parents, of a loving home with family, and it seemed a shame if no one was willing to step up and give them at least one good day to celebrate.

'We do get donations for that, and the local food banks contribute. I know we shouldn't encourage them to be materialistic—'

'It's only natural though, isn't it. They're kids. They want what everyone else has, and it's not their fault they don't have anyone to give them the Christmas they deserve.'

She remembered all too well when all of her friends were getting the latest must-have doll, and she'd prayed so hard to get one. Only to unwrap a cheap pound-store version on Christmas morning. She couldn't help the disappointment that settled into her bones. After all, she'd still believed in the magic of Christmas. That Santa and his elves would make her everything she wanted. She didn't want any other child to experience that same sort of disappointment if she could help it, and given Gabe's own history, she was sure he'd want to help.

The lift pinged open and she led the care home worker down the dark corridor towards Gabe's office and knocked on the door.

'Come in,' he shouted gruffly.

Aurelia led them both in to find him staring sternly at his computer screen. He always seemed to be in a foul temper when he was at work, compared to the man she'd come to know at home. It made her wonder what went on behind the scenes here, and what it was which seemed to cause his bad mood on the premises.

'Good afternoon, Mr Delaney. This young lady would like to have a quick word with you, if that's okay?' She made the introduction, then stood back from the desk.

'Please, take a seat. Both of you,' Gabe commanded.

'My name is Louisa Mallen. I'm from the local children's home, and I wondered if we could persuade you, Delaney's Department Store that is, to donate some toys for our children?'

Gabe leaned back in his chair with a sigh and held his hand up. 'I'll stop you there. Delaney's as a rule doesn't affiliate itself with any charities. I'm sorry. If we give to one, it's often expected that we should give to all who come to the door.'

'We're not a charity, sir. I'm just asking for a one-time donation of toys.' Two red spots appeared on Ms Mallen's cheeks as she fought to be heard.

Aurelia could feel the heat in her rising too. She couldn't believe what she was hearing.

'I'm very sorry you've had a wasted trip.' Gabe rose from behind the desk and strode across the office floor to open the door, effectively dismissing them.

Aurelia got up and escorted the young woman back out. 'I'm so sorry. I really thought he would help.'

'It's okay,' she said, her bottom lip quivering. 'I'm getting used to it. No one seems to want to help. Thanks anyway.'

Aurelia watched her walk away, upset on her behalf, and for the children. She couldn't understand how Gabe could turn his back on them when he hadn't hesitated to step up for her when she'd needed help.

And she wouldn't be able to live with herself if she didn't say something about it. Even if it cost her dearly.

She didn't bother knocking on the door again. Her rage dictated that she simply fling the door open to confront him. 'What on earth was that all about?'

Eyebrows raised, he looked at her over the top of his laptop. 'Excuse me?'

'We're talking about children who have nothing for Christmas. You should be able to relate to that.' It was below the belt, but this wasn't the time for subtlety or diplomacy. Louisa's gentle approach hadn't achieved anything so it was time for a different tact.

She knew she'd got his attention when his brow furrowed into a frown. 'That was personal information shared with you in my home. It's not something I expect to have thrown back at me when you don't get your own way. Unless you've forgotten, Ms Hughes, I'm still your boss. Here at least.'

He made it sound as though she was throwing a tantrum, though as she took stock of her folded arms, pursed lips stance, she supposed that was what it looked like. In the heat of the moment she'd forgotten herself, and how much he'd done for her personally when he really didn't have to. She unfolded her arms.

'I'm sorry. I shouldn't have said that. I just… I don't understand why you're so reluctant to help.' More than anything, she was disappointed to see this side of him when she'd taken him for a kind, generous man who cared about more than himself.

'It's store policy. My father didn't agree with charity.'

'And you're your father's son, right?' Aurelia braced her hands on his desk and leaned across it. Struggling so hard to contain her anger that she was practically vibrating.

'Nobody gets anything for free in this life. You have to work for it.' The way he said it, Gabe must have had those words drummed into him from an early age.

'What about me? You gave me a home for Christmas. Do I have to repay that? Have you been itemising everything I've used these past couple of days so you can invoice me at the end of my stay?'

Gabe tutted. 'Of course not.'

'Then how is this different? These children need something to get them through and are you really going to miss the price of a few toys from your pocket? I'm sure it's tax deductible anyway…'

'Why do you care, Aurelia? I'm sure I would've heard if you'd had this same argument with my father before.

This probably isn't the first time someone has come in with a begging bowl, so what made you think this time was different? Did you think that because I fell for your sob story I'm a pushover for every needy soul who comes looking for a handout?'

Aurelia blanched at the verbal punch to the gut. It was the first time he'd made her feel like that pathetic loser forced to sleep in the store because she'd lost everything. After the personal things they'd shared, she thought he'd come to see her as something other than a charity case. Apparently not.

'You're right. We turn people away every year. I wouldn't have dared face up to your father because I knew he wasn't a charitable man. I just thought you were different.'

The rage ebbed away until she was left with a sense of disappointment that almost made her want to weep. The insult she'd hoped to leave with him sounded more like a teary realisation she'd got him wrong. Yet again the Hughes curse had reared its ugly head to remind her she knew nothing about men.

She had to leave before she either cried, or said something else liable to get her fired or make her homeless again. If it wasn't already too late.

Gabe should have been mad at Aurelia's outburst, and for bringing someone to his office without an appointment. Initially, he had been. He didn't want her acting as though she got special treatment at the store simply because they were living together at present. That was one way the rest of the staff would be sure to notice that something was going on. Certainly his father wouldn't have stood for the unscheduled interruption, nor her unprofessional behaviour towards him personally, and she would have found herself on the end of an official warning. She was right about one thing, though, he wasn't his father.

On some level he actually respected the fact that she'd stood up to him for something she felt strongly about. In his position he was used to people giving in to his authority without ever voicing their own opinion, but he didn't want to be surrounded by sycophants. It was important to him that when it came to making these big decisions about the store's future, that he had all of the information at hand, not just the stuff people thought he wanted to hear.

His father had never wanted to listen to anyone else's voice but his own. Which is why he'd never changed the store, or his style of running it, in decades. Gabe didn't want to be the same. He wanted to be open to new ideas which could improve the store's fortunes if possible. If he decided to keep it as an ongoing interest. The alternative was simply bulldozing the place to make a quick sale and pocket the profits.

Although the emotional attachments he had towards the store were something he was simply going to have to deal with himself.

Aurelia was clearly passionate about the store helping these children, and he understood why. She probably knew what it was like to miss out on the toys her peers had. Although Gabe had never wanted for anything materialistic, he still had some experience of feeling neglected, left out of Christmas celebrations.

More than anything, he found himself wanting to make her happy. She'd had a rough time of it recently, and she'd told him herself that she appreciated his help. Aurelia had expected him to help these children. That was the kind of man she expected him to be, and that was the kind of man he wanted to be for her.

Perhaps he had been too hasty, rejecting the idea of helping because he'd been put on the spot and resorted back to his father's way of dealing with such matters. Before he'd had time to think things through clearly and realise the difference he could make for a few children at Christmas.

He did a search for the children's home contact details and hoped it wasn't too late for some damage limitation, and save his reputation with Aurelia as well. The more a plan formed in his mind of what he could offer to the children, the more excited he became. Discovering himself how good it felt to give something back to the community which had kept the store going all these years. Something his father had neglected to do, and giving him somewhere new to make his mark on the business.

This could be the start of a new charitable arm. If he could get the board to agree to it they could open up all sorts of avenues. Internships, sponsorships, and, of course, donations to good causes, should Delaney's live on. It would be down to him to convince everyone it was a good idea. Starting with Louisa Mallen and Aurelia.

'Hello, is that Louisa? This is Gabe Delaney, of Delaney's Department Store. You called in earlier, and after having some time to think about it, I'd like to help after all...'

Aurelia waited in the usual spot for Gabe to pick her up after work, though she was tempted to reject his offer of a lift and get the bus back. Except this wasn't some lover's tiff and she couldn't afford to get him offside in case he did throw her out on the street. As justifiably angry as she'd been that he'd refused to help the children's home, he was still her boss, and she had crossed the line today. She didn't want to inflame tensions any more. The best that she could hope for tonight was to go back to his place and disappear off to her room, and hopefully by the morning, tempers would have cooled down.

She didn't speak as she got into the car, not trusting herself to hold her tongue. He'd really let her down today, but she was annoyed at herself too that she'd got him so wrong. Clearly her radar was as bad as her mother's when it came to finding reliable men.

'I'm going to need you to pack a few things,' Gabe said eventually, failing to ease the tension in the car.

She should have seen it coming. It hadn't been a good move questioning his character and insulting him in front of Ms Mallen today. She had no one to blame but herself for outstaying her welcome already. Just because he'd opened up to her last night, it hadn't given her the right to speak to him the way she had this afternoon. Though she didn't regret a word she'd said.

'I understand,' she said, knowing there was no point in fighting his decision when she'd pushed him to it. Tried to take advantage of his generosity by getting involved with matters which didn't concern her. At the end of the day she was merely his employee, and he'd already been extremely charitable towards her.

She just didn't know where she was going to go now.

As they drove up the long driveway towards the house, that heaviness of uncertainty weighed on her shoulders. She hadn't realised how settled she'd felt in Gabe's home until she had to leave it. Especially when the Christmas lights twinkled their welcome inside.

'Is an hour enough time? Just grab your nightclothes and toiletries and I'll meet you back here. Do you need a sleeping bag?'

She'd really overestimated this man's character when he was being so calm about the fact he was throwing her out on the street in December. 'I might need a little longer to get all my things together. Thank you for letting me stay. I'm sorry it had to end this way.'

Aurelia turned to walk upstairs but he caught her by the wrist and spun her around to look at him again.

'What do you mean?'

'I'm sorry I made life so difficult for you at work that you feel the need to get rid of me, but you're perfectly within your right. You don't owe me anything.' It was the other way around and she'd never be able to pay him back for the kindness he'd shown her. She just wished it had extended to others who'd needed it, then she mightn't have found herself in this position so soon.

He frowned at her. 'Who said anything about getting rid of you? Didn't Louisa get in touch? She said she would call you to confirm details because I had to go and deal with all the paperwork and insurance palaver so this could go ahead. I suppose she was busy sorting out arrangements at her end...'

Aurelia held her hand up for him to stop. Her head buzzing with the snippets of information he'd given her, trying to piece them together. 'No one phoned to tell me anything, or at least I didn't get any messages through.'

It was possible that either one of the junior staff hadn't

remembered to pass on any messages, or they'd been so busy they hadn't heard or had time to answer the phone.

'Sorry…wait, did you think I was actually going to throw you out?' His half-smile was in contrast to his furrowed brow and she couldn't tell if he was angry or amused by the misunderstanding.

'Yes. I know I overstepped the mark today. You're my boss. I should've remembered my place. I have no right telling you how to run your business. Clearly you know what you're doing.' She had a cheek to give anyone advice when her life was a complete mess. Especially to someone who was one of life's successes.

He was definitely smiling now, and she put her little heart flutter down to relief that perhaps he wasn't going to make her homeless in the next hour.

'I like to think so, but on this occasion I'll admit to being wrong.'

'Pardon me?'

'I'm so used to doing everything the way my father did, I forgot who I was. What I want. And that's to help where I can.'

'So you're going to donate some toys to the home?' Aurelia was as happy for those children as she was for herself that Gabe wasn't going to let anyone feel abandoned again.

'I am, but I've also got something special planned for tonight. It was inspired by you actually?'

'Me?' She couldn't think what he possibly had in mind unless it was a tree decorating party.

'Remember that first night, when I found you sleeping in the store?'

'How could I forget? Not one of my finest moments.'

In fact, it had to have been one of the lowest points of her life. Knowing she'd lost everything she'd ever worked for and had to resort to sneaking into the store like a thief.

'Well, I'm hoping to turn it into something with happier connotations. Some of the children from the home are having a sleepover at the store. We're going to get takeaway, play some games and they can take a toy with them at the end.' The breadth of Gabe's smile made him look like an excited child himself. It was a lovely idea and such a turnaround from the conversation they'd had this afternoon, that Aurelia couldn't understand what had changed his mind.

Although, one other thing he'd mentioned had caught her attention. 'You said, "we."'

'Yes. There will be chaperones from the home for the children but I also need to make sure the store is protected. Plus, I thought it might be fun.' It was difficult to imagine this handsome businessman enjoying a sleepover on his own shop floor with a bunch of over-excited children, playing games, when up until yesterday he hadn't even wanted a Christmas tree on display.

'Fun? You?'

He pouted at that. 'We had fun last night, didn't we?'

The memory of sitting on the sofa sharing the pizza came to mind, along with that urge to kiss him, and she had to mentally shake it away. 'I suppose so.'

He rested his hands on her shoulders and she did her best not to react to feeling the warmth of his body on hers. 'Look, I know I wasn't exactly responsive to the idea today, but I had time to think. You're right, I'm not my father. It just takes me a moment to realise that sometimes. I can afford to let a few children enjoy themselves for one night.'

They both knew he could afford it, but this wasn't about money. It was about so much more. This said more about his character than his bank balance. Yes, she'd had to give him a nudge in the right direction, but he could easily have gone the other way. He could have doubled down and not only denied any donations to the home, but denied her entry to *his* home. That's exactly what she thought was happening, and thank goodness she'd got it wrong.

He'd completely surprised her with what he'd actually planned. Going above and beyond to give these children some happy memories. He didn't have to do that just to make her happy, and it was a sign he'd put genuine thought in how to make this a night to remember.

However, it also meant she was having a sleepover with Gabe too. Something which likely wasn't going to help get any inappropriate thoughts about her boss out of her head.

'I'm sure they'll be over the moon. So, er, what's the plan?'

'Like I said, grab your PJs and a toothbrush. I've never had a sleepover before.' Gabe bounded up the staircase ahead of her, clearly looking forward to the night ahead.

This was a completely different side to him. Every moment she spent with him, the more she could see the man behind the corporate suits and the stern Delaney façade. If she wasn't careful she might start to think he was someone worth sticking around for. Someone she could rely on.

All the more reason she should keep trying to find alternative accommodation, instead of accompanying him to sleepovers.

CHAPTER FIVE

'I'M PUTTING YOU in charge of games,' Gabe whispered, clearly intimidated by the group of hyped-up children looking at them expectantly.

'Not after you've filled them up with sugar and E numbers.' Aurelia tried to keep her focus on making this a night to remember for the children, and not Gabe in the cotton blue-and-white-striped pyjamas he'd insisted on stopping to buy before they got here. It had only made her wonder what he usually slept in, and why it wasn't appropriate for tonight. Boxers? Nothing?

Focus. This is the children's fantasy, not yours. She reminded herself.

'Well, what's a sleepover without junk food and ice cream?' Gabe was bouncing almost as much as their charges, after the spread he'd laid on in the home section of the store.

Louisa and some of the other staff from the care home had arrived en masse with the children, everyone dressed in their pyjamas and wide-eyed as they'd walked into the quiet store. Aurelia had to admit, she was having fun too, and this would have been a dream come true for her as a kid. Looking at Gabe, adorable in his stripy PJs, she felt as though she was in a dream now.

She was glad she had at least one pair of respectable pyjamas she'd been able to wear, which didn't have holes, or pictures of cartoon characters on them. Her button-down, navy silk nightwear had been a gift from her ex. The only reason she hadn't thrown them out along with everything else that reminded her of him was because she knew how expensive they'd been, and she was glad she'd held on to them now. She hadn't missed Gabe's eyes assessing her attire when she'd changed into them, or the nod of approval.

'What about a game of hide-and-seek?' Aurelia suggested to a round of enthusiastic cheers.

'As long as we keep it just on this floor, and everyone's very careful,' Louisa insisted. She had adopted the sensible adult role, whilst Aurelia and Gabe had thrown themselves into the mêlée with the same childlike enthusiasm as the kids they were entertaining.

They'd sat down at the staged dining room table with the other kids, eating burgers and fries, and generally making pigs of themselves. She couldn't remember the last time she'd felt so carefree. Remarkable, given her current personal circumstances.

But Gabe had been able to give her that. Not only had he provided her with somewhere to stay and peace of mind over the holidays, but he'd indulged her inner child, and in turn she thought he'd discovered his own. She never would have believed that the same man who'd inspected the staff like they were in a police line-up, only a few days ago, was now running around the store in his pyjamas.

'You're it!' Brian, one of the children who looked to be about nine years old, tipped Louisa and ran off giggling. The rest of the children followed suit.

'I guess that means I'm "it,"' Louisa sighed, then started counting. 'One, two, three…'

Aurelia and Gabe looked at each other, then took off running in different directions. The whole thing was absurd as everyone scattered, the little ones screaming with glee, and the adults trying to find a hiding place where they would fit.

'Four, five, six…'

Aurelia spotted a large wardrobe in the bedroom section and immediately jumped inside, pulling the door closed behind her. Her heart was already racing when the door opened again and Gabe appeared.

'Sorry. I didn't realise you were here, Aurelia.'

'Ready or not, here I come!' Louisa shouted to let them know time was running out.

'Get in, quick,' Aurelia said, grabbing Gabe's arm and pulling him inside the wardrobe with her.

It was only when they were both standing almost nose to nose and she could feel his hot breath on her skin, that she realised how big he was, and how little room there was inside the wardrobe.

'Hi,' he said, looking down at her with a little smile.

'Hi.' Aurelia couldn't believe how intimate this suddenly felt. They were playing a game of hide-and-seek for goodness' sake.

'What are we doing?' Gabe shook his head, and she could see he was trying to stifle a laugh.

'I can honestly say this is not where I saw myself two days ago.'

Never in her wildest dreams, when she was on the streets with her worldly belongings, did she think she'd end up hiding in a wardrobe with her boss. Nor did it ever cross her mind that there would be some sort of weird sexual tension crackling between them.

'I wonder what everyone at work would—' Before she could finish the sentence, Gabe placed a finger on her mouth to quiet her.

He pointed towards the door. Footsteps sounded past the door, followed by a happy squeal, and a, 'Gotcha!' Louisa had clearly uncovered someone's hiding place, only upping the tension of the moment.

Her heart was racing. Especially as his finger still lingered on her lips, and his eyes were locked on hers. As though there was more going on between them than the need to outwit their captor.

When the door was wrenched open, light flooding into their intense, dark surroundings, it came as a relief. These feelings she was having towards Gabe were unsettling, and she needed some space from him to get them under control.

'Gotcha!' Louisa, followed by the rest of the children she'd apparently already caught, was grinning back at them from the other side of the open door.

Aurelia held her hands up in surrender and stepped out, with Gabe coming out behind her.

'You were the last to be found, and now I think it's probably time we brushed our teeth and all got some sleep.' Louisa's decree was met with a cacophony of boos, and a lot of sad faces.

Although it was obvious everyone had been enjoying themselves so much they didn't want it to end, Aurelia didn't like the idea of anyone going to sleep unhappy. It soon became apparent that Gabe felt the same way.

'We have one last surprise for you here at Delaney's,'

he said, immediately grabbing everyone's attention. 'Follow me.'

He really seemed to be getting into the role of children's entertainer, and it made her wonder what he would have been like as a father. Gabe had unlocked that childlike enthusiasm his father had probably done his best to suppress, and Aurelia would happily encourage. She hoped this was a side of him he'd embrace more. Although it would probably be better for her if it wasn't around her. Then she wouldn't be thinking about what it would be like to have his babies.

Children and adults alike traipsed after him as though he was some kind of Pied Piper. He led them towards the toy department, causing a lot of excited chatter among the group.

'Before everyone goes to bed, I want you all to have a present. You can take one thing to keep.' Gabe's announcement brought a lot of gasps, happy smiles and wide eyes as the children scattered around the floor to pick out the gifts.

'That means you too,' he said to Aurelia, and the rest of the adults.

He was really enjoying being the benefactor, and Aurelia wondered if the store policy might be about to change.

'Are you sure you want to do this?' she asked, as Louisa and her colleagues joined the children on the floor.

Gabe shrugged. 'It's just a few toys, and it will make them happy.'

'As far as I can see, you've already done that.' Aurelia offered him a grateful smile on their behalf, knowing how much it would mean to them that someone cared enough to do this.

Though she did try to make a mental note of what everyone picked out, so she could mark it off their stock. This was her department after all.

'Thank you, Mr Delaney.' A little girl ran up and threw her arms around Gabe's legs, a soft squishy animal hanging from her hand.

'You're very welcome,' he replied, clearly quite touched by the gesture.

One by one, the children, and staff all came to offer their gratitude. Everyone wearing a great big smile, including Gabe.

'It looks as though everyone has chosen their gift,' Aurelia noted as the children filed past clutching art sets, board games and cuddly toys.

'Everyone except you,' he corrected her.

'I don't need anything. Besides, you've given me plenty already. As well as somewhere to stay, and a Christmas to look forward to, he'd also given her some very lovely memories to keep.

'Just a minute.' He disappeared back onto the floor, and came back carrying a huge, soft teddy bear. 'For you.'

'Gabe, you don't have to give me anything.'

'I want to,' he insisted, holding her gaze so she knew how important it was to him that everyone here tonight had something to remember it.

It was likely the only gift she would receive this year, and the thought spurred her to accept it.

'Thank you,' she said, snuggling into the bear, knowing she'd treasure it forever.

Gabe was on a high. The endorphins from sharing this night with the children and staff from the home, as well as Aurelia, were probably going to keep him awake until morning. Along with the fact he was sharing a bed with Aurelia. Well, he had the sleeping bag next to her on the floor.

He'd kitted everyone out with sleeping bags and pillows, and it was almost like camping out. Though it was warmer than being outside in December, with less chance of being bitten by midges.

He couldn't imagine his father ever doing anything like this, and he'd probably be turning in his grave at the amount of money this would cost. Regardless that Gabe could easily afford it. It was difficult to move away from his father's influence, but Aurelia's perspective was helping him to do just that. And experience the joys of simply being able to give.

It was making the future of Delaney's more complicated than ever. With the marketing boom and the need for accommodation in prime city centre location at an all-time high, it was obvious where the money lay. However, the store had been opening up so many new opportunities for him, his heart was telling him to keep it as an ongoing interest. He could make a difference to so many people here, but he knew if his father's genes won through, this would likely be the end of his altruistic tendencies.

It was hard to know what to do when he'd spent his whole life being told making money was the name of the game. That being rich was the only way he could be loved. Now he found that generosity was winning him a new legion of fans as well as giving him a buzz from doing the right thing, he was torn over his next move.

'I hope you enjoyed tonight too,' Aurelia whispered to him in the dark. He could see the glint in her eyes, and the soft glow of the fairy lights at least enabled him to see her smile, even though there was a massive teddy bear wedged between their bodies.

It had taken a while for everyone to settle down, and they'd turned the lights off in the end, just leaving the Christmas tree lights on so they weren't in complete darkness. But now the sound of gentle snores let him know exhaustion had claimed most of tonight's residents.

He and Aurelia were in a corner away from the rest of the group, letting Louisa and her colleagues stay with the young children for propriety's sake.

'I did. Thank you.'

'What are you thanking *me* for?' she laughed. 'You were the one who organised everything.'

'I would never have thought to do anything if you hadn't berated me in my office.'

She buried her face in her teddy's tummy and groaned. 'I'm so sorry about that. I just wanted to be able to help and it wasn't in my power to do so.'

'But it is in mine. I understand. In future, don't hesitate to come to me again. I will try and have an open mind as well as an open door.'

'And I will try to cool my temper in future,' she said, peeking out from her hiding place.

'No need. It's a novelty to have someone say what they think to my face. Usually people are too afraid.'

'Well, I didn't have much to lose, did I? Only my job, and somewhere to stay,' she joked, but he could tell she'd been worried that she'd risked everything by speaking her mind.

'It showed you were passionate about these children. I'm glad they had you to stand up for them, Aurelia.'

Gabe only wished that he and Aurelia had had someone to do the same for them when they'd needed support. Needed to be children.

'And you.' They were looking deep into one another's eyes, and Gabe felt something shift between them which went far beyond mutual respect.

'I suppose we should get some sleep,' he suggested, though he knew it was going to prove next to impossible when he was so aware of her next to him. Effectively sleeping together, albeit in separate sleeping bags, and on the store floor with a bunch of other people.

'Good night, Gabe,' she said, though her eyes were still open, watching him. Her face only millimetres from his.

'Good night, Aurelia.' His whispered voice was husky, and likely a sign of the way he was beginning to feel about her.

Not only was he attracted to her looks, but her kindness, and the passion with which she stood up for others as well as herself.

That realisation seemed to overwhelm him, short-circuiting his usual self-control. Before he knew what he was doing, he leaned in and kissed her softly on the lips. He watched her wide eyes flutter shut at his touch, and as much as he wanted to carry on kissing her, reality had already set in. Gabe pulled back and rolled onto his side, facing away from her. Every muscle in his body tense, aware of what he'd just done.

He thought it best not to acknowledge what had happened, and hoped she saw it as simply a friendly good-night kiss. Regardless that it felt much more than that.

He could almost feel her eyes boring into his back, questioning why he'd done it, but he couldn't tell her when the answer was simply because he'd wanted to. The only thing more disturbing than that, had been her response, and the knowledge that she'd wanted it just as much.

CHAPTER SIX

AURELIA WAS ZONED out from all the usual chatter in the store. Still trying to come to terms with the fact Gabe had kissed her last night, and what it meant.

'Earth to Aurelia.' Her colleague Suzy clicked her fingers, trying to bring her back to the present.

'Sorry. Did you say something?'

The older woman rolled her eyes. Suzy had been here for decades, though on a part-time basis. She knew everything there was to know about the store, and practically everyone who came through the doors. The ideal person to provide all of the local gossip, but also the worst person to catch her daydreaming about the boss.

'I said, apparently there was some kind of children's party here last night. The cleaners were saying about the mess they had to clean up this morning before opening. Someone said something about young Mr Delaney having a sleepover for residents of the local children's home, and letting them help themselves to toys.'

'Oh?' Aurelia played dumb. It was clear she was angling for more information, or confirmation of the rumours. Neither of which Aurelia was prepared to furnish her with. What had happened last night was private. Especially the bit when he gave her a good-night peck on the lips and her body responded as though it was a passionate embrace.

She'd been on fire the moment he touched her. Not ideal in the confines of a nylon sleeping bag, but she'd suffered in silence so he didn't think she was reading more into it. Even though she was.

Why had he done it? Would it have gone on longer if they hadn't been surrounded by other people? Why did she want him to do it again? Did he want to?

Well, she'd had one of those questions answered when their night together was over and they'd gone back to his house in virtual silence this morning to get ready for work, with no mention that it had ever happened. Obviously it had meant nothing more to him than a kiss good-night. It was her fault she couldn't wipe it from her memory, or her lips.

'I thought you might know more about it. Anyway, his father would never have dreamed of doing the like. He'd be turning in his grave.' Suzy folded her arms across her ample bosom, now in full flow.

'Surely, it's a nice thing for him to do?' Aurelia didn't see the problem with Gabe doing something completely uncharacteristic of the Delaney name.

'Yes. Of course. That's what I mean. Old Mr Delaney wouldn't give you a penny out of his pocket unless he had to. I'm hoping that means the store might mean more to him than the ground it sits on. Hopefully we'll still have jobs to come back to in the New Year after all.' Suzy turned away to serve her next customer at the till, leaving Aurelia to ponder her words.

Since getting to know Gabe better she would never have expected her position at Delaney's to be in jeopardy.

She desperately wanted to believe that he wouldn't see them all out of work but it seemed it was probably a common worry with her colleagues. The thought of losing her job on top of everything else made her feel sick. Whilst she was worrying over non-issues such as a good-night kiss, she should have been focusing on the real problem she might have to face.

Apart from anything else, once Christmas was over, she was going to be out on the streets. She'd been relying on Gabe too much to make her feel good, and it was about time she starting taking steps to protect her future herself. The problem was, she didn't know where to start. And there was a piece of her that still wanted Gabe to be a part of that future in some way.

As she was beginning to despair that she was getting back into old habits, she spotted Louisa walking into the department with one of the children from last night.

'Hello. Nice to see you both again,' she said, moving out from behind the counter to greet them.

'You too, Aurelia. We just wanted to come and say thank you for last night.'

'Well, it's Mr Delaney who organised everything, but I'll pass on the message.' She didn't want to disturb him again. Besides, some space might be good for her peace of mind right now.

'I made this for him.' The little girl who was holding Louisa's hand gave Aurelia a hand-drawn card with a picture of Gabe, and who she assumed was the little girl beside him, clutching the same blond-headed doll which was peeking out of her coat pocket.

'I will make sure he gets this right away. Thank you very much.' Aurelia knew he'd be touched by the gesture. Very like the one he'd made for his mother which had made him emotional and had very likely helped him to discover his inner child.

'All of the children wanted to show their gratitude. I can't tell you how much it meant to everyone.' Louisa opened up the bag over her shoulder and withdrew a stack of cards and drawings.

'I'm so glad everyone had a good time.' There wasn't anything else she could say when she was so choked with emotion that these children had been allowed to experience some Christmas magic at least once in their lives. All because of Gabe.

'Oh, we did. It was nice for the grown-ups to have some fun too. I'm looking forward to using the art set I got when I have some spare time.' That look of childlike wonder was still on Louisa's face from last night, and it made Aurelia think about the gift Gabe had given her too.

That ridiculous, huge teddy bear which made her feel all warm inside when she looked at it. It was a reminder that someone had thought about her. Cared enough to give her a moment's happiness. She traced her fingers over her lips. Well, two moments, she supposed.

'I hope you enjoy it. I'll let Mr Delaney know you called, and I'll leave these cards with him. Thanks for stopping by.' Aurelia waved the pair off, the little girl skipping away with her dolly in her hand.

Once she got someone to cover her place on the floor, she hurried towards the lift to share the news. She couldn't wait to tell him how much the evening had meant to everyone in the hope it would spur him to do more. Perhaps even make this a regular event for disadvantaged children. Something that would cement his place at the store, and hopefully the emotional investment would mean he would see more than pound signs when it came to any business decisions.

It hadn't escaped Gabe's notice that he was working out of his office in Delaney's more than anywhere else. He always had other projects on the go, other properties demanding his attention, but he'd started to feel more comfortable here. More so than when his father had been in charge here. He was beginning to realise a lot of that was down to Aurelia.

Before he'd met her, everything had seemed straightforward. It made financial business sense to shut Delaney's store for good, and develop the land into desirable luxury apartments in the city centre. Belfast was growing in popularity both with students and upwardly mobile twentysomethings. It would be easy to capitalise on that.

He'd always wondered why his father seemed to have an attachment to it when his sole purpose in life had been to increase his coffers. Perhaps he had channelled his love and attention into the store which should have been directed towards his only son.

The Delaney men weren't good at relationships. With good reason. Both had lost people they'd loved. Though he'd never really felt close to his father, Gabe was beginning to see that after losing his wife, he too had been afraid to show love and have his heart broken again too. The same reason Gabe was struggling with his attraction towards Aurelia.

On paper, it shouldn't be a problem. They were both single, and clearly had a lot in common, even though they were on opposite sides of the financial divide. If last night's kiss was anything to go by, the attraction was mutual too.

The problem was the other things they had in common: the store, and currently his home. Any dalliances he had with the opposite sex tended to be casual and short-lived. Current circumstances made that impossible. All he could really hope for at the minute was that this chemistry between them would burn itself out soon. He had some business meetings abroad in the next few months, with one planned in Finland the next day. Perhaps some distance would put things into perspective and he'd realise that all the sentimentality she'd unlocked in the house was making him over-emotional. The very reason he was acting so out of character.

There was a knock on the door and he focused his attention back on his laptop to give the impression his mind was where it was supposed to be. On business, and making money. Making his father proud, and building on the Delaney name. Literally.

'Come in,' he shouted, and waited to see who, or what, was demanding his attention.

'Sorry to bother you. Are you busy?' When Aurelia poked her head around the door he couldn't help but smile. He was always happy to see her, even if last night had made things a little awkward between them. He'd decided not to address the fact he'd kissed her, and since she hadn't mentioned it, he hoped they were both able to forget it ever happened. Or at least pass it off as a simple good-night kiss that shouldn't warrant the time he was spending thinking about it.

'Nothing that can't wait. What can I do for you?' He

knew she wouldn't have ventured up here without good reason.

'Louisa and one of the children from the home stopped by to say thank you for last night. I didn't want to bring them up and put you on the spot in case you were too busy, but they left these for you. Some of the children wanted to express their gratitude. It's rather sweet.' She set a stack of papers on his desk.

Gabe rifled through them and soon realised it was a pile of thank you cards and drawings the children had made for him. He had to swallow the lump of emotion suddenly forming in his throat. 'That's...that's so nice of them to take the time to do that for me.'

Though he felt guilty he was the one getting all the love when Aurelia had been instrumental in him helping at all.

'They all wanted to do something for you in return for the lovely night everyone had. In fact, I think you deserve a treat too. Let me take you out for a coffee and something sweet when you have time.'

'You don't need to do that. Save your money.'

'It's okay. I have accrued a considerable amount of loyalty points over the year. I usually save them for hot chocolates and mince pies, so you're welcome to join me.'

'Sounds good.' It was an innocuous enough offer that he knew she was moved to do now that the children had shown their appreciation.

'Just let me know the next time you're free and I'll shout you.' She looked so chuffed with herself that she was able to do something for him, Gabe knew he had to accept.

'I'm free now, if you are?' It wasn't as though his mind

was on the job at the minute anyway. A time out might help him refocus.

Aurelia checked her watch. 'I finish in an hour, if you can wait that long?'

'Sure. I'll meet you in the usual place.' It would give him a chance to make some arrangements for his trip so he'd done something productive for the day.

'No need. It's just around the corner. We can walk there.' She paused, a look of uncertainty crossing her face. 'Unless you'd rather people didn't see us together.'

He hadn't thought about that, but it was different having a coffee with an employee, than people knowing they'd had a sleepover in the store. Besides, he didn't want to hurt her feelings when she was trying to do something nice for him. Given her current circumstances he understood there wasn't a lot of opportunity for her to do much for anyone else.

'Of course not. I'll meet you downstairs in an hour.' This was going to be a real step out of his comfort zone, for numerous reasons, but in the end it all came down to one thing: He wanted to make Aurelia happy.

'I'll see you tomorrow,' Aurelia called, as she went to grab her bag and coat to make a hasty exit.

Although she would have been grateful for the extra money from a longer shift, she was glad of the opportunity to duck out early for a festive cuppa in Gabe's company. It was something new and exciting to go somewhere with him outside of work, even though it was only for a thank-you coffee. The least she could do when he'd given her so much.

Still, the fact that he'd agreed to it had made her

pleased to think she was giving something back. She'd seen how happy those simple cards from the children had made him and found herself wanting to contribute to that feeling for him too. Given that he seemed unperturbed by the thought of anyone seeing them together also solidified the notion that she'd read way too much into that good-night kiss. If it had been anything more he either would have pursued it, or wanted some space from her. It turned out to have been no big deal to him at all. Perhaps she needed to get out more when any attention from the opposite sex was making her pine for more.

She rushed out the door past the security guard, trying to get out before anyone could stop her to talk. Only to rush head first into a solid male chest.

'You're keen.' Even if she hadn't recognised Gabe's voice, she'd come to know the very shape of his body. The way his broad shoulders tapered to a V at his waist. She knew the smell of his cologne. A fresh citrus scent with accents of spice which seemed tailor-made for him.

And now she realised she knew way too much about him. Had been paying more attention than she knew.

'Sorry.' She stood back, blinking up at his smiling face. A welcome sight in the late winter afternoon gloom. 'I didn't want to have you standing out here waiting for me.'

Really, she didn't want him to know how keen she'd been to finish those last dragging moments of her shift so she could get out and see him. It wasn't just because they'd shared a kiss, that he was easy on the eye or the fact that he was the only thing keeping her from living rough on the streets at present. She enjoyed his company. And there was an ease between them that made her feel comfortable in his presence, regardless that he was her boss.

'Shall we?' He stood back and motioned for her to walk on ahead of him. Making her suddenly conscious of him watching her.

The rain started to fall heavily then and they ended up having to make a run for it towards the coffee shop, only stopping once they had shelter in the doorway. Both laughing as they shook the rain from their hair.

Aurelia couldn't help but notice his wet, white shirt was clinging to his chest, inadvertently showing off his muscular build. She gulped, trying to swallow down the sudden swell of yearning.

This was supposed to be her chance to thank him for being so charitable to her and the children from the home. Not an opportunity to ogle him some more.

'Coffee?' She pushed the door open, strangely eager to get into the bustling coffee shop. She hoped the crowd inside would distract her from her companion's entry into the best wet shirt competition.

'Er, I think I was promised a hot chocolate and a mince pie.' He pointed towards the glass display case where the sweets were waiting.

'Of course.' She flashed the app on her phone which was enabling her to provide the holiday treats for free.

The team of efficient baristas set to work immediately on their order whilst they waited at the end of the counter. Eventually they were presented with two tall glass mugs topped with copious amounts of cream and marshmallows. It was definitely decadent, and Aurelia was happy Gabe seemed to have a sweet tooth just like hers.

'Wow. You really are spoiling me,' he said, carrying the tray carefully across the coffee shop floor.

'I reckon you're worth it.' She spotted a couple just leaving the table in the corner and quickly cleared away the cups they'd left behind, so she and Gabe could sit down.

'I can't remember the last time I had one of these. Probably when my mother was still alive. Father would've been disgusted at the very sight.'

Gabe held up his hot chocolate and took a sip, coating his top lip with cream, and completely going against type. This wasn't the stuffy, uptight boss she'd mistaken him for on first impressions.

Aurelia reckoned up until she'd crashed into his life he would never have even thought to take a coffee break with an employee, never mind being seen as anything other than immaculate in public. His father had always been neatly groomed, without a speck of dust to sully him. Then again, he'd never appeared much fun to be around. Unlike his son, whom she couldn't seem to get enough of.

'This was one thing my mum was good at. Although she made her own.' Aurelia supposed she and Gabe had been deprived in different ways. The simple, everyday things she'd taken for granted, were likely the moments he would have preferred to have with his father instead of building up an empire. She, on the other hand, had longed for a bricks and mortar home to call her own. Perhaps their ease together came from finally having those needs met in one another. Even for a little while.

She had to remember not to get too comfortable though, because it would all be over in just a matter of days, and if she wasn't careful leaving Gabe's house was going to exacerbate those wounds she was already carrying.

Aurelia took a sip of her hot chocolate, trying not to end up covered in cream, and failing.

'You've got a little something on your lip.' Before she realised what was happening, Gabe reached over and brushed the cream from her top lip with his thumb. There was something in that move that electrified her. The soft touch instantly bringing memories of his lips being there only last night. She knew he felt it too as their eyes locked and neither seemed able to look away.

'Oh, I see why you haven't been too worried about keeping your job.' The loud accusation jerked them both out of their daze to find Suzy staring at them, arms folded and lips pursed.

'What? No. What are you talking about?' Aurelia was flustered as she jerked away from Gabe's touch.

'In bed with the boss, are you? That's one way to keep him onside.' Suzy's allegation brought a picture of lying next to Gabe on the store floor to Aurelia's mind, along with that kiss, making her blush. Doing nothing to help her refute the charge.

Gabe got to his feet, looking as angry as she was embarrassed by the confrontation. 'I think you should be careful about what you're implying, Ms Daley. Miss Hughes and I are simply having our coffee break. Not that we have to justify ourselves to you. As head of her department, Miss Hughes and I have some decisions to make on its future. In fact, we have a business meeting in Finland tomorrow and we were discussing who should be temporarily promoted in her absence. If you're hoping to be in the running, I suggest you walk away now.'

He was cool and calm, at least on the exterior. Aurelia could see his hands clench and release as he fought to restrain himself from saying anything else. Although it was all lies to cover the fact that they'd been seen together, and Suzy was jumping to the wrong conclusion, his words had the desired effect.

Suzy simply nodded, a red flush spreading up her neck and into her cheeks. 'Apologies if I got it wrong. I would of course like to be considered for any extra hours of responsibility in your absence, Aurelia.'

'Okay,' Aurelia managed to utter. Enough to make Suzy exit the coffee shop altogether.

Gabe sat down again, and Aurelia felt as though she was melting into her chair, the tension exiting her body after the confrontation and leaving her exhausted.

'Sorry about that,' he said, then continued to drink his hot drink and take a bite of his mince pie as though nothing had happened.

'I shouldn't have put you in this position. I'm the one who should be sorry.' She should have known this would backfire. In hindsight, this had been inevitable when they were spending so much time together. It would be all around the store by tomorrow morning that she and Gabe were an item, and just wait until they found out she was living with him. Ugh. The only thing she dreaded more than the gossip mill getting things wrong, would be having to explain what had actually happened—that she was homeless and living on his charity.

Gabe reached across the table and took her hand. Sending a tingle of electricity across her skin. 'Hey. You haven't done anything wrong. Neither have I. Don't let her spoil this.'

He took another drink, making sure his mouth and chin were covered in cream, assuring her smile in return. When he was able to forget who he was to everyone else around him, he was quite disarming.

'You're such an eejit,' she said, handing him a napkin and trying not to make any further body contact liable to get them into more trouble.

'Words I'm sure you never thought you'd be saying to your boss.' Gabe grinned as he wiped his face.

'I know. Sorry.' Apparently she did need constant reminding of that fact.

'Stop saying sorry.'

'But I am sorry. If I hadn't suggested this, Suzy would never have seen us together, and you wouldn't have had to make up those lies so she wouldn't get the wrong idea.' Aurelia sighed. It was all such a convoluted mess to cover up the mistakes she had made in her personal life.

'Lies? What lies? I do have a meeting in Finland tomorrow as it happens, and I could use your input.'

'Seriously?'

'I'm always serious when it comes to business. It also happens to be close to Lapland. Home of Santa Claus, and I thought perhaps you might like to visit.' He finished his mince pie, as though he hadn't just made all of her Christmas dreams come true.

When she was a little girl she'd always wanted to go to Lapland, to see Santa and the elves, and play in the snow. Now, as an adult, she still wanted the magic, and couldn't believe Gabe was simply handing it to her.

'You don't have to do that.' It occurred to her that he hadn't mentioned this trip until Suzy had put them on the spot and he'd needed some way to get her to back off.

The likelihood was that he'd had no intention of bringing Aurelia along at all.

'I'm not doing anything. I have a business trip, you are head of the toy department, and there's a place available if you want it.' He shrugged as though it was no big deal and that she was trying to read more into it.

For once she just wanted to throw caution to the wind. She didn't have anything to lose, but everything to gain. For a little while she could forget all of her troubles here and simply indulge her inner child a little more. It would be fun to see Gabe in that environment too. She could just imagine him sitting on Santa's lap, telling him what a good boy he'd been.

'If you're sure you don't mind me tagging along, I'd love to go with you. I don't know how I can pay you back though.' She may as well be upfront when she couldn't offer any sort of payment or contribution to her stay.

Gabe waved away her concern. 'It's all paid for. I'll simply add you on. I'll just need to cover your flights but it's a work trip so just call it a perk.'

Aurelia knew he was only saying that so she didn't feel bad. He might be working, but it had been a spur-of-the-moment decision to add her into the mix. 'A work trip how?'

Gabe sighed. 'Aurelia, you don't make it easy for people to help you.'

'It has been said...' She liked her independence and it had taken her a long time to trust her ex. Look where that had got her. These days she was learning to look out for herself. Even if she'd been relying on Gabe a little too much recently.

'It's Christmas, you work in Toys... I'm sure you can

get some inspiration for a Christmas display, or get some sort of exclusive deal with the elves or something.' He was being facetious but if she was going on this trip, Aurelia wanted to get something from it other than a longing to be a child again herself. She needed to prove herself not only to Suzy and her other colleagues, but to Gabe too.

'I have your permission for that?' She would love to have some real input into the store to bring in more customers and put Delaney's on the map. It was the sort of responsibility, and faith in her, that could really give her an ego boost when she needed it most. Not least because it suggested an investment in the future of the store. An idea that perhaps Gabe was leaning towards saving her job along with all the others in keeping the store going for a while longer.

It felt like a huge responsibility to not let him down, but also to come up with some money-making ideas to convince him the store was a viable future prospect. Her future, along with everyone else's, might be safe if she could prove her worth on this trip.

'You don't need my permission, Ms Hughes. I trust you.' Those pale blue eyes trained on her made her gulp. She knew what a big step it was for him when he was the kind of man who liked to take charge, and she didn't want to let him, or her colleagues, down.

Going away with him brought a sense of excitement and anticipation she didn't want to analyse too closely in case it was about more than making her mark on the store.

CHAPTER SEVEN

OKAY, SO GABE'S plan to put some distance between him and Aurelia by going to Finland hadn't quite worked out. Mainly because she'd ended up accompanying him.

He'd tried to tell himself it was a knee-jerk reaction to being caught in the coffee shop with her in an intimate moment, and trying to cover his tracks. Deep down he knew she was always going to go on this trip with him, because he knew how much she'd enjoy it.

To him it was simply a business trip overseas, but it represented so much more to someone like Aurelia, who was very much in touch with her inner child.

They'd both experienced a certain kind of neglect growing up, and each had dealt with that very differently. Where he'd learned to try and ignore Christmas was even happening, Aurelia had fully embraced the season and everything that went with it. That very much included the idea that Santa Claus could be real. What better way to treat her than to take her to the home of the man himself?

As long as he remembered things between them couldn't go any further, that this was supposed to be a business trip, he couldn't see the harm in letting her enjoy the magic.

The flight alone had proved that. It had been full of excited children and families. Like Christmas Eve in the air. With no escape. Although he'd reluctantly admit to being amused by Aurelia singing along with the Christmas songs being belted out by the children. He'd even let her put a set of flashing antlers on his head when she'd insisted he try and get into the Christmas spirit with her. Of course, whilst he was dressed in his suit for his meeting, Aurelia had donned a very fetching ugly Christmas sweater. Although, on her it looked nothing but adorable.

It was unfortunate they'd had to cover up with snowsuits and layers of clothing more suitable for the minustwenty-degree temperature.

He'd had to leave her in the lobby of the hotel where he was meeting potential investors for a chain of international hotels he'd been planning. Despite the importance of the meeting, his thoughts were very much with Aurelia and his plans for his time with her. He'd been relieved when everything was done and dusted and after shaking hands, he was free to return to her.

Gabe wanted to put on that ridiculous snowman suit and get out into the snow to have fun with her. Something he hadn't known he was even capable of doing until Aurelia had come into his life.

He found her where he'd left her, in the lobby, drinking hot chocolate with her cosy Christmas romance she'd been reading. When she saw him her face lit up with a smile, and he felt the warmth of it right down to his bones.

'Hey. Sorry to keep you so long.'

'That's okay. It's not often I get some downtime to simply enjoy the quiet and read.' She packed her book into her bag and finished her drink.

'So, what's next, Boss?' she asked as she got to her feet.

'Checking in to our accommodation before it gets dark.' He'd phoned ahead for a taxi to take them to their resort, and he was hoping Aurelia was going to love it. 'There's out transport now.'

The minivan pulled up outside the hotel and he loaded their luggage into the boot before jumping into the back seat with Aurelia.

'Why didn't we just stay here? It seemed nice enough.' She looked back at the luxury hotel with longing and Gabe hoped he hadn't got things wrong with the plans he'd made for them.

'I'm sure it's perfectly fine, but I thought we should do something special. It's not every day you get to visit the Arctic Circle.' He'd booked the place on a whim after seeing all the rave reviews saying it was the perfect place to stay.

Aurelia smiled, though she looked a little disappointed. 'I'm happy to go wherever you have planned. This is supposed to be a business trip after all, it's not a holiday.'

'I'm hoping it can be both. I think we could do with some time away from everything going on back home.' Between his grief and the decisions he was facing over Delaney's, and Aurelia's financial and relationship problems, an escape was much-needed. Even just for a little while.

Aurelia sighed and leaned against the window, watching the snowy landscape as they passed. Even Gabe had to admit it was pretty. The snow-tipped forest and clean, untouched marshmallow surround were peaceful and inviting, despite the cold.

The most pleasing sight however was the wonder on

Aurelia's face as she took it all in. Her forehead pressed against the glass so she didn't miss a second of the sights. It only made him more excited about their accommodation and how much she was going to love it.

'What on earth is this?' Her eyes were wide as they drove into the resort, pulling up outside their glass apartment.

He'd looked into the glass igloos which seemed so popular for tourists to enjoy the dark skies at night, but he figured they would be too compact, too intimate for their purposes. Instead, he'd opted for the stylish studio-style, self-catering apartment, which featured a full length glass front and roof. The building was kind of shaped like a tepee, supposedly influenced by the indigenous Sami people of Lapland.

'I thought it would give us the best views. We might even get to see the northern lights if we're lucky.' It was such a departure from his usual trips, and he attributed that entirely to his determination to please his travel partner. Normally, he was straight onto the next flight available after an overseas business meeting, never taking the time to do any sightseeing. The most he ever saw was the inside of the closest hotel to the airport. This trip was definitely different.

He found himself wanting to explore not only the country he was visiting, but a different side to him too. The side he hadn't known existed until Aurelia helped him uncover it. The part of him his father had never encouraged, or loved.

He helped her out of the van along with her luggage as she seemed hypnotised by the sight before her. 'It's amazing, Gabe. Magical.'

'Wait until it gets dark,' their driver/guide commented, beckoning them inside the accommodation.

He gave them a quick tour. Leaving Gabe and Aurelia both open-mouthed. 'This is the kitchen area, the living room, and upstairs we have the bedroom. There's a glass ceiling so you can see the skies.'

'Er, there's only one bed,' Aurelia noted as she walked in, flicking her gaze at Gabe.

'It's a king-size. We don't do singles. Although, if you'd like to upgrade to our family accommodation, I'm sure there will be enough rooms for you to sleep separately.' Their guide couldn't hide the smirk on his face. Looking at Gabe as though he'd tried to finagle this trip so he and Aurelia would have to sleep together. He didn't want her to think the same thing.

'That won't be necessary. I'm happy to sleep downstairs. It's likely I'll be making some international calls late into the night anyway.' That seemed sufficient for Aurelia to relax, knowing that he wasn't planning some great power play seduction, as well as wiping the grin off the guide's face.

He led them back downstairs in a hurry. 'Okay, so outside you have your own hot tub and sauna and there's a restaurant up in the main building. Any questions?'

'No. I think we'll be happy enough for the night. What do you think, Aurelia? Will this do?'

'Yeah. I think we could rough it here for one night.' Her grin matched his.

'Good. If you need anything, just contact us at the main building.' The young man clapped his hands together as if to signal his time with them was done and they were now on their own. It suited Gabe.

'You don't think perhaps this was a little over the top for a business trip?' Aurelia went and stood at the front window, which had a clear view of the snowy landscape around them.

Gabe shrugged. 'I thought it was a once-in-a-lifetime thing you wouldn't want to miss.'

Without any prior warning, Aurelia threw her arms around him and kissed his cheek. 'Thank you.'

'You're welcome.' His cheeks were burning from where her lips had touched his skin and he moved away to take another tour of the apartment and steal a moment to compose himself again.

It was a sleek, modern space with a fully incorporated kitchen on the ground floor, along with a comfortable sofa and huge wall-mounted television in the living area. Though why anyone would need that when they had such a beautiful view, he had no idea. The sofa was large and comfortable-looking, and he'd be happy to sleep there in this instance to let Aurelia enjoy the full dark sky experience herself.

He opened the door and walked out to the hot tub, fluffy white robes and towels provided next to it.

'I wondered why you'd told me to bring my bathing suit, but I just figured it was in case I wanted to use the hotel's indoor amenities. I had no idea this was what you'd planned.' Aurelia appeared beside him and pushed the button on the Jacuzzi to start the bubbles.

'Well, they do tell you to embrace the local culture and I think they like their hot tubs and saunas out here.'

'I think they like their ice baths too. Are you up for that?'

Gabe grimaced at the very thought. 'The purpose of

this place is to enjoy the stay. Not to endure torture. Now, what do you want to do this afternoon? They have all sorts of activities to take part in.'

He handed her the leaflet their guide had left on the kitchen worktop listing everything available to them on-site.

'Ooh. Can we take the sleigh ride down into the Christmas Village? That sounds like fun.' Aurelia's eyes lit up, and it was easy to see how she would have looked as a child on Christmas morning, when the smallest thing made her so happy. It was an intoxicating feeling knowing he had the power to do that. To make someone light up from the inside out, when Gabe felt as though he'd spent his whole life trying to elicit the same response from his father and failing.

'Sure. Though you'll have to make sure you've got plenty of layers on. There will be no central heating on that trip.' It was a different experience being driven through the snow in a warm, enclosed vehicle, than the cold reality that awaited on an open sleigh. But it did leave opportunities for them to cuddle up together for warmth…

An idea that Gabe had to chastise himself for even thinking about, considering Aurelia's worry over the fact he'd accidentally booked them into couple's accommodation. Subconsciously, or not.

Aurelia was beside herself with excitement. She couldn't believe everything Gabe had done to make sure she had a wonderful time, and she was doing her best not to analyse it too closely. He was simply a generous man deep down as he'd already proved with the children from the home. She was simply just another in need of his charity and he'd gone all out to make sure she had a memorable Christmas.

By the time they'd both layered up in their brightly coloured snowsuits, gloves and mittens to protect them from the cold, all evidence of Mr Delaney the businessman had disappeared. Now he just looked like any other tourist here in Finland to have some fun in the snow. Something dangerous in itself, but she wasn't about to get too caught up in that and lose out on this trip of a lifetime.

'I've never felt cold like it.' As she stepped onto the sleigh next to him, she swore her very eyelashes were freezing over, along with every other part of her that wasn't covered.

'Now we know why there's a hot tub provided. It's to thaw us out at the end of the day.' He pulled up the blankets which had been provided for their comfort, making sure she was as cosy as she could be in the freezing temperatures.

The hot tub had been a surprise, along with every other aspect of the accommodation he'd booked. Initially, she'd been concerned about the prospect of changing into a bathing suit and climbing into the hot tub with him, but now she was looking forward to it. Only to get warm again, of course. It wasn't as though she was looking forward to seeing him in a lot fewer layers...

It hadn't helped seeing that huge bed and briefly thinking for a moment that he'd expected to share it with her. The way she was feeling lately, she couldn't be sure she would have objected. A night with Gabe, away from everything, underneath the stars was a temptation it would be difficult to resist.

Aurelia tried to shake away the image she was conjuring in her mind but it wasn't easy snuggled up so close to him she could smell his now familiar aftershave. This whole trip really was a dream come true and she had to pinch herself as they slid across the icy plains pulled by reindeer which looked as though they'd walked off a Christmas film set. Even the driver of the sleigh, in colourful traditional dress, made the whole experience special. Though Aurelia was glad it was a short journey, and the sights and sounds of the nearby village let them know it had come to an end. It meant they could get inside and warm themselves for a little while.

They thanked their driver and trekked their way through the snow towards the gift shop, making sure to stomp off the excess snow from their boots at the entrance. She wished she wasn't so strapped for cash and she could really go to town buying souvenirs of such a lovely trip. Things she could bring out every year to remind her of this time with Gabe. Ornaments, baubles, soft toys and ceramics, all stamped with the name of the town to be treasured forever. All she could do was look and sigh. Though when Gabe disappeared into an adjacent store to buy himself a leather belt, she took the opportunity to purchase a small gift for him. A small glass igloo complete with a tiny penguin ice-fishing outside.

A silly trinket which would hopefully make him smile, and show her appreciation in some small fashion.

She waited impatiently for the cashier to wrap it up in tissue paper, then shoved it in her pocket. Just in time before Gabe came back to meet her.

'Where's all the unnecessary tat? I expected you to

have bags of Christmas decorations to take home,' he said, frowning at her.

'I'm trying to be financially responsible. You should be thankful I'm not frittering away this month's wages, and having to outstay my welcome even longer.' That thought which had been hovering close to the surface suddenly burst through, reminding her that she would soon have to move out of Gabe's house. She would be back to standing on her own two feet. And that was what she wanted, wasn't it?

His lips tightened into a thin line, although he disapproved, but thought better of saying something. Maybe she'd already outstayed her welcome and this trip had been his way of saying goodbye.

The thought caused her stomach to plummet, even though it was inevitable. He'd baled her out for Christmas and she should be thankful for everything he'd done for her, not expect more.

'The post office is across the way. I thought you might like to pay a visit before we head back.' He pointed over to the log cabin with Santa's Post Office proudly displayed in red letters across the signage.

Aurelia knew it was primarily for children to post their Christmas lists to the man himself, but she couldn't resist. 'Yes, please.'

She hadn't expected the noise and colour that waited beyond the doors. Rosy-cheeked elves dressed in green tunics and stripy red-and-white socks were helping the young visitors colour and glitter to their hearts' content, whilst some of the older children were posting cards back home.

Aurelia selected a picture postcard of the snowy landscape, complete with full-sized snowmen, and scrawled Gabe's address on the back. 'A little souvenir of the trip.'

She handed it over to one of Santa's helpers behind the counter who stamped it and let her post it in the postbox herself. Gabe didn't take part himself, but the fact he'd waited whilst she did, let her know he was willing to indulge her. She didn't know many men who would. Her ex certainly wouldn't have had the patience, and Gabe was surprising her every day.

'You know, we could put something like this in the toy department. I know it's nearly Christmas, but it's something we could do every year in the future. It could become a feature.'

As she was putting the idea to Gabe, she could just imagine a little postbox set up for visiting children to post their wish list every year. She'd love to be the one overseeing it, and could even send a reply to make it even more special. As long as there was still a store for her to be working in.

'It's your department, Aurelia. I'm sure you could make it work.'

She wanted to believe that this was a sign that he hadn't given up on the idea of the store continuing. That the longer he spent immersed in the business, with his employees, and perhaps even with her, he would see there was more to life than making money. If she could do one small thing to convince him the store was worth saving, it would make her feel as though she hadn't simply blagged a free holiday. That it was a business trip, not the romantic fantasy which she was gradually getting caught up in.

'You're very quiet,' Gabe commented as they made their way back to their accommodation.

'It's been a long day.' It was the truth, though she was enjoying it and wasn't ready for it to be over.

'Why don't we make something to eat and relax for the rest of the evening. We can slob out at the apartment instead of getting dressed up to go to the restaurant again.' Although Gabe's suggestion meant they'd be alone for the remainder of the night, taking it easy and enjoying the comforts provided was very tempting.

'Sounds good. Though I have to tell you, I'm not really an haute cuisine chef. My specialty is a spag bol.' Aurelia didn't know what food was provided but she was pretty sure it would be fresh, and Gabe was used to fine dining.

'As good as that sounds, maybe some other time. I think we have a barbecue and I am quite the master at that, if I do say so myself.' He let them back into the apartment and both stripped off their outer layers at the door.

'A barbecue? In the snow?'

'Why not?'

'Um, because it's freezing outside.'

'And here I thought you were the adventurous type, Aurelia. I've already asked for the kitchen to be stocked with food, so I'm sure there's something I can cook for us. I tell you what, whilst I'm slaving away over the barbecue, why don't you relax in the hot tub?'

'Are you sure you don't mind? That sounds heavenly.' The cold in her bones was aching for a little warm relief.

'Of course. You go and get changed and I'll get set up for dinner.'

She put up a feeble protest, which Gabe quickly shot down, insisting that she should relax. So, Aurelia rushed to unpack her bag upstairs and quickly donned her swimsuit. Making sure to cover herself with the complimentary robe and slippers before returning back outside.

Gabe was turning some sizzling chicken breasts and salmon fillets on the barbecue, humming to himself when she appeared on the deck which was protected from the snow by a small canopy.

'The food shouldn't be long,' he said, politely turning his back as she disrobed and stepped into the tub.

'Would you like me to get anything, or set the table?' she asked, though she was already leaning back and sinking into the blissful bubbles. The revitalising warmth welcome in the midst of the frozen tundra.

It was surreal watching Gabe barbecue in his winter woollies, with snow drifts all around whilst she was luxuriating in a hot tub, but it was also amazing.

'Not at all. You stay where you are.' At Gabe's insistence, she let him carry on, and closed her eyes, giving herself into the moment.

She only opened them again when she felt a nudge against her arm and found Gabe beside her, handing her a glass of champagne.

'Cheers,' he said, raising his glass to her.

'Cheers.' The more special he was making this trip for her, Aurelia knew the harder it was going to be getting back to reality. This sort of thing might be the norm for him, luxury travel abroad and enjoying the good life, but she didn't want to get too used to it. In another week or so she was going to be back on the street if she didn't find somewhere else to stay soon.

Apart from all of the wonderful experiences she was having here, simply having someone taking care of her the way he had was more than she could have ever expected. In fact, it had been an age since anyone had done that for her. Taking her feelings and comfort into consideration instead of just focusing on his own, the way her ex and her mother had always done. That sense of having someone in her life that she could depend on, who was looking out for her, was something she was going to find hard to let go. But she was going to have to. That ended with their deal once Christmas was over.

She didn't know how on earth she was ever going to get back to simply being his anonymous employee, as though none of this had ever happened. As though Gabe had never been such a wonderful part of her life. All of these memories they were creating packed away with the Christmas decorations, only to be brought out if she was feeling especially sentimental.

Somehow, he'd managed to turn the worst time of her life into the best, and that's what scared her. That she wouldn't want to leave him behind, and wouldn't be able to get back to her real life. The transition was going to hurt like hell, but she had to thank him for helping her temporarily forget the dire circumstances her ex had left her in.

As always, that sense that she was leaving herself vulnerable, simply by letting him be part of her life, made her want to push him away. To protect herself, and likely her heart too. She knew she was coming to like him more with every passing moment and act of generosity.

He wasn't just her boss, or a good Samaritan. Gabe was becoming the sort of man she wished she'd met instead of her ex. The man she had let into her life, only for him to ruin it. The very opposite to how Gabe had acted. Perhaps if she'd met him first, things might have been different.

She almost choked on her champagne at that ridiculous notion. As if he saw her as anything other than someone to be pitied.

'Food's ready, if you don't mind eating out here? We have an outdoor heater. Or, you know, I can just serve you where you are.' He was grinning as he teased her and it obviously hadn't gone unnoticed how easily she was adapting to his lifestyle. By either of them.

Aurelia narrowed her eyes at him. 'I wouldn't want to put you out any more than I already have.'

She grabbed a towel to wrap around her body as she stepped out of the tub, tucking it to make it into an ad hoc strapless dress, then donned and belted the robe. Whilst she'd been lounging in the water, he'd been busy. The picnic table was laden with salad and freshly barbecued chicken and salmon. It looked and smelled divine.

'I can't remember the last time I cooked for anyone else.' He topped up her champagne, and poured himself another glass.

There was something strangely thrilling in his comment. Even though she knew these were unusual circumstances, and he was not cooking for her in the same way he might make a romantic meal for a love interest. She wanted to think he was doing this because he thought of her as someone special. The way she was beginning to think of him.

'You probably don't need to when you have minions to do that sort of thing for you,' she teased, as she tucked into the tasty meal he'd made specially for her. Feeling a little smug that she was receiving special treatment which would certainly upset more than a few people back home if they knew.

A memory of a bitter Suzy confronting them in the coffee shop came to mind, but she didn't want to let anything spoil this time. That jolt back down to earth would come quick enough.

'Yes, next time I'll make sure to pack a couple so I can lounge around in the hot tub with you.' He attacked a chicken wing with gusto, his words yet again proving sufficient to get Aurelia's blood pumping.

Not only at the mention that there could be another time, but also because her imagination was conjuring up a picture of him half-naked in the small tub with her. Cosy. Intimate. Wet. And very, very hot.

'Yes, bring someone to do the dishes too.' Aurelia set to work tidying away the remnants of their dinner in an attempt to direct her attention elsewhere.

She was supposed to be avoiding getting any closer to Gabe, not thinking of him as the main character in more erotic fantasies. When she ventured back outside, he was bent over picking something up off the deck, offering her a view of his peachy backside. On impulse, trying to avoid any more inappropriate thoughts, she scooped up a handful of snow from the ground, and packed it into a ball. Without taking time to think about what she was doing, and to whom, acting only on the opportunity presented to her, she launched the snowball. It hit his backside with a satisfying smack. Worth the stinging cold in her fingers.

'What the—' He reeled around, completely taken by surprise.

She should have feigned innocence, but the sight of his bewilderment made her laugh out loud. 'I couldn't resist.'

'Is that so?' Before she realised what was happening,

Gabe had fashioned his own snowball and chucked it back at her.

It hit her in the chest, completely taking her breath away. 'Oh, this is war now.'

She was glad they'd moved away from any romantic illusion towards somewhere she felt more comfortable as they began chucking snowballs at one another like overgrown children.

Their hearty laughter filled the frosty air, along with shrieks as each snowball landed on its target. They gradually moved closer to one another, the play becoming faster and more furious in their bid to outdo one another. Until they were breathless, wet and freezing from the interaction. Aurelia managed to get one last hit as she dumped a handful of loose snow on Gabe's head. Though, in her hurry to get away before he could get revenge, she slipped and ended up falling.

Things seemed to happen in slow motion then as Gabe reached out to try and catch her before she hit the ground, only for him to lose his footing too. Leaving them tumbling down, limbs entangled, in a heap of snow.

Their laughter gradually died down as they found themselves almost nose to nose, with Aurelia practically lying in Gabe's arms. A perfect first kiss moment if they hadn't already shared that one good-night kiss at the sleepover in the store which she'd overanalysed a thousand times. Perhaps it was her imagination working overtime again. Projecting what she wanted to happen when he was likely oblivious.

Besides, there was also the matter of her being his employee, currently living off his mercy and goodwill. Aurelia couldn't run the risk of losing everything for the sake of an ill-timed, ill-judged, romantic notion. Especially when all she had left was wrapped up in the relationship she did have with him right now.

'We should get in out of the cold,' she said, scrabbling to her feet and rushing inside.

Gabe followed, leaving his sodden boots and coat by the door.

'You're shaking like a leaf. I'm so sorry. You must be frozen. We need to get you warmed up again, and quick.' He took her by the hand and led her to the small sauna room, where she had no choice but to take off her wet robe and slippers, leaving her shivering just in her swimsuit.

Gabe set to work getting the steam going once he'd wrapped her in clean, dry towels. 'I'll go and get changed, then I'll join you.'

'There's no need. I'll be fine on my own.' The whole point of a snowball fight had been to put some distance between them, but it was beginning to seem as though that had backfired spectacularly.

He fixed her with a determined look. 'It'll be my fault if you end up with hypothermia. I'm not going to risk you passing out in a sauna.'

There was little point in arguing any more with him, it would simply delay the inevitable. Her and Gabe, alone in the sauna, wearing very little.

Whilst he went to change into something more uncomfortable for her, Aurelia said a little prayer, hoping for strength to carry her through whatever the hell they did next.

Gabe was annoyed at himself, not only for putting Aurelia in real danger of becoming ill, but also for making things even more difficult for him on a personal level. He knew he was taking a chance by bringing her out here in the first place, but instead of creating any sort of space between them, he appeared to be doubling down on the time they were spending together. It was possible he was simply enjoying being with her a little too much.

A snowball fight, for goodness' sake. He was a grown man, her boss, and he shouldn't have enjoyed the sparring as much as he had. Or the aftermath when they'd collapsed in the snow together. For a moment he'd forgotten who he was, who Aurelia was, and almost given in to the urge to kiss her. If there weren't so many complications and consequences involved in that small act, he wouldn't even have thought twice about doing so. Now, however, he was going to be testing his restraint even further being in even closer confines with her. Especially when a simple black one-piece had suddenly become the sexiest item of clothing he'd ever seen.

Past lovers had been fond of silk and lace lingerie to drive him to distraction, but all it took was apparently a modest swimsuit which merely hinted at the curves beneath. Gabe knew he shouldn't have been looking, but he was a red-blooded male and her stunning figure couldn't fail to grab his attention. There was something about Aurelia which made him feel like a hormonal teenager again who couldn't seem to keep a hold of his urges. Though he was trying his best. She didn't make it easy when the hungry looks she directed at him sometimes reflected his own, he was sure.

Like now for instance. When he'd joined her in the sauna in his shorts. There was nothing remotely sexy about a pair of baggy navy swim-shorts, yet the way she devoured the sight of him when he walked in made him walk a little taller. Albeit, also making other parts of him a tad uncomfortable.

'How are you feeling now?' he asked Aurelia, as the steam filled the small room along with the relaxing scent of lavender.

'I told you, I'm okay. You don't need to worry.' She smiled, doing her best to put his mind at ease. Impossible when he was having feelings towards her which were decidedly disturbing his peace of mind.

'Can I get you a glass of water, or anything else?'

'No. Relax. I'm not shivering any more. If anything I'm beginning to sweat now.' She fanned her face as the heat really began to ramp up.

The action only drew attention towards the small rivulet of sweat which was making its way steadily down to the valley between her ample breasts. When he looked up again, it was to find her watching him with equal fascination. And dare he say it, lust? Suddenly at a loss for words, a silence descended between them, thick with unspoken desires.

He waited for Aurelia to decide what she wanted to happen next, because his willpower was weakening by every passing moment between them. Attraction gradually erasing all of those concerns about why they shouldn't take the next step and act on this obvious chemistry between them.

'We should probably get out,' she finally said, rising to leave. Decision made.

'Yeah,' he said immediately, needing some fresh air, and a chance to cool down.

'Er, Gabe, I just wanted to check again with you about

sleeping arrangements.' Her cheeks were pink as she asked the question. It was sweet, but he avoided teasing her when it was clear she was uncomfortable about whatever was happening between them. Although it seemed as though her thoughts had strayed to the same place as his. The bedroom.

'I told you, I'm happy for you to take the bed. Don't worry about me, I can sleep down here on the sofa.'

'I don't like asking you to do that when you've already given me so much.' She looked genuinely upset by the idea that he should be roughing it down here, but it had always been the plan for her to enjoy everything their accommodation had to offer. He'd spent so much time in luxury hotels he took them for granted. Whereas it seemed as though Aurelia had very little opportunity to be indulged in this fashion.

'It's my treat. I'll have to follow up on the meeting I had today anyway. It can't be all play and no work.' He grinned, remembering how much fun they'd been having in the snow until he'd almost given her hypothermia.

'Only if you're sure...' She was hesitant to accept the offer, but that was her nature. Gabe had come to learn that she wasn't used to people doing things for her, at least not without an ulterior motive, because she always looked at him with a certain degree of suspicion when he did her a kindness. It was a wonder she'd ever left the store with him that first night.

'I'm sure.' To be honest he didn't know why he felt compelled to do so much for her in the first place, when he'd never had this reaction to anyone else before. Perhaps it was because he'd recognised someone else who'd been lacking in love, and didn't want anyone to feel the way he'd felt growing up. He wanted to be the one who could offer that warm fuzzy feeling of having someone there during life's low points.

'In that case, I'm going to head up to bed now. I'm exhausted. Thanks for everything today.' She stood up on tiptoe and gave him a kiss on the cheek to express her gratitude.

A dangerous move in the current climate. As highlighted by the sudden frisson in the air between them, and the hesitation in moving away from one another. As though they were two magnets consistently drawn to one another, yet fighting the obvious attraction.

'You're very welcome,' he said, eventually, cutting through the tension and effectively ending the moment. Surprised by his own fortitude when everything inside was screaming at him to make a move. To finally give in to this chemistry between them and damn the consequences. He was sure it would be worth it.

It was just as well Aurelia was already climbing the wooden staircase, leaving him alone to wrestle with his growing feelings for her. So he could hopefully get them under control and get back to focusing on business, instead of his personal life.

CHAPTER EIGHT

DESPITE THE HUGE comfy bed, her body limp with exhaustion and the tranquillity of her surroundings, Aurelia couldn't sleep. Things between her and Gabe were hotting up in more ways than one. Sitting so close to him in that sauna, wearing so little, had been torturous. Especially after their fun in the snow which had been exhilarating to say the least.

This had been such a wonderful trip she knew there was one thing which would complete it. She and Gabe had sailed close to the flames a few times, getting closer and closer to getting burned. If she was honest she was finding it harder to care. That want to close the distance between them and give in to temptation was overriding all common sense at present. Though the fact that he'd decided to sleep on the sofa said it all, she supposed. He'd made it clear from the outset that they wouldn't be sharing a bed.

At least one of them was keeping a clear head. If he'd wanted more, the one bed, two lonely people scenario would have played out the way every romantic would imagine. Forced together, temptation would prove too much and the evening would end with a passionate tryst neither saw coming.

She sighed. Chance would be a fine thing. Since Gary

had left, she'd spent the past months trying to get over his betrayal. And simply trying to survive. Getting involved with anyone else had been the last thing on her mind. Perhaps these thoughts about Gabe were simply a symptom that she was ready to pursue a romantic interest again. It was only natural given everything he'd done for her that he'd become the target of her blossoming libido. Once Christmas was over and she had to move out, those feelings would likely subside again. She hoped.

The problem was what she did about them in the meantime.

For an age she simply lay in bed staring up at the bright night sky, as though she'd find some answers in the twinkling stars above. The magical sight further improved when she saw the unmistakable green glow of the northern lights. Mother Nature provided an awesome display of brilliant pink, purple and green rays flickering and dancing. A celestial ballet she felt guilty about letting Gabe miss. Impossible to enjoy completely knowing he was downstairs, oblivious to the wonder.

With a frustrated huff of breath, she climbed out of bed, and made her way downstairs, clad only in her pyjamas. She peered into the living room area, deciding that if he was asleep she'd simply go back to bed without disturbing him.

However, Gabe was very much awake, leaning over the coffee table, typing on his laptop. She gave a subtle cough to let him know she was there.

'Oh, hey. Is everything okay for you up there? Are you warm enough? I think there are more blankets in the wardrobe if you need them.' He immediately forgot about his work to focus on her, and what she might need, and Aurelia's heart simpered. Before she'd got to know him, she would have figured him for a workaholic who would've hated being inconvenienced by anyone.

It might have been better for her peace of mind if he had turned out to be that person.

'It's actually lovely and cosy up there. Thank you. I, er, thought you might want to come up. To see the view, I mean. The northern lights.' Aurelia was stumbling over her words, trying not to make it sound as though she was propositioning him.

Gabe smiled, clearly amused by her bluster. 'I'd like that. If it's okay with you?'

'Sure.' Aurelia took the lead back up the staircase with Gabe following close behind.

'Believe it or not, I've never seen the aurora borealis.' Trust Gabe to give the spectacle its proper name. Though it did come as a surprise to hear that he'd never experienced it before. Aurelia thought a man like him would have seen all the sights the world had to offer someone with unlimited funds.

'I don't believe that with your extensive business contacts and travel history that this is the first time the lights have appeared for you.' They were standing awkwardly in the bedroom, craning their necks to look up at the sights above.

Even in the unearthly green glow from the lights, Gabe looked a little ashamed. 'Maybe not, but it's the first time I've even taken time out from work to look.'

She could believe that. After all, it had been her first impression of him. That Gabe Delaney had no interest in anything other than money and nothing was more beautiful, or magical, to him than making more of it.

'Why now?' She was curious that, given he was still on a working trip, he should take the time out tonight to take an interest. It also brought into question his motives for indulging the other activities they'd enjoyed over their stay.

Gabe fixed her with his smile. 'Because you asked me to.'

'Oh.' Warmth flooded her skin at the implication of that simple comment. She wanted to share the experience with him and he was apparently happy to oblige. Prioritising being with her over his work. A new experience for her.

Her own mother had always put the needs of the men in her life before Aurelia's best interests, and even Gary had decided what he wanted was more important than what they had together. If he'd considered her feelings at all, he would have at least talked to her before disappearing. There'd been plenty of chances for him to tell her he didn't want to be in a relationship any more, that he didn't want to live in domestic bliss, but to explore the world, and his freedom.

That's what an adult would have done. Given her some warning, and a chance to sort her life out too. Instead, he'd just upped and left, throwing her life into turmoil the way her mother used to. A pattern she apparently couldn't break.

Since that night in the store, Gabe had gone out of his way to make her life better. This latest comment had all sorts of connotations. Not least that he seemed to be content in her company. She'd seen for herself how different he was when he was with her, and though Aurelia was trying so hard not to read anything into that, it was difficult not to. Especially when she found herself wanting to share special moments like this with him.

'It is amazing though, isn't it?' Gabe had moved his gaze from her to the skies, and Aurelia realised she'd forgotten all about the spectacle going on above their heads, in the light of what was going on inside hers.

'You can see it better from the bed.' She was nervous as she said it, essentially inviting him to join her, but she didn't have an ulterior motive.

Nevertheless, when she lay down on one side of the bed, he did the same on the other side. Making sure to keep a respectable distance between them. Regardless that she was in her pyjamas and Gabe was wearing a loose T-shirt and sweatpants, for some reason this seemed even more intimate than the sauna.

The atmosphere between them seemed more charged than the phenomenon they were witnessing above them.

'I've been missing out on so much.' Gabe's wistful whisper eventually penetrated the silence.

'You're a busy man.' Aurelia understood that. Not only was he working to put money in his own pocket, but he was now dealing with his father's legacy. The whole Delaney name. That meant a responsibility not only to the company, but to the employees who relied on him for financial stability. Aurelia included.

Up until now she'd only been thinking about herself, the impact everything was having on her own circumstances. With hindsight, she could see he was dealing with a lot too, on top of the grief for his father. It was no wonder he hadn't had time for anything else.

He sighed. A sound so full of regret it made her ache for him.

'It's not just that. My father had it drilled into me from an early age that nothing mattered except money. Having it, and making more of it. He didn't seem to take joy in anything else. Not Mother Nature, or even his only son.'

Aurelia had to swallow the giant lump in her throat before she embarrassed herself by openly sobbing. It was obvious how deeply affected he'd been by his relationship with his father, and she could empathise. She knew her own childhood had heavily influenced how she lived her life. At least how she'd wanted to live her life.

'I'm sorry. You deserved more. But perhaps it has moulded you into the man you are now. I know you're not like your father.' She hoped he would take it as the compliment she meant, and not as an insult about his father. Especially when he'd been so open with her about how much he'd wanted his father to be different with him. To love him.

Gabe rolled onto his side to look at her, forcing her to do the same. The light display forgotten as they gazed at one another instead. 'But that's who I always wanted to be.'

'Why? If he was so cold towards you, why would you want to emulate him?' She'd been the opposite. Trying her best not to end up like her mother, and failing anyway. Just as penniless and dependent on other people's charity, with no idea of what the future held. The only consolation being that Aurelia hadn't inflicted that lifestyle onto another generation.

'Because that was the only way I could ever get his approval. By being as work focused and money driven as he was.'

'You must know though, that was your father's problem not yours.'

Gabe made a face. 'I don't know…it seems to matter to most people.'

'That's not the only reason people like you.' Aurelia felt guilty in that moment, thinking about all the money he'd spent on getting her out here and making it all so special. Although she hadn't asked for any of it, it had made her think about him in a different light. Was she just as guilty as his father?

She hoped that her growing feelings for him were more to do with getting to know him as a person, and less to do with his bank balance. As glorious as this trip had been, if he'd been as sweet to her at home, prioritising her comfort and needs over everything else, she was sure she'd have felt the same way towards him.

The one thing that was muddying the waters was the fact that she was living off his generosity at present because of her situation. Albeit temporarily. She just didn't want him to think she was using him or, valuing his worth based on his financial status. He was coming to be an important part of her life and it scared her just to admit that to herself.

'Isn't it? My first, and I suppose only, real relationship kind of emphasised that idea. I thought Emma and I were going to get married and have kids of our own one day. That I'd be the dad I'd always dreamed of having growing up. I'd rebelled a bit I suppose from my father at that time, wanting to be a success in my own right, for my own reasons. Proving my own worth. So I set up my own business, ignoring all the advice he'd spouted over the years, thinking that I knew best. That I didn't need anything from him. Especially not his approval.'

'What happened?' As far as she was concerned he

was a success in his own right, sure he'd made his own fortune before he'd inherited Delaney's along with the family estate.

'The business inevitably failed. I was young, naive and optimistic. A bit of a daydreamer. All of that was knocked out of me when I found Emma half-naked in my house with my more successful best friend. I was doing my utmost to save my business but she'd already moved on to the next best thing. It was my fault. I'd let her down. Failed her the same way I'd failed my father. As soon as the money was gone, so was she. Well, I threw her out, but you know what I mean. I think if I'd have been as successful then as I am now, she would still be in my life.' It was clear what had happened with his ex still hurt. The pain, there in his eyes.

She couldn't help but wonder if that was what he wanted. If losing Emma had spurred him on to be that success, and if, given a chance, he would have this woman, who was making Aurelia irrationally jealous, back in his life. Although, in her opinion, someone who would cheat on a man like Gabe didn't deserve him in any circumstances.

'So, when things didn't work out, you reverted back to type and followed in your father's footsteps.' She could see why. It was a defence mechanism. A safety net. Where there were no unnecessary risks.

He nodded. 'It was easier that way. Kept everyone happy when I was making money.'

'Except you.'

A lopsided smile. 'Don't get me wrong, I enjoyed the trappings of success. Still do, as you've discovered. But the experience of losing everything validated that idea that my worth was tied up in my finances. Since then I've made sure to keep my head, and my heart, in check. I don't do serious relationships. My work is my mistress.'

Aurelia could understand why he would take that approach, and it felt like an ominous warning. Even more reason not to get any more involved with him. He was a commitment-phobe. One she'd been relying on way too much as it was. Having any romantic feelings towards him was only going to lead her down the same path which had caused all the problems in the first place. She was supposed to be an independent woman, yet here she was completely at his mercy. Apparently unable to maintain those defences around her heart when he seemed just as wounded by life as she was.

'Things don't always work out the way we want though, do they? I'd promised myself I wouldn't end up like my mum, sofa-surfing, with no security in my life. Although I'm in luxury at present, that's because you took pity on me. My ex leaving destroyed me in every way imaginable. I let myself depend on him, and when he decided to take off, my world crumbled around me. I don't want to make the same mistake ever again.'

She swallowed hard, never feeling as vulnerable as she did right now, even when she'd found herself out on the street. This was a conversation she probably should have had with her ex, but she'd put on a mask for him. Pretended to be a strong independent woman, when deep down she'd been frightened of someone letting her down again.

If she'd told him her fears, perhaps he would have thought twice about ending their relationship the way he had. Maybe he thought she didn't need him. Either way, if she'd had some warning she could have prepared herself, planned what to do. Instead of having her world ripped from under her and making her feel like that young girl again who'd had to move time and time again wherever the wind blew her mother. Never knowing what was coming next.

At least Gabe was being honest with her. He hadn't promised her anything beyond Christmas.

'So what are we doing here?' He gave her an uncertain smile she was sure matched her own. Sometimes it felt as though they were two parts of the same puzzle meant to be together, and she was beginning to wonder why she'd been fighting it for so long. She felt safe with Gabe, and since he'd been hurt in the past too, she didn't believe he would deliberately hurt her. It was exhausting keeping up the pretence that she didn't need anyone in her life, because admitting she did made her vulnerable. Gabe knew everything about her now and she thought she could finally drop that façade. For once she simply wanted to feel safe.

'I don't know, but it feels nice.' Even that admission made her tingle all over. Something was changing between them, and heaven help her, she wanted it to.

Gabe leaned in and kissed her softly on the lips. Aurelia's eyes fluttered shut as her body went into swoon mode, melting into the mattress. She should have had the common sense to put a stop to it, make sure things didn't go any further, knowing things couldn't end well between them. But she convinced herself that she deserved some happiness, no matter how short-lived.

So, instead of keeping herself protected, she leaned farther into the kiss.

As Gabe wrapped an arm around her waist and pulled her closer, a little moan escaped her lips. He was kissing her harder now, with a passion that took her breath away. As though finally giving in to this attraction between them had unleashed something wild and wonderful, and she was enjoying the benefits of the release. She cupped his face in her hands, claiming him as hers, just as possessively as his hand was claiming her.

Her tongue danced with his, tasting and teasing, as they rolled on the bed, limbs entwined. They could have put an end to it then and there, put it down to a moment of madness. Carried away by the romance of their surroundings, and finding solace in one another's arms.

However, she simply didn't want to, and she definitely got the impression that Gabe felt the same. They wanted this. Needed it. And nothing else seemed to matter.

Giving over to the inevitable, they began clawing at one another's clothes as animal instinct took over. Aurelia couldn't wait to have him naked beside her, literally stripping away everything between them so they could be as close as possible. She was a slave to her libido as she tugged his shirt over his head, revealing the smooth contours of the broad chest she knew was waiting for her. Fascinated by the hills and valleys of his pectoral muscles, she traced her fingers over his warm skin. Felt him suck in a shaky breath as she did so; letting her know he was every bit as affected by this interaction as she was.

Aurelia dipped her head and flicked her tongue over his flat nipple, bringing it to attention at her behest, garnering a very male growl. As though she'd flipped a switch, Gabe was suddenly upon her. Nibbling at her neck, almost ripping at her pyjama top in his haste to undress her. She'd never felt so wanted, so aroused and so ready all at once.

Undone and exposed, emotionally as well as physically, Aurelia surrendered her body to Gabe's ministration. Still kissing her with that same intensity, he cupped her breast in his palm, kneading, squeezing and teasing, until her nipples were aching for attention too. Gabe put her out of her misery quickly, latching on and sucking on her taut pink tip until she was gasping in ecstasy.

'Gabe—' It was a plea for complete release. She needed him to give her everything, and take all she had in return.

'Are you sure?' He was asking for permission, consent to let those urges take over, and leaving no room for misunderstanding or regret. She understood why when they'd already veered so close to the edge before, only to retreat at the last second. This was different. They'd taken that next step, only to find they both wanted more.

Aurelia knew what was going to follow was going to be amazing. Foolish? Perhaps. But amazing all the same. It was a risk worth taking when it was making her feel this good already.

'I'm sure.' To illustrate the point she hooked her legs around his waist and pushed his sweatpants and boxers down over his hips with her feet.

He flashed her a devilish grin, which succeeded in sending a ripple of anticipation through her entire body, making her ready for whatever he had to offer. Gabe took his sweet time taking his clothes off the rest of the way, giving her a front row seat for the striptease. She wasn't disappointed. In fact, if she had a stack of fifty pound notes she'd be throwing them at him right now. Gabe Delaney was an impressive specimen of the male physique.

'You're staring,' he said almost bashfully, though she was sure he knew exactly why the sight of him had left her open-mouthed.

'Well, I'm just taking everything in.' She swallowed hard.

Gabe dropped his head with a laugh, then began stalking along the bed with intent towards her. 'My turn.'

With one smooth motion he pulled her down the mattress by her feet and divested her of her pyjama bottoms and panties. Leaving her completely naked beneath him. His glistening sapphire eyes swept over her body, darkening with desire.

'What?' she asked, anxiously, wondering why the haste to get to the next step had suddenly stalled. Perhaps he'd changed his mind, or didn't like what he saw. Aurelia knew she was likely a little curvier than the supermodels a man like Gabe was used to dating, and therefore not as attractive to him. Although the hunger in his eyes said different.

'I'm just taking everything in.' He grinned and gave her a cheeky wink, which helped her relax and make her feel less self-conscious about being exposed to his scrutiny.

'And?' She feigned bravado, and a confidence she wanted to have in bed with him. Here, she wanted them to be equals. Both enjoying the experience.

Gabe nodded. 'And, I like it.'

He was back on her, covering her naked form with his, and making her squeal with delight as his hands and mouth worked overtime exploring her soft contours. There was no need for any more words as they let their bodies take control. Showing one another what turned them on, and what they needed. Until they both seemed ready to burst with desire.

When he briefly left her to search for a condom she thought she would combust from sheer frustration. Contraception wasn't something she'd even thought about when packing for a business trip, but apparently a man like Gabe was always prepared. Although she didn't think he'd come away with the sole intent of seducing her, the idea that he was ready to sleep with someone at any time was something she had to put aside to be in the moment with him. They weren't a couple, it wasn't cheating, yet she didn't want to think of him being with anyone else.

'What is it? What's wrong?' He was braced above her, obviously seeing the shift in her from wanton lover, to the anxious, insecure woman she really was. The Aurelia whose ex hadn't wanted her.

'Nothing.' The last thing either of them needed right now was for her to come across as jealous and clingy, when this had started out as a spontaneous, passionate tryst which was bound to happen. If either of them considered this anything more than a lust-driven liaison, it would be over.

'You can still change your mind if you want.' His worried forehead made her want him all the more.

'No. I want this. I want you, Gabe.' She smoothed her hand across his brow until it evened out.

He kissed her palm before kissing her lips again. A slow, tender reassurance that he wouldn't do anything she didn't want him to. Things had changed between them from their raw, passionate urges to something more... meaningful. This was no longer about fulfilling a need, and racing towards that final release. It was the joining together of two people who had found something special in one another, and were afraid to explore it other than physically.

Perhaps this should have been a warning sign to stop before things got any further, but her heart, and every other body part, was overruling her head. She just wanted Gabe.

Slowly, carefully, he forged their bodies together, making her gasp at the tight fit.

'Are you okay?' he whispered in her ear, unmoving until she was able to relax and confirm again that she was ready for this.

Some men in Gabe's position, where money and power meant they were used to getting what they wanted, didn't care about anyone else but themselves. To find he was still showing her so much consideration almost brought tears to her eyes. Aurelia could honestly say that Gabe was the only person in her life who'd ever seemed to put her first. It was difficult not to get swept off her feet by that, so she thought it better to try and keep things on a purely physical level from now on. This was sex. It couldn't be anything more, for her own protection.

He moved slowly inside her, filling her, stretching her, making love to her. At first Aurelia was content with his gentle touch, his butterfly kisses maintaining that emotional connection, because it felt so good. But the more she enjoyed it, the further she knew she was falling for him. She needed that untamed version of him to keep her safe from herself, and so consumed with need that every other thought was blocked from her mind. So she wouldn't find herself whispering sweet nothings into his ear and ruining everything.

He didn't do serious commitment, and she wasn't about to let another man into her life who could rip it all apart. That should have been reason enough to keep things casual and purely sexual.

To let him know she wanted a change of pace and dynamics between them, she wrapped her legs around his waist and tilted her hips upward to meet his every thrust.

Tightening her inner muscles, squeezing and releasing, until she knew he was incapable of coherent thought too. With his head buried in the crook of her neck he drove into her with increased fervour. His actions and grunts of primal satisfaction combining to push her further and further towards that final release.

'Aurelia—'

She covered his mouth with hers to swallow that gasp of familiarity. This needed to feel like anonymous sex. Ridiculous given the current circumstances, but she was clinging to that lifeline to try and protect herself.

Gabe was barely holding it together as Aurelia tugged at his bottom lip with her teeth, whilst driving the rest of his body crazy too. He'd had no idea she would be this passionate, sexy or capable of completely undoing him the way she had.

From the moment she'd invited him upstairs he knew they'd likely sleep together when this attraction between them refused to abate. He simply hadn't accounted for how else she could make him feel: out of control. Yet she was matching him thrust by thrust, refusing to let him be a gentleman, and sending him soaring towards the edge with her. He knew she was close by her breathy moans, increasing in frequency and pitch, as she rode with him. Her body slick with desire beneath him.

He was a man used to being in charge. In business, and in life. Relationships were brief, leaving both parties satisfied with no regrets or commitment. Everything about being with Aurelia was different, and threatened all he knew. As though those defences he'd build around his heart to protect him from experiencing that searing pain inflicted once too often, were crumbling with every surprise she threw his way.

Yet that didn't stop him from wanting this. Wanting Aurelia. He was barely clinging to that last of his control when Aurelia rolled them both over until he was lying flat on his back. She was in charge now, and though he should have wanted to challenge that, he didn't. Gabe was content to see that confidence in her as she rode his hips. Hands braced on his shoulders, her breasts bouncing so tantalisingly close to him, she drove them both towards that final peak.

Gabe anchored her buttocks with his hands and thrust upwards, still a very active participant in this passionate game. Aurelia cried out, her eyes locked with his, letting him see, and feel, as her orgasm slammed through her body. It was enough to send Gabe hurtling into the abyss with her. He had his own personal light show going on behind his eyelids as his neural pathways seemed to short-circuit from the intensity of his climax.

Gabe had always enjoyed a healthy sex life, never short of a willing partner. However, he couldn't remember it being this intense with another woman. The act leaving him completely and utterly spent. Having given everything of himself, and holding nothing back. Perhaps that was what was scaring him right now.

Aurelia wasn't just some casual acquaintance he'd bedded. As well as being his employee, someone he was going to see frequently, she was also currently living with him. This was never going to be a wham, bam, thank you ma'am. They were connected, emotionally. Something he'd done his best to avoid when it came to sex.

'Don't do that,' Aurelia said as he lay beside her, staring up at the ever-changing night sky.

'Don't do what?'

'Disappear into your own head. Don't overanalyse what's just happened and make it weird.' Clearly Aurelia was thinking along the same lines, doing her best to write this off as something less than it was so she wouldn't freak out either.

'Okay... How do we stop it becoming weird?' He needed to know so he could relax and enjoy this for what it had been. Amazing, and not something he wanted to come to regret.

Aurelia rolled onto her side too to face him. 'Look, this doesn't have to be anything more than just sex. Neither of us wants that.'

He tried to read into anything that might be going on beyond the words, worried she was only saying what he wanted to hear, but finding nothing. She was still smiling, and seemingly as content with things the way they were. Perhaps he wouldn't have to leap out of bed like a scalded cat after all, pretending he had some very important business which would keep him occupied until they got back home. If they both knew where they stood, no misunderstandings, than they could simply enjoy this for what it was. A very nice distraction from reality.

'And what do you want, Aurelia?' He grinned at her, comfortable to remain where he was now that there was no threat to his bachelor lifestyle. She'd been through a lot and it was clear that she wasn't looking for romantic complications any more than he was.

'Isn't that where we came in?' Aurelia trailed a finger down the centre of his chest, dipping dangerously low and reminding him that question was why they'd given in to temptation in the first place. They'd done exactly what they'd wanted, ignoring any possible consequences.

Gabe had to admit it had felt good to simply go with those urges for once without having to weigh up future risk, and not only physically. He hadn't had to do mental gymnastics to try and keep his feelings at bay, letting his body have the full workout for once. Even now he was leaning in for another kiss, another taste of her on his lips. Glad that she couldn't seem to get enough of him, and that he'd proved himself worth taking a chance on.

Thankfully, their evening hadn't yet come to an end, and they were free to pretend a little longer that nothing else mattered beyond this bed.

'I'm always happy to oblige, although I might need some time to regain my strength first.' After that epic release he would need some time before he was back at full strength. There was no way he was giving some lacklustre performance next time around and make her think that had been a one-off.

It wasn't his reputation he was concerned with, but the chance to perhaps continue this when they got back home. Although they hadn't discussed it, as long as they were of the same mind, he didn't see why they couldn't extend this until their Christmas deadline.

Once Aurelia moved out they'd be able to put this be-hind them as simply a good time, but until then they could keep enjoying one another. This kind of chemistry didn't come along every day.

'That's okay. I'm happy just to lie here with you.' Au-relia shifted over beside him, and ordinarily that move would have caused him to freeze. To panic and find an excuse to leave. Cuddling, snuggling and anything which wasn't simply foreplay were usually warning signs that things were going in a different direction than he was comfortable with.

This was different. They'd drawn their boundaries, knew where they stood, and he doubted sharing body heat was going to change anything now.

He lay on his back and let Aurelia cuddled into his side, her head resting in the crook of his arm. Despite the central heating in the building, his natural instinct was to pull the blanket up around their naked bodies. Cocooning them together even more in their love bubble.

Gabe couldn't remember the last time he'd done this. Simply lay in bed post sex and enjoyed the moment. There was a reason, he supposed. It made him vulnerable. In that moment his guard was down and he'd always been afraid of feelings creeping in to spoil things. So he'd pre-empted that moment and made his getaway before showing any weakness. There was no need for that tonight.

'It is pretty awesome,' he said, staring up at the fluctuating neon lights.

'The northern lights, or just being here with you?'

'Both,' he teased, squeezing her close, the softness of her naked body against his already re-energising him.

His sigh of contentment surprised them both but he didn't want to dwell on it through fear he'd have to leave her bed after all. Instead, they simply lay in silence, in one another's arms, as the night skies continued to dance.

It wasn't long before they'd both drifted into a deep, peaceful sleep.

CHAPTER NINE

AURELIA COULD FEEL the sun on her eyelids but didn't want to open them. That would mean her night with Gabe was effectively over, and she wasn't ready to leave it behind just yet. Not least because he'd promised her a replay, but exhaustion had robbed her of it. She didn't even want to move in case she disturbed him, though she knew their time together had to end at some point. And soon. Their flight home was in the afternoon.

So when he did stir beside her, her emotions were mixed.

'Morning,' he said through a yawn as he scratched his head, mussing his hair to make him even sexier. That sleepy, just-had-sex look apparently her new turn-on. Although he didn't have to do much to get her engine revving when his naked body was pressed against hers. Evidence of his whole body waking up, pressing into her flesh.

'Morning. What are your plans today?' She suspected he probably had more work meetings to go to and she wouldn't be able to monopolise any more of his time.

He stretched and rubbed the arm she'd been lying on for most of the night, likely trying to get the circulation back in it. 'No plans other than being here with you. There's no hurry, is there?'

'Not at all.' She realised she'd been tense, waiting for a dismissal now their night together was over, but his nonchalance enabled her to relax for a little while longer.

'Good.' He dropped a kiss on her nose before throwing the covers back and striding magnificently naked across the room to the bathroom.

Aurelia watched his muscular backside and his thick leg muscles as he walked away, lusting after him just as much now as she had last night.

'Should we get some breakfast?' She really didn't know what the protocol was after this sort of thing. Did they pretend it had never happened? Spend the day lazing in bed? Or find some middle ground and simply get up and continue the day? She supposed Gabe had more experience and would take the lead.

He walked back out of the bathroom drying his hands on a towel. 'We have enough supplies to make breakfast here. You stay there. You look beautiful.'

It was the sort of comment he probably paid every woman he woke up next to, but Aurelia blushed all the same. If nothing else, he was certainly giving her ego a boost. Something much needed after everything she'd been through. Making her feel as though she wasn't one of life's failures after all.

Once Gabe disappeared down the stairs, she let out a sigh, a smug grin on her face as she replayed last night's events in her head. Her body was still pleasantly tingling from their exertions, and she felt thoroughly ravished and satisfied.

When she thought about her sex life with her ex she realised she'd never quite been left with this same contentment. He'd been mostly concerned with his own fulfilment, hers an afterthought, if thought of at all. Aurelia supposed she'd been so starved of love and affection at home, she'd taken whatever crumbs he'd offered.

It was tragic, really, that she'd settled for so much less than the passion she'd experienced from one night with Gabe. If nothing else hopefully she'd realise she deserved more. A satisfying sex life was just as important as the stability a partner could provide. Though she doubted she'd be seeking either in the near future. Once she moved out of Gabe's place, the emphasis would be very much about getting her life back on track and standing on her own two feet again. That did not leave room for anyone else in her life who could potentially mess things up for her again.

'Breakfast is served.' Gabe swept back into the room, wearing an apron to cover his modesty, and carrying a full tray.

He set it down on the bed with a flourish, and climbed in beside Aurelia.

'Do you do this for everyone you spend the night with?' It killed her to ask it, even though she was trying to make it sound like a joke. She hated to think of him being this free, this sweet with anyone else. Anyone but her.

He handed her a small glass of freshly squeezed orange juice. 'I can honestly say I've never done this before. Apart from the fact I'm usually too busy to stop for breakfast, I'm not in the habit of sticking around after a one-night stand.'

The sweet orange was overpowered by the taste of bitterness in her mouth, as he relegated her to just another one of his conquests. 'Is that what this is? Just a one-night stand?'

Gabe took a bite out of his wholegrain toast. 'Well...' He chewed before he spoke again. 'I was thinking about that. It doesn't have to be if you don't want it to.'

'What do you mean?' Just when she thought he was making it clear she was merely another notch on his bedpost, Gabe was alluding to something a lot more between them. An idea which both excited her, and made her wary. After all, the only reason she'd slept with him last night was because she believed he wasn't looking for anything serious.

Aurelia knew she was a mass of conflict, but that was the effect Gabe had on her. She wanted more, but not to the point where it would put her in danger of getting hurt again.

He offered her a bite of toast, and though her stomach couldn't settle until she knew what was happening, she chomped down on the buttery slice.

'I think we both enjoyed last night—' He seemed to wait for her approval before carrying on, so Aurelia nodded. 'I don't see why we can't continue this until after Christmas. We both know things will be coming to an end, but we may as well have some fun until then, don't you think?'

It was so very tempting. He was suggesting a casual fling for the duration of their time together. Something she wouldn't ordinarily entertain, certainly not with her boss. But last night had been incredible and it would seem churlish to deny herself the chance of having that again and again. Especially when they'd drawn those boundaries to ensure things wouldn't go beyond the physical, or the New Year.

'I don't know... I was under the impression this was a one-off. I might need some persuading.' She was teasing, trying to keep things light-hearted to avoid any over-analysing, or over-complicating things. It would be easy to say yes, but she had to make sure she didn't start to believe they had a future beyond Christmas.

'I have to prove myself, huh? Again.'

'Yeah, I've got a terrible memory. You'll have to remind me if you were up to par.' It was a direct challenge she was hoping he was willing to take on.

For a moment she thought she'd taken the joke too far and wounded his male pride. Until he practically rugby tackled her down onto the mattress, making her squeal with a mixture of surprise and glee that she was getting what she wanted.

Breakfast was forgotten about and in the midst of their renewed desire for one another, the tray and the dishes landed on the floor, orange juice spilling everywhere. Aurelia noticed and felt guilty about the mess.

'We'll have to clean that up,' she said, in between fevered kisses.

'I'll do it later,' Gabe growled, more focused on renewing their connection, and showing Aurelia why they should continue with this arrangement for a while longer.

Not that it was going to take much persuasion, but she was happy to let him try.

He'd pulled away the sheet covering her naked body, staring at her as though seeing her for the first time. The blatant lust in his eyes for her, mixed with appreciation for what he saw, fuelled her ardour. And when he cupped her breast, used the flat of his tongue to tease her nipple, before tugging the taut peak with his teeth, she all but climaxed there and then.

It was ridiculous how in tune he was with her body, and how she responded to his touch so readily. In all the time she'd been with Gary she didn't think they'd had such a strong physical connection as the one she had with Gabe. He was already proving last night hadn't been an exception to the rule when she was writhing in ecstasy before he'd even taken off his apron. Something she made sure to rectify quickly, exposing the fact he was just as turned-on as she was.

Aurelia took him in hand, finding satisfaction in his sudden intake of breath and knowing that she was having as great effect on his body as he had on hers. That chemistry between them caused an explosive reaction with every touch, every caress and kiss. At this moment in time she'd prefer if Christmas never came. A big deal for someone who deemed it the highlight of the year. Though she'd definitely found a new favourite time. Every moment she spent in this bed with Gabe.

Her hand rhythmically pumping his shaft, she kissed and nibbled the skin at his neck, until she could feel him shaking with restraint.

'What are you doing to me?' he groaned into her shoulder.

'Do you want me to stop?'

'Definitely not.'

She could sense his mischievous grin even though she couldn't see it when it was clear how much he was enjoying what she was doing to him. Before they went any further, Gabe sheathed himself with another condom. If they were going to continue their arrangement they needed to make sure they were stocked up on contraception when they seemed unable to keep their hands off one another. As though once they'd given in to that first temptation, they hadn't been able to rein it back in.

She wasn't complaining. It was going to be one hell of a Christmas, though she hoped the shadow of their arrangement ending wouldn't spoil everything. What she wanted was to enjoy this for what it was and have something memorable from this period in her life for all the right reasons. A bright light shining in the darkness her ex had left her treading in his wake.

This time, when Gabe forged their bodies together, she was more than ready for him. Her body already getting used to how he felt, accommodating him at once, and making her feel as though a missing piece of herself had been found.

She didn't want to think about how the loss was going to affect her when it was all over for good. For once she was going to take a leaf out of her mother's book and go with the flow. There was something to be said for acting on impulse every now and then when the dopamine hit made everything seem worth the risk.

Perhaps she was fated to be like her mother after all. Despite all of her attempts otherwise, she'd still ended up in a life of uncertainty and instability. Gabe was the oasis in that desert of rejection and insecurity, providing her with everything she needed to survive. Even though it couldn't be sustained on a permanent basis. It would be easy to mistake gratitude for something else, though her body's reactions told her what she felt for Gabe was more than simply thanks. Why else would she be considering risking getting hurt by keeping this going?

Hips rocking together, hot breath on her face, mutual groans of satisfaction filling the air, Aurelia and Gabe found their rhythm together once more. Another breathtaking display of fireworks to rival last night's light show. As she climbed higher with every thrust, she made sure to take him with her, until the air was filled with cries of satisfaction.

Aurelia didn't know what lay ahead for them once they returned home, but she did know she couldn't give up the chance to have this with Gabe on a regular basis. For however long he remained in her life.

CHAPTER TEN

THEY'D ALMOST MISSED their flight. Though Gabe would have quite happily spent the rest of the day in bed with Aurelia and booked the next one, she'd insisted they needed to get back. It was uncharacteristic of him not to put work before everything, but it had felt good to play hooky from life for a little while. Snuggled up with Aurelia, he didn't have any responsibilities or worries about the future of Delaney's. For once he didn't have to make excuses and leave after a night of passion, because Aurelia knew he didn't want anything more than that. In fact, Aurelia knew more about him than people who'd been in his life for years.

They had that sort of connection which had made it easy to open up to one another and stop pretending to be strong and impervious to hurt. There were all sorts of firsts with Aurelia. He was sure they looked like a loved-up honeymoon couple as they'd boarded their flight, always touching, hugging and kissing. All of those intimate public displays of affection he usually shied away from but out there, with Aurelia, Gabe had been content to express his feelings. As long as he remembered it couldn't last, he should avoid catastrophe.

He knew Aurelia too was **aware** of that time limit on

their arrangement. He'd even felt her withdraw from him as the plane had touched down at the airport, when the lights of the city below guided them back to real life. As she'd turned away from him to watch out of the window, he had a feeling the fantasy was coming to an end, and he wasn't ready to let it go just yet.

It had been nice being a part of a couple for a while. Having that intimacy he was usually afraid of letting develop with a partner. Gabe had begun to wonder about the life he could have if he wasn't so affected by his past. A wife, a family, surrounded by love in that big house was something he longed for, but had always been too afraid of wanting. It would have left him vulnerable to getting hurt again by someone who didn't love him as much as he loved them. Someone who mightn't stick around if things didn't work out because he'd failed in some way. Again.

He'd already been rejected by Emma, and his father, and there was a fear of that happening again. It was safer to be on his own, but sharing his life with Aurelia had made a lot of things in his life better. He realised how lonely his life had been until she'd moved in with him. The trouble was going to come when she left him again, and that was something he should be planning for, knowing it was a definite.

Any normal person would give himself a chance, and tell her how he felt to see if they could have a future together. However, Gabe was worried that his past had left him too scarred to ever fully open up his heart to anyone again. After how much she'd gone through in the past, and how many people had let her down, Aurelia deserved better than that. She needed a partner who could commit themselves completely to her.

For now he was simply going to enjoy being with Aurelia and try to at least have one good Christmas. It wasn't going to be easy when he had the future of the store weighing heavily on him. Not when it was about more than money and severing that tie with his father. These past days of getting to know everyone at the store, Aurelia most of all, he was more emotionally invested than ever in the place. He knew that if he decided to close Delaney's it was going to put her into an even more precarious financial position, along with her other colleagues. Gabe didn't want to do that to her when she was going through an already difficult time. Letting her move into his home, and getting to know her, had complicated everything.

He didn't want her to hate him, but he also wanted to make that final decision with his business in mind, instead of his heart. It was all going to come to a head after Christmas, and he had a feeling that if he closed the store he might never see Aurelia again. At present, he didn't want to imagine that scenario. He wanted to live in this bubble they'd created for a little while longer.

'Home, sweet home,' he said, pushing the front door open. A quiet Aurelia followed behind.

'Oh, your housekeeper must have left the lights on for us.' The sight of the Christmas tree lights seemed to cheer her and grab her back from wherever she'd drifted off to.

'I have to admit it is nice to come back to this. It makes it feel more homely. Perhaps I'll keep it up all year.' Although he'd been resistant initially to Aurelia's insistence about bringing Christmas into the house, it made the place more welcoming. Less lonely.

Aurelia stared at him open-mouthed. 'I can't believe I've actually converted you.'

'I know, what can I say? I'm easily influenced.' They both knew that wasn't true, but in terms of Christmas he'd let Aurelia lead the way when it made then both happy. It would never have crossed his mind to do any of those wonderful things in Finland if he hadn't been trying to get in the Christmas spirit with her. Something he was glad he'd done, even if it didn't last beyond this year.

He already knew subsequent Christmases without Aurelia here were never going to hold the same appeal.

'I doubt that.' Her tone sounded a little flat, and Gabe wondered what had changed her buoyant mood over the last few hours. He hoped it was more to do with the fact they had to get back to reality, than having doubts about continuing their new, temporary relationship.

'Is everything okay?' He set his bag down and gave her his full attention.

She sighed. 'It's just…we're back to work tomorrow. I know this is only a casual thing going on between us, but is it going to make things difficult for us? I mean, not just now, but in the future.'

It was clearly something which had been on her mind since their plane had taken off in Finland. She wasn't asking him to go public or expecting any favours, but obviously she was concerned about the impact this could have on her job. Gabe was ashamed that he hadn't even considered that. Not least because he hadn't yet made the decision on Delaney's future. There was still a possibility that he'd sell the place and Aurelia would be put out of a job along with everyone else.

Not that he wanted to have that conversation. It would cause an argument and he had to have a clear head when it came to making that important decision. It was out of his comfort zone even for his personal life to be led by his emotions. Apart from anything else he didn't want any ill feeling between them when their time together was limited.

In some ways his life pre-Aurelia had been easier. He'd made decisions based on financial sense. These days his conscience was beginning to creep in. Emotions were getting involved and complicating everything.

'I don't see why it should. We're both adults, going into this with our eyes open and no expectations of one another beyond Christmas. No one has to know if that's what you're worried about.' He was sure that the way Suzy had jumped to conclusions before anything had happened was on her mind, and he certainly didn't want to cause any friction between her and her colleagues.

'So, we pretend this never happened?'

'In work at least. At home, we're free to do as we please.' Gabe slid his arms around Aurelia's waist and pulled her towards him, keen to do just that.

'I'm a little tired after the flight. I might just go to bed.' Aurelia was making it clear that there was no funny business on the agenda tonight.

It should've been his cue to say good-night with them both retiring to their respective rooms. Instead, he uttered something he never thought he'd say in his life.

'We don't have to do anything. We can just cuddle if that's what you want?' The idea of not spending the night with her seemed worse than not having sex. That was the moment Gabe realised he was getting in deeper than he was prepared for. Yet, he didn't want to take it back.

Not when she smiled, took his hand and led him upstairs saying, 'I'd like that.'

Gabe had no idea how things were going to pan out long-term, either at the store, or between them. Until decisions were made, and deadlines were met, he didn't want to think about it too much either. He meant it when he said they should carry on as normal at work, but he hoped when they were at home, at least, they could still make believe that they were in that little Finnish love bubble.

It hadn't escaped his attention that he was referring to the old house as 'home' since Aurelia had moved in. Whether it would still feel the same once she was gone remained to be seen.

It had been oddly comfortable waking up in Gabe's bed and getting ready for work, as though it was perfectly normal. Aurelia had thought that with sex off the table he wouldn't have wanted to spend the night with her, but he'd seemed equally as comfortable simply being together.

The flight back had been a worry for her, knowing that they would have to adjust to real life again. That Gabe might change his mind about wanting to continue with their arrangement, jeopardising her job and her future in the process. She hadn't been testing him when she said she didn't want to do anything physical, she'd been merely exhausted.

Still, it had proved a point. He wasn't just using her for sex. Which should have rung alarm bells when it came to protecting herself, but she was glad. Happy that this wasn't only physical for him after all. She didn't feel so bad, then, for letting a few emotions get involved. If he didn't like her for who she was or enjoy her company, having her sleeping in his arms wouldn't have been enough. He'd shared his bed and not banished her to his spare room like the unwanted guest she'd started out as.

Though she was going to have to be careful at work, where rumours had apparently started before they'd as much as kissed. If word got out about their 'arrangement' she was sure she wouldn't be looked on favourably by her colleagues, and she was sure they were going to remain in her life long after Gabe. She had no doubt when things settled down and she'd moved out, he likely wasn't going to become as much of a fixture at the store.

After their 'business' trip, the very least she could do was try and implement some new ideas in the department so it looked as though she'd been doing something more than the boss.

There was also the not-so-small matter of the store's future. Whether or not Gabe was going to sell up. If he did, it would completely devastate her when her job was the only thing she had left in her life. It was a subject they hadn't discussed, likely because neither wanted to spoil what they had at present. If she didn't like what he had planned she knew she couldn't in good conscience live on at his house pretending everything was okay. Aurelia supposed if he had made his decision already, he wouldn't want word to get out before he was ready. She'd feel a duty to inform her colleagues if their world was about to be ripped away, knowing how devastating a lack of warning could be on these matters.

For now, all she could do was carry on as normal, and do her best to show off her department at the store's most important time of the year. After all, it could be their last Christmas here.

The thought alone made her want to weep.

'Suzy, I'm just going to put this here for the children to use.' Pulling herself together, Aurelia placed the make-shift postbox she'd cobbled together from a cardboard box and some poster paint, beside the sales desk.

'Don't you think it's a little close to Christmas for the children to be writing to Santa?' Suzy didn't look convinced, but neither was she a big fan of Christmas, or children. She was the definition of someone only here for the pay cheque, but she was as much a part of Delaney's as the out-of-fashion décor. Fussy, flocked wallpaper in a world of clean lines and minimalism.

Aurelia shrugged. 'Maybe, but they might like to use it anyway. I'll make it into a proper feature next year.'

'If we're still here next year,' Suzy muttered under her breath.

Aurelia understood her colleague's cynicism, she had her own concerns. However, after spending time with Gabe, she wanted to think he would look after his employees when he'd been so compassionate and kind to her. He took his responsibilities seriously, and she hoped the Gabe she knew would look out for everyone's interests, not just his own.

'I'm sure we will be. Now, can you merchandise the board games for me please before the afternoon rush?' Aurelia smiled sweetly as she dismissed Suzy from the conversation.

She didn't need anyone's permission to do anything here except Gabe's and he'd been more than happy for her to implement some elements of their Lapland trip in her department. He'd even helped her with her little art project this morning before she'd come into work. Though they'd got more paint on one another than on their postbox.

Throughout her shift, she drifted off into daydreams as she recalled their shower together afterwards which soon ended with them in bed again. Making up for a night of cuddling. Which, although had been sweet, had somehow felt more intimate than their previous bedroom antics. It took their relationship beyond just sex. That should have frightened the life out of her, yet she was excited.

If Gabe wanted to move their relationship towards something more meaningful, she might be tempted. He'd already proved time and time again that she could trust him, that he cared about her, and even from that first night she'd known he wouldn't abandon her. Aurelia was venturing into dangerous territory, starting to believe that Gabe could be more than a passing phase, but taking that risk was more appealing than being without him.

However, she wasn't brave enough to make that call. She would wait until he was ready, if ever, to move on to something more serious between them. That way she could be sure she wasn't going to be the one left nursing a broken heart, sleeping on the streets and regretting ever getting involved.

'The place looks great.' The sound of Gabe behind her made Aurelia jump.

Mostly because he was never far from her thoughts these days and she'd thought she'd somehow managed to manifest him.

'Oh, hey. Thanks. I'm doing my best to bring a little of Lapland to Belfast.' The paper snowflakes she'd cut out on her break now hanging from the ceiling weren't exactly the sort of quality Delaney's prided itself on, but it gave the department a snowy vibe. The kids loved it.

'I'm pleased to know our business trip wasn't wasted.'

Gabe didn't have to say anything else to make her blush, recalling their recent activities.

'I think I learned a few things I was able to bring back with me.' She was teasing him right back, taking pleasure in the wry smile he was trying to suppress.

'Good. I look forward to seeing what you've got planned.' That mischievous twinkle in his eyes did things to her that a million aphrodisiacs couldn't hope to emulate.

Aurelia caught sight of Suzy glaring over at them from the floor and she knew they had to put an end to the flirting, even though it seemed they couldn't help it. Anytime they were in a room they ended up in one another's arms, and knowing they couldn't do it here simply made it seem like foreplay. The main event later after work was sure to be just as explosive as their first time together when the anticipation was building with every passing moment.

A little girl and her mother appeared by the postbox and Aurelia decided it was safer to move back into assistant mode for both their sakes. 'Hello there. Can I help you?'

'Daisy wanted to send Father Christmas her drawing. Is that okay?' The mum was holding the child back from posting the piece of paper in her hand until she had permission.

'Of course.' Aurelia bent down so she was at Daisy's eye level. 'Can I see?'

The little girl proudly showed off her picture of a Christmas tree surrounded by presents. A beautiful, colourful crayon rendition of the child's excitement for the big day. Aurelia felt her heart catch, the emotion of being able to share in the little girl's contribution.

'That's beautiful. Now, have you got your name and address on it anywhere? Then Santa Claus can thank you for it himself.' Aurelia was already imagining the fun she'd have replying to the letters and adding to the Christmas magic for them.

'Yes. I wrote it on the back over at the letter writing station.' The mother pointed over to the table Aurelia had set up with paper, crayons and stickers for the children to write their letters.

'Good. So, Daisy, you can go ahead and post your picture. We'll get it to Father Christmas before Christmas Day.' Aurelia stood back and let Daisy have her moment, with Gabe looking on from the sidelines.

Until Lapland she would have had him down as a complete cynic, but the fact that he'd accommodated her whimsy here said a lot about him. Even now he was watching with a smile. He definitely had a sensitive side and in that second she thought he would have made a great father. Aurelia remembered the hopeful letters and wishes she'd made at Christmas as a little girl, all revolving around having a family and a home. Given the chance now, she'd probably still take it if she could be guaranteed a happy-ever-after.

Aurelia clapped as Daisy posted her precious picture, surprised when Gabe joined in. Even more so when he strode over and lifted the jar of candy canes they had for sale on the counter.

'Every artist deserves a treat for their hard work,' he said, bending down to offer Daisy a candy cane.

She looked at her mother, who nodded her permission, and Daisy stuck her little mittened hand into the jar and pulled out a candy cane. A wide smile on her face.

'One for Mum too.' Gabe bestowed his charms on Daisy's mother too, who blushed from his attention before helping herself to a treat.

Aurelia felt an unwanted surge of jealousy at the interaction and it flustered her. Proving once and for all she was in deeper than a simple casual fling.

The happy duo uttered their thanks and walked away smiling, leaving her and Gabe alone again.

'I think you deserve one too,' he said, presenting her with a candy cane of her own.

'Why, thank you, Mr Delaney.' She was tempted to make an erotic display of enjoying it, but thought better of it with her already suspicious colleague lurking nearby.

'I actually wanted to ask a favour from you, Ms Hughes. I need you to do some overtime tonight if that's not too much trouble?'

'Not at all. What have you got planned?' Despite her imagination trying to turn it into some raunchy after hours romp, Aurelia knew this had to be work-related. He wouldn't be so blatant, or take a risk of getting caught in the store when they had the freedom to do what they wanted back at his place.

It was important he knew that she could still keep business and pleasure separate, and remain professional when it was called for.

Gabe looked almost embarrassed about being asked the question and Aurelia wondered if she'd got things wrong after all.

'I, er, wondered if you'd help me pick out gifts for the children at the home? Not all of them were able to stay over that night and I thought it would be nice to donate some toys. You would have a better idea of what's popular, or suitable.'

'Of course I'll help. That's a wonderful idea.' She was genuinely blown away by his thoughtfulness. Gabe was so different from his father and she hoped he could see that. The fact that he'd obviously given the matter a lot of thought spoke volumes about his character. His generosity of spirit wasn't reserved just for her, it was a part of him that had simply needed to be unlocked.

She imagined that such gestures wouldn't have been encouraged by his father, who had apparently prioritised wealth above all else, but Aurelia knew that this level of thoughtfulness meant so much more.

'I phoned the home and got a list of names and ages, so hopefully we can tailor gifts individually.' He unfolded a piece of paper where he'd jotted down the information. Again, the effort and thought he'd gone to, proving this was more than an empty gesture. Gabe wanted to give these children a special memory, and make Christmas day something to be cherished.

The only thing about his gesture that made her sad was that it had come from his feelings associated with the day. Like her, he'd felt left out of the celebrations and remembered the disappointment he'd experienced when Christmas hadn't lived up to expectations. Aurelia hoped in some way she'd be able to make the time special for him this year too. He deserved to have someone in his life who could show that they cared about him. Although she was worried about where her feelings would lead her long-term, the one thing she knew was that she cared deeply for him. Otherwise she wouldn't be so afraid of getting things wrong.

Even if she didn't have much to look forward to after

Christmas, she wanted to be part of this. To make someone else's day special. It might also prove to be another tradition he would carry on year after year and she could only encourage that, knowing they would all benefit from the gesture. Making other people happy at Christmas was more important to her than any material gifts she might receive.

'That's great. I'm sure they will all really appreciate your generosity. Once I get cashed up we'll get started on that list.' Aurelia was already looking forward to it, as she always did whenever she was going to get to spend time with Gabe.

Not least because she knew they'd get to go home together at the end of it all.

Gabe didn't know who he'd become lately. He smiled to himself as he pushed a cage for the gifts down towards the toy department in the closed store. Perhaps this was who he'd always been, a generous benefactor to local children. The real Gabe had simply been lost in his quest to please his father. Or, it was possible this change in him had come completely from having Aurelia in his life. Her influence making him realise how important it was to help others less fortunate than himself. She made him want to be a better man.

'I thought it would be easier to load the toys on here so we can take everything directly to the car when we're finished,' he told Aurelia, who was waiting for him, her department the only light in the store now. Like a beacon in the darkness, beckoning him to safety. That was how he felt when he was with her, and he had to admit it was nice after so long being on his own.

He'd always felt as though he had to have that strong, impenetrable shield around his heart so he'd never get hurt again. There had already been so much pain in his life, losing his mum, being rejected by his partner, and never truly having his father's love. It had been easier to simply shut down and accept he'd never be close enough to anyone to truly share his life with. Aurelia had made him begin to wonder if he could be satisfied if that was all there was ever going to be in his life. Loneliness, work, and casual, meaningless encounters didn't hold the same appeal when he'd seen a glimpse of how his life could be with her in it. He was happy, content with the domesticity of going home with her every night, waking up together to start the day anew and making love whenever they felt like it.

The thought of it all ending soon was almost too much to bear. Especially when she was helping him open up to the idea of having something more in his life. Even seeing her with the little girl tonight and how she'd lit up at the idea of helping keep the Christmas magic alive in the child's life, made him think about how she would be as a mother herself.

He'd closed off the idea of having a family himself, because he didn't think he'd ever meet someone who would make him want to open his heart to that. Worried he'd end up with the same disjointed family he'd grown up in. The more time he spent with Aurelia, the more he wanted it all.

He knew it was a big leap from a casual fling to thoughts of settling down and having a family, but he thought he might be ready to take the next step with Aurelia at least. That meant something more serious between them, making a commitment beyond their arranged agreement. He didn't know how she'd react to that idea and it was a risk for him even to go there with her. Hopefully, tonight would show her the kind of man he was at heart, the kind of man he wanted to be for her, and just maybe they could lay all the ghosts of their pasts to rest and move forward together.

There was only one problem casting a shadow over everything, and that was the future of the store. He was under pressure to make a decision before the housing market changed and the window for making that huge profit disappeared. The difficulty was now that his heart was completely open, not only to Aurelia, but to the employees who were depending on him. It was difficult to make that sudden change from a logical businessman focused on profits, to a man with a sentimental and financial responsibility to those who worked for him.

'Earth to Gabe.' Aurelia waved her hands in front of his face, trying to get his attention.

'Sorry. Did you say something?'

Aurelia huffed out a breath with a roll of her eyes. 'I asked where you wanted to start? With the younger children, or the teenagers? Do you want us to split the task, or choose everything together?'

'I need your guidance, so we'll do it together.' He also wanted the time together to perhaps broach the subject of extending their deal. It was a risk when they'd agreed to the time limit for very good reasons. To keep emptions out of the equation, but it had turned out an impossible task for Gabe. He could only hope that Aurelia might feel the same way about him.

'Okay, well, the little ones will enjoy anything that

makes a noise or has flashing lights.' Aurelia walked along the aisles selecting items she deemed suitable and handed it to Gabe for approval. He promptly put everything in the metal cage they normally used for transporting stock but which tonight was serving as a stand-in sleigh.

'I have a note of some of the older children's likes. I thought maybe some craft sets for the artists among them.' This was all new to Gabe but he was enjoying picking out gifts, doing his best to choose items he thought the recipient would love to open on Christmas morning. It made him think about Aurelia, and what he could give her for Christmas. It had to be something special. A generic piece of jewellery or bottle of perfume simply wouldn't do. It would have to be something meaningful so she would know how much thought he'd given it, and realise how much she was coming to mean to him.

'Nice, and we'll have some cuddly toys too. You can't go wrong with those.' As though they were on a game show Aurelia was piling toys into the trolley. Not that Gabe cared. He could see how happy it was making her, and he was looking forward to putting smiles on the faces of those children too. The cost was definitely worth the reward.

By the time they'd both finished, there were probably enough toys to give to half the children in the city. It looked as though they'd won a trolley dash competition and grabbed as much as they could off the shelves in a short space of time.

'We might have overdone it a little. Do you want to cut it down bit?' Aurelia must have been feeling guilty about the cost as she looked through the presents filling the cage.

'It's fine. We'll send everything over to the home and let them decide what they want to do with everything.'

'Don't you want to be there? To be the one handing out the gifts?'

Gabe supposed if his father had been talked into this kind of gesture he would've tried to find a way to make it pay. Turn it into a PR stunt for the store in the hope that revenue would increase. That wasn't Gabe's motivation.

'It's not about me. It's about making the day special for the children. They don't need me there for that.'

Aurelia stood up on her tiptoes and kissed his cheek.

'What's that for?'

'For being you,' she said, melting his heart. It was the first time he could ever remember anyone showing him affection without an ulterior motive. Yes, this little enterprise would cost him a few pounds, but he hadn't been manipulated into it. He'd done it because it was the right thing to do and it made him feel good.

'Can I leave you to do the paperwork here? I've got an errand to run.' It was half true. After having her help, and the lateness of the hour, he thought dinner was called for.

Aurelia sighed. 'Sure. I'll wait here.'

Gabe headed to the homewares department, making a call on the way. He set a table for dinner, lit a couple of candles and put some music on low in the background. He just wanted to show Aurelia his appreciation, and show he did have a romantic side. If it was too much, it would give him an indication that she wasn't ready to move their relationship to something more serious. When the food arrived, he collected it at the back door and sent her a text to meet him on the floor. He was just dishing out dinner when she arrived.

'What's all this?'

'Dinner. We haven't eaten, and since we can't go out in public, I thought this was the next best thing.' At least it made a change from his place. Hopefully, if they both agreed they wanted more, they would be able to go out in public and wouldn't have to sneak around after dark any longer.

'Thank you.' Instead of laughing in his face, she smiled. Appearing genuinely grateful for the gesture.

Gabe breathed a sigh of relief. 'Sit down. I just ordered pasta. I hope that's okay.'

'Lovely. It's my favourite comfort food.' Aurelia was already digging her fork into the creamy pasta and sauce whilst he poured them both a small glass of wine.

'That's good to know.' He'd file that away with everything else he knew about her, because it was important to him. He was interested in getting to know her better so they could have that closeness he'd always been afraid of. That was the effect she'd had on him.

'Thanks for letting me be part of this tonight. It was fun playing Mrs Christmas for a while.'

'There's no one else I would rather have done it with. It feels good doing something selfless. My father would be most displeased at how I turned out.' At one point that would have killed him, but now Gabe was realising there was a lot more to life than money. And he wanted to share it with the woman sitting across the table from him.

'You talk a lot about your father, and what he wanted. I think your mother would have been very proud of the man you've become. I know I am.' Aurelia reached across to take his hand in hers, and Gabe thought this could be the moment to raise the subject of their arrangement.

He turned up the volume on his phone so the easy listening music filtered through the store. Then he scraped his chair back and moved over to where Aurelia was sitting. He held out his hand.

'Would you like to dance?'

Without hesitation she got to her feet and took his hand. 'I'd love to.'

He took her in his arms and they swayed together. Aurelia sighed and rested her head on his shoulder and a feeling of complete contentment settled over Gabe. As though he was right where he wanted to be. Who would have thought that he would be dancing in the middle of his father's store with one of the employees? And it had nothing whatsoever to do with money.

'I've been thinking...' He swallowed hard, knowing the next words that came out of his mouth would be leaving him vulnerable. Something he'd avoided for a long time.

'Hmm?' Aurelia's sleepy response almost made him lose his train of thought. It reminded him of her being curled up in bed next to him, seeking his warmth in the middle of the night and making him feel wanted. Loved.

'I know we both decided that we would only be together until Christmas was over—'

'Yes?' She was looking at him with anticipation rather than suspicion. This felt very like make or break time.

Gabe summoned all the strength he had. 'I'm not sure it's what I want any more.'

'Okay. Then there's no point in dragging this out then, is there?' She pushed away from his chest, breaking that connection between them. Her face looked pained, and her eyes full of sadness.

It took Gabe a moment to realise what she was thinking. He grabbed her hand again. 'Wait. No. I'm not saying I want to end things. Quite the opposite.'

'Then what?' Aurelia's obvious upset at the notion that he'd been about to break up with her made him sure he was doing the right thing after all.

'I thought… I thought perhaps you might want to stay a bit longer?' He watched her worried brow as it morphed into a look of surprise.

'Really?'

'Really. I mean, we don't have to live together or anything if you still want to get your own place. Though you're welcome to stay. I just… I like being with you, Aurelia. Maybe we could see where this goes.' He was putting himself out there, but her smile was able to calm the frantic beat of his heart waiting for her response.

'I'd like that.'

It was such a welcome relief to find she clearly wanted the same thing, that Gabe immediately kissed her full on the mouth. He didn't have to hold anything back now. Especially when Aurelia was kissing him back with such fierce passion, and blowing every other thought out of his mind except how much he wanted her. It was as though finally expressing their desire to be together had unleashed that animalistic side in both of them again.

'Do you want to stay here, or take this back home?' It would be easy to throw caution to the wind once more and make use of the bed department here in the store, but they'd agreed they wanted something more meaningful. Sleeping together here would be impulsive, reckless and the sort of thing he might do with someone he'd never see again.

However, they did have a place to go together. Somewhere more private and comfortable that they could both call home now.

'As happy as I am that you never updated the security in the store, I think I'd be happier if we slept in your bed. But what about all the mess?' Aurelia pointed towards the dirty dishes they'd left behind from their romantic dinner.

'That can wait. I can't,' he growled, and grabbed her for another passion-fuelled kiss. 'I'll come in early and clear it all away.'

'In that case, what are we waiting for?' With a grin, Aurelia took his hand, and let him lead her through the store, making sure everything was closed down before they left.

As they got into the car, Aurelia lay her head on his shoulder and said, 'Take me home.'

For Gabe, that was exactly what she was to him. Home.

CHAPTER ELEVEN

'WE'RE GOING TO have to be quick before everyone else gets here,' Aurelia giggled as she and Gabe hurriedly cleared away all evidence of their evening in the store.

'Well, if someone hadn't dragged me back to bed we might have got here earlier.' Gabe finished wiping down the table before wrapping an arm around her waist and pulling her in for a kiss.

'You know we're not going to be able to do this when you upgrade the security in this place.' She was only teasing, but she thought she saw a flicker of a frown cross his face at the mention of the store in the future.

Although he hadn't told her of his plans yet, she imagined Delaney's could go from strength to strength with Gabe at the helm, and that he would be as ingrained in the fabric of the building as his father had been. She would do her best to show him that regardless of all the emotional implications of keeping the place, that it could still be a savvy investment. The postbox she'd implemented was already a success, drawing more customers to the toy department than ever, and she was planning on spending the night drafting replies to all of the excited children who'd written to Father Christmas. Maybe next year they might be able to run a competition to win a trip to Lapland. Now, that really would draw a crowd.

On a personal level, she could see the difference the store was making to Gabe, and the wider community. She hoped the sleepover they'd held with the children from the home would become a regular event. Even this morning when they'd dropped off the gifts they'd chosen last night, he'd promised he would donate again next year. Aurelia was proud of Gabe and the good name he was making for himself in the city.

Perhaps he was simply still a little wary of her getting involved in his business affairs. It was one thing helping to make decisions where her department was concerned but he likely didn't appreciate her getting involved in things which didn't concern her. Like security, and spending more money on things which his father had never deemed necessary.

He dropped a kiss on her lips, and his smile made her wonder if she'd imagined the worrying look, trying to convince herself there was a problem and she needed to hold back. 'But we can do it at home.'

Home. Every time he said that word it sent shivers across her skin and made her forget any doubts. She couldn't believe how lucky she was, not only that Gabe had opened up his house to her, but also his heart. It was exciting and terrifying all at once investing in someone again. This man she was falling for deeper every day had her job, her home and now her heart in his hands. A position she swore she'd never put herself in again. Yet, being with Gabe was the happiest time in her life she could ever remember.

The hubbub of staff arriving reminded them they

weren't on their own any more and they quickly separated. Although not before Gabe gave her one last peck on the cheek. Enough to set her up for the day, and look forward to the time when they could be together without having to worry about who might see them.

Aurelia was looking forward to the day when perhaps they could go public. Even though she knew it wouldn't go down well with some of her colleagues. Still, she could keep work and her private life separate, and it would be a while before she told anyone they were together. She wasn't going to tempt fate until she was sure that things were going to work out. Until then, she intended to get on with her job, and go home with Gabe at night. The best of both worlds.

She tried to ignore that niggling feeling that it was all too good to be true and she was simply setting herself up for another fall.

It turned out Aurelia was having a hard time keeping her distance from Gabe. The store was buzzing with frantic shoppers all trying to get those last-minute gifts in and she was rushed off her feet, but her thoughts were never far from her boss.

She couldn't believe he wanted to be with her. It was a huge step for both of them to make a commitment to one another beyond their Christmas deadline, even though they were effectively living together anyway. Perhaps she should still try the council again to find somewhere of her own, just to give them a little space. It was one thing staying in his house when they weren't anything serious, but now it might be forcing them somewhere in their relationship they weren't ready to go just yet.

When there was a lull in sales around five o'clock she decided to go and have a chat with him and get his opinion. It was a good excuse to see him too.

The door to his office was open and she was about to knock when she heard him talking. Deciding to wait until he was free, she found herself hovering in the doorway. The apparent one-sided conversation made her realise he was on the phone with someone.

She hadn't intended to eavesdrop but his voice had carried to her nonetheless.

'I know the land is worth more than the store has made in decades. Why do you think it has taken me so long to make the decision? It's not easy to make dozens of people redundant. One last Christmas, we agreed.'

Aurelia backed away. She didn't want to hear any more. All the time she'd spent with Gabe, getting to know each other, and opening up, she thought would somehow make a difference. That by seeing what the store meant to her, her colleagues and the community, it might influence his decision. It seemed as though he'd made up his mind long before that, and nothing had convinced him to change it. She'd imagined he'd fall in love with the place just as she had. Thought that the softer side she'd seen to him would win out over everything his father had ingrained in him. What a fool she'd been.

Blinded by everything she thought he could offer, so that she couldn't see what was really happening. Ignoring her instincts in favour of everything her libido had wanted instead. When all along he'd been planning on selling everyone out. Taking away their livelihoods so he could make even more money. She wondered if everything for the kids at the children's home and the trip to

Lapland had all been to keep her onside so she wouldn't rock the boat. After everything they'd shared together, it felt like a personal betrayal more than an astute business decision.

She'd opened her heart to him. Told him things she'd never shared with anyone. Yet, he apparently still hadn't thought twice about making her unemployed as well as homeless.

Even if that emotional connection had been genuine, she couldn't be with someone who could be so callous. Who didn't think twice about putting people out on the street when he had no use for them. There was no doubt in her mind that he'd do the same to her when he inevitably grew bored of any commitment.

The revelation that she'd put herself in the very same situation she'd been trying to avoid, caused her to stumble in her haste to get away. Kicking over a box of papers sitting in the hallway.

Before she could get away, Gabe was at the door, frowning at her. His phone call apparently over. 'Aurelia? Is everything okay?'

'You're going to sell the store?'

He sighed. 'You knew that was an option.'

'I didn't think you were seriously considering it.'

'I'm a businessman. I have to consider everything before making a decision.'

'And what about all your employees? What about me?'

'This was never anything personal, Aurelia, and I would always have made sure that you were okay.'

She didn't think that made things any better for her. It wouldn't make her any better than him if she should only be worried about herself.

'One last Christmas…you should have told me, Gabe.'

'I don't see why. This is my store, my business.'

'And I'm just an employee. I get it.'

'That's not what I meant—'

Aurelia held up her hand to signal for him to stop. She couldn't listen to any more when her heart was breaking with every word. 'It doesn't matter, Gabe. You're not the person I thought you were, and I'm sorry but I can't do this any more. I need some space.'

Gabe looked as though he was about to protest, then dropped his head, apparently thinking better of it. 'Where will you go?'

It was disappointing, even in the circumstances, that he wasn't even going to fight for her. To tell her that she'd got it wrong, or that he would do anything to keep her in his life. It confirmed to her that she was making the right decision. He couldn't have cared enough about her if he wasn't trying to stop her now. At least she was getting out now before she'd begun imagining settling down with him forever. There might be a little part of her heart left she could salvage, though it was hurting like hell right now.

'I'll find somewhere.' She didn't know where she was going to go. This time she couldn't even sneak into the store when he knew she might try that. Though at this point in time she just needed out of his home. To start over again on her own, wherever that may be.

'At least let me try and get you a good hotel or something. You're not going to get anything else this close to Christmas.' Money was the answer to everything where Gabe was concerned.

As much as Aurelia wanted to say no, she genuinely

didn't know what else to do. Christmas in a hotel room would be slightly less depressing than spending it freezing to death on the street.

'Only if you let me pay you back when I can.' It would make her believe that she was still in charge of her own destiny in some small way. She needed that, after almost losing herself and her independence to someone else who was only going to let her down.

'Whatever you want, Aurelia.' Gabe's seeming indifference to her departure from his life made her spin on her heels and walk away before he saw her tears.

She couldn't believe she'd got it so wrong, so soon after her last disastrous relationship. It seemed she was doomed to repeat her mother's mistakes after all.

'I'm sorry, Aurelia.' Gabe didn't know what else to say as he deposited her bag at her feet outside the hotel he'd booked for her. It had taken almost as much persuasion for him to do that, as to accept his offer of a lift. But he wouldn't take no for an answer where either her accommodation, or transport were concerned. Not when it was snowing and he knew how upset he'd made her.

Everything inside him wanted to beg her to stay, but that little voice of reason won out. The one that said because he hadn't given her what she wanted and she'd left, Aurelia couldn't love him as much as he wanted. There was no reason to fight to have her in his life, to tell her he hadn't made the final decision, if she wanted to think the worst of him. It was better for him to find out now than to wait and have his heart completely broken in the future.

The truth was, he was still torn between his heart and his head when it came to making that decision. Sure, it would be easier for him personally to let things carry on as normal. Let the store continue the way it had always done, and remain in Aurelia's good books. But, that wasn't a good, financial move when the place was barely keeping its head above water the way it was. However, he had a feeling it was his relationship with Aurelia which was primarily stopping him from securing the store's future. He knew that if he did that, he was making a commitment to her too in some way. And she'd been right about one thing: He was still keeping things from her. Unable to open himself up completely, governed by his fear of being too vulnerable to being hurt again. She needed someone in her life who was truly open to her emotionally, because loved ones in the past had betrayed her trust so readily.

Aurelia calling a halt to things now seemed best for them both in the long run. Although it hurt to let her go, he was sure it would protect them both from more pain when being together seemed fraught with too many dangers.

'Me too,' was all she said as she turned and walked into the hotel, leaving him standing outside in the snow. A sad ending to what had been the most amazing time of his life.

She'd had her bag packed within ten minutes of being back at his place, apparently unable to wait to get away. It was ironic that he hadn't even made a decision yet where the store's future was concerned, but he was being punished regardless. Of course the future of his employees was important to him but this was business, and he couldn't quite shake off that need to follow the money rather than his heart.

Gabe headed home with a sense of dread, knowing it was full of reminders of Aurelia. Not least the fairy lights blazing away on the Christmas tree—the good parts of the season which she'd reminded him of, only for them now to be associated with loss again.

He walked over to the mantelpiece and lifted up the crudely made ornament she'd left behind. A reminder of her enthusiasm for all things Christmas, and how much she'd helped him to open up. He wasn't the same man he'd been before she came into his life, but the only thing he regretted was that things hadn't worked out between them. For a short while he'd imagined settling down and having that family he'd always wanted, but it had proved a dream too far.

'Has Miss Hughes gone? I went into her room to change the bedding but I see the room is empty.' Mrs Kent's voice stopped him from wallowing too much.

'Yes. She, er, decided to spend Christmas elsewhere in the end.' It wasn't the Christmas either of them had envisaged. For the first time in his adult life he'd been looking forward to it, to spending it with her. Now the day would feel lonelier than ever.

'I'm sorry. I liked her. She reminded me a lot of your mother.' The housekeeper's words came as a surprise. Physically, his mother and Aurelia couldn't have been farther apart. His mother had been a petite blonde, whilst Aurelia was a tall, curvy brunette.

'How so?'

'Well, she's fun and she brightened this place up. I've never seen you so happy and relaxed.'

Gabe couldn't argue with any of that.

'Of course, she was a shopgirl just like your mother too.'

'Pardon?'

'Your mother worked in Delaney's before she married

your father. Didn't you know that?' The revelation made Gabe look at everything he'd known about his parents in a different light.

'No.' It explained a lot. For someone so obsessed with money, his father had never wanted to part with the store and Gabe had never understood why. His father certainly hadn't been the sentimental type. Or so he'd thought.

He'd never shared tender anecdotes about how he'd met Gabe's mother, or really talked about her at all.

'Your father loved your mother deeply. I know he didn't always show you a lot of affection, but her death hit him hard. I think he simply closed himself off after she'd gone. He put all of his love and attention into the store because it reminded him of her.'

'I guess it explains a lot.' It was a difficult truth to take in. His father had directed all those important emotions into a bricks and mortar building instead of the most important person left in his life. He didn't want to be guilty of doing the same. Aurelia made him feel things he'd never felt for anyone before, and no amount of money could compete with that.

Gabe didn't want to make the same mistakes as his father, missing out on an important relationship because he'd been so wounded by the past. It made him want to put himself out there because he and Aurelia might have another chance together. Risking his heart seemed like a small price to pay if it meant he might have her in his life after all. All he could hope for was that she wanted the same.

It had been a couple of days since Aurelia had moved into the hotel room. Tomorrow was Christmas Day, yet she felt more despondent now than when she'd been evicted and had nowhere to go. Because she didn't have Gabe.

Coming to work was difficult, wondering if she'd catch a glimpse of him, and how it would make her feel. In the end she hadn't had to worry. He'd been conspicuous in his absence. Still, it hadn't stopped her looking for him amongst the crowds all day.

'Have a lovely Christmas,' she said to a customer for the umpteenth time that day, handing over the purchases with a forced smile.

Christmas Eve had always been the happiest time of the year for her, but she felt as though she was just dialling it in this time. She wasn't feeling anything except sadness, and the thought of spending Christmas Day in a hotel room wasn't helping that.

They were closing early today, and as the last customer drifted out, Mr Thompson locked the doors before addressing the staff gathered.

'Mr Delaney would like to see everyone on the ground floor before we leave for the Christmas holidays.'

The announcement made Aurelia's blood run cold. Surely Gabe wouldn't tell everyone they were losing their jobs on Christmas Eve? Despite how they'd left things between them, she didn't believe he would be so deliberately cruel.

He was waiting for everyone in his office door as they assembled in the hallway. She was disappointed in the fact her heart still leapt at the sight of him. It wasn't as easy to simply shut off her feelings as much as she wanted to.

'Thanks for coming, everyone. I won't keep you too long as I know you're all eager to get home and set out some milk and cookies for Santa coming.' Gabe's joke brought a chorus of anxious titters.

'I'll get straight to the point. I know everyone is worried about Delaney's future. Yes, it's true, the land the store is sitting on would be worth more as a development site for new city apartments.' That comment was met with a rumbling of discontent, but Gabe continued. 'That being said, Delaney's is a Belfast landmark. We have a history here that's important, and working alongside everyone here has made me see that some things are more important than profit.'

Aurelia felt his eyes upon her, and she held her breath, waiting for his next statement.

'I've made the decision to carry on here. There will be a few improvements and I want to modernise the place over the next years, but I can assure everyone that your jobs are safe.'

A relieved cheer echoed around the walls, but Aurelia found that she couldn't speak. Her heart was so full for what he was doing that emotion was choking her. Gabe was putting everyone above profit, she knew that, but his decision also made her sad for everything she'd lost.

She'd convinced herself he was as selfish as everyone else in her life, and had written him off before he could have a chancc to prove himself. Now he had, she could see she'd been looking for an excuse to end things before she inevitably got hurt. If she'd waited, talked things through, perhaps they could have salvaged a relationship, but she'd pre-empted the end and finished things before he could. This announcement only made the loss feel even greater. She'd thrown away the chance to be with this good man.

'Okay. Go home and be with your families, and enjoy Christmas.' Gabe waved off everyone else, but moved towards Aurelia. She remained rooted to the spot. 'Can I have a word with you in my office?'

'Sure.' Aurelia forced her feet to follow him, worried she was about to find herself jobless as well as homeless again. Back where she'd started.

Once she'd followed him into the room, Gabe closed the door and gestured for her to take a seat. It felt very much the lead-up to getting fired. Probably for ranting at the boss about business matters which didn't concern her.

'For the record, I'd never made the decision to sell the store. We had talked about one last Christmas for the place, but that was before I'd spent time here, and before it had come to mean so much to me. Before you came to mean so much to me. I was torn, yes. My heart telling me to keep the place, whilst my head was telling me to take the route which actually made financial sense. I just needed a little time to realise what it was I really wanted.' His little smile only made her want to cry more.

She had got him wrong. The Gabe she'd come to know these past days would never have sold them all out for money, but her wounded heart had made her decision on their relationship before it had ever got off the ground. Telling her to get out before he could abandon her like everyone else in her life.

Looking back, she wondered if she'd chosen Gary to be with because she'd known all along that he'd let her down, confirming that she'd be better off alone. Perhaps it was that kind of self-sabotage which had caused her to make rush judgements with Gabe too. Pushing him away to protect herself. Now she was more alone than ever.

'I'm sorry.' There was nothing else she could say. At least, not without breaking down in tears and begging him to give her another chance. She loved him and she knew that was what had scared her so much about getting things wrong. Gary had abandoned her and broke her heart and she hadn't felt a fraction of the love for him that she felt for Gabe. So she'd found a reason to get out before he did. Now he was telling her she'd got him wrong, she knew what she'd thrown away.

Gabe moved behind his desk and rummaged in the drawer.

'You left these behind.' He produced the handmade ornaments from her childhood which she'd placed on the mantelpiece when they'd been decorating for Christmas. It seemed like a lifetime ago now. A life she was missing.

'Thanks. For what it's worth, I'm sorry I got things so wrong. I think I was still hurting from my ex, and thought I was protecting myself. Subconsciously, I must have been looking for a reason to push you away before you had a chance to hurt me like everyone else in my life.' Aurelia knew he deserved the truth when she'd been so quick to think the worst of him. He hadn't done anything wrong.

Gabe nodded sagely. 'I understand that. I guess that's why I didn't tell you what was really going on either. I could have erased all doubt, fought for us, but I was afraid too that I wasn't going to be enough for you.'

'Never.' Aurelia forgot herself and went to him, needing to convince him that she hadn't been rejecting him. Simply trying to prevent herself from getting hurt.

'I was worried I'd let you down because I couldn't open up to you fully. Emotionally.'

'And what are you doing right now?' She gave him a half-smile, afraid to believe that they still had a chance if they could both be brave enough to leave the wounds of the past behind them.

Gabe smiled back. 'I guess I'm not ready to lose you after all.'

Aurelia's heartbeat quickened at the thought that perhaps all wasn't lost.

'I miss you,' Gabe said, tucking a strand of her hair behind her ear. That tender touch sending shivers across her skin. Reminding her why it was so hard to walk away from him. Gabe Delaney made her feel wanted, safe. Something she'd never found with anyone else. She'd just been afraid he was too good to be true.

But did she really want to lose him through fear? That felt as though she was punishing herself for falling in love. Maybe, just maybe, she deserved to take her happiness where she found it, and that was with Gabe.

'I miss you too.' Her voice was thick with emotion. Those feelings she'd tried so hard to deny, now forcing their way to the surface.

'Can we try again?' he asked, his eyes pleading with her to give him another chance.

'I want to, but how are we going to go forward? How do we stop letting the past get in the way of our future?' Aurelia didn't want to rush foolishly into some romantic notion of a happy-ever-after when she knew the reality too well.

Gabe cupped her face in his hands, forcing her to look directly into his eyes. 'Nothing else matters to me except being with you, Aurelia. If I have to tell you every single little thing that's going on in my head I will, if it means you'll trust me. I love you, and I want you to be in my life. If that's what you want too.'

There was no doubting that Gabe meant every word he said, Aurelia could see it in his eyes. It was there in his actions too. Not only was he baring his heart to her, but he'd proved he was the sort of man who would put people before profit by saving the store. Gabe Delaney was the real deal. Now all she had to do was put her faith in him, and her feelings, once more.

She nodded, not trusting herself to say the words he was waiting to hear without sobbing like a baby. There was nothing she wanted more than to be with Gabe. She'd just been too afraid of the strength of her feelings.

He hugged her tight. 'Best Christmas present ever,' he whispered.

Aurelia had never felt so wanted, so cherished, and she was going to let herself revel in it. They were going to have the best Christmas either of them had ever had. Together.

EPILOGUE

A Year Later

'THIS LOOKS AMAZING,' Aurelia said, tucking into the Christmas dinner she and Gabe had made together. He'd thrown himself completely into Christmas this year and she loved it. She loved him.

Last year had been nice in the end, spending the day together and making plans for the future, but they'd had plenty of time this year to prepare for the big day. The tree had gone up at the end of November and they'd decorated the house for Christmas together. With her sentimental handicrafts, and the glass igloo she'd bought for him in Lapland taking pride of place on the mantelpiece. December had been spent buying presents and distributing them to needy children.

'It should be Christmas every day,' Gabe exclaimed slicing into the turkey.

'You can have too much of a good thing, you know.'

'Never. I could never have too much of you.' He leaned across the table and kissed her hard on the lips.

Even after a year, every touch melted her. She'd never moved out in the end. Things between them had been so good since they opened up to one another, it seemed like a step backwards for her to leave again. So they'd worked together and gone home together every night. Her colleagues had got used to seeing them together and it hadn't turned out to be such a scandal after all for them to be a couple. Aurelia supposed everyone was simply glad they still had jobs to go to.

Gabe had invested in the store, modernising it, but still maintaining that atmosphere that made Delaney's special. Although he still had other business interests, he was taking on fewer projects, insisting he would rather spend more time at home with Aurelia than working day and night. He'd even implemented some of the ideas she'd had, not only for her department, but for the store too. Proving how much he respected her opinion. When it came to Delaney's, they worked pretty well as a team. She couldn't believe how lucky she was.

'So, after dinner I'm thinking sofa, film and maybe some chocolate.' This was their day and she'd been looking forward to simply relaxing with Gabe in the comfort of their own home.

'Sounds good to me. Now, what about the crackers?' Gabe lifted the silver foil-wrapped handmade cracker from the table and held it out to her.

They'd decided against gifts to one another since they had everything they needed. Though they'd agreed to make one another crackers with a token gift inside.

Aurelia had been hiding her present to Gabe for a few weeks and was anxious to see his reaction, but she could see he was equally excited about his gift. She took the other end of the cracker and pulled, hearing the satisfying snap before the contents clattered onto the table.

Aurelia picked up the shiny gift and turned it over in

her hand. It was a ring. And not one of those pink plastic ones either. This looked to be real gold and diamonds.

When she looked up, Gabe was kneeling beside her chair and taking her hand in his. Her heart was almost pounding out of her chest.

'Aurelia Hughes, I love you from the bottom of my heart. Will you marry me?'

She knew how much it took for him to make that sort of commitment and it meant everything to her. It was a promise that he'd always be there for her. Everything she needed.

'Yes. I'll marry you, Gabe. I love you too.' She watched with tears in her eyes as he slid the ring on to her finger.

'Now it's your turn.' She presented him with the cracker she'd made specially. Although it wasn't as expensive as a gold-and-diamond ring, it had the same impact.

Gabe's mouth dropped open as he held up the positive pregnancy test. 'You're pregnant?'

'We're having a baby.' It hadn't been planned but as sometimes happened, passion had overtaken them. The consequences of which she hoped he would look forward to as much as she was. Before Gabe had come into her life she didn't think she'd ever want the responsibility of being a parent, but life with him was so settled and happy, not to mention passionate, that she'd found herself wanting the impossible. A family. And now he'd given it to her.

He pulled her into a hug, a huge smile on his face. 'Best Christmas present ever.'

Aurelia loved that he was so happy. She just didn't know how she was going to top this one next Christmas, now they both had everything they'd ever wanted.

* * * * *

If you enjoyed this story,
check out these other great reads
from Karin Baine

Spanish Doc to Heal Her
Temptation in a Tiara
Tempted by Her Off-Limits Boss
Nurse's New Year with the Billionaire

All available now!

MILLS & BOON®

Coming next month

CHRISTMAS WITH THE SECRET TYCOON
Rhoda Baxter

'I'm so sorry!' Maddie scrambled down the ladder.

Unfortunately, one of the baubles had ended up on the bottom step. She slipped and fell, arms flailing, onto the poor man she'd just covered in tinsel.

She closed her eyes, expecting a crash. Instead she landed against something soft. There was a grunt and a soft 'ow.' She opened her eyes to find that she had been caught by the man who had been standing there.

For a moment all she could do was stare. He had silver streamers hanging over one eyebrow and his glasses were askew, but there was no mistaking those blue eyes. This was the guy who had been looking out the window. At the time she hadn't been able to make out his features that well, but up close, he was spectacular. Sharp cheekbones, strong jaw. It was the sort of face that wouldn't look out of place on an advertising billboard. She opened her mouth to apologize, but nothing came out.

'Are you okay?' His voice was soft and deep. It seemed to connect to something under her lungs.

Continue reading

CHRISTMAS WITH THE SECRET TYCOON
Rhoda Baxter

Available next month
millsandboon.co.uk

COMING SOON!

We really hope you enjoyed reading this book.
If you're looking for more romance
be sure to head to the shops when
new books are available on

Thursday 20th November

MILLS & BOON

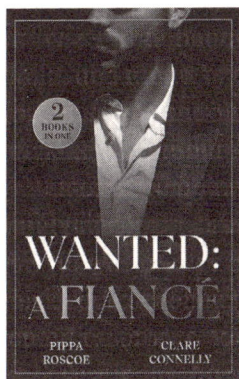

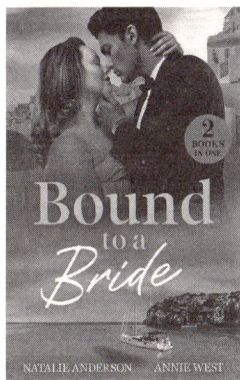

afterglow BOOKS

Afterglow Books is a trend-led, trope-filled list of books with diverse, authentic and relatable characters, a wide array of voices and representations, plus real world trials and tribulations. Featuring all the tropes you could possibly want (think small-town settings, fake relationships, grumpy vs sunshine, enemies to lovers) and all with a generous dose of spice in every story.

♪ @millsandboonuk
☉ @millsandboonuk
afterglowbooks.co.uk
#AfterglowBooks

For all the latest book news, exclusive content and giveaways scan the QR code below to sign up to the Afterglow newsletter:

SCAN ME

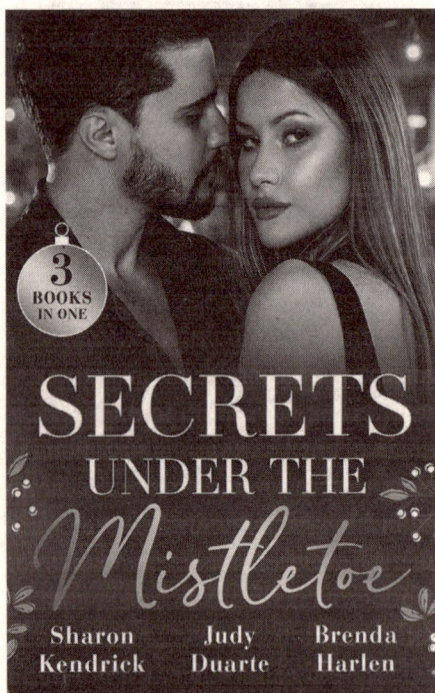